According to author JOHN WILCOX, an inability to do sums and a nascent talent to string words together steered him towards journalism – that and the desire to wear a trench coat, belted with a knot, just like Bogart. After a number of years working as a journalist, he was lured into industry. In the mid-nineties he sold his company in order to devote himself to his first love, writing. He has now published, to high acclaim, eight Simon Fonthill novels and two works of non-fiction, including an autobiography.

www.johnwilcoxauthor.co.uk

By John Wilcox

The War of the Dragon Lady

Starshine

THE WAR OF THE DRAGON LADY

JOHN WILCOX

Allison & Busby Limited
13 Charlotte Mews
London W1T 4EJ
www.allisonandbusby.com

First published in Great Britain by Allison & Busby in 2012.
This paperback edition published by Allison & Busby in 2012.

Copyright © 2012 by JOHN WILCOX

A CIP catalogue record for this book is available from
the British Library.

10 9 8 7 6 5 4 3 2 1

ISBN 978-0-7490-1208-3

Typeset in 10.5/16 pt Sabon by
Allison & Busby Ltd.

The paper used for this Allison & Busby publication
has been produced from trees that have been legally sourced
from well-managed and credibly certified forests.

Printed and bound by
CPI Group (UK) Ltd, Croydon, CR0 4YY

To Peter Jackson, editor, writer, critic,
teacher and old friend.

CHAPTER ONE

Chihli Province, China. June 1900.

Simon Fonthill eased himself in the saddle, stood a little shakily in the stirrups – he was tired but, at forty-five and even after twenty-four years of hard campaigning throughout Queen Victoria's empire, he remained an uncertain horseman – and looked around him. The plain of Northern China presented little to see. There had been no rain that spring and no corn had been sown. Two years of drought had sucked the moisture from the rice fields and the sun's rays flinched back from the hard earth as though even they were burnt by the touch. In the distance the white road wound towards the roofs of a village, but no other living thing stirred: no people, no animals, not even a bird, for there were no trees or bushes to give it perch.

Jenkins urged his mount alongside. ''Otter than bleedin' Africa, I'd say.' He sucked in his great moustache as though to gain moisture from it. 'Don't remember it bein' as 'ot as this in the Sudan, look you.'

He sniffed. 'Can't see why we've come, to be honest, bach sir.'

'Don't let's get into that, for God's sake.' Fonthill pulled down his white topee, the better to shield his eyes, and nodded ahead. 'Should be able to find a bit of shade in that village. Stop for a cup of green tea or something.'

He relaxed back into the saddle but his mind remained on edge. It wasn't just the heat. The temperature must be well over ninety degrees, even in the shade – that which could be found – but the feeling of oppression that sat above him in the yellow sky had nothing to do with the sun. In truth, he had been uneasy since they had landed at Tientsin a week ago. China, or at least this Province of Chihli, had not been welcoming.

The teeming streets of the inland port had seemed to lack that cheerful bustle that so characterised Bombay, Alexandria or Cape Town, where white people, particularly the British, were accepted and even welcomed as traders and bringers of wealth. In Tientsin, the people had hurried by, their eyes downcast under their wide, conical straw hats and their features sullen, and the peasants glimpsed as they penetrated deeper inland seemed to share this same resentment. Fonthill had served in Zululand, Afghanistan, the Transvaal, the Sudan and Matabeleland and he recognised aggression when he met it. Here, he could almost smell it.

His unease communicated itself to Jenkins. 'There's trouble about, ain't there?' he said. 'D'you think it's them boxing blokes?'

'What, the Boxers?' He grinned. 'Well, we haven't exactly met any of them yet, have we? But something's up. I can feel it. But then, perhaps I'm imagining it. Too much sun and bloody dust.'

'Are you all right, Simon?' His wife called from the cart at the back of which she perched less than comfortably on their baggage, trying to find shade beneath a parasol. Their Chinese servant and guide slumped on the single seat before her, letting the reins leading to the mules fall into his lap. He seemed as glad as the animals to stop for a moment.

Fonthill turned his horse and let it amble back to the cart. 'Yes, fine, my love. I thought we might stop at that village up ahead and see if we can get some tea. Yes?'

'Oh absolutely. Find some shade.' She smiled at her husband.

Alice Fonthill was exactly the same age as her husband but there was very little sign of middle age in her face or figure. Dressed in a loose, white, cotton shift with sandals on her feet, she seemed neither plump nor slim but sturdy rather, with her midriff pulled in tightly by a lime-green bandana. Her face was open, her features regular and her eyes a steady grey; indeed, she could have been called beautiful if it had not been for a certain squareness to her jaw which bestowed a sense of purpose. Under her floppy white hat her hair was fair with only the lightest dusting of grey and her skin was unfashionably tanned. Not for her the protected pallor of the Raj's memsahibs. Mrs Fonthill, known to her readers of London's *Morning Post* by her maiden name of Alice Griffith, was as comfortable out of doors as her husband.

In fact, the two of them made a handsome couple as they smiled at each other in the heat. He was of middle height at five foot nine inches, though now he slumped in the saddle. His shoulders were wide and no fat had encroached to widen his waist, for a life spent farming and campaigning had made his body hard. His eyes were brown and normally showed traces of reserve, but not now as he looked at his wife with a tenderness that had survived years of sadness as well as joy. The most prominent feature of his face was the nose, broken years ago by a Pathan musket and now hooked, giving him a predatory air, that of a hunter looking for his prey. Yet his mouth, though thin-lipped, was soft and betrayed sensitivity; perhaps that rarity in Queen Victoria's great empire – a warrior with a conscience?

Fonthill jerked his head towards their guide, now seemingly asleep as he sat, hunched. 'Has he said much?' he mouthed.

She shook her head. 'Not a sausage,' she whispered. 'He's not exactly sociable, is he?'

'Ah well, we can't be far from your uncle's place. This should be the last stop. Let's get on.'

He pulled on the rein and gently leant over and gave the sleeping man a prod, pointing ahead. 'We'll stop at that village,' he said slowly.

The Chinaman opened his eyes. He said nothing but he jerked the reins and flicked his whip and the two mules shuffled ahead, hardly disturbing the dust on the road.

They had ambled barely a hundred yards when they heard the noise. It was difficult at first to tell the origin; then it became clear. Voices raised, Chinese voices, of course, but with that distinctive sing-song pattern now lost and merged into a high-pitched howl. It came from the village ahead and it personified hate and anger. The communal voice of a mob.

Fonthill turned and shouted to their driver, 'Stay here.' Then to Jenkins, 'Come on.'

They spurred their weary horses into something resembling a canter and rounded the bend that wound into what seemed like the main street of small dwelling houses, more a hamlet than a village. The place was deserted except for some dozen Chinamen who were surrounding a youth, who stood, befuddled, as abuse was hurled at him as he twisted and turned to find a way out through the ring.

The men were dressed all alike. They were barefooted and wore the loose pyjama-type garment of the Chinese peasant. But the pastoral effect of their clothing was completely dissipated by the red cloths tied round their heads, the red ribbons that fluttered from their wrists and ankles and the scarlet girdles that circled their waists. Two of them carried swords, others large sticks.

'Boxers!' breathed Simon.

The boy in their midst was probably no more than sixteen and he raised his hands in a desperate attempt to defend himself as the blows began to rain down on him. Then the lad went down on one knee under the force of the attack from all sides and, as he did so, two of his assailants drew their swords.

'That's enough,' shouted Fonthill. 'Stop that!' He dug his heels into his horse's flanks and rode straight into the crowd, scattering them. He was conscious of Jenkins riding closely behind him as he groped behind his saddlebag for some kind of weapon. He found only the end of his ash walking stick and drew it as he burst through the crowd. Wheeling his mount around, he realised that the mob had scattered only momentarily. The boy lay dazed on the ground but the Boxers now ignored him and approached the two horsemen, fanning out to surround them.

'Watch out, bach sir.' Jenkins's vocal Welshness always seemed to increase in proportion to the danger faced. 'The buggers 'ave got swords and they'll come at our backs, look you.'

'We mustn't let them attack the wagon.' The pitch of Fonthill's own voice now betrayed the peril of their situation. 'Dammit. Shouldn't have left the revolvers with the baggage. Only one thing for it. Cavalry charge. You ready, 352?'

Jenkins's eyes were black and cold under the rim of his wide-brimmed hat. 'Most certainly. But don't fall off, 'cos I might not 'ave a chance to pick you up, now, see.'

'Rubbish. I'm as good as a dragoon now. Use your stick as a sabre. Right at 'em, then – and shout. Now. Charge!'

The two lowered their sticks, put their heads down and urged their horses into a startled gallop. As they charged, they shouted – or rather, screamed. Jenkins's was a high-pitched, Celtic cry that seemed to come from deep within him; a prehistoric place of dark valleys and hills. Fonthill's seemed half embarrassed, more a desperate appeal for a catch from first slip on the cricket field than a battle cry. Both, however, were effective, for the Boxers broke and ran. Not, however, before one of them swung his club backhandedly at Simon's horse, catching him on the rump and causing him to rear.

Fonthill, with only one hand on the reins, was unable to control his mount and he felt himself slip backwards and then crash to the ground, temporarily winding him and sending his stick clattering away. Within moments, as he attempted to scramble to his feet, he realised that Jenkins was beside him, a knife gleaming in his hand.

'I just knew you'd fall off,' muttered the Welshman. 'On your feet, boyo, they're coming at us again. 'Ere, 'ave my stick, it's better than nothing. Back to back now.'

Taking deep gulps of hot air, Fonthill tried to regain his breath. The Boxers had whirled around and the two swordsmen were advancing on them now, preparing to take easy prey. Simon noticed that neither betrayed the slightest expression as he stepped forward.

Their eyes were completely dispassionate, like those of two snakes, preparing to strike.

'Bit of dust in their faces when they come in, bach sir,' muttered Jenkins. 'Might just give us a moment. If I can get close, I'll slit their gizzards, so I will. See if you can get be'ind me, like.'

'Certainly not. I'll fight my own bloody battle, thank you very much.'

The partners knelt down slowly, as though in supplication, but each gathered a handful of dust in his free hand and then they rose equally slowly to face the swordsmen.

Fonthill's mind raced. He knew that Jenkins was a superb close-quarters fighter. He had seen him confront and subdue a strapping assegai-carrying Zulu warrior, fighting only with his hands. But he himself had no such skills. The agony was that, if they were killed, Alice would be left completely defenceless in the wagon just outside the village. The Boxers would surely take it and she, too, would perish, for their guide would be useless. He must use what skills he had. The ash walking stick would become a rapier.

Slowly, he raised it and adopted the fencing *en garde* position, as he had been taught to do so many years ago at Sandhurst, the training school for young British officers. The ridiculous posture – side on, feet planted fore and aft and knees bent, while the stick was presented, horizontal to the ground, to the opponent – caused the Boxer to pause in his advance. The man stood for a moment, his mouth gaping, perspiration pouring down his chest in the gap shown by his open vest and his pigtail moving, pendulum like, as his head moved from side to side. Slowly he absorbed the situation. Then he grinned and jumped forward, swinging his sword in a silver arc.

Fonthill moved back and immediately crashed into the posterior of the Welshman, who judging by the clang of steel on steel was now engaged in his own fight for life. Somehow, however, Simon deflected the swing of the sword with his stick, so that it passed harmlessly to his side. Moving to his left, he lunged forward classically, taking the Chinaman firmly in the midriff with the point of the stick, causing the man to gasp and fall away, holding his stomach.

Seizing the moment, Simon attacked, thrusting with his ash as though it was an épée made of finest steel. Except that, of course, it was not. With a contemptuous swipe, the Boxer swung his blade across his body, cutting Fonthill's staff in half and leaving only a shattered stump in his hand.

'Dammit to hell.' In desperation, the Englishman sprang forward and threw the sand into the face of his opponent, causing the man to clutch at his eye. Before the Boxer could recover, Fonthill thrust the stump of his stick into his face. The splintered end grazed the cheekbone, producing a cry of pain and anger.

But it was the aggression of despair, for the Chinaman was not hurt. He backed away for a moment, wiped his eye and then sprang forward, raising his sword for one last and surely fatal attack.

Suddenly a shot rang out and the man clutched at his shoulder, blood spurting between his fingers. The sword dropped from his hand and he turned and looked with astonishment at the figure of Alice, standing some twenty-five yards away, the long barrel of an American Naval Colt revolver smoking in her hand.

For a split second the scene became frozen, like some mimed tableau, all movement stilled as though the actors were waiting for applause at the end of the drama. The rest of the Boxers were standing around in various postures, waiting for the swordsmen to end the entertainment by killing their men. The youth knelt on his hands and knees in the centre of the road, his mouth open. Jenkins had somehow turned his man and now had him from the back, his long knife at the throat of his assailant, whose sword lay on the ground.

All was still and then, as though acting on some hidden

signal, the scene broke up: the Boxers ran as fast as their bare feet could take them, led by Simon's wounded opponent, clutching his shoulder as he loped away. The boy stood to his feet, swayed for a moment and then approached the two Englishmen.

Incongruously, he stood before Simon and held out his hand. 'How do you do?' he asked in impeccable, if mannered, English. 'Am I right in believing that you are English, sir?'

'Bugger that.' Jenkins's interruption was low and gutteral. 'Do you want me to kill this bloke, bach sir? Might as well. He tried to kill us and I don't think I can 'old 'im much longer. Got a bit of a cut on me arm, see.'

'What?' Fonthill wiped the perspiration from his eyes. 'Good God, no. Let the swine go.'

Jenkins relaxed his grip and immediately the Boxer ducked away, like a trout returned to a stream, and ran after his fellows. In a few seconds the dusty street was deserted except for the boy and his rescuers.

Fonthill ignored the extended hand and ran towards his wife. 'Oh, wonderful shooting, Alice. I'd have been cut in half if you hadn't arrived.' He embraced her. 'Are you all right, darling? Where's the cart?'

Gently she pushed him away. She was shivering slightly, despite the heat. 'Perfectly all right, thank you. I am so used to rushing about China in this heat and shooting at the peasantry.' She handed the Colt to Simon, wiped her brow and then frowned. 'Ah, Jenkins is hurt.'

The Welshman was clumsily attempting with one hand to tie a very soiled handkerchief around his upper arm, where blood poured from a deep cut in the biceps. Alice ran to him.

'Sit down, 352.'

'No, missus. I'm all right, really. Just a scratch.'

'Sit down, I say.' Alice eased the man to the ground and knelt beside him. With a gesture of disgust, she threw away the rag, took her own handkerchief from a pocket in her skirt and folded it onto the wound, then bound it with the scarf taken from her throat. 'Hold that tightly to stop the bleeding, and we'll get back to the cart and wash the wound and dress it properly. Now, can you stand?'

Jenkins sniffed. 'Course I can. As a matter of fact, I never wanted to sit in the first place, if you remember, Miss Alice. I'm all right, thank you very much.'

Alice grinned at him. Jenkins had long since lost his hat in the affray – in her experience he rarely retained a hat for longer than a couple of hours in any one day, anyway – and, now covered in dust, he looked like some labourer from a stone mine, his thick hair standing up like grey stubble and his great moustache bristling with grit. Jenkins stood at only five foot four inches but he was not a small man. In fact, he seemed almost as broad as he was tall, so wide were his shoulders and so deep his chest. It was no surprise that he had turned the tables on the Boxer. Even at forty-nine, he was as quick on his feet as a fox, and throughout his life he had fought: in his early days in British army barrack rooms, detention centres and bars throughout the length and breadth of the Empire and then, for the last two decades, at the side of Simon Fonthill, his former subaltern, turned mentor and comrade, in a dozen adventures around the world. Formally employed now as gentleman's servant, Jenkins was part of the family. His Christian name long since forgotten, he was known as '352' – the last three numerals of his old army number, used to distinguish him from the seven other Jenkinses in his company in the old 24th Regiment of Foot, that most Welsh of army units – and he formed an essential third leg of the Fonthill stool.

Now he grinned back in gratitude at Alice as she and Simon helped him to his feet. Then Alice suddenly became aware of the Chinese youth, standing by deferentially. His shirt was torn, blood was trickling from several head wounds and swellings were appearing on his face. As she regarded him, he began to sway.

'Oh, my goodness,' cried Alice. 'Quick, Simon. He's going to fall.'

Fonthill sprang forward and caught the young man in his arms.

He lifted him easily. 'Back to the wagon,' he said. 'This chap needs a bit of shade under your parasol, darling. Here, take the Colt, Jenkins. They might come back. We need to get out of here. Alice, bring the horses.'

They hurried, as best they could, round the bend to find to their relief the cart standing at the side of the road where the mules had dragged it to find shade. Of their guide and driver there was no sign.

''E's buggered off,' panted Jenkins.

'Good riddance.' Fonthill lowered the boy onto the bags and jammed Alice's parasol so that it provided some shade for his head.

'Now, water, Alice, if you please.'

She unscrewed her water bottle and offered it to the youth's lips. At first the water trickled down his chin and then, as his eyes flickered open, he drank.

'Good,' muttered Alice. 'Now lie still and let me bathe those bruises.'

As she did so, Simon retrieved his own canteen and, removing the temporary dressing on Jenkins's arm, began to dab gently at the wound beneath.

'Bloody 'ell,' swore the Welshman. 'That's a bit sharp, see.'

'Don't be such a baby. You said yourself it was only a scratch. Here, you do it. I'm no nursemaid. I'll hitch the horses up to the wagon. We must get moving. I don't want the Boxers back.'

Jenkins looked up. 'Why are they called that, then? They don't seem to fight by the Queensbury Rules, now do they?'

Fonthill gathered the reins of the horses and attached them to the rear of the cart. 'I'm told that they're mainly young men,' he said, 'all supposed to be fierce patriots who hate foreigners and who practise martial arts, though I don't think they include boxing as we know it.' He climbed into the seat of the wagon and cracked the whip over the mules. 'They've adopted this Japanese form of wrestling, called ju-jitsu, or something. Anyway, I don't want to fight 'em again with the stub of a walking stick.'

'Simon,' Alice called. 'Have you noticed something strange about this place?'

'Well, it's bloody hot, for one thing.'

'No. Despite all the noise we haven't seen one single person from the village. No one has come out of the houses. It's like a ghost village.'

'Ah,' the boy struggled up onto his elbow and spoke. 'That is because they frightened of Boxers. Watch from windows. They in terrible funk, you see.'

Simon grinned over his shoulder at the colloquialism. 'Goodness me, young man, your English is very good. Where did you learn it?'

'At school and at home with father and mother. They my teachers.'

'Do they live near here? Can we take you to them?'

The boy raised a smile. 'I think you go there, anyway. I think you Captain Fonthill, Mrs Alice and Sergeant Jenkins. Am I right?'

The three looked in amazement at the young man, whose smile had broadened into a grin. 'You are, indeed,' said Alice. 'Who are you?'

The lad squirmed until he was sitting upright. 'My name is Chang. There is more to it than that, of course, but it is difficult for English to say rest of name. So call me Chang.' His grin lapsed into a frown. 'But you not supposed to be here.'

'What do you mean?'

'I go to Peking last week to send you cable to ship in Tientsin, saying too dangerous to travel here because of Boxers. Cable from my father, Reverend Griffith.'

'Your *father* . . . ?' Alice was incredulous. '*My* Uncle Edward is your . . . er . . . *father*?'

20

'Oh yes.' The boy nodded his head, the most earnest expression on his face. 'And Mrs Griffith my mother. They buy me from warlord when I was a baby and bring me up. My real parents dead. So I think we are all cousins, or something like that. I am very glad indeed to meet you all.' And he extended his hand.

They each took it solemnly.

'Well that's solved the problem of finding the mission,' said Fonthill. 'It must be near here. What were you doing when the Boxers found you?'

'I was going to buy rice, if I could find someone in village to sell.' He looked round earnestly. 'It is very scarce, because of drought. Drought a bally nuisance, you know.'

Simon smothered a smile. 'I am sure it is. But why did the Boxers attack you? I thought they were only against foreigners, and you are Chinese.' He coughed. 'Albeit a very English one.'

The boy fingered beneath his torn shirt and produced a crucifix hanging on a chain. 'Because I am Christian, follower of Lord Jesus Christ. Boxers hate Christians in particular, and they hate missionaries most of all. Reverend Father had been warned that Boxers were coming. That is why he sent me to capital to cable you not to come. Why you come, then?'

Alice resumed her treatment of the bruises. 'Your cable must have arrived after we left the ship in Tientsin – in fact, after we left the port. Now lie still.'

'No.' Fonthill turned his head. 'Can you come up here, Chang, and show us the way? If you are feeling up to it, that is?'

The boy squirmed onto his knees and crawled across the baggage until he was kneeling behind Simon. 'Oh, I am very up to it, thank you very much. Yes. You follow this way and then, in a moment, you will turn right. I will show you. Mission about five minutes away now.'

The cart with its attendant horses slowly wound its way through the barren countryside. There was no question of distancing themselves from the Boxers, for Simon could summon up nothing from the mules other than a slow trudge. But it seemed as if the insurgents had been deterred by Alice's pistol shot, for no one followed them and, indeed, the members of the little party felt as though they were the only moving life on that empty, dry plain.

Eventually, they meandered their way into another village, virtually a small town, for it was considerably larger than the place of their attack. The road led them into a warren of alleyways where, at last, people were evident, moving through the narrow streets and staring with a singular lack of benevolence at the cart and its exotic cargo of white-skinned foreigners. The party passed the open doorway of an indigo dye works, where rising steam obscured the workers within, and then a large, three-storey building, the smell of which confirmed to Jenkins, at least, that it was a rice-wine distillery.

Following Chang's very explicit directions – 'Now, cousin, pray take this next turning on the left' – they emerged into a small square dominated by a two-storeyed, wooden church, unmistakeable from the crucifix attached above the doorway.

Next to it was a small house, built, like those fronting the square, of cream-coloured mud brick and featuring ochre-coloured window shutters closed against the fierce sun and a rippling roof of purple tiles. Outside the house, looking anxiously up the street and rubbing her hands together in obvious anxiety, stood an elderly woman. She was small and dressed, Chinese fashion, in a shapeless cotton garment, her smock buttoned up to the chin and her long skirt ending just above wooden clogs. Unlike other women in the square, however, she wore no straw hat and her grey hair was scraped back into a serviceable bun at the nape of her neck. Her high cheekbones and the walnut-grained skin of her face made her appear Chinese, but the set of her eyes, distinguishable to the occupants of the cart as it came closer, confirmed her as European.

Alice let out a cry, 'Aunt Lizzie!' and leapt from the cart before it had stopped, engulfing the woman in her arms. The two stood rocking together on the doorstep of the house before the old lady gently pushed her niece away and peered anxiously over her shoulder into the wagon.

'Oh, thank the Lord,' she cried. 'You've got Chang.' And she held out her arms to the lad, who scrambled down and embraced his adoptive mother. The two stayed locked together for a moment before Mrs Griffith let him go and stretched out her hand to Fonthill.

'And you must be Simon,' she said. 'Oh, forgive me.' She pulled up a corner of her apron and wiped away a tear. 'You must think me so rude but,' she smiled at the boy, 'I was so sure that something had happened to . . .' then her voice

23

tailed away as she saw the cuts and bruises on Chang's face. 'Ah, I knew it. He has been hurt. What happened? Tell me.'

'Oh, I am all right, Mother. But I fear I would have been killed but for the intervention of my . . . er . . . my cousins. They were very brave. It was a party of Boxers, you see . . .'

'Enough,' cried the old lady. 'It is best to come inside, all of you. These are dangerous times. Simon, can you and your young man,' she indicated Jenkins, who beamed at the compliment, 'take the cart and mules into the courtyard through that door there. I will send someone to unharness the mules and take your bags. But it would be wise to get off the street as soon as possible. Come, dear Alice. This way. We tried to stop you coming but obviously our message did not get through. I thank God that you have not been harmed. Come in. Come in.'

Fifteen minutes later, they were all seated in the shade of the courtyard, drinking tea beside a large stone basin within which three white and gold koi carp circled languidly.

'Edward is making a visit to a sick parishioner,' explained Lizzie, 'but he will be here soon. Like me, he will be sorry but happy to see you. Our other son, Gerald, has been on a trip to Peking but he should be back tonight.'

'Have the Boxers bothered you, Mrs Griffith?' asked Simon.

'No, but we have been told that they have targeted us and that they are on their way here. That must have been the party that attacked Chang.' The old lady sniffed. 'Edward has refused to leave but we have just had a message from the bishop in Tientsin, ordering us to leave the mission and go to Peking.'

She put a brown-speckled hand to her brow and Simon marvelled, not for the first time, at the courage of these missionaries who spent their lives abroad, usually in discomfort and often in danger, to spread the word of their God. But Mrs Griffith was continuing, 'Mind you, I am not sure that the capital will be entirely safe, for I understand that the insurgents have burnt down the grandstand at the racecourse just outside the city.' She pursed her lips. 'It was the centre of social activity for the Europeans in the city, you know. Such a disgraceful thing to do. So uncalled for. I think we must leave now, though.'

Her voice tailed away and she looked around the courtyard. A shard of sunlight had been allowed to creep through the overhanging roof and it fell on the osmanthus plant in the corner, which she had proudly shown to her visitors and boasted that it was said to be more than four hundred years old. Simon realised what a wrench it would be for the Griffiths to leave their home, where, Alice had explained to Simon earlier, they had worked for thirty-two years, building the wooden church with their own hands and confirming hundreds of Chinese into the Christian church.

His reverie was interrupted by the arrival of the Reverend Edward Griffith, who expressed both the inevitable consternation and joy at their arrival. A tall, broad-shouldered man, Griffith presented as hearty and healthy a figure as his wife offered up frailty. It was clear that, unlike his spouse, he had prospered physically in the harsh climate of Northern China and, with his side whiskers and red face, he reminded Simon very much of the dominating presence of the clergyman's brother and Alice's late father, Brigadier Cecil Griffith, also of Simon's and Jenkins's old regiment, the 24th of Foot.

It had been the deaths, disconcertingly close together, of both Alice's and Simon's parents that had prompted the Fonthills to embark on the round-the-world trip that had led them to this small town in China. Some six years before, after taking part in Cecil Rhodes's invasion of Matabeleland and surviving the clash with King Lobengula's impis there, they had returned to Norfolk to farm Alice's estate. Restive with the unaccustomed tranquillity, however, and financially buttressed by inheritances from both sets of parents, the couple had decided to make a first visit to America and visit Alice's uncle in China on their way home. They were enjoying the vastness of the prairies of North America when news reached them of the outbreak of war in South Africa. Simon was anxious to hurry to Cape Town to join in the fight against the Boers, but Alice – not unsympathetic to the cause of the Afrikaner farmers – persuaded him that the war would be over by the time they reached Africa, so they continued their journey to China. It was only when they reached Tientsin that they heard of the Boxer Rebellion.

They were all changing for dinner when Gerald Griffith arrived, dusty from his journey to Peking. He was a tall, thin young man in his early twenties, English but dressed as a Chinaman and wearing the beginnings of a beard. He washed for dinner but did not change and seemed less than delighted to see the visitors as they assembled around the table.

'It is dangerous here, you know,' he said. 'You should not have come, for the downtrodden people of China do not like the *yang kuei-tzu*.'

'The *yang* . . . ?' enquired Alice.

'The foreign devils.' The young man spoke with a curl of his lip.

'That will do, Gerald,' said his father quickly. He turned apologetically to his guests. 'My son has grown up with the Chinese people – in fact he has never been home – and he shares an affinity with them. It is,' he shrugged, 'understandable and he has a point.'

'Of course,' said Simon. 'Perhaps you would explain a little of the background to this uprising – if that is what it is.'

'I will tell you what I know but first let us eat. Shall we say grace?'

They ate a surprisingly delicious dinner of herbal pancakes, a hotpot of fish and braised tofu – Simon surmised that Aunt Lizzie had raided what was best of her drought-denuded pantry to put on a show for her guests – and as their Chinese servant cleared away the plates, Simon repeated his request. The clergyman wiped his whiskers and settled back in his chair. 'It's all our dashed fault, really, you know,' he said.

'What?' asked Fonthill. 'Do you mean the British? The Opium Wars and all that?'

'Well partly, I suppose. But I really mean all the European imperial powers who have imposed themselves on this country. Dashed disgraceful, if you will pardon my language.'

'*Damned* disgraceful,' echoed Gerald. His face was flushed.

'Please watch your own language, Gerald,' Mr Griffith rebuked. 'There is no excuse for that.'

'Sorry, Father.'

Edward Griffith took another sip of rice wine and continued. 'The Manchu dynasty – it still rules, of course – always exercised a blind, reclusive xenophobia and until 1848 the only part of the Chinese Empire on which foreign merchants were permitted to set foot, and then only between October and March, was a plot of land on the Canton waterfront. Things began to change after we – the British, that is – forced the First Opium War on the Chinese in the 1840s. It was a shameful act on our part, you know.'

'Incredibly shameful,' added Gerald.

Griffith sighed and frowned at his son once again at the interruption. Mrs Griffith, however, took Gerald's hand and squeezed it. 'Let the boy speak, Edward,' she said gently. 'He has a right to his opinion.'

'Hmm. Now, where was I?'

'The Opium Wars, Reverend.' Jenkins was leaning forward, his chin on his fist, listening intently.

'Yes, thank you. Well, after the Treaty of Nanking which settled the war, the Chinese were forced to cede to Britain that barren lump of rock called Hong Kong, pay a swingeing indemnity, remove the most vexatious restrictions on commerce at Canton, open four other ports to trade and grant foreigners the right to reside in them. We had our foot in the Chinese door and we pushed it wide open.

'You see,' the clergyman filled his pipe with tobacco and stared at the ceiling, 'imperial expansion was the order of the day. China was weak.' He began thumping a large finger into the palm of his other hand in emphasis. 'Portugal had got Macao; France occupied a large part of Annam; in 1862 Britain annexed Lower Burma, just across the frontier; France then took three provinces of Lower Cochin-China and gained control of the Mekon basin; Russia then occupied a large tract of Chinese Turkestan; Japan took the Liu Chiu Islands; Britain annexed Upper Burma; and then, in 1887, the rest of Annam, Cochin-China and Cambodia were sequestered to form French Indo-China. It was a land grab of epic proportions.'

Griffith blew a blue cloud of tobacco smoke to the ceiling. 'Then came the war with Japan of 1894 to 1895 which ended in crushing defeat for this country and set off the land scramble again. It seemed as though it was China's destiny to be carved up, just as Africa has been.'

He gestured with his pipe. 'By 1895, most of the outlying dependencies of the Empire – I mean the Chinese one, not ours – had been lopped off. I don't know the figures, but the size of this vast country had been severely reduced. But it didn't stop there. The Germans were probably the worst. Two German missionaries were killed three years ago in the interior near Kiaochow. Instead of negotiating with Peking, the Kaiser rattled his great sabre and threatened war. As a result, he gained a ninety-nine-year lease of Kiaochow Bay, the city of Tsingtao, a whacking great indemnity for the two dead missionaries and extensive railway and mining concessions in that province. Then everybody jumped in.

'Spheres of influence became the thing to have. Germany

claimed exclusive influence here in Shantung, Russia in Manchuria, of course, Japan in Fukien and Britain in the Yangtze Valley. Can you imagine that sort of thing happening in the British Empire? Eh?'

A silence fell on the gathering. Gerald took a deep breath to speak, but his mother laid a quietening hand on his arm.

Eventually, Simon broke the silence. 'And the Boxers?' he asked.

'Ah yes, the Boxers. Well something had to give – or more precisely something had to rise. They first appeared in this province about two years ago, when the Germans were pressing hard on the Kiaochow Bay business. They are mainly young men, often youths, and they call themselves . . . er . . . what is it, Chang?'

The youth cleared his throat to answer but a glowering Gerald intervened. 'The *I Ho Ch'uan,*' he said, as though with pride. 'The Society of Righteous and Harmonious Fists.'

Jenkins let out a great guffaw, to be silenced by a glare from Fonthill.

'Quite so,' continued the clergyman. 'Strange, of course, to us. White people called them "Boxers" because they were so fit, although they would never know how to fight with their fists in a skilled manner, as we do. Like uneducated insurgents the world over . . .' he gestured with his pipe towards Simon – 'you in particular will remember the Mahdi's followers in the Sudan—'

Fonthill nodded.

'—they all think that they are "the chosen ones" and that no bullets can harm them. They hate Europeans and particularly members of religious groups and poor devils like us, the missionaries.'

He puffed at his pipe. 'Although it is the Catholics who seem to have caught it in the neck most. I suppose you could say that the priests had it coming to them. Back in 1860, the French had negotiated a treaty under which their Roman Catholic missionaries were given all kinds of rights denied to others – rights of residence in the interior, the building of churches and the establishment of orphanages. The last bit has caused all kinds of problems, giving rise to rumours that the priests were stealing Chinese children and killing them. But it was worse than that . . .' He gestured with both hands. 'All Catholic bishops were granted the same rank as provincial governors, they were allowed to wear a mandarin's button and carry the umbrella of honour and even,' he blew out his cheeks in disgust, 'awarded the discharge of a cannon when they come and go. It had all got out of hand. As a result, we are all being tarred with the same brush.'

Mrs Griffith took up the story. 'You see, all this has coincided with terrible times here,' she said, her eyes glistening in the lamplight. 'The drought is the worst for decades, ruining the rice crop and putting water at a premium. We – the so-called foreign devils – are getting the blame for this, including the mining and railway engineers here. It is being said that the laying of railway tracks is desecrating the graves of ancestors and the new telegraph poles cause moaning in the wind, which the peasants on whose lands they have been erected say is the crying of the dead. We foreigners are being

31

blamed for upsetting the balance of nature, as well as killing the cotton market by importing cloth and garments.'

'The British are the worst.' The truculence in Gerald's voice was evident. 'Although the Empress has banned the opium trade,' he said, 'the British traders keep it going, of course, and make much money from it. Everyone knows that.'

The visitors all looked down at the table, unsure of what to say. Then Fonthill looked up and studied the young man for a moment. There was none of his father's fortitude in his face, nor any of his mother's sensitivity. His features reflected intelligence, there was no doubt of that, but his mouth was weak and his eyes showed only antagonism.

Simon cleared his throat. 'What about the Empress?' he asked of Griffith. 'Does she approve of the Boxers or try to suppress them?'

The missionary smiled. 'A good question. She's a formidable woman. Oiled, black hair pulled straight back, skin like porcelain and long, manicured fingernails, curved like claws. They call her "The Dragon Lady". You may know that the old girl – she's actually the Empress Dowager – deposed her nephew the Emperor Kuang Hsu about eighteen months ago, for being too much in favour of Western modernisation?'

Simon shook his head.

'Well, she's as clever as a fox leading the hunt. Officially she disapproves of the Boxers, but in reality she is encouraging them, there's no doubt about that. She thinks that they will teach the foreigners a lesson or two without her getting the blame and, anyway, they would be too expensive to put down.' The old man sighed. 'They're spreading out quickly, you see.'

'And coming this way,' added Gerald, his eyes alight. 'They told me in Peking that the Boxers who burnt the racecourse pavilion are only the vanguard. It is said that the army might join them.'

'Ah, I doubt that,' said Edward Griffith. 'The Empress would never allow that. It would upset the apple cart completely with the British and the other foreign ministers at the Manchu court—'

'Who are complete ciphers,' interrupted Gerald. 'Weak men representing weak regimes.'

'Blimey,' muttered Jenkins in a whispered aside to Fonthill. ''Oos side is 'e on, then?'

Another silence fell on the little gathering. The shadows flickering across the faces of the group seemed to presage and emphasize the dangers that lay outside the walls. A sense of impending disaster permeated the room. 'Well, sir,' asked Simon. 'Will you leave your home here?'

At first it seemed as though the old man was ignoring the question. He leant across the table and took up his wife's hand. He addressed her in a low voice: 'I think, my dear, that we now have no alternative.' He nodded towards Chang, who sat listening intently to everything that was being said. 'What has happened to our son today confirms the danger. I have been stupid in delaying so long. But now, I think we must leave before dawn. These people are so close. They could come tomorrow.'

Lizzie Griffith put a hand to her mouth. 'That quickly! We can never pack in time.'

Her husband squeezed her hand. 'We cannot take much with us, Lizzie. I am so sorry, but we must leave almost immediately. Time for a little sleep and then we must away. Of one thing, I promise you . . .' He looked into her eyes. 'We shall return.'

Tears were now trickling down Mrs Griffith's cheeks. 'But where shall we go?'

'To Peking. We shall find shelter there and we can stay until this trouble blows over. It will be transitory I feel sure.' He looked up at his visitors. 'I am so sorry, dear friends, that I must ask you to leave as soon as you arrive. But there is no other choice.'

Alice stood and moved behind her aunt's chair, putting her cheek next to hers and embracing her. 'My dear aunt,' she said. 'It is lucky we are here, for we can protect you on the journey. And I shall help you pack the few things you can take. We can jettison the things of ours we don't need to make room in the cart. All will be well, you will see.'

And so the little gathering broke up. In a corner of the room, Simon detained the Reverend. 'Do you have any weapons, sir?'

The old man gave a wan smile. 'One rather old fowling piece. I fear that is all. But I do not favour violence. I speak fluent Mandarin and, if we are accosted, I think I can reason with them. I believe I am known for doing good work in this region for many years. And anyway,' he put his hand on Simon's shoulder, 'I know that the Good Lord will protect us.'

34

As he stepped away, Jenkins moved to Fonthill's side. 'The Good Lord,' he growled, 'plus one old fowling piece and two Colt revolvers. It's not much, bach sir, is it?'

Simon nodded and gave a half-smile. 'Alice has a small pistol, but no, not much. I fear it could be quite a journey. Gird your loins, 352, gird your loins.'

'Ah yes.' Jenkins frowned. 'D'you know, I've never been quite sure what loins are . . . ?'

'They're things that have to be girt. Bed now.'

CHAPTER TWO

They were on the road well before sunrise. There were no tears on Mrs Griffith's face now as she organised the departure with calm efficiency, as though they were merely making a summer visit to the capital. The crude cart that had carried the visitors was left behind and the Griffiths' much larger wagon was put into service to carry both sets of baggage. As the little party wound through the narrow alleyways, Simon on horseback took the lead, with a surly Gerald on his pony alongside to point the way; the Reverend Griffith drove the wagon, with Chang at his side, the two women sitting amidst the baggage and a mounted Jenkins rode behind as rearguard. Fonthill and Jenkins each carried a pearl-handled Colt revolver, and the sporting shotgun, which the missionary chose not to load, lay amongst the bags at the back of the wagon.

'How far to Peking?' asked Fonthill.

'About fifteen miles,' replied Gerald. 'The road gets better nearer the city, of course.'

'Is it open country?'

'Most of the way.'

Simon thought for a moment. 'Is there one place where we might be ambushed – where there is cover on either side?'

'Er . . . yes. Probably.' The young man's eyes widened. 'It's a small village. We have to go through its centre.'

'Can we get round it?'

'No, not really. Fields are too rough on either side.'

'Right. Tell me when we near it.'

The sun rose to make the world a heat bowl once again and Griffith stopped to stretch a tarpaulin over the rickety frame on the wagon to give its occupants some shade. The barren nature of the plain afforded them no relief from the sun, of course, but it gave them an excellent view all around, enabling them to detect any sign of pursuit, even from far away.

They skirted two villages without incident. Outside one, they met two peasants, attempting to work in the hard ground. Griffith called to them and asked for news of Boxers but the men's faces remained quite impassive and he received no reply, even when the question was repeated by Chang in a more colloquial dialect.

Jenkins rode up. 'I think people are comin' up be'ind us, bach sir,' he reported.

Fonthill whirled round in the saddle and squinted back down the road. 'Dammit. I wish I had field glasses. Can't see a sign of anyone. Can you, Gerald, you've got young eyes?'

'No. Nothing.'

Jenkins sniffed. 'Oh, they're there all right. Look 'ard. There's a bit of a dust cloud, way back.'

Simon shielded his eyes and squinted. 'Ah, yes. I see what you mean. Boxers, do you think?'

'Who else would be travellin' in a crowd, like that?'

'Gerald?'

Fear showed in the man's eyes. 'Yes. I should think so. They're coming after us, all right. We shouldn't have left. We could have stayed and spread ourselves round amongst neighbours. That way they probably wouldn't have found all of us.'

Fonthill eyed him keenly. 'Just your father, eh?'

'No. I didn't mean that.'

'Right. We'll wait here for them.'

Gerald's jaw dropped. 'You must be mad. We have four mules. If we whip them hard, we might be able to outpace them, if they're on foot.'

'Not in this heat – and mules don't like to run. Neither do I, for that matter. No, we'll wait here for them. Reverend,' he walked his horse over to where Griffith was tying up a loose part of the tarpaulin, 'it seems that we are being followed and they are probably Boxers.'

Mrs Griffith drew in her breath sharply but her husband's face betrayed no emotion. 'Very well,' he said. 'Even in this heat, the Chinese travel fast on foot, so I doubt if we can outdistance them. What do you propose?'

'I agree that we can't run. I suggest that we wait here for

them. The road is narrow and there are quite wide ditches on either side, so it could be difficult for them to surround us. I think we might deter them with our pistols.'

'Ah no.' The clergyman shook his head. 'No violence. Let me talk to them. Some of them could be locals and they will know me. We must put our trust in the Lord.'

Simon eyed him for a moment, then nodded. 'Very well, sir. But I reserve the right to shoot if things get nasty. From what I've heard, the Boxers don't have firearms, they rely on swords and clubs, so we might have a chance of putting them off, anyway. Right. We don't have much time. Jenkins.'

'Sir.'

'Hitch your horse to the far side of the wagon – not the rear, close to the ditch – and take that shovel. See that declivity in the field over there . . . ?'

'What's a declivity when it's at 'ome?'

'Oh Lord, I do wish sometimes that you had finished that Army Certificate of Education that you started on.'

'Well, I would 'ave, wouldn't I, if you 'adn't taken me off to fight the savage Zulu, see.'

'All right. That dip in the ground over there? See it?'

'Oh yes.'

'Dig a hole in it, sufficiently deep to give you cover. Don't pile up soil, though. I don't want the Boxers to know you're there. Take ammunition for your Colt from the box in the wagon and then go quickly. There's little time. If firing starts I want you to give covering fire. But don't fire unless I do. Understand?'

Jenkins's eyes had become cold and hard again. Fonthill

knew the signs. The Welshman was ready for – was about to revel in – action and danger.

'Very good, bach sir.'

'Good. Double away.'

'What do you want me to do?' Gerald Griffith's voice was querulous.

Simon looked back at the wagon. The missionary was sitting on the driving seat, slowly turning the pages of his Bible. Alice, Lizzie and Chang were now out of sight behind the tarpaulin, although, of course, the wagon was open fore and aft. Fonthill turned to Gerald.

'If fighting does start,' he said, 'we will be fairly useless on horseback, for gunfire will disturb the horses and make it difficult to fire accurately. So we will hitch the horses to the side of the wagon to stop them boarding from that side. Please tie your horse and then load the fowling piece. We will wait under cover while your father speaks to these people. But we will demonstrate that we are armed. We must not fire unless we have to. However . . .' he now spoke with emphasis '. . . Do not fire until I do. And when you do fire, aim to kill. There can be no hesitation once the fighting begins – if it does, that is. Now, tie your horse and then get into the wagon.'

Wide-eyed, Gerald nodded and led his horse to the far side of the wagon. Fonthill followed him, hitched up his own mount and climbed inside. As he did so, the Reverend Griffith stepped down and, Bible in hand, walked a little way down the road towards where the dust cloud could now be clearly seen.

'What is happening, Simon?' asked Alice. Mrs Griffith

was by her side. Anxiety was reflected in both their faces. Chang, sitting at their feet, seemed quite unperturbed.

'I think there is no need for alarm yet,' said Fonthill. 'However, it looks as though the Boxers have followed us and are approaching. We cannot outdistance them so we shall wait for them here. Mr Griffith is confident that he can talk them out of violence and so there will be no shooting unless we really have to defend ourselves.'

Mrs Griffith shot a glance over her shoulder. 'I do not like Edward going among those people,' she said. 'He should stay in the wagon.'

Simon nodded. 'I quite agree. I will ask him to return. In the meantime, Alice?'

His wife nodded.

'Do you have that little popgun of yours that was so useful in the Sudan?'

'It is not a popgun, Simon. It is a very effective French officer's side arm, a very fine, eleven-millimetre Chamelot-Delvigne, that served me well in Egypt as well as the Sudan.' She withdrew the scarf that lay across her lap to reveal the little, steel-blue automatic.

Fonthill gave a smile that didn't reach his eyes. 'Good. I am sorry we can't give you a Colt, because you are probably a better shot with it than me. But have your little gun ready. Don't shoot until I do.'

Then he bowed his head. 'Sorry, Mrs Griffith. I promise that we will try and avoid violence.' He climbed down from the wagon and walked towards where the clergyman was standing, looking down the road. Their pursuers could now

41

be seen and flashes of scarlet revealed their identity.

'I think it would be safer if you addressed them from the wagon, sir,' he said.

Griffith smiled, a little wistfully. 'No, Simon. I want to show that I am part of them. So I shall walk towards them, in peace, and speak to them from their midst. I think it is the best way.'

Simon's heart fell. If the clergyman formed part of the crowd, it would be extremely difficult to defend him if the mob turned on him. He turned to his right and looked across the field. There was no sign of Jenkins, except what could be a ripple of fresh earth, some thirty yards away. Good. That flank was covered, anyway. He smiled confidently at the missionary.

'Of course, sir. Good luck. Don't be afraid to run back to the wagon if you have to. We will cover you.'

'I will.' Griffith held out his hand. 'God bless you, nephew.'

They shook hands and Fonthill climbed back into the wagon. He addressed Gerald. 'Have you loaded the fowling piece?'

'Yes, but I can't see me harming anyone with it. It only shoots pellets.'

'It doesn't matter. It will have a deterrent effect. Now,' he addressed the others, 'Mrs Griffith please keep low. The rest of us will show our weapons when the Boxers come up, I will pull back the tarpaulin to show them that we are armed. Gerald, you take the rear of the wagon, Alice you guard the front, Chang you hold the reins of the mules and attempt to quieten them if shooting starts. I will guard the side facing the road. The horses hitched on the other side should stop them climbing aboard from that side. Let me repeat – do not fire unless I do.'

'Where is 352?' asked Alice.

'He is hidden out in the field. If we have to shoot, firing coming from the flank should disconcert the Boxers.'

Gerald's face was white. 'What if they have guns? We could be mown down.'

'I doubt if they will have rifles or anything like that. If they do, shoot at the marksmen first. Here they come. Good luck everyone.'

Fonthill finished unfurling the tarpaulin, so that the interior of the wagon was revealed. As he tied the last cord, he caught a glimpse of the Reverend Griffith stepping forward to meet the Boxers, his hand upheld in the universal gesture of peace. Simon bit his lip as he watched. He tried to count the Chinamen and gave up at fourteen. Perhaps there were twenty. Far too many, anyway. A Daniel – a very old but brave Daniel – was about to enter the lion's den, with only his Bible to protect him.

Fonthill adopted what he hoped was a commanding posture: one booted foot on the sideboard of the wagon, one arrogant hand on his hip and the other holding the Colt at his side, the sun glinting on its long barrel. He nodded sharply to Gerald.

'Show your gun, young man. You too, Alice.'

Small beads of perspiration were now showing on his wife's upper lip, but she nodded and moved to the open rear of the wagon and began making a great show of loading her little automatic pistol. Gerald Griffith crept up behind her and held up his fowling piece as though about to shoot a passing bird. Mrs Griffith knelt a little unsteadily on an old leather case, her hands clasped together and her eyes tightly closed as she prayed. Chang, one of whose eyes had partly closed following yesterday's affray, had taken up his post on the driver's seat, waiting in silence.

Simon turned his gaze back to the missionary. He had now reached the Boxers, who immediately opened their ranks and allowed him to mingle with them. He stood out, tall and erect, in their midst, both hands held high, one of them holding his Bible. The Chinese had fallen silent now and the missionary's voice could just be heard, speaking quite slowly and evenly and sounding even more mellifluous in Mandarin. To Fonthill, he cut a biblical figure, as though he were a medieval preacher addressing his flock. His mind went back to an old painting that had hung in his father's study. The metaphor was made even more apt by the rapt, open faces of the young men surrounding him. Simon was reminded that they were peasants, many of them seemingly still in their teens. As far as he could see, few of them wore shoes or sandals. Violence suddenly seemed far away on this warm, sunlit morning.

Suddenly, there was a sharp report from within the wagon and Fonthill swung around to see Gerald Griffith staring at the smoking barrel of his gun.

'What the hell—?' snarled Simon.

'It just went off.' The young man's mouth hung open.

The heads of everyone in the group turned towards the wagon and the scene froze for a split second. Then a chant began from the back of the rabble, '*Sha! Sha! Sha!*'

'What does that mean?' asked Alice, wide-eyed.

'Means kill,' called back Chang. 'I think they come at us now.'

'Reload your gun,' Fonthill ordered Gerald. 'Quickly now, man, for God's sake.'

The chant was taken up by the rest of the Boxers and Simon caught a momentary glimpse of Edward Griffith holding out his hands in a placatory gesture, when a sword flashed and he disappeared into the crowd.

'Ah no!' cried Alice.

'Get to the front, Alice,' shouted Simon.

Several more swords were swung high in the middle of the crowd and then the Boxers turned towards the wagon. 'Don't fire yet, 352,' yelled Fonthill. 'I'll try and warn them off.'

He held up his free hand, palm facing outward towards the mob, and then fired his revolver above their heads.

It had the reverse effect to that intended – indeed it seemed to act like the starting gun in a race, for the front row of the Boxers immediately produced swords and began to run towards the wagon.

'Fire, Jenkins,' cried Simon. There were only about sixty yards between the attackers and the defenders and Fonthill realised that he had only six shots with which to deter the charge, for there would be little time to reload. He took careful aim, fired and brought down the leading man.

Cocking back the hammer with his thumb, he fired again, and then again and again. Behind him, he heard the bark of Alice's automatic and the deeper report of the fowling piece.

The front row of the attackers seemed to melt away and the second line tripped over five bodies on the ground and the remainder halted, their swords held aloft still truculently, but their aggression now replaced by indecision.

In those few precious seconds, Simon thrust three more rounds into his Colt. Coolly, he aimed again and fired, then twice more. At almost the same time, he heard firing from the field to his right and glimpsed an erect Jenkins, hammering back the cocking mechanism of his revolver with his left hand as he let off round after round in rapid succession.

It was enough. The surprise of the attack from the right – although at too great a distance for Jenkins's handgun to be a killing piece – broke whatever resistance was left among the Boxers and they turned and fled back up the road from which they had come. In an amazingly few moments, they had shrunk to diminutive figures in the dusty distance. The attack was over almost as soon as it had begun.

Fonthill leapt down from the wagon and ran towards where he could see the Reverend Griffith lying in a pool of blood.

He bent down. 'Oh my God.' Suddenly, Alice was by his side. 'Are we too late?'

Simon gently turned the missionary over. His left shoulder bore a deep gash and his right arm had been almost completely severed at the biceps, although the fingers of the hand still clutched his Bible. Blood oozed from a sword thrust to the breast and another to the stomach. A half-smile remained fixed on the old man's face, as though something in that vicious outburst of violence had amused him. Or perhaps he was pleased at the end to be exchanging one world for another, for he was quite dead.

'Don't let Mrs Griffith . . .' began Fonthill. But he realised that he was too late. The missionary's wife was looking down at her husband, her hands clasped before her, one tear threading its way down her cheek.

Alice rose and gathered her aunt into her arms. But she was gently pushed away. Mrs Griffith gestured over her shoulder to where the Chinese lay in the road.

'Some of these poor people are wounded,' she said. 'We cannot help Edward now, but we may be able to reduce the suffering of those whom we have injured. Alice, in my main case, there is a little leather first-aid box. Please bring it and you and I will do what we can. Now, Simon,' she looked up at him, 'perhaps you would be kind enough to leave me for a moment with my husband, so that I can say goodbye. Thank you.'

Fonthill bent his head and walked towards where Jenkins was picking his way back across the field. 'A bit bloody late with your covering fire, 352,' he said. 'What happened? Did you doze off?'

'Doze off be buggered, beggin' your pardon, bach sir.' He gestured to his Colt. 'This bloody thing jammed, just as the firin' started, see. That's why, once I 'ad it cleared, like, I started blazin' away in case they 'adn't noticed me. Sorry about that, but it wasn't my fault, see.'

He gestured towards where Mrs Griffith was kneeling beside her husband. ''As the Reverend copped it, then?'

'I'm afraid so. Come on. I want a word with young Mr Gerald.'

They found the young man rather too frantically helping Alice to find his mother's first-aid box. Chang was kneeling by the front wheel of the wagon, quietly sobbing.

When the box had been found and Alice ran with it to her aunt, Fonthill addressed Gerald Griffith. 'Why the hell did you fire your piece,' he demanded, 'when I told you *not* to fire until I did?'

'I didn't fire it. It sort of went off on its own.' Gerald's eyes were staring and his mouth set hard under its thin moustache. 'It's all your fault. If you hadn't told us to show our weapons – for all the good *that* did – the thing wouldn't have gone off. I wouldn't have had to wave it about.'

Jenkins clenched his fist and took a pace forward. 'Don't you talk to the captain like that,' he growled. 'You're not fit to clean 'is boots.'

'That will do, 352.' Fonthill's voice was low with disgust. He addressed Griffith again. 'Now, I am afraid that you have lost your father and your mother will need all the help you can give her. I suggest you go to her now and help her in what she is doing – and I suggest you take your brother with you.'

'He's not my bro—' He broke off when he saw the light in Fonthill's eye. 'Oh, very well.'

Simon and Jenkins watched the two walk slowly to where Mrs Griffith and Alice were now tending two Boxers, who were sitting up in the road. 'As far as I can see,' said Fonthill, 'not one of the people who attacked us was hit by buckshot from that lad's piece. He must be a particularly bad shot. It would have been almost impossible to have missed at this range.'

'Ah.' Jenkins sucked in his moustache. 'And do you think 'e let off that thing deliberately early?'

'What?' Fonthill looked at his old comrade sharply. 'And *deliberately* cause the death of his father?'

'Hmm. Wouldn't know about that, bach sir. That's a serious thing to say about a feller, ain't it? I wouldn't know.'

'Neither would I. Come on. Let's wrap up the reverend in a sheet or something and lay him in the wagon. We can't leave him here. But we can leave them,' he indicated the dead Boxers. 'Best put them in the ditch. No time to bury them for we must be on our way. I shall be glad to be out of here.'

Simon looked around him reflectively. There was no one else to be seen, for the Boxers had long since disappeared and, for all the firing, nobody had materialised from a village that could be glimpsed about half a mile away. The fields were barren. Five dead bodies, in addition to the missionary, lay in the roadway. Alice was tying a bandage around the calf of one of the wounded Chinamen and Mrs Griffith was fixing a sling to the other's arm. Both men looked bemused but submissive. No danger there. He sighed. It had been six years since he had last experienced violence; since he had last seen men cut down in their prime. Now, within nine days of landing in China, he had experienced it twice. He wrinkled his brow in dismay. Was he born to attract it, he wondered? Did his life now *have* to be a choice between the boredom of a pastoral existence in Norfolk and the undoubted excitement of the last two days, with its concomitant sadness of the killing of a good man like the Reverend Griffith? Wasn't there a middle road he could tread? He sighed. One thing was sure: the answer wouldn't be found on this bloodstained road. Best to get out of here as fast as possible. There might be other bands of Boxers in the vicinity. Within fifteen minutes, the body of the clergyman had been wrapped in a waterproof sheet and gently placed in the rear of the wagon, and the dead Chinese rolled into the ditch. A crutch had been fashioned for the man wounded in the leg and he and his comrade had been told to retrace their steps back to the nearest village behind them – not, Simon insisted, that which lay ahead.

That, in fact, proved to be as deserted as the others they had passed through and Simon wondered whether its inhabitants were staying indoors, for surely they must have heard the sound of gunfire. Or had they fled at the threat of trouble? Chang, peering through his good eye, which was still weeping tears at the loss of his 'father', was proving to be a skilled handler of the mules and they made good progress through the village and also through that which Gerald had warned could be a place of ambush. It was as though they were journeying through a landscape torn by war, although there was no obvious sign of conflict or depredation.

The terrain changed somewhat, however, as they neared Peking. Shallow canals, which still retained a vestige of water, crossed the fields and crops of *kaoliang*, a form of millet, some of it ten feet high, were standing tall around them. They gave Simon cause for concern for they could easily conceal parties of Boxers.

His anxiety increased when Gerald was able to question one worker in the fields not afraid to talk with them.

'He says,' reported the young man, his face animated, 'that Boxers have attacked and set fire to Fengtai, the railway junction not far from here, and that the rail link has been cut. He says we are in danger.'

'Well,' snorted Jenkins from his post riding behind the wagon, 'we didn't need 'im to tell us that, now, did we?'

Alice looked up from the rear, where she was cushioning the head of Mrs Griffith on her shoulder. 'How far to Peking now, then?' she enquired quietly.

Chang sniffed and answered, 'Not far, cousin. Say three, four miles. Should soon see city.'

And so they did. It rose from the plain like some medieval fortress, surrounded with walls of stone some forty feet high and topped by castellated battlements. Towers with the distinctive flared roofs of the Chinese stood out like sentinels from deep within the city and, unlike the surrounding countryside, there was much traffic through the high gates within the walls.

'Where do we go?' asked Fonthill, riding alongside Gerald.

'We must make for the Legation Quarter in the heart of the city. This is almost a city within a city and houses the diplomatic corps.' His lips curled at the words.

'How many legations are there?'

'Eleven. All the fat birds that have been picking clean the bones of the Chinese Empire for so many years are there.' He numbered them by ticking off his fingers. 'The British, the Austro-Hungarians, the Americans, the Belgians, the French, the Germans, the Dutch, the Italians, the Japanese, the Russians . . .' He paused, attempting to recollect the last. 'Ah yes. The Spanish. They are all represented by these pompous ministers with their fancy uniforms and plumed hats. No wonder the Empress hates them all.'

'Does she?'

'Oh yes.' The young man smirked. 'If she had her way she would let her army clean them all out. But the Boxers will probably do it for her.'

At this point the wagon trundled through the deep opening of one of the gates and they were immediately among narrow streets that teemed with humanity. Fonthill frowned. The Legation Quarter did not sound like much of a sanctuary.

'Is the Quarter walled?' he asked.

'In some places. Peking is a city of walls.' Gerald became animated. 'The Legation Quarter is an enclave about . . .' He mused for a moment, his forefinger on his chin. 'Roughly about half to three-quarters of a mile square, I suppose. Part of it borders on the Imperial City – the palace and the Forbidden City, you know?'

Fonthill nodded, although he didn't know.

'Alongside the legations the *yang kuei-tzu*—'

Simon interrupted. 'The *yang* what?'

The young man shook his head impatiently. 'I told you. The *yang kuei-tzu* means the foreigners. The foreign barbarians.'

'Wait a minute.' Fonthill put his hand on Gerald's arm. 'Barbarians! Gerald, *you* are a foreigner. Your father was. Your mother is. I am. We are not barbarians.'

Gerald Griffith flushed. 'That is what the Chinese call you . . . us. But I am not a foreigner. I was born in China. That makes a difference, you know.'

'Really. Very well. Now continue to tell me about the Legation.'

'Well, within the enclave and all around the legations the foreign commercial houses have established themselves: the Hongkong and Shanghai Bank, the Russo-Chinese Bank, two shops, Imbeck's and Kierulff's, the Peking Hotel and the Club.'

'The Club?'

'Yes. All of the people who matter – the white people, that is – are members.'

Fonthill thought for a moment. 'The Quarter – the enclave – could it be defended?'

Gerald gave a lofty smile and indicated the houses all around them. 'You see how closely the houses are built. They go right up to the edge of the Quarter. It would be difficult, I think.'

'Is the Quarter completely walled?'

'Oh no. There is the Tartar City to the north, in which the Forbidden City and the palace is built, and this is walled where it meets the Quarter, and in the south, the great Tartar

53

Wall acts as a boundary to the Quarter, but these are the only places where you could say big walls help to protect it. But I don't know. I am not a soldier.'

'Hmm. And how many people – foreigners – are there working and living within the Quarter?'

'I think about five hundred.'

'I see. Thank you, Gerald.' But Simon was not at all reassured. A 'city within a city', with houses pressing up close to the boundaries and sides seeming comparatively open. Not exactly a fortress . . .

Soon they entered the Quarter and approached the British Legation, the largest of all the diplomatic buildings, by the look of it, built of stone but with the distinctive Chinese roof tiles sweeping low and turned up at the gutters. A Union Jack fluttered from a flagstaff outside. There they dismounted and the ladies were handed down, Mrs Griffith standing upright and firm, no tears now evident on her rough cheeks, although her eyes remained moist.

Within minutes the members of the party were seated before a large desk behind which sat the British Minister to the Chinese Court, Sir Claude MacDonald. He was a tall, raw-boned man, in his late forties, with a thin face and the ruddy cheeks of a highlander, framed by a wide sweeping moustache, the ends of which had been waxed so that they stood out like the wing tips of a bird of prey.

He listened with fierce concentration, his bulbous eyes fixed intently on Simon's face as the details of their journey, including the two encounters with the Boxers, were related.

At the end, he stood, took Mrs Griffith's hand and bowed low over it.

'How frightful, madam,' he said. 'I am so sorry. I never had the pleasure of meeting your husband, but I heard much of his good works in the province. You have my deepest condolences.'

Mrs Griffith inclined her head in acknowledgement. 'We must make immediate arrangements,' he rolled his 'r's slightly on the word, 'for your husband's interment here in the Legation's cemetery. I presume, ma'am, that is what you would wish?'

'Thank you, sir.'

Sir Claude rang a bell and a Chinese servant in an impeccable loose, white tunic entered. The minister spoke to him in Mandarin and turned back to the visitors.

'I have given instructions for your things to be taken to the Peking Hotel, a short walk from here, and for rooms to be booked for you all. I suggest that you go there immediately – my servant here will show you the way – and take some rest and refreshment. I will be here at your service should you need anything. We can talk later about your future. I hope that it won't be long before you will be able to return to your house and church, Mrs Griffith.'

They stood but the tall man laid a hand on Simon's arm. 'I believe you were a captain in the British army, sir?'

'I was, Sir Claude, but some years ago now, I fear.'

'Yes, I have heard of you. Good work in Afghanistan, the Sudan and Matabeleland, I understand. I would be grateful if you could tarry a moment to talk with me.'

'Of course, sir. 352, go with the ladies and make sure they are comfortable.'

'Very good, bach sir.'

Once the two were seated, Sir Claude offered a cigarette and requested that Fonthill go through the details of the attack once again. At the end, he nodded, blew a blue cloud of smoke up to the ceiling, watching it, his head back.

At length, Simon broke the silence. 'Do you anticipate that the Boxers will attack the Legation Quarter, Sir Claude?'

The minister shrugged. 'It really depends on the Empress, Fonthill. It is rumoured that she might sit back and quietly encourage them to have a go at us, don't you know. But I rather doubt it. She wouldn't dare to flout the Foreign Powers in that way.'

'But aren't the Boxers on their way here? I understand that they have torched the railway junction near here and cut the telegraph wires.'

'Quite so. In addition to Mr Griffith, I hear that two more British missionaries have been murdered in the province. Worse than that, however, the Empress has replaced Prince Ching, a most amenable chap, as president of China, with a feller called Prince Tuan. Now, he's a reactionary of the worst kind. Hates all foreigners and he could well encourage the Boxers.'

Fonthill frowned. 'Good Lord. So it all looks rather bad?'

MacDonald stood. 'Not at all. No need for funk at all, my dear fellow. However, as a precaution, I telegraphed Tientsin and asked that a detachment of military should be sent here without delay. Some three hundred officers and men – mainly sailors and marines from European warships lying off Taku Bar – have been despatched. They should be here very soon. Should be enough to ward off any nonsense from these Boxer fellers.'

He held out his hand. 'But good to have you here, just in case, Fonthill. You could well be damned useful if we do have a spot of bother. So I hope you will stay a day or two, what?'

'Of course, sir.' They shook hands.

The minister walked him to the door and laid a hand on his shoulder. 'By the way, I have just heard some good news from home. Mafeking has been relieved.'

Fonthill stared back bleakly. 'Mafeking? What…where…is that?'

'Good Lord, don't you know? Ah, but of course. You have been travelling. The war in South Africa, this trouble with the Boers. You must know that they have been besieging Mafeking, this town in the Transvaal, for ages. Well, we've relieved the siege at last. It's been a source of great rejoicing back home.'

'Yes, of course. I know *that* Mafeking. But . . . do you mean that the war in South Africa is still on?'

'Oh yes.' Sir Claude gave a wry smile. 'My dear chap, you really must have been out of touch. These Boers gave us a terrible hiding in the first few weeks. They brought off three major victories, but the tide has turned, as we always knew it would. The matter should be brought to a close very soon now, I would think. But it was touch and go for a time.'

Simon frowned. 'Yes. I always thought that the Boer

farmer was the best light-cavalryman in the world.' And then, almost to himself, 'I should have been there, dammit. I should have been there.' He looked up at the Scotsman and smiled. 'Ah well, can't be helped. Let's hope it's over soon. And this affair, too.'

'Quite so. I am sure it will be. I don't really anticipate trouble, you know. We should all be quite safe within the Legation Quarter and I trust Her Celestial Highness to sort out the Boxers if and when they get here.' He gave a paternal smile. 'Now go and get some rest, my dear chap. You've had quite a day of it.'

'Thank you, sir. Goodbye.'

Fonthill walked out into the hot sun and looked around him. Unlike the teeming streets outside, the Quarter seemed somnolent. A cluster of cream-suited Europeans wearing solar topees walked by and, despite the heat, several tight-waisted ladies, with smart straw hats tied under their chins by coloured scarves, sauntered past, holding parasols above their heads. Simon doffed his hat and they smiled back. It was all so civilised. Then he remembered the hundreds – the thousands – of Chinese on the other side of those high walls and he heard again the cries of '*Sha! Sha!*'

He strode away, a troubled frown on his face.

CHAPTER THREE

The next evening the detachment from Tientsin, mainly sailors, arrived. They marched through the streets of Peking into the Legation Quarter with bayonets fixed, a fine sight. Yet their journey had not been uneventful. They had to be transported from their ships in the bay by lighters and other shallow-draught vessels past the Chinese forts guarding the River Pei Ho to the small river port of Tangku, from which they were able to entrain for Tientsin and travel on, via the now repaired railway, to the line terminal at Machiapu, just outside the walls of Peking. There, however, six thousand Muslim soldiers from the northern province of Kansu had been concentrated by the Chinese authorities to await the arrival of the foreign force.

Throughout that day, Fonthill and his companions had grown increasingly aware that the residents within the enclave did not share Sir Claude MacDonald's sanguine view of events. Crowds could be heard in the streets outside the Legation walls chanting and shouting. It was said that many of the missionaries in their compounds out in the Chinese City had donned native dress, twisted their long hair into pigtails and prepared for flight.

It was a huge relief, then, when, at the last minute, the Kansu troops were withdrawn and the polyglot contingent was allowed to pass unmolested through to the Yung Ting Men, the main, gated entrance to the city, and then through the streets to the Quarter. In all, 337 officers and men, comprising guards specifically for the British, French, Italian, Japanese and Russian legations, marched in, led by a tiny contingent of the United States Marine Corps.

Fonthill and Jenkins watched them, silent among all the foreign residents around them who were waving and cheering the arrivals.

'It's not much, is it?' sniffed Jenkins.

'No, it's not,' Simon agreed. 'And it's a mixed bunch of nationalities, always difficult to command in action. Still, they look professional and I would back trained troops any day, however small, against a mob.'

A further contingent of fifty-two German and thirty-seven Austrian sailors arrived three days later and the presence of the troops had an almost magical effect on the city. The mobs outside the Quarter dispersed, the tension eased and those missionaries who had taken refuge within the Legation went back to their compounds in the city. Mrs Griffith, who with the rest of her party had attended the burial of her husband, began making plans to return home with her two sons.

Fonthill took advantage of this one evening to ask the old lady about Gerald. The young man had continually absented himself during the first days after their arrival, only returning for the evening meal at the hotel. Why, asked Simon, did he seem so antagonistic to his fellow ex-patriots in Peking?

Mrs Griffith smiled and nodded. 'I understand your question,' she said. 'He can be dogmatic on the point sometimes. But, you know, Simon, he is a good boy at heart, even though his father used to despair of him sometimes.'

'I'm sure he is, Mrs Griffith, but sometimes he almost seems to favour the Boxers. And where does he go during the daytime here?'

'Well, you should know that, since he graduated from university here, he has wanted to join the Chinese foreign service.' Her eyes, which had remained sad since their arrival, now briefly shone with pride. 'Gerald is a very good Mandarin speaker, you know, even better than his father. He has made some very good friends at court and has always admired the Empress. He has had this ambition to serve this country, but, of course, it is terribly difficult for someone who is not born of Chinese parents to work in the court here. But he still has hopes.'

'I see. But surely this is a difficult time to do that?'

'Oh quite. But he feels that this is when he could be of most service. Seeing both sides, you see.'

Fonthill fought back the desire to answer 'or just one'. Instead, he nodded and smiled acquiescence. 'Well, I wish him luck,' he said. 'He is obviously a bright lad.'

She smiled. 'Yes, isn't he? He will be a great comfort to me, now that . . . now that Edward is gone.'

'And Chang?'

'Ah, Chang. He has been with us since he was a baby and we have always tried to treat him as one of our own – the same as Gerald.' Her brow clouded for a moment. 'But in the last couple of years Gerald seems to have taken against his brother. It is something that had begun to worry Edward quite a lot. We had hoped that they would both go into the ministry together, you know.'

'What now?'

Mrs Griffith pushed a stray strand of hair back into its bun. 'Chang is still quite young, of course, but he may take holy orders. Perhaps, once he is ordained, he could take over his father's mission. That would be nice, if it is God's will.'

They were interrupted by the arrival of an agitated Alice. She sat next to Mrs Griffith and took up the old lady's hand. 'Bad news, I'm afraid. We have just heard that another two British missionaries have been murdered by the Boxers at a place about forty miles south of Peking.'

Mrs Griffith put her free hand to her mouth. 'What are their names? We are sure to know them. Where, did you say?'

'I don't know, Aunt. But there is worse. The Boxers have made another raid on the railway. A heavier one this time. Stations have been burnt, the Chinese troops guarding them have fled and the rails have been torn up. The line to Tientsin is definitely broken. More and more missionaries are coming into the Legation. You can't leave now, I fear, my dear.' Alice turned her face to Simon. 'It is rumoured that the Boxers are marching on the city.'

Fonthill put his hand on her shoulder. 'That rumour has been rife since we got here, my love. But I agree. You can't leave Peking, my dear Aunt, even though this heat has got so much worse. I will try and see Sir Claude and find the true position.'

Outside, he met a perspiring and indignant Jenkins. ''Ere,' he said. ''ave you 'eard what 'appened when they burnt down that racecourse place?'

'No.'

'These boxin' chaps got 'old of one of the native Christian blokes and roasted 'im alive in the ashes of the place.'

'Good Lord. Look, I think trouble is definitely coming here.' Simon looked with affection at his former batman and his comrade in so many tight corners. '352, you once were the best scavenger in the British Army. Do you think—'

'What's a scavenger, then, like?'

'Thief. Well – more the picker-up of unwanted trifles. A taker of things from people who don't need them and the giver of them to friends who need them.'

'Well, I did my small best, bach sir, when that sort of . . . er . . . skill was needed. What do we need now, then?'

'We need rifles, 352. We need rifles. Two of them, as modern as you can get but we will put up with older ones, if need be. A couple of Martini-Henrys would be fine. One for you and one for me. If trouble comes, those Colts will not be adequate, I fear. Here, take this money. It should be enough.'

'Very good, sir. I shall go scrimmaging. Personally, I'd

be much 'appier with a proper rifle than with them pea-shooters. I've made a couple of drinkin' mates who might be able to 'elp. No promises, mind you.' Mopping his brow, he walked firmly away, a sense of purpose in his step.

At the British Legation, Simon found that Sir Claude was in conference with the heads of the other delegations. John Sims, however, an aide who had once served with Simon's old regiment, the 24th of Foot, and with whom he had consequently struck up a friendship, was forthcoming about the situation.

The young man, working in his shirtsleeves in a small office as hot as an oven, was emphatic. 'We've heard that the Boxers have seized and are in the process of destroying the railway bridge at Yangtsun, just about the one irreplaceable link in the line between Peking and Tientsin,' he said. 'The heads of the legations here can't agree on concerted action and we're getting absolutely no change from the Manchu court. So Sir Claude has telegraphed to Admiral Seymour in Tientsin to send a large force to us here before it's too late.'

He held up a telegram. 'Haven't been able to show this to the old man yet, because he's still chewing the fat with the other ministers, but it says that two thousand armed men of eight nationalities have steamed out of Tientsin this morning. They should be here tonight.'

Fonthill blew out his cheeks. 'Thank God for that. Look, just in case they can't get through . . .' he held up his hand to stop his friend from interrupting '. . . it sounds as though it's going to be damned difficult to come the eighty miles by train. Just in case they have to slog through on foot, how many men do we have who could defend the Legation Quarter until they arrive?'

Sims frowned and shook his head. 'Afraid I have no idea, sir. Apart from the sailors who arrived the other day, there is just a handful of Legation guards, don't know how many.' He looked up at Fonthill ruefully. 'I know what you're thinking. There should have been some sort of contingency planning, but Sir Claude has been so busy trying to push his colleagues from the other legations into some kind of agreement . . .' His voice tailed away and he wiped his brow. 'It's been like trying to get a bunch of opera prima donnas to sing all together in tune.'

He was interrupted by the arrival of Sir Claude, resplendent and perspiring in his high-buttoned blue jacket, replete with polished buttons and gold braid. He shook Fonthill's hand.

'Been to the Spanish Legation,' he said. 'The minister there is officially the doyen so we meet there, but, he is elderly and, as a leader, he is useless. We are getting nowhere with the palace. Do you know, Fonthill, when I went to protest formally about the deaths of our British missionaries, one of the Tsungli Yamen, that's a sort of Foreign Office, went fast asleep openly.'

He put up a silencing hand to Sims who was waving his telegram. 'I've been trying to get us to demand that the Empress receives all the members of the corps diplomatique in a formal audience, but we couldn't agree unanimously even on that.' It seemed as though the ends of Sir Claude's moustache were quivering in frustration. He turned to Sims. 'Yes, John, what is it?'

Wordlessly, the aide offered him the telegram. Sir Claude read it and then looked up. 'Thank God for that,' he exclaimed. He sat down on the edge of Sims's desk and eased open the gold-embossed high collar of his tunic, allowing his Adam's apple to leap, it seemed, with relief. He addressed Sims. 'Tell the commanding officer of the force that arrived the other day that I want him and his sailors and marines to turn out in force tomorrow, with carts, to march to the station to escort these troops in. Make a bit of a show of it, you know.'

He turned back to Simon. 'Well, Fonthill, we should be all right now. Two thousand troops is more than enough to put down these renegades if they attack us – and more than enough to impress the Court.' Then he frowned. 'If they can repair the railway, that is. But even if they can't, it's not a huge distance to march and I don't see a force like that being deterred by an undisciplined mob.'

Simon's face remained impassive. 'What about the Chinese army, though, sir? Would they join forces with the rebels?'

MacDonald shook his head firmly. 'Most unlikely. That would amount to a virtual declaration of war on the Foreign Powers. The Empress would never do that. No. I'm getting up early to welcome the troops in just after dawn at the station. Won't you join me?'

'Of course, sir.'

Well before dawn the next morning, Fonthill and Jenkins joined the small party of ministers, dressed in their finery,

66

who waited, amongst a crowd of Chinese – unusually silent – for the arrival of the troops. The sailors and marines had drawn up carts to convey the two thousand newcomers into the Quarter and, as the sun came up, European civilians on horseback pushed their way through to get a better view. Also present were the Kansu soldiers, drawn up outside the city, in the park-like grounds near the Ha Ta Men Gate.

But no trains were reported as pulling into the station. The sun grew higher, the heat increased and the waiting became more and more uncomfortable for the officials and other Europeans.

'I knew it,' breathed Fonthill to Jenkins. 'The main bridge is down in the south-east, the line is up and there's no way a force like this can get through by rail. It could be some time before they get here.'

The Welshman nodded, his great moustache half sucked under his lower lip. 'Just as well, then,' he whispered, 'that I've managed to get us two rifles, ain't it?'

Simon grinned. 'Oh, well done. I knew you would. Where are they?'

'Under me bed, next to me potty. I'll show you later.'

'How old?'

'Well, I reckon they was used at Waterloo, but I think they'll do. They are only single-shot Martini-Henrys, like we used in Zululand. But they were good enough for us against them black fellers, so I reckon they should be able to knock over a few Chinks, look you. I've tested them and they fire 'igh, so remember that. I also bought two lungers – bayonets, just like we 'ad in Zululand – and two 'undred rounds of ammunition each.'

'You're a miracle, 352, that's what you are. I only hope we don't have to use them.'

'So do I. Oh, I've got some change for you.' He dug in his pocket and produced a handful of Chinese coins.

'Oh no. You keep that. As long as you don't spend it on the demon drink.'

'Who, me, bach sir? Never.'

'Well, I wish we'd got the things with us now.' Fonthill looked about him. 'There could be trouble here.'

The crowd of Chinese milling about the gate had grown now and were beginning to press in on the waiting troops. The Muslim troops from the north were beginning to stamp their feet and jeer. The crowd took up the chant and the commander of the sailors and marines looked up at MacDonald. The minister nodded his head and the troops shouldered their arms and began to escort the empty carts back through the gate. At this, the jeers grew louder but no one attempted to prevent the movement and within minutes the carts, the waiting dignitaries, the mounted civilians and the troops were safely back inside the Legation wall.

Sir Claude took off his plumed hat and wiped his brow. 'Damned disappointing,' he confided to Fonthill. 'They must have been delayed repairing the line. But they will get here – and at least we didn't have any actual trouble down there.'

The trouble came, however, that afternoon, as, back in the hotel, Jenkins was showing Simon the rifles. Once again it was Alice who was the harbinger. Her face was white.

'It's the Chancellor of the Japanese Legation,' she said. 'For some reason, he chose to go down to the station this afternoon. He went alone and was dressed formally wearing a tailcoat and bowler hat. Outside the Yung Ting Men Gate he was dragged from his cart, *by the Chinese troops*, and hacked to pieces, with the crowd all around urging them on.' She gulped and went on, 'His corpse was left lying in the gutter and they say that his heart was . . . was . . . cut out and sent to General Tung Fuhsiang, the commander of the Muslim troops.' She sniffed. 'So much for the Empress's troops protecting us.'

Chang had entered with Alice. He nodded his head. 'It is true,' he said. 'I hear it from one of the guards at Japanese Legation. He say that commander of the guards was going to commit hara-kiri because of dishonour, but was persuaded against. It is frightfully distressing, don't you think?'

'Oh, I do, Chang,' said Fonthill. 'Frightfully distressing indeed.'

Alice looked up sharply at Simon. But there was no hint of sarcasm on his face. Instead, he took Chang by the arm. 'Sit down . . . er . . . old chap,' he said. 'What do *you* think about all this?'

'Well, old fellow,' said the Chinaman, 'I most disturbed that my countrymen should do this sort of thing. I know that they not Christians but this violence is not in Chinese religion. Confucius would not approve, oh dear me no. Not approve at all. And Empress surely cannot approve. Very, very distressing.'

Simon studied the young man's face intently. Chang looked, of course, completely Oriental. His face was oval-shaped and his eyes shone from slits set in the smoothest of skins, from which the bruises sustained in the affray with the Boxers had now disappeared. He wore a conventional pigtail and the customary white smock buttoned at the throat. A black skullcap completed the picture of a lower-middle-class Chinaman. Only the choice of the occasional, startlingly British phrase betrayed his upbringing. But these were strange times. Was he to be trusted? Fonthill decided to probe deeper.

'Gerald,' he said, 'seems to have some sympathy with the Boxers. And, indeed, I can understand his position, to some extent. The Great Powers have not behaved very well in carving up large portions of China for themselves. Some sort of uprising, given the circumstances, is not unexpected.'

Chang shook his head vehemently, so that his pigtail swung behind him. 'I not agree with Gerald,' he said. 'Manchu court has also behaved badly over years in trying to prevent intercourse with foreign traders . . . er . . . you would say, "intercourse"?'

'Perhaps "discourse" would be a better word.'

'Ah so. Discourse, yes. I must remember. Anyway, my father always say that she too old-fashioned for this year of 1900. Must move with . . . er . . . years.'

'With the times?'

'Precisely, cousin. She must move along with times.'

Simon stifled a smile at the young man's earnestness. He was sure that there was no dissembling there. Chang was a true son of his father.

He turned back to the others. 'Well that settles it,' he

said. 'If there was any question of Aunt Lizzie returning to her home, that has gone now. It looks as though things are getting worse. I do hope that Sir Claude and his colleagues in the corps decide to pull their fingers out at last and begin to arrange some sort of defences. The Quarter is very vulnerable, as things stand now. And if he doesn't know that, I'm afraid I shall have to tell him.'

Despite the murder of one of their number, however, all the members of the corps diplomatique seemed to remain sanguine and Sir Claude continued to shuttle back and forth to the Spanish Legation. The streets outside the Legation Quarter's walls were now ominously quiet. From within the enclave, Chinese servants, grooms, gardeners and chair-bearers were slipping away, to be replaced by an influx of missionaries from the surrounding areas and from the many missions within the city itself. The Legation Quarter was now becoming crowded, with accommodation having to be found for the refugees, as well as the four hundred military who had arrived. The discomfort was compounded by the heat and the drought, still unbroken after many months.

Then, at last, the Boxers arrived. They burst through the Ha Ta Men Gate, to the east of the Legation Quarter. Here, there was no targeting of Christians. The red-sashed horde ran through the narrow streets, pillaging the shops and houses and killing any who stood before them. The shopkeepers and residents fled before them, crowding the streets and shrieking in fear as the Boxers began burning the buildings. The many missions, customs offices and the homes of the teachers at the Imperial University were fired and the East Cathedral went up in flames, its old French priest and many of his flock perishing within.

The flames could be seen from the Legation and, as night fell, torches could be seen bobbing in the distance towards the Austrian Legation, which lay outside the walls of the Quarter. From the eastern wall of the enclave Fonthill, Jenkins and Chang watched the torches approaching.

'Are the Austrians still within the legation building?' Simon asked Chang, who had become the most reliable source of information about the city.

The young man nodded. 'Oh yes. But they have seven guards there to protect the building – and a machine gun.'

Fonthill grunted. 'That may not be enough. Go and get the rifles, 352. We must help them. But there is no need for you to come, Chang. It could be dangerous.'

The Chinaman looked offended. 'Of course I come, cousin. May I have loan of one of your excellent revolvers, please?'

'Er . . . yes. Do you know how to use it?'

'I watch you in the wagon. You just point and fire, yes?'

'Well, ah, something like that. I'll show you. One Colt as well, then, Jenkins. Get a move on.'

The three, now armed, slipped through the Legation gate and ran up Custom Street towards where the Austrian building stood at the north-eastern corner of the Legation enclave. Could they get there before the Boxers? They did so, but it was a close thing, for the torches could be seen bobbing down the narrow street towards them.

'Where's the machine gun?' demanded Fonthill of the young Austrian sergeant in charge of the guard.

'On zer roof, sir.'

'No. No good up there. Bring it down here. To shoot up the street. Quickly now. Er . . . *schnell jetzt!*'

The young man nodded, immediately responding to Simon's air of authority, and he doubled away, taking two of his men with him.

The Boxers were now some three hundred yards away and the cries of '*Sha! Sha!*' could clearly be heard. Fonthill clipped the old, triangular-shaped bayonet to the end of his rifle and nodded to Jenkins to do the same. With the lunger fitted, the rifle became a stabbing weapon six feet long, which even the Zulus had feared.

The Austrians had protected the door of the Legation with mealie bags. 'Drag 'em out so that they give us some protection facing up the road,' Simon shouted. 'Quickly, before they are on us.' The three laid aside their weapons and pulled six of the bags out into the road so that they formed a rough, low bastion.

As Fonthill knelt, resting his rifle on top of one of the bags, he had a momentary impression of Chang, standing very erect and extending his arm holding the Colt and pulling the trigger – with no result.

'Safety catch,' he yelled, 'just by the trigger.' Then, 'Rapid fire!'

At one hundred yards they could not miss, and three of the leading figures fell, their torches scattering across the road before them, burning on the cobbles. The Boxers halted for a moment and then came on again. But their hesitation was enough for Fonthill and Jenkins each to thrust a round into the breech and fire again and then again. Four more of the red-banded figures fell again, causing the mob to stand irresolutely.

Except for one brave man. Screaming 'Sha!' and brandishing a large sword, he bounded forward, red bands at forehead, wrist and ankles flying behind him, presenting a terrifying figure by the light of the burning brands. Simon was still fumbling to thumb another cartridge into the breech of his rifle and Chang was clumsily attempting to reload his revolver. Jenkins, however, put one hand on top of the mealie bag and vaulted over, in time to present his rifle and bayonet to the Chinaman, who stopped, puzzled with how to deal with this strange, crouching man with the large moustache.

'Come on, yer yeller bugger,' coaxed Jenkins. 'Yer not so brave now it's not a woman or child or some poor little bugger of a clergyman facing yer, are yer? Come on, boyo.' And he made a feint to the right shoulder, which the Boxer clumsily countered with his sword. Immediately, the Welshman brought up the butt of his rifle and caught the Chinaman on the chin. As he staggered back, Jenkins reversed his rifle and plunged his bayonet into the man's chest. For a moment the two stood, seemingly connected umbilically, before Jenkins twisted the bayonet and withdrew it, allowing the Boxer to slump to the floor with a sigh.

Fonthill heard a sound behind him and swung round in consternation. The three Austrians were staggering through the doorway, carrying the heavy machine gun.

'Quick!' shouted Simon. 'On top of the bag. Come back, 352. We're going to fire.'

Laboriously, the Austrians mounted the gun on its tripod and fed the ammunition belt into the breech, while the Chinese watched, unsure, it seemed, whether to charge or run away. Then the soldier at the handles depressed the trigger and the gun chattered into life. It was enough. The Boxers turned and fled, casting aside their torches and showing the white soles of their bare feet in the flickering light. Fonthill watched, expecting the gun to cut a swathe through the running horde. Instead, telegraph poles in the distance were severed, falling and bringing down the wires.

'You bloody fools,' screamed Simon. 'You're firing too high!'

But the Austrians paid no heed. Exhilarated by the clatter of the bullets, the gunner kept firing, bringing tiles down from the buildings at the far end of the street and causing showers of plaster to rain down on the retreating Boxers. Soon the attackers were out of sight, leaving their dead lying on the rough surface, their blood soaking into their like-coloured ribbons and sashes.

Chang was looking at Jenkins with a mixture of horror and fascination. 'You are indeed extremely good fighter, Mister Jenkins,' he said. 'You frighten me.'

Jenkins had the grace to look embarrassed. 'Well, son, it was 'im or me. I 'ad to go at 'im with the lunger 'cos I didn't 'ave anythin' up the spout, look you.'

The Chinaman was puzzled and turned his head around. 'Where do I look, Mr Jenkins? Where is spout?'

Simon sighed. 'Never mind, now, Chang. You did well.' He turned to the Austrian sergeant, speaking slowly. 'The Boxers might come back,' he said. 'Is your minister inside?'

'No, *mein herr*. He is in der Legation Quarter.'

'Very sensible of him. Well, tell him that I do not think it possible to defend this building here, outside the Legation walls. He should evacuate it.'

'I will tell him. Excuse me, *mein herr*. Who are you?'

'I am formerly a captain in the British infantry and this is my comrade, formerly a sergeant in the army. We are . . . er . . . advising the British minister. I know what I am talking about, Sergeant, I assure you. Evacuate this Legation. It is indefensible. Oh, and tell your men to fire lower with that Maxim.'

'*Ach so*. Very *gut*, sir.'

The three walked back down Custom Street, their weapons at the ready, but there was no sign of Boxers. They met, however, a small band of European civilians, armed with an assortment of sporting rifles and similar weapons. They were on their way, the Frenchman at their head explained to Fonthill, to the exposed South Cathedral, which seemed to lie directly in the path of the advancing Boxers. A cluster of Catholic missionaries were sheltering there who needed to be escorted to the Legation enclave, if it was not too late.

'We'll come with you,' said Simon. 'You may need us.'

In fact, the cathedral was not under immediate threat when they arrived. But the little party rounded up more than twenty Catholic missionaries sheltering within the

76

venerable cathedral, plus five Sisters of Charity and twenty Chinese nuns. As they turned back towards the Legation walls they saw the glow of the Boxers' torches to the north and heard the distant chanting, growing nearer. Hurrying through the silent streets back to the Legation gates, they saw the old cathedral go up in flames behind them.

Back in the Legation compound, they were met by an anxious Mrs Griffith and Alice. Of Gerald, once again there was no sight.

Alice put her hand on her husband's arm. 'The whole commercial quarter – the richest part of the city – has been burnt down,' she said. 'All those lovely pearl and jewellery shops, the beautiful textile stores, the silk and satin warehouses have been destroyed. Simon, I would prefer it if you would not go out again outside the Legation walls. It is clear that the Boxers are starting now to infiltrate the city and, if they come at you from all sides, even you and the mighty 352 would not be able to defend yourselves. And I do not wish to be left alone in this strange country, if you don't mind.'

Fonthill seized her hand and kissed it. 'I'm afraid, darling, that we shall have to go again, although not tonight. We cannot give up the streets to the Boxers. They should be patrolled. I also think we shall have to start erecting some defences. The Quarter is very vulnerable, particularly from the south. I fear I must start laying down the law a bit with Sir Claude.'

So it was that the next morning Fonthill requested an interview with the British minister. He found the tall Scotsman very preoccupied.

'Thank you for your work last night, Fonthill,' he said. 'I knew you would be useful. I have to report to you that we are now completely cut off. Our last telegraph link, running north to Russian territory, has been severed. I have no idea what has happened to the relief contingent from Tientsin, so we are very much on our own now, I fear.'

Fonthill nodded. 'I see. This gives added urgency to what I have to say, sir.'

'And what is that, pray?'

'So far there has been no direct attack on the Legation Quarter. But if there is, it would be very difficult to defend the whole of the perimeter with the few troops we have at our command.'

'What do you suggest?'

'We should destroy those houses that come up close on the other side of our wall and which would give cover to any attackers. This would give us a field of fire. From what I can see – and I do not know all of the geography of the place – there are parts of the perimeter that are virtually indefensible anyway, so we should abandon them, so shortening our line, so to speak. We should build a second, tighter, line of defence inside that we could man more adequately – digging trenches, erecting barricades and so on – and we should begin patrolling the streets outside our walls, bringing in those who are being threatened.'

The minister frowned. 'Good Lord, Fonthill. We cannot just bring in people willy-nilly. We are overcrowded as it is. Where would we put them all? And it could be dangerous. We could be importing spies and malcontents within our midst.'

'It's a risk but we can't leave people out there to be murdered. The Boxers outnumber us. So far, they do not appear to have guns. But, from what I hear of the Manchu court, they will soon get them and things will then be very different. There is also the matter of the Imperial Army. If they side with the rebels – and there have been indications of this, the assassination of the Japanese minister, for instance – if they turn on us, then we shall be in a pretty pickle.'

MacDonald mused for a moment. 'Very well. My responsibilities are heavy and I must be aware of them. I agree that we must improve our defences. The problem, of course, is getting all of the nationalities represented here to move in unison, for we are a rather uneasy coalition, you know, and it is difficult to find agreement. However, I retain some influence and I will see what I can do. I value your advice, my dear fellow.' He gave a melancholy smile. 'After all, in my army days, before I joined the diplomat service, I was only a subaltern. You were a captain.' He fluttered a mock salute. 'So – very good, sir.'

In fact, events moved quickly. Within the next few days, some two thousand Chinese Catholics found their way into the legations and the Methodists followed suit, evacuating their own compound near the Ha Ta Men. As Sir Claude had predicted, the overcrowding became acute, but one great benefit accrued. These Chinese proved to be a willing and hard-working labour force. Within the next few days, houses near the walls were burnt to the ground; barricades were erected at strategic points; trenches were dug; and shell-proof shelters were erected – all under the supervision of Fonthill and Captain Strouts, of the Royal Marines, the British Legation's guard commander.

The Peking Hotel, although it remained open, was considered by Simon to be too close to the eastern defences, so his party – Mrs Griffith, her two sons, Alice, Jenkins and himself – were given shelter inside the walls of the British Legation.

After the original sorties of the Boxers, a strange quiet had descended upon the beleaguered Legation Quarter. Rumours and counter-rumours flew. The Empress issued an edict blaming the death of the Japanese chancellor and the burnings upon 'brigands and seditious characters'. Troops of the Imperial army continued to remain passive and her ministers continued to send flowery messages to the heads of the legations assuring them of their safety and deprecating the need for foreign troops to be sent from the coast.

Then events took a dramatic turn. Each of the heads of legations received an ultimatum from the Chinese Foreign Office. It reported that the Foreign Powers had demanded the surrender of the Taku Forts at the head of the River Pei Ho, the sea gateway to Tientsin. If the demand was not met, the powers would occupy the forts by force. As a result, said the ultimatum, emotions were running high among the people of Peking and the Imperial Government could no longer be responsible for the safety of the ministers and their families in the Legation Quarter and they should leave the legations for Tientsin within twenty-four hours. Imperial troops would be provided as an escort.

These letters threw the ministers into a state of confusion – and indignation. Firstly, they had no idea that hostilities had broken out at the coast and they blamed their compatriots there for compromising their position at the capital. Secondly, and predictably, they could not agree on whether or not to surrender to the ultimatum. Equally predictably, they decided to play for time. A letter was sent, agreeing to depart but pleading for more time and asking for details of the protection to be provided and of the transport being made available.

Sir Claude, however, confided to Fonthill that, whatever the reply, he had no intention of 'moving an inch'. Nevertheless, the ministers and staffs of some legations began their packing, although in fear of what might happen once they had left the walls of the Quarter.

'It would be madness to leave,' confided Simon to Alice. 'Once out there on the plain we would all be attacked and butchered by the Chinese troops, just like the Japanese chancellor. We must stay with Sir Claude and, if necessary, concentrate our forces on defending the British Legation.'

'Wherever you are,' replied Alice calmly, 'I will be.'

The denouement of the situation, however, arrived in a quite different way. The ministers fulminated for hours around their large table in the Spanish Legation awaiting a reply but none came. Finally, the bellicose German minister, Baron von Ketteler, declared that he would wait no longer, but journey to the palace himself and demand an answer 'if I have to sit there all night'.

He set off with his Chinese secretary to the Foreign Office, both travelling in sedan chairs with canopies of red and green proclaiming their status and with two liveried servants riding on ponies as outriders. Half an hour later, his dragoman, who had been shot through both legs, dragged himself into the American Methodist mission near the Ha Ta Men Gate and declared that the minister had been shot in his chair by a Manchu solider 'in full uniform with a mandarin's hat and button and blue feather'. A patrol of fifteen German sailors went out to try and retrieve the minister's body but were driven back. The word spread throughout the legations. There was no more talk of accepting the offer of evacuation.

Instead, and with belated speed, the legations prepared to defend themselves at last.

It was agreed that the British Legation, by far the largest and, by its position, not commanded by the Great Tartar Wall but with a good field of fire, should be a kind of central redoubt. It would be a place where, if the worst came to the worst, all the defenders of the legations could fall back for a last stand. However, it was decided that it should also offer shelter to non-combatants.

As a result, the whole of the foreign community of Peking, together with ponies and mules, a small flock of sheep and one cow, gathered within the compound. An area of some three acres, which normally housed sixty people, was now occupied by nine hundred.

The separate buildings of the Legation had been hurriedly allocated to the different nationalities. The missionaries who had fled their missions in the Chinese City were crowded together in the Legation's chapel. The elegant front pavilions were stacked with all kinds of luggage, the most notable being provisions and wine; the stable-house was allocated to Norwegians; the rear pavilion was divided into small rooms for miscellaneous use, and in one of the tiniest Mrs Griffith and Alice made their new home, with Gerald, Chang, Simon and Jenkins housed together next door.

All was activity in the other legations, too. As a squadron of Chinese cavalry, in their black turbans, galloped down Custom Street past the isolated Austrian Legation, guards of all the threatened nationalities were busy strengthening makeshift barricades, laying out primitive firefighting equipment and, near the American and German legations, manning the outposts that had been erected on the Tartar Wall.

At four o'clock – the hour at which the formal Chinese ultimatum was due to expire – Fonthill and Jenkins stood on the front lawn of the British Legation, once marked out for clock golf, while Simon consulted his watch. At exactly the hour, firing broke out from the outlying Austrian Legation, which, despite Fonthill's advice, had not been evacuated.

'Well,' frowned Simon, 'I'm afraid we are now well and truly under siege. Will we be able to hold out, I wonder?'

Jenkins sucked in his moustache. 'We'll just 'ave to, bach sir. I wouldn't want to think about the alternative if them yeller bastards break through.'

CHAPTER FOUR

The ending of the formal ultimatum brought a sense of reality to the besieged foreigners and their dependents within the Legation Quarter. It was as though the defensive precautions already taken under the direction of Fonthill and Captain Strouts had been a game, the withdrawal to a secondary line away from the outer walls merely a harmless diversion to relieve the boredom of waiting for the relief column to arrive. Now, it became clear to Simon on a quick tour with Jenkins that the instructions that had been given for the erection of the fallback defences had been carried out quite inadequately. The barricades mainly consisted of overturned carts, with gaps between them, and the trenches were little more than shallow scoops in the earth. A concerted attack on the Quarter would surely have resulted in these flimsy defences being overrun.

Luckily, that attack did not come. The lull gave the

defenders time to retreat from the indefensible positions outside the fallback line. After that immediate flurry of firing on the Austrian Legation, no attack was pressed home and Simon's call to leave the Legation was heeded at last and the defenders were able to scurry back to within the reserve line. Similarly, the other outlying legations – the Dutch, the Belgian, the Italian and the French – were also abandoned, as was the Peking Club and the large offices of the influential trading house, Jardine Matheson. Immediately, most of these buildings were torched by the Chinese and firing broke out, sometimes heavily, around the hastily manned new perimeter of the defences. Nevertheless, the Chinese seemed reluctant to press home any direct attacks.

'This is ridiculous,' confessed Fonthill to Jenkins at the end of the first day of the siege. The pair had spent the hours helping to direct the reinforcing of the flimsy defences: the piling of rubble upon and in between the upturned carts, the loopholing of these walls, the deepening of the trenches in the open land on the exposed sides of the line, and the making of sandbags from pillowcases and cushions. 'The trouble is,' continued Simon, wiping his brow, 'there doesn't seem to be anyone in overall charge. It's like the Tower of Babel, with everyone shouting in different languages. It's no way to conduct a defence. I have to see Sir Claude.'

'Be careful,' said Jenkins, 'don't get too close to 'im because if 'e turns round too quick, like, 'e'll 'ave your eye out with the end of them moustaches. Shall I come, too?'

'No. Get back and see if the ladies are all right.'

There was little sign of chaos, however, in the small, dimly lit office of the British minister. He sat at his desk writing quietly, his severe tunic unbuttoned at the neck and a small glass of port at his elbow.

'Ah, Fonthill,' he said, standing and extending his hand. 'Good Lord, you look a bit dusty. Take a glass of this Taylor's '79. I can commend it.'

'No thank you, sir.'

'I insist. You look hot and bothered. Now sit down and tell me what is on your mind.' He fetched another glass from an upended suitcase and filled it. 'Here.'

Fonthill took it and perched on the only other chair in the room. Then he unburdened himself of his doubts: the lack of leadership, chain of command and coordination; the still-inadequate state of the defences and the paucity of firepower. Then he took a sip of the Taylor's. MacDonald was right. It was delicious.

The minister listened without interruption, then twisted the wax more firmly into his moustache ends, as though to marshal his thoughts.

'First point,' he said. 'Leadership. You are quite right, there has been little of it, because our Spanish doyen has lacked the . . . ah . . . sense of purpose, shall we say, to provide it. This has now been recognised. I've just come back from a meeting of the corps diplomatique and I have been elected to take over the direction of the defence.' He smiled apologetically. 'Not exactly a general, don't you know, but, as I told you, I did serve in the British army years ago and actually fought in a couple of campaigns in Africa. Nothing like your experience, my dear fellow, but in the land of the blind and all that, you know . . .'

'Good. I'm delighted to hear it, sir.'

'Secondly,' he waved a languid hand to his desk, 'I am just in the middle of setting up a system of committees to delegate authority. I have already appointed a fortifications committee, under a feller called Gamewell. A missionary, of course, but he used to be an engineer and I've got faith in him. These missionaries are the most resourceful people. We have appointed as military commander, Captain von Thomann, the captain of the Austrian cruiser *Zenta*, who is here on holiday, poor chap,' he gave a wan and rather apologetic smile. 'We're diplomats, you see, and we have to appoint on seniority. Thomann is the senior officer here, so it had to be him. But he will report to me.

'As for resources, I have drawn up here what we have. Our total strength of trained fighting men is twenty officers and three hundred and eighty-nine men, split into eight nationalities. This is the breakdown. Here, take a look.' He thrust a piece of paper towards Fonthill, who read:

	Officers	Men
British	3	79
Russian	2	79
Americans	3	53
Germans	1	51
French	2	45
Austrian	7	30
Italians	1	28
Japanese	1	24

'Very much a mixed bag, I fear,' said the minister, 'but beggars can't be choosers, what?'

Simon frowned. 'Quite so, sir. What about civilians? Can't we mobilise the fit men?'

'Indeed. I have already made them fall in, so to speak. There are two categories. The first is composed of ex-soldiers and sailors who between them have quite a bit of experience of war. There are seventy-five of these chaps, of whom thirty-two are Japanese. The second,' his wry smile returned, 'are rather colourful. There are fifty of 'em and they are mainly British students at the university. I call 'em "The Carving-Knife Brigade", because they lash these . . . ah . . . culinary objects to whatever weapons they've got: old rifles, shotguns, one elephant gun and so on. But they're rarin' to go, although,' his faint smile broadened into a grin, 'their experience of battle is confined to one chap who once saw the trooping of the colour in St James's Park, London. As Wellington said of his troops, "I don't know what they will do to the enemy, but they frighten me to death."'

Then the grin faded on the tall man's face. 'Trouble with this business of commanding the defence,' he went on, 'is that I have to observe the niceties of corps diplomatique communications. I don't exactly give orders. I must send polite little notes to the other heads of legations, requesting certain courses of action – usually written in my best French.'

Fonthill took another sip of port and suppressed a smile. 'What about ammunition – and do we have any artillery?'

'Very little, I fear. We have four light pieces, the best of which appears to be an Italian one-pounder, for which we have . . . let me see . . .' he replaced his spectacles and peered at another piece of paper '. . . one hundred and twenty shells.

Hopefully it should be enough. Then the Americans have a Colt heavy machine gun with twenty-five thousand rounds, the Austrians have their Maxim and we have a five-barrelled Nordenfelt, which is almost as old as me and incapable of firing more than five rounds before jamming.'

'What about other ammo? Didn't the men who marched in from Tientsin bring reserves?'

'Not enough, I fear. The Japanese brought only one hundred rounds for each man and the rest only three hundred. Trouble is, since every contingent uses a different type of rifle, we can't create a common reserve of ammunition.'

MacDonald rose from his chair with the bottle of port and refilled Fonthill's glass, then his own. 'However,' he went on, 'there is *good* news. The most important thing is that I have nine more of these bottles left.' He smiled at his joke. 'We do have reasonable supplies of food and water. I have ascertained that we should be able to feed some three thousand people within the compounds for quite some time. There are four wells of sweet water within the British compound alone, and one shop has provided nearly two hundred tons of wheat, rice and maize and, because the spring race meeting has only just been held, we have more than one hundred and fifty ponies and a few mules in the stables to provide meat, with fodder to feed them for some weeks yet.'

He leant across the table. 'I would have liked to have put you in charge of the defences, Fonthill,' he said. 'But I must observe the damned niceties. However, I would like you to be free to approach me at any time and bring to my attention matters that concern you. As, indeed, you have already done.'

'Thank you, sir. I shall take advantage of that, when I see fit.'

'Good. Now, I have prepared a map of the Quarter, with our new line of defences marked. Come here and show me where you think we are weakest.'

Fonthill rose and stood by the minister's side and looked over his shoulder. MacDonald had marked the new perimeter that had been created by Simon and Captain Strouts. It showed a reduction of the enclave strongly on the west and eastern boundaries, where new defences had been erected along winding streets where rows of Chinese houses had been demolished to give a good field of fire, and across open spaces, particularly to the west, looking across the Imperial Carriage Park and the old Mongol Market. To the north it used fairly substantial walls and to the north-east it enclosed an open space called the Wang Fu, a traditional park. The south was dominated by the huge Tartar City Wall, some forty feet wide. Here, faced by lack of resources, Fonthill and Strouts had been forced to erect barricades across the top of the wall to enclose just the length of it which looked down on the American Legation.

Simon jabbed his finger onto the map. 'It is here, in the south, along the Tartar Wall,' he said, 'that we are weak. Those barricades must be held and, of course, they are exposed. The second point is here, to the north, where we are forced to stretch out to enclose the Wang Fu. We may have to retreat inwards here, if we are pressed hard.'

'Hmm,' said MacDonald. 'What about the canal?' This ran directly from north to south through the centre of the legations. The defences here looped southwards on each side of it from the north, with a small bridge over it, halfway down, defended. At its egress from the Quarter at the south, the canal ran under the Tartar Wall, at the very point where the barricaded 'European section' formed a bridge over it.

'Should be safe enough,' said Fonthill. 'The sides of the canal are steep and can be defended easily enough and we should be able to fire down from the two bridges if the Chinese try to enter from either north or south.'

'Good. I shall bear in mind what you have said.'

Fonthill moved away from the map. He was tired from his exertions during the day and the port, although welcome enough, was beginning to make his head throb. In addition, however, he was becoming a little impatient of the amateurish nature of the plans he was hearing for the defence of the Quarter. 'Polite notes in French' indeed! He ran his hand over his face, mixing white dust with perspiration, so that he looked clown-like.

'Do you have a reserve, sir?' he demanded.

'Reserve? What do you mean?'

'Well.' Simon exhaled in an exasperated sigh. 'There are clear weak points in the ring of defences. If one of these starts to crumble, you will need to speed reinforcements to it to prevent a breakthrough by the Chinese. How will you do this?'

Sir Claude's eyes seemed to grow more bulbous as he stared at Fonthill in silence for a moment. 'Each legation,' he said eventually, 'has the responsibility for protecting the area of the perimeter near to it. Given the circumstances you mention, I would ask the nearest commander to move troops along to defend the point of pressure.'

Fonthill nodded. 'So weakening the area from which the troops have been sent. No. It won't work. You need, Sir Claude, a small reserve of trusted troops that you can rush to the threatened points to avert the danger. Can you create such a reserve?'

The tall man put a hand to his chin. 'I see your point. As you know, we are stretched very thinly as it is. But let me see . . .' He thought for a moment. 'Look. I think Strouts could spare twenty-five of his marines from here to form such a body. I shall instruct him accordingly . . . and,' he gave a half-smile, 'I shan't have to write to him in French. Now, look here, Fonthill. Would you stay here in the Legation with your experienced chap, what d'yer call him, 325, is it?'

'352, sir.'

'Ah yes. Not far out. Yes, stay here to command this reserve and take it wherever it is needed. Will you do that?'

'Of course, sir. Honoured to do so.'

'Good man. Now. Another glass?'

'No thank you, sir. I must get back to see how my wife is faring.'

'Of course. Give her my regards.'

The next day, however, Sir Claude's system had its first test and failed it. After an uneasy night during which the Boxers had kept up an incessant, if inaccurate, fire upon the defenders – either the Chinese army had joined them or issued them with firearms – Captain von Thomann, the commander of the military forces within the Quarter, received a report that the American Legation, an important bastion in the southern defences, had been abandoned. Without attempting to confirm the report, he ordered all the defenders on the eastern side of the compound to leave their posts and fall back on the British Legation. Immediately, the Americans, still manning their posts on the Tartar Wall, joined in the retreat and took the Russians in the adjoining sector with them.

All became chaos within the British Legation, where Sir Claude, realising that great stretches of the defences were unattended, immediately ordered the men to return to their posts. They did so with alacrity and, for some strange reason, the Chinese did not take advantage of the situation, contenting themselves merely with burning down the Italian Legation and occupying one abandoned barricade.

'They're as bloody useless as we are,' observed Jenkins with a sniff.

There was one beneficial outcome, however. The inexperienced and fallible von Thomann was immediately relieved of his command and Sir Claude MacDonald, once a second lieutenant in the Highland Light Infantry, took direct command of the defending force.

It soon became clear that, whatever the pretences of the Empress, the Chinese army was now fully engaged in the attack on the Quarter, for two days after the ending of the ultimatum and the beginning of the siege, two nine-pounder Krupp artillery pieces began firing on the American and Russian legations from the burnt-out tower over the Chien Men Gate to the south-west of the Quarter.

This was a serious development, for the fire was accurately directed – clearly the work of skilled artillerymen – and if it continued and if other guns were brought into play it could bring down the makeshift barricades erected around the perimeter and the defences could be overrun. With only the little Italian cannon available there was no way the defenders could reduce the fire of the Krupp pieces.

The defences could be strengthened against shellfire, however. Under the direction of Lady MacDonald, assisted by Alice and Mrs Griffith, the grand ladies of the legations – all of whom were now sheltering within the British Legation – were set to making sandbags. There was no hessian available but every fabric that could be found was pressed into service. The result was that the barricades and hastily erected bombproof shelters were buttressed by bags made of fine silks, best curtains and lustrous satins, all in bright and erstwhile fashionable colours, so giving a surreal appearance to these patchwork defences.

For some reason, the shellfire slackened and fell away completely, but then it was replaced by fierce activity to the north of the British Legation. Here stood a mainly wooden, very old building called the Hanlin Yuan, a place venerated by the Chinese, for it was in essence a library, housing some of the great manuscripts from the past, a veritable treasure house of learning. Although this virtually abutted onto the buildings of the British Legation, the defenders made no attempt to destroy it. The Chinese respect for tradition and for learning, it was felt, would prevent any attempt to use it to burn out the British.

Not so.

Fonthill was the first to see a trickle of flame rise from the roof of the Yuan, where its eaves overhung and virtually touched those of the Legation. The wind was blowing from the north, sending sparks and smoke swirling above the Legation's roof. Simon blew his whistle, so summoning his marines, always on standby, and turned to Alice, with whom he had been sipping coffee.

'Rally the ladies, children and as many of the Chinese coolies as you can,' he cried. 'Organise buckets, chamber pots – anything that can carry water – and form a chain from the well to the wall. Tell Sir Claude, but tell him that I said we shouldn't take soldiers from the defences. That's what the Chinese will want us to do. Quickly now!'

She nodded and ran back inside. The marines, with Jenkins, had now fallen in outside the front pavilion and Fonthill led them at a run to where the flames were now leaping from the old wooden roof of the Yuan. As they neared the conflagration, they realised that Boxers and some of the Muslim infantry were firing through the smoke from nearby upper windows, so making it dangerous for firefighters to approach.

Fonthill called Jenkins. 'See those snipers,' he pointed. 'Take six of the marines onto the roof of the Legation and clear them out of those windows.'

'Very good, bach sir. What are you going to do?'

'We have got to break through and try and prevent the fire from reaching the Legation.'

When improving the defences, Simon and Strouts had

taken the precaution of burrowing a hole through their own wall, leading through to the nearest of the Yuan cloisters but leaving a thin pile of rubble as a temporary closure. With his marines, Fonthill began tearing at this barrier, throwing the bricks behind them. They had soon broken through and Simon directed two marines to stand as guards in the cloister. He heard a rattle of musketry from the roof of the Legation, showing that Jenkins and his men were doing their work, and he scrambled back to meet his wife, her face blackened by smoke, leading a line of boys, coolies and some of the Legation ladies all beginning to pass water along the line in an eclectic variety of receptacles.

Alice handed him a brimming chamber pot.

'Get back,' he shouted. 'Let the coolies take this end. It's dangerous.'

'Take the damned thing,' she shouted back. 'I'm not standing here all day ruining my hair in this smoke. Come along. Here's another one.'

Fonthill frowned in annoyance but quickly ordered his marines to extend the line through the gap and into the cloister. There they began throwing the water onto the flames creeping towards them along the shingles of the cloister's low roof. For almost an hour they toiled, the line stretching some two hundred yards from well to the hole in the wall, the colourful dresses of the ladies interspersed with the dun-coloured tunics of the coolies and the shirts and shorts of the boys. Jenkins and his sharpshooters had done their work to protect the line and they slung their buckets and pots in comparative safety, but all of their efforts would have been in vain against the encroaching flames had not the wind changed. Suddenly, miraculously, it veered from the north to the east, blowing flames, sparks and smoke back towards the Hanlin Yuan itself. With a roar the old building went up in a pyre of flames.

Fonthill brought back his marines and they walled up the hole again. Then he directed them to douse the western walls of the Legation buildings with water.

At last, what was left of the Yuan collapsed in a shower of sparks. Simon became aware that Sir Claude was at his shoulder, his buttons sparkling somehow and his moustache still spiked amidst the smoke. 'Well done, Fonthill,' he said. 'Good work. The Legation could have gone up in smoke and then we would all have been finished.'

'Don't thank me, sir.' Simon nodded towards where the women, boys and coolies in the line were all slumped to the ground in exhaustion. 'Thank them. And the wind.' He looked behind him. 'At least we've got a good field of fire in this direction now.'

'Yes.' The minister's face was drawn. 'I got your message, of course, and you were right. As soon as the blaze started, firing started all around the perimeter. The American and Russian barricades on the Tartar Wall were attacked directly. So this was more than just an attempt to burn us out, it was a diversion to attract men away from our line.'

'Any breakthroughs?'

'No. We held fast all the way around. But it is quite clear that the Dragon Lady is throwing her army into the battle now. Things are hotting up in more ways than one. Where, oh where, is that damned relief column?'

Fonthill wiped a hand over his blackened face and then held it out to Alice, who now approached him. 'Have no messages got through, sir?'

'Not a damned thing . . . oh, forgive me, Mrs Fonthill.' The minister took her hand and bowed over it, with highland courtesy. 'Splendid work you did there, me dear. Way beyond the call of duty.'

Alice frowned. 'It was not that, Sir Claude. In these conditions the call comes to us all.' Her frown changed to an ironic smile. 'So we "feeble women" all play our part. We are all in this together.'

'Quite so, dear lady. Quite so.'

Alice shot a quick glance to Simon and then said, 'May I ask you a question, Sir Claude?'

'Of course, my dear.'

'You will know that I have a nephew here, Gerald Griffith, the son of Mrs Griffith?'

'Yes. I believe I have met him.'

'Have you, by any chance, commissioned him to slip outside the Quarter since the siege began, to, perhaps, gather information for you?'

'Good gracious no. That would be putting him in some particular danger, I would have thought.'

Fonthill intervened. 'What are you getting at, Alice?'

She turned a wrinkled and blackened brow towards him. 'I didn't like to tell you, Simon, but Gerald has been absenting himself from the Legation almost every day since well before the siege began. At first, I thought he was helping to stand guard at the perimeter walls, as is Chang, but my aunt tells me that is not so and that he has been slipping out of the Quarter for most of the days. She has no idea where he goes and I cannot help wondering what he is doing. Then it occurred to me that, given his fluency with the language and his contacts with the court here, he might be on some mission for Sir Claude. But clearly not.'

The three exchanged glances. 'Nothing suspicious at all, I would think,' said MacDonald, 'given his parentage.'

'Hmm.' Simon shook his head slowly. 'I'm not sure. I think I had better have a word with that young man. Come on, Alice,' he shook his wife's hand in his, 'you had better go and clean up. You look like a coal-black Mammy.'

She laughed. 'A literal case of the pot calling the kettle black. Good day, Sir Claude.'

'Good day, Mrs Fonthill.'

As they walked back, hand in hand, they passed a small man in a large white hat and elegantly suited. He was talking vehemently to one of MacDonald's aides.

'Who is that?' enquired Simon.

'That, my dear, is Monsieur Pichon, the French minister. He is universally loathed, because he is continually pessimistic, saying that we shall all be overwhelmed and beheaded. What's more, he is a coward. All of the ministers have now withdrawn to the British Legation, but most of them spend much of their days with their guards on the perimeter.' Her lip curled. 'This one is always here, usually with the women, or he takes a walk pretending to visit what's left of his legation, where his troops are. But he never arrives there.'

'What a cad!'

'Quite.' She nodded towards the Frenchman. 'Now, he'll be complaining about something, mark my words.'

Fonthill had no opportunity to talk with Gerald, for the young man did not return that night and the next day saw the fiercest fighting since the siege had begun. Early that morning Simon received an urgent message from Sir Claude: 'Americans on the Tartar Wall are under strong attack. Please reinforce immediately.'

His marines paraded at the double and, led by Simon and Jenkins, ran to the southernmost part of the Quarter, where the great Tartar Wall loomed over everything and everyone.

The road that ran along the top of the wall was forty feet wide, providing enough room for four carriages to ride along it side by side. On the western end of their sector, the Americans had piled upturned carts, splintered bunks, rubble and sandbags to cut off the road from that end, and the Germans had erected a similar barricade some two hundred yards to the east. This had prevented the Chinese from occupying all of the wall, and so from firing down on everyone in the southern end of the Quarter, and also from commanding the southern bridge over the canal. But, as Simon had predicted, it was one of the weak points in the defences and it was vital that it should be held.

Fonthill and his marines, the latter wearing their wide-brimmed straw hats so redolent of the seaside, arrived just as the Americans were involved in fierce hand-to-hand fighting on the barricade itself.

'Fix bayonets,' he yelled. 'Climb the barricade and pitch in. Come on!'

The barricade, however, although only breast-high, was not easy to climb, not least because some of the American dead and wounded had slid halfway down it on the defenders' side. Slipping and sliding on the debris, Simon climbed to the top and ducked under a sword, swung horizontally by a tall Boxer. He thrust with his bayonet and caught the man in the breast, freeing his lunger and pushing the Boxer down the barricade by thrusting with his boot on his chest.

He was conscious of Jenkins at his side deflecting a pike thrust with the butt of his rifle and spearing his man with his own bayonet. All along the top of the barricade, the marines and the remaining Americans were engaged in hand-to-hand combat with a mixture of Chinese: a sprinkling of young Boxers with their red head-and-hip bands far outnumbered by troops of the Imperial army in blood-red and green uniforms and the less-bizarrely attired Muslims from the north in their dun-coloured overalls. Looking ahead, Simon saw further troops doubling along the Chinese part of the wall to reinforce the attackers.

'Marines!' he screamed. 'Give them a volley. Fire!'

Not all of his party were able to disengage to fire but enough were able to do so and some sixteen or seventeen of the Chinese, either on the barricade or at its base, fell. 'Reload,' shouted Simon. 'Another volley. Are you ready? Fire! Reload. At the men running towards us – Fire!'

At such short range the volleys were completely effective and all the men in the first and second ranks of the reinforcements fell. Their comrades hesitated and stood for a moment irresolutely.

'Now's the time, boys,' shouted Fonthill. 'Straight at 'em. Charge!'

As one man, the marines, plus a few of the Americans, tumbled down the barricade, levelled their bayonets and ran towards where the Chinese stood. A volley from the attackers could have done incomparable damage in that small space but none came. Instead, the Chinese broke ranks, turned and ran along the road in full retreat.

'Halt!' ordered Simon. 'Reload and give them one more volley to send them on their way. Right? Fire!'

Once again the Martini-Henrys, mingled with the Americans' Springfield rifles, spat fire and more of the running Chinese fell.

Fonthill turned to look for the familiar figure of Jenkins, but the Welshman was not at his side. Whirling round, his heart in his mouth, he saw his comrade sitting on a pile of masonry at the foot of the barricade, holding his foot.

'What's the matter with you?' he called.

'Twisted me bloody ankle on this bedstead thing, look you. You can't fight a war like this, see, climbin' all over stuff. It's askin' too much.'

Grinning, Simon looked at his panting marines. 'Any casualties?' he called.

A sweating sergeant nodded to the barricade. 'Marine Robson got a sword thrust in the belly, sir. But I think that's all. I 'ope we don't 'ave to do much more charging in this 'eat, sir.'

Fonthill shook his head. 'Back to the barricade. But it looks as though we shall have to build it up a bit. I just hope the Chinese don't direct artillery fire on it, that's all.' He turned to one of the gaitered Americans who had charged with them. 'Have you been shelled?'

'Noo.' He spoke in the lazy tones of the Deep South. 'Ah guess they was afraid of knocking down this old wall an' all. Say, we all sure are thankful for your help heah. Might have let 'em in iffen you hadn't shown up.'

'Don't mention it. Do you have an officer with you?'

'Did have. But the cap'n got himself shot,' he nodded his head, 'back there. We sure took some casualties.'

'Ah. I'm sorry to hear it. Call the Legation if you get into more trouble. We're a sort of firefighting company. Come on now. Back to the barricades in case the Chinks recover their nerve.'

But they did not, and after shoring up the barrier, giving first aid to the marine with the wound in his stomach, which turned out to be only superficial, and tying a tight bandage around Jenkins's ankle, Fonthill took his men back to the British compound. There, where the Welshman's ankle was treated – despite his protests – it was found that the slight arm wound he had sustained in the affray with the Boxers near the Griffiths' village had turned sceptic. Jenkins had lived and fought for three weeks without complaining.

'It's the lack of beer, see,' he explained. 'It's poisoned me system. I've gone so long without a pint that my body is complainin'. An' so am I.'

* * *

103

In fact, as the days progressed under the hot sun with steady firing, some sporadic shelling and occasional direct attacks on the perimeter, the defenders' casualties increased. The little hospital that had been set up within the British Legation soon became overcrowded and the small medical staff were supplemented by the ladies of the Legation, led by Mrs Griffith, whose life as a missionary's wife had given her some basic medical skills, and Alice, who herself had acquired knowledge of first aid from her campaigns with Simon.

Pony meat and rice had become the staple diet for most in the Legation, washed down by copious draughts of champagne from the two stores within the Quarter, Imbeck's and Kierulff's. These also supplied seemingly limitless quantities of cigarettes, for now everyone smoked to combat the foul smells that rose from the bodies of the dead Chinese left outside the defences. It was no longer safe to venture beyond the perimeter to bury them – and there was nowhere to inter them, for that matter. Bathing was a thing of the past. And the sun continued to blaze down from a yellow sky.

Tensions mounted among the defenders and the non-combatants. At least the men mounting the walls and barricades had something to take their mind off the heat and the flies, for the Chinese attacks were becoming more determined, proving that the Empress had finally decided to gamble on wiping out the foreign devils so stubbornly holding out in her city.

Fonthill and his marines were called out when a mine was exploded under what was left of the French Legation and the

Chinese poured through the wreckage, almost overwhelming the Frenchmen who had for so long defended their line there. The fighting was fierce there for a time – Jenkins firing, stabbing and clubbing like a wild thing, despite his bandaged arm – until the defenders gradually consolidated their bridgehead and the attackers retreated, setting fire to the ruins of the Legation as they went.

The situation was worse, however, to the east of the British compound, in the Wang Fu, where the Japanese had the responsibility of defending this rambling park, dotted with small palaces and pagodas. If it had been lost, the Chinese would have poured through the centre of the Quarter, cutting off the British Legation from the others. The original defensive line there, established by Fonthill and Captain Strouts, had had to be abandoned, and the Japanese – who were turning out, Simon judged, to be the best of the defending troops – established a series of defensive positions from which they doggedly retreated in turn, fighting over every inch of the ground. Here, the 'Carving-Knife Brigade' were proving their worth, fighting with their primitive weapons as fiercely as their smaller, professional comrades. Even so, after days of attack and counter-attack, three-quarters of the Fu was in enemy hands.

At this point, ammunition for the little Italian one-pounder – small in size but valuable, for it was the only real piece of ordnance possessed by the legation soldiers – was down to fourteen rounds. And then two pieces of great good fortune occurred to give relief to the hard-pressed defenders.

The first occurred when Fonthill and Jenkins were

scavenging within an old foundry within the lines, searching for overlooked ammunition. There, lying in a corner, was a rusty but still serviceable-looking barrel of an old gun, a relic, by the look of it, of an Anglo-French expedition of 1860.

'Will it still fire?' asked Jenkins.

'I've no idea,' said Fonthill. 'I'm no gunner. But we will damned sure find out.'

A French artilleryman was consulted and, after inspecting the muzzle, he pronounced it still clearly rifled, with the firing mechanism still in place. The rust was chipped off and the barrel was mounted on a wooden base and a set of wheels originally intended for the Italian gun. Miraculously, some old nine-pound Russian ammunition was found which actually fitted.

'We have artillery,' Simon proudly announced to Sir Claude.

What's more, it worked, either when loaded with the nine-pound shells or filled with grapeshot formed of old nails and bits of iron and fired over open sights at the advancing hordes, particularly in the open spaces of the Fu. The diplomats called their gun 'The International'. To the marines, she was 'Betsy'.

The second piece of good fortune came out of the blue, from the unlikely source of the Imperial Palace.

At four o'clock on a day when every yard of the perimeter defences was under heavy attack, horns and bugles were suddenly heard from the direction of the palace, to be answered by similar sounds from all around the Chinese lines. Instantly, the firing from the attackers died away, leaving an eerie silence. A sentry on the roof of the British Legation stables reported that a large board carrying Chinese characters was being hoisted on the North Bridge. Translators with field glasses read out the message:

'*In accordance with the Imperial commands to protect the ministers, firing will cease immediately. A despatch will be delivered at the Imperial Canal bridge.*'

Watch was kept on the bridge, but no messenger arrived. Nevertheless, the ceasefire held and the cicadas could be heard chattering again in the Legation Quarter.

'What does it mean?' Alice asked of her husband, as she stood outside the sickbay, her sleeves rolled to the elbow and a bloodstained apron tied around her waist.

'God knows.' Then Simon's eyes lit up. 'It just could be that the relief column is nearly here at last. It would be typical of the Dragon Lady to bend the knee only when she had to and to pretend that she had the welfare of the diplomats at heart all the time. The crafty old . . . It's the only reason I can think of.'

Alice smiled. 'I wonder if he might know the reason.' She nodded her head to indicate someone behind Fonthill.

Simon whirled round. Walking by on the other side of the path, moving quietly as though anxious not to attract attention, was Gerald Griffith. He had long ago shaved off his incipient beard, leaving only his moustache, which now hung down on either side of his mouth, in mandarin style. He had allowed his hair to grow and had it gathered together at the nape of his neck and twisted in the beginning of a pigtail. He wore the loose trousers, sandals and buttoned-to-the-neck tunic of an indigenous peasant. He looked, in fact, completely Chinese.

Fonthill's previous attempts to question him on his movements during the day had met with monosyllabic replies. He went out, he said, 'to talk with friends'. While Chang had long ago attached himself to Fonthill's marines, turning out when required, still armed with Simon's revolver, Gerald seemed to take no part in the defence of the Quarter. His mother, however, would hear no criticism of him. 'He is a good boy,' she said. 'Just a little withdrawn, that's all, and does not wish to be a soldier.'

Now Fonthill walked across and caught up with the young man. 'Ah, Gerald,' he said, slipping into step. 'Been for a walk?'

'Yes.'

'It seems we have a ceasefire.'

'So it seems.'

'Do you know why?'

'Why should I know?'

Simon grasped his arm and brought him to a halt. 'Because I believe that you slip through the defences regularly and talk to your friends in the Imperial Palace.'

Gerald held up his head defiantly. 'That is not against the law.'

'It's damned near it, my friend. We are at war, Gerald. Those people on the other side of the barricades and walls are Chinese, my lad, and they are trying to kill us. Your friends. They are *the enemy*, dammit. Don't you ever consider that?'

For a moment the young man paused. 'I do not consider them to be so. They are doing what they consider to be right.'

'And do you tell *your friends* of the disposition of our defences here?'

'No. I do not know them, anyway.'

For a moment, the two men stood in silence, glaring at each other in the hot sun. In the distance, a pony could be heard whinnying from the butchery and from within the hospital a wounded man cursed in pain. Simon sighed. 'Let me ask you again. Do you know why the Empress has called a truce?'

'No. I do not.'

'Is it because the relief column is near?'

For the first time Gerald became animated. He threw back his head and laughed. 'Where did you get that idea? There's no relief column. Tientsin is surrounded and under siege – just like here. If you and these stuffy ministers think you are going to be rescued, then you are all living in dreamland.' He shook his arm free, gave a direct and lubricious grin to Alice, who had been listening to the conversation from outside the hospital, and walked on.

Alice crossed the path and grasped her husband's arm. 'Oh, Simon. Do you think he's right – that there's no relief column, I mean?'

Fonthill shook his head. 'Of course not. The Old Dragon has called a halt because she's sustained too many casualties. There must have been about two thousand of her soldiers who have been killed trying to break in here. She knows she's gambled and lost.' He smiled reassuringly. 'There's no way that that cocky young devil can know more than MacDonald.'

That night the defenders on guard dozed uneasily around the perimeter, the quiet more unsettling than the continual firing had been. The next day, the shelling and the rifle fire from the Chinese resumed, with even more intensity than before.

The brief truce – called and held for no apparent reason – was over. The siege settled in once more.

CHAPTER FIVE

The brief interval, although refreshing while it lasted, had the overall effect of depressing the defenders of the Legation Quarter. It seemed as though the Empress, in her palace not so far away, was playing with them, as a cat plays with a mouse: letting it spring away for a moment and then clutching it back again in its claws. Certainly, the firing from the Chinese lines had been resumed with a fierceness that, if accuracy had been added to intensity, would have seriously reduced the defenders' capacity to resist. It was the absence of serious shellfire, however, that caused the most puzzlement.

'Why don't they use those Krupp cannon more?' Fonthill demanded rhetorically of Jenkins. 'They each give us about six rounds a day, which causes more damage than that produced by all their other pop-shooters put together. Then they lay off. It seems strange.'

Jenkins sniffed. 'Short of ammunition, p'raps?'

'Don't think so. MacDonald tells me that before all this started he saw thousands of Krupp shells stacked in a warehouse in the Imperial City. If the Chinese wake up and really begin to bombard us, I don't think we would be able to hold out much longer. The Quarter would be in ruins.'

'Why can't we make a sortie, like, and put the bloody things out of action?'

'Because they are too far away, on a roof somewhere to the south. I doubt if we would be able to get to them.' Fonthill mused for a moment. 'It's a thought, though. I'll talk to Captain Strouts about it.'

The captain in command of the British marine guard was sceptical at first, but he too began to warm to the idea. 'I know where they are,' he said, 'they're firing from the top of the Chien Men, that partly burnt-out pagoda tower on the other side of the Tartar Wall. It would be terribly risky but we might just be able to reach the place and destroy the bloody things.'

'At night, I think,' suggested Fonthill.

'I agree. A smallish party, moving fast.'

'I'll put it to Sir Claude.'

The minister was unimpressed. 'You would take the marines, I suppose?'

'Yes, sir.'

'But you know, Fonthill, they are among the most effective and best-trained of all the troops in the Quarter. If you lose them – not to mention yourself – we would be bereft. I really can't allow it.'

Simon sighed. 'I don't know why the Chinese haven't used these guns at all so far. Once they realise what an advantage they have with them and start bombarding us consistently, they could reduce virtually the whole Quarter to a heap of rubble within, say, two days. They could destroy the barricades on the wall and beyond and we would be defenceless. The siege would be over. I really feel we should try to take them out before their advantage is realised.'

'Hmm. Is Strouts with you on this?'

'Completely.'

'How will you get out?'

'Through the sluice gates at the southern end of the canal.'

'Will you need any . . . um . . . diversionary activity from us?'

'No thank you, sir. A good idea, but we will get out through the sleepiest part of the night. Nothing is ever quiet through the night here but it all tails off a bit about three-thirty. That's when we will go. Running like hell through the streets, in plimsolls, not army boots. Hit 'em before they know what's happening.'

There was silence for a time, while Sir Claude's eyes seemed to grow more bulbous by the heartbeat. Then he stood and held out his hand. 'Very well, my dear fellow. May God be with you.'

Strouts and Fonthill trained their men for two days as best they could, within the confined space of the compound. They practised running in plimsolls and sandals, carrying rifles and fixed bayonets, and they rehearsed – with the help of the French artillery officer – how to destroy cannon.

'Throw zem off ze tower as well, if you can,' he urged. 'But zey will be 'eavy.'

On the afternoon before the sortie, Simon told Alice about the plan. She stood for a moment, very still, with tears in her eyes. Then she put her arms around her husband's neck and nuzzled his ear. 'I know it is no use me trying to dissuade you from this ridiculous exercise,' she said. 'But, you know,' she pulled back her head and looked him in the eyes, 'one day you will push your luck too far. You cannot continue to get away with these ridiculous enterprises. Let someone younger go, my dear. You have done far more than your bit in this siege. I do so not want to be a widow at my age.'

He kissed her briefly. 'Don't worry. Dear old 352 will look after me. But one thing.'

'What?'

'Don't let Gerald or his mother know about this.'

'Of course.'

They assembled just as the moon was beginning to settle over the rooftops, looking like a rather exotic Chinese lantern, low in the sky.

The marines had exchanged their scoop-brimmed straw hats for a variety of knitted skullcaps and their boots for training pumps. They wore dark clothing and they had blackened their faces. Each man carried a rifle and bayonet at the trail, except for Jenkins, whose arm having recovered had volunteered to spike the guns and bore the bag of spikes and a large hammer. At his belt, however, hung his large knife. Fonthill and Strouts wore revolvers tucked into their own belts and carried naval cutlasses in their right hands, the blades blackened to prevent moonlight reflecting from them.

Sir Claude had risen to wish them Godspeed and stood shivering slightly in his dressing gown, although the night was not cold. 'You look like pirates,' he observed, with a sad smile. 'Good luck.'

The two officers saluted him with their cutlasses and Simon blew a kiss to Alice, who stood erect in the shadows. Dry-eyed but tight-lipped, she acknowledged it with the merest nod of her head. Then the little company moved away with a quick step.

Fonthill had chosen the sluice gates for their exit from the Quarter, not only because he knew it was lightly guarded from the Chinese side – the besiegers now never thought that the defenders would try to leave their ramshackle fortress – but because it was the nearest point of egress to the Chien Men, some three hundred yards away. The gates were not raised, for it would have been too noisy a process to carry out without alerting the guards. At either side of the grills, however, in the tunnel at the base of the Tartar Wall, there was a space big enough for one man to slither through. Simon took one side and Strouts – a burly, well-moustached man – the other. The rest of the party waited, huddled against the dripping walls of the tunnel.

Peering through the grill, Fonthill saw two guards, squatting on the pavement at the far side of the road. They did not move and it seemed that they were asleep. No one else was to be seen, although gunfire sounded from quite near. Nodding to the captain, Simon slithered through the gap and bounded across the road.

But, despite their posture, neither of the guards was asleep. They were, however, surprised to be suddenly set upon by two darkly dressed men with black faces emerging from the canal and they were just a little slow to gain their feet. The blade of Fonthill's cutlass wrought a slashing cut across the right shoulder of the nearest man. But he, like his fellow, was a Moslem Kansu from the north, toughened by years of campaigning for his brigand chief, Tung Fu-hsiang. He grunted with pain but rolled away from Simon's next swing and, drawing a knife from his belt, thrust at Fonthill's stomach. But it was a weak blow with his left hand and the blade point caught in Simon's cummerbund without penetrating. The next blow from the cutlass nearly severed his head.

Strouts had similarly finished his man and the two marauders stood for a moment, their blades dripping red, while they anxiously scanned the street on either side of them. There was no sign of life. Fonthill beckoned and the marines, led by Jenkins, began slipping past the sluice gates and running across the road to join them.

'Ever used a cutlass before?' grunted Strouts.

Simon shook his head, still panting.

'Thought not. Everyone uses the blade, just because it's curved. No good. The swing gives yer man time to duck. Use the point. Stupid weapon. Don't know why it's curved. Only good for thickheaded sailors.'

'Still, wish I'd got one,' sniffed Jenkins. 'All I've got is a ropey old bag.'

'You'll be lethal with that,' said Fonthill. 'Now. Everyone here? Good. Remember no firing. If we get into trouble, use the bayonet. Right. Follow me.'

They set off at a fast trot, making little sound and with no light reflecting from their blackened lungers.

No one was about in those narrow streets, although rifle fire sounded all around them. Simon realised that the musketry was coming from the upper floors of the houses, where snipers were directing a desultory fire on the American and German defenders on the ramparts of the wall. No one was looking down. It was just as well, for the raiding party would have been hard-pressed to have fought their way through the streets if met by stubborn opposition.

As it was, they found their way to where the Chinese had reduced the jewellery and fine furs quarter to blackened rubble with their indiscriminate torching of the shops earlier in the siege. It was flames from these buildings that had set fire to the fine, old brick and wooden pagoda of the Chien Men tower, leaving it a stumpy ruin of charred bricks, now some forty-five feet high. Somehow, however, the Chinese had managed to swing the two guns up to the top, giving the guns sufficient height to fire across the Tartar Wall and directly into the Legation Quarter. The two cannon could now be seen, silhouetted against the night sky.

Fonthill halted the raiding party at the end of the ruins of the shops. A scattering of soldiers lay, huddled in blankets, sleeping at the base of the tower. Others could be seen, standing by their guns at the top. To reach the tower, however, the raiders would have to cross a stretch of open ground.

''Ow the bloody 'ell do we get up there?' whispered Jenkins. 'I didn't knows we'd 'ave to do any climbin', see.'

Simon frowned. He knew that Jenkins was as brave as a lion. Hardened by a hundred fights with a variety of weapons around the world, he would take on anyone in combat. He was aware that the Welshman was as strong as an ox, a crack shot and a surprisingly good horseman. But he also knew that he was afraid of water – he could not swim – crocodiles and, perhaps most of all, heights. Standing on the smallest ladder made his legs tremble.

'For God's sake, 352,' he hissed. 'There's bound to be a ladder and, anyway, it's not very high. Just follow me – and don't look down.' He turned to Strouts. 'Will you please keep about half the party here and try and pick off the guards up on top if they see us as we climb the ladder. Stay here under cover and shoot anyone who tries to run across this space to get to us. Whatever happens, though, don't fire until we have seen off these chaps sleeping down below.'

The marine nodded. He had generously granted Fonthill the leadership of the sortie, in view of his greater experience.

Simon addressed the rest of the party. 'These men here,' he indicated about twelve, 'will come with me. No firing, now. We will double across this open space and bayonet the men sleeping. Not a nice thing to do, I agree, but it is very necessary. We don't want them to give the alarm. So everything must be done quietly and quickly. Then it will be a case of following Jenkins and me up the ladder – there's bound to be one, perhaps two – and seeing to whoever is left on top and then putting the guns out of action. Understood?'

The men nodded, the whites of their eyes standing out in their darkened faces.

'And, look you,' whispered Jenkins, 'will somebody catch me if I fall, like?'

'Stop being a baby, 352,' hissed Fonthill. 'Right. Bayonets only, remember. Get the bastards before they wake. Now, *go*!'

Like wraiths from a fire, heads down, bayonets presented, the little party sprinted across the open space towards where the sleeping figures lay. The only sound they made was the faint clunk from the spikes in Jenkins's hessian bag. The Chinamen had no chance. Remembering Strouts' advice, Fonthill plunged the point of his cutlass into the first recumbent form and then into the next. All around him he was aware that bayonets were being thrust into the sleepers, as though they were sacks of corn, being spiked before being tossed onto a pile. Two attempted to rise but they were easily cut down. It was all over within a matter of seconds. The massacre had taken place with hardly a sound being made.

Fonthill flattened himself, his back to the base of the wall. Sure enough, a ladder to his right led up to the top. There seemed only one. He gulped. They surely must be seen from the top as they began to climb up and it would be so easy for the guards up there to shoot down, or even push the ladder away. They would surely shoot before he could gain the top and use his cutlass. Better to rely on his revolver – and on the marines in the shadows opposite to cut the guards down before they could shoot.

He gave a sweating Jenkins a weak and less-than-comforting grin and waved at Strouts. Then he tucked his cutlass into his belt, drew his Colt revolver and began to climb.

On the first few rungs the only sound he could hear was a muffled 'Oh my God' as Jenkins followed him. Then, a loud challenge in Chinese came from the top. Simon gave a cheery and, he hoped, a reassuring wave to whoever was above him. It was immediately followed, however, with a loud report and a bullet cracked into the brickwork near his head and pinged away. Fonthill raised his revolver and fired virtually blindly directly above him. At the same time, two rifle shots rang out from the ruins and the man above gave a grunt and toppled over, passing him and crashing to the ground.

'Keep goin', bach sir, for God's sake.' Jenkins's voice came from below him. 'I think I've peed me pants and I've got a bloke below me, see.'

Fonthill was now at the top of the ladder and, cautiously, he raised himself up and peered over the edge of the tower. Four men were silhouetted against the moonlit sky in various postures. The first, on his knees, was in the process of thrusting a cartridge into the breech of the rifle. The next two had obviously just crawled from their bedrolls and were looking around them in some consternation. The head of the fourth could only just be glimpsed between the wheels of the Krupp guns.

Gripping the top of the ladder as it projected upwards, Simon presented his revolver at the kneeling man, fired and, predictably, missed him.

'It fires high, dammit,' shouted Jenkins from down below. The man was now on his feet, fumbling with the bolt mechanism of his rifle. Fonthill adjusted his aim and shot the man in the breast. Cocking the revolver with his thumb, he fired at the nearest of the two men standing and brought him down too. The third man held up his hands in surrender and Simon waved him aside. He looked along the sights of the Colt for the fourth but he had disappeared behind the two cannon.

'Can you get up, bach?' hissed Jenkins. It was always a sign of great anxiety when the Welshman omitted the 'sir' when addressing his comrade. 'Me trousers are soaked and me 'ead's spinnin' up 'ere. I think I'm goin' to fall.'

'No you're not. Hang on. I'm climbing up.'

Attempting to keep his revolver levelled at the standing Chinaman and wary of the man hiding behind the two cannons, Simon hauled himself over the edge and, on knees and one hand, crouched on the top of the tower. There was a clunk as Jenkins threw his bag of spikes ahead of him and a cry of 'Thank God!' as the Welshman scrambled away from the edge.

His arrival distracted Fonthill and the standing man ducked away, reaching down to pick up a rifle. Simon's first shot caught him in the shoulder, spinning him round, and the second took him in the forehead, causing him to fall.

'I keep telling you, it fires high,' grunted Jenkins, now his normal, cool self again. ''Ere, let me 'ave it.' He put out his hand and Fonthill was happy to hand over the Colt.

'Just two more shots left,' he said. 'Be careful. There's another man behind the guns.' As he spoke, he was aware of firing breaking out down below, near the edge of the burnt-out shops. Strouts and his men were obviously under attack. They must hurry.

121

The thought had hardly crossed his mind when a rifle barrel poked through the spokes of one of the guns and a bullet zipped through the edge of Fonthill's jacket, prompting him to roll away. It immediately galvanised Jenkins, who sprang to his feet with amazing alacrity for a man who, moments before, had been wetting himself with fear. Ducking under the barrel of the nearest gun, the Welshman fired one shot from the revolver. As the sound echoed away, he called out, 'All right, bach sir. We've cleared this top, like. The others can come up.'

Fonthill crawled back to the ladder. His men were lined up it, presenting a perfect target to whoever was attacking the marines in the ruins. 'All right,' he called. 'Climb up, as quick as you like.'

Jenkins was already examining the guns. 'Where did that Frenchie say we should stick the spikes?' he asked, perspiration dripping down his face.

'In the priming hole, at the top. Give me a spike. I'll hold it while . . .' His voice tailed away. There was no priming hole, this was a modern, breech-loading gun. One that could not be spiked.

'Damn that Frenchman,' he swore. 'Must have fought at Austerlitz.' Then he became aware that eight of his men were now on the top of the tower. 'Where are the rest of you?' he demanded.

'Got picked off comin' up the tower,' replied a corporal of marines. 'We was strung out like paper ducks at the fairground. 'Ow are we goin' to get down again, sir?'

'We'll get down all right, don't worry about that.' In fact, the thought of climbing back down that ladder under gunfire

122

perturbed him considerably. 'Right. Four of you line the edge. See if you can get a sight on whoever is firing at us and take a few out. They'll be in the ruins. You four give me and Jenkins a hand to see if we can tip these bloody guns over the edge. Come on.'

It took some time before they could move either gun. They had been propped up by bricks to ensure that the recoil did not send them back over the edge. All of the bricks therefore had to be cleared away, together with the bodies of the dead Chinese, before the heavy guns could be shifted.

'Now,' said Simon. 'Spin them round on their wheels and simply push them over the edge – but one at a time, in case we cause the tower to collapse further. And not the ladder side, for God's sake . . . !'

All of this was being done while the four marines were delivering a steady fire on whatever Chinese they could see amongst the debris down below. Fonthill looked over their shoulders. Strouts and his men had spread out among the ruins and were engaged in a lively exchange with mainly hidden adversaries. Looking down, Simon had a sudden idea.

He turned round. The marines were on the point of tipping the second Krupp gun over the edge. 'Stop,' he shouted. 'Pull it back.'

With ill grace, the sweating men did so. 'What's up?' asked Jenkins.

'I think we can use this thing before we throw it over.'

'Ah . . . what? Fire down on them lot, down there?'

'Why not? If we can depress it enough to fire down – and if we can find out how to load and fire it.'

123

Jenkins wiped the back of his wrist across his perspiring brow. 'Aw, it's just a matter of shovin' in a shell and pullin' the trigger, ain't it?'

'I doubt it.' He turned to the marines, standing at the wheels. 'Anyone know anything about artillery?' He was greeted by blank faces. But one of the men firing from the edge turned his head.

'I was a gunner for a time, sir.'

'Good. See if you can load this thing. You,' he indicated the men standing, 'pull the gun back, swivel it around and build up bricks under its trail to see if we can depress the muzzle.' He looked to the east. Was the sky brightening there? 'Come on, lads. Look lively. We haven't got much time. The rest of you keep firing.'

A shell was soon found and the marine opened the breech and inserted it into the groove, slamming the breech block over it. The gun was inched carefully on its wheels toward the edge facing the ruined retail area. Then the bricks were built up under the wooden trail that would normally attach it to the harness of the horses pulling it. This, of course, depressed the barrel. There seemed to be no sophisticated sights, so Fonthill directed the men to move the gun so that its barrel was roughly aimed at the middle of the rubble and timber from which the flashes of rifle fire could be seen.

A sudden thought struck him. 'Do we have to fuse the shell before we fire it?' he asked of the ex-gunner.

'Dunno, sir. Never had to do that bit.'

'Well, we'll just have to take a chance on that.' He sighted down the barrel of the gun. 'Come and look at this,' he ordered the marine. 'Laid like this, should we be able to land a shell amongst those riflemen?'

The ex-gunner squinted down the barrel. He waved his hand. 'Bit more elevation, sir.'

Fonthill removed a couple of bricks.

'That should do it, sir.'

'What's your name, marine?'

'Oakley, sir.'

Simon grinned. 'Let's hope you're a relative of . . . what was her name? Ah yes. Little Annie Oakley. Deadliest shot in the west. Can you fire this thing?'

'Oh yes, sir. That's the easiest part.'

'Right men. Stand back.'

Fonthill looked around him quickly. The space on top of the tower was rectangular, the size of a large tennis court, but much narrower. If the gun backfired in some way, then they could all be blown off the top, for it was firing from the narrowest part. If the bricks wedged under the wheels proved inadequate, then the recoil could take the gun and Oakley back over the edge. Would it work? There was only one way to find out. He nodded at Oakley. 'Fire!'

The report was deafening and the muzzle of the gun spurted flame. The bricks were sent scattering as the whole thing recoiled – but less than a foot and it did not implode. Instead, the explosion came from the middle of the ruins below them, roughly where the gun had been aimed. An inverted triangular-shaped sheet of flame sprang up, sending a shower of debris high into the air.

The marines on the tower sprang to their feet and waved

their woolly hats, cheering. A similar but fainter cheer came from Strouts' men, down below.

'Oakley,' shouted Fonthill. 'Get another shell. I'd like to give 'em one more round to make 'em think we are going to keep up the shelling.'

The shell was found and inserted into the breech.

'Right, Oakley,' said Fonthill. 'Lay the gun to fire just a little back of where the last shell landed. You three, pile up the bricks again. You lads at the edge, keep up the musketry until we fire the gun, but start shimmying down that ladder like hell as soon as we have fired. The rest of us will cover you from up here.'

Once more the barrel was adjusted and once more the shell exploded satisfactorily in the target area.

'Good shot, Oakley,' shouted Simon. 'You'll be awarded a coconut when we get back. Now, let's all tip this gun over the edge. We can't hang about up here. You others, down the ladder as fast as you can. Once down, all of you sprint across to join Captain Strouts. Jenkins and I will cover you as best we can. Off you go.'

With an effort, the gun was reversed, wheeled to the opposite edge and given a final push that sent it tumbling down to land on its mate with a satisfying, metal-tearing crash.

Simon picked up two of the rifles left by the Chinese and the bandoliers that lay by their sleeping bags. Throwing a rifle and a bandolier to Jenkins, he crouched on the edge, joining the marines waiting to take their turn down the ladder. 'Can you see any of the men firing on our chaps?' he asked the man next to him.

'They were over there, sir,' said the marine, pointing. 'But I think the shells may have got most of them.'

'Good. Get down the ladder.'

Soon, only Fonthill and Jenkins were left on the top of the tower. Dawn was colouring the sky to the east. Simon looked to his right, to the south, away from the ruins, where the narrow streets criss-crossed the Chinese City. Was it his imagination, or could he see figures running along them in the direction of the open space and the tower?

'Down you go, 352.'

'No, bach sir. I'll follow, look you.'

'No. You go first. Get on that ladder or I'll push you over. Here, give me that rifle and bandolier. I'll carry them. Get onto the first rung, face the wall and hold on to the side pieces. Oh, and think of the Queen. Go on, man. I can see Chinese troops running towards us. We don't want to be stuck up here. I promise not to pee on you.'

Jenkins forced a ghastly grin. 'Very kind, I'm sure.' But his legs were trembling as he reached with a tentative foot for the top rung.

Fonthill selected a couple of rounds from the bandoliers slung around his shoulders and inserted them into the breech of one of the Mausers – a rapid-firing rifle, much better than the old Martini-Henrys they carried. He fired them in the general direction of the figures he could now see running through the nearest street. The range was too extreme, of course, but it made him feel better. Then he swung himself onto the ladder.

Climbing down that ladder was one of the most frightening and frustrating journeys of Simon's life. His progress, of course, had to be geared to that of Jenkins who, with eyes tightly shut, seemed hardly to be moving as he groped his way down, one foot slowly feeling for the rung below it. At any moment, Fonthill felt that a hail of bullets would thud into their bodies. Looking down, he could see that all of the marines from the tower had been able to reach their comrades in the ruins, some hundred yards away. And they had stopped firing, presumably because the enemy had fled. Or had they, themselves, fled? He shuddered and plodded down, after Jenkins.

At last a cry of 'Oh, thank God for that' from below him showed that his comrade had reached the ground safely. The cry that quickly followed of 'Throw me a rifle, quick' showed that the Welshman had regained his normal equanimity. He tossed a rifle down, followed by one of the bandoliers.

It was at that moment that a bullet thudded into the brickwork to his left, followed by another, high above him to the right. Immediately, they were answered by Jenkins, who was now kneeling and coolly firing at figures running across the open ground towards them from the Chinese City. At the same moment, his shooting was supplemented by firing from the ruins. As Fonthill clung to the ladder, he saw at least a dozen Chinese soldiers brought down.

'Come on, bach,' called Jenkins. 'You're only a few feet up. You can jump down now. We've got to get out of here quick, see.'

Simon, encumbered by rifle, bandolier and cutlass, swivelled round and jumped, landing on all fours next to the Welshman. 'Right,' shouted Jenkins, 'our lads over there will cover us, look you. Run like hell.'

They did so and gained the cover of the ruins, where about fifteen marines were spread out behind the debris firing steadily.

'Where's Captain Strouts?' asked Fonthill of a stout, hugely moustached sergeant.

The man nodded. 'Over there, sir. Gone, I'm afraid. Bullet through 'is 'ead. Are you all down now, sir?'

'Yes.' Simon's voice was half choked with grief. 'Is this all you've got left of the party?'

The sergeant coolly sighted and let off another round. ''Fraid so, sir.' He nodded over his shoulder. 'Got caught from be'ind us, so to speak. We've lost about 'alf our number. If you 'adn't started your fireworks up there, the rest of us would have got it, too. I think the Chinks be'ind us took fright at that.' He wiped his moustache with a dirty handkerchief. 'They don't like artillery, y'see, sir. Pity we don't 'ave a few more guns.' He regarded Fonthill respectfully. 'If I may say so, sir, you did a good job up there. But I do suggest now that we should bugger off back to the compound.' He nodded across the space to where flashes of rifle fire could be seen coming from the streets. 'I think we've got the rest of the Chinese army comin' after us.' Then he nodded behind him. 'And a few more be'ind us still to get through.'

Fonthill nodded. 'Of course, Sergeant. Do we have any wounded?'

'Only scratches, sir. Their firin' was quite good for savages. Got most of our blokes through the 'ead.'

'Right. I'm afraid we can't stay to bury them. I will take the lead, Sergeant, and I would be grateful if you would bring up the rear, with another good man. We may have to do a couple of bayonet charges to get through.'

'Very good, sir. Quite right. The Chinks don't like the bayonets, either. After you, then, sir.'

Three abreast, led by Fonthill and Jenkins, the remnants of the raiding party began their retreat. It became clear that the troops who had closed in behind Strouts' group as the tower was scaled had not been led efficiently, for they all seemed to have dispersed as a result of the shelling. There was no attempt to hinder the party as they trotted back towards the Tartar Wall. Not until, that is, they reached the point where they could see the sluice gates to their right and just ahead of them. Suddenly, with a howl, the street ahead was filled with Chinese troops, brandishing swords and pikes.

Fonthill gulped. 'Fall into two lines across the street. Now,' he yelled. 'Front rank, kneel.'

The mob in front of them paused for a moment, as though mesmerised by these strange movements.

'Two volleys by ranks,' cried Simon. 'Front rank, fire!' The volley from eight rifles thundered out. 'Front rank, reload. Second rank, fire! Second rank, reload.'

The front line facing the little party seemed to disintegrate, leaving sixteen bodies lying on the harsh surface of the road. Fonthill looked up and saw anxious faces peering down at him from the top of the great wall. He prayed that they would be Americans. He hailed them: 'Open the sluice gates when we charge 'em.' There was no response. Had he been heard? He felt a tap on his shoulder.

'Beggin' your pardon, sir,' said the marine sergeant, as

though interrupting a conversation at an officers' tea party. 'But a party of the enemy seems to be comin' up fast be'ind us. P'raps a bayonet charge, sir?'

Fonthill swallowed and tried to answer as coolly as the question had been put. 'Splendid idea, Sergeant,' he said. 'Thank you for your advice.' Then, turning, 'Marines! One more volley from the front rank then we all charge with the bayonet. Make for the sluice gates. Now, front rank, fire!' Then, as the smoke curled upwards: 'All ranks, charge!'

The marines bounded forward as one man, spreading out across the width of the street, their rifles and bayonets extending out in front of them, like a fast-moving, prickly hedge. The Chinese facing them immediately broke. Just two sword-wielding warriors attempted to get through the bayonet wall and were cut down for their bravery. Within seconds, the British had broken through and were running towards the canal opening where, thankfully, the sluice gates guarding it were gradually being winched open. From the ramparts up above came covering fire from the Americans lining the wall.

Jenkins, the sergeant and Fonthill were the last to splash through the opening before the gates began to close. The three stood with their backs to the wall, their breasts heaving.

'No more casualties, Sergeant?' gasped Simon.

'None since we left poor old Captain Strouts, sir.' He puffed out his cheeks. 'I'd call it a well-carried-out strategic withdrawal.'

'Good, thank you. Let's all go and have a cup of horrible coffee.'

Word had got out about the sortie and, despite the early

hour, the party's return was greeted at the British Legation by an applauding group of diplomats and other civilians. Sir Claude clearly had not gone back to bed since seeing off the marines and he was waiting on the Residency steps. He shook Fonthill warmly by the hand and then his face dropped as he looked over his shoulder.

'Yes,' said Simon sadly, 'heavy casualties, I'm afraid, sir. We lost roughly half of our strength, including Captain Strouts. But we did destroy the guns.'

MacDonald's drooping face took on even more the expression of a bloodhound. He said nothing but retained Fonthill's hand, continuing to shake it.

Eventually, he said, 'It was a heavy price to pay, Fonthill, but I do believe that it will prove to have been worth it. Now go and get some breakfast and perhaps you would report to me in some detail when you feel up to it.'

Alice had not slept either and he found her, white-faced and crouching in her dressing gown, outside her sleeping quarters. She had not dared to see who were among the returning party and she could not restrain her tears when she saw him. For a time they did not exchange a word, merely holding each other.

'So you see, my luck has not run out yet, my love,' said Simon nuzzling his nose into her long, loose hair. 'Dear old 352 did look after me, although I have to report that he ruined his trousers.' She looked at him in some consternation. 'I'll tell you later,' he added hurriedly. 'Is there any very old, roast pony to be had?'

CHAPTER SIX

As though incensed by the success of the sortie, the Chinese stepped up their attacks on the perimeter, particularly on the Fu, where the Japanese held on stoically, giving ground when they had to, retaking it when the opportunity occurred. The defenders' casualties grew, however, and it became dangerous to walk across open ground within the compounds. A marine, a survivor of Fonthill's sortie, was shot and killed just outside the guardhouse by the main entrance to the British Legation. The Australian machine gun and then the American were hauled back to the Legation as a final precaution.

From the general direction of Tientsin, it was reported that searchlights could be seen probing the sky. The relief expedition, at last? Two rockets were sent up from the German compound but no reply was seen in the southern sky.

Overcrowding was becoming a problem in the British

Legation, which housed most of the European civilians. The Dutch minister slept in a cupboard in the small house allotted to the Russian minister and the fifty-one members of his family and staff. Forty people now sat down to dinner each evening in Lady MacDonald's dining room. Cooking itself became a problem and the ornamental rockwork in the Legation grounds became an outdoor kitchen, where large kettles and pots were used for boiling the horsemeat by Chinese cooks, incongruously wearing frilly aprons.

The strain of the overcrowding and the growing danger from snipers' bullets and shrapnel fragments was particularly hard on the women. In the case of Mrs Griffith and the Fonthills, however, this was supplemented by the latters' resentment of Gerald, causing a rift to appear between them. The young man had ceased making his mysterious disappearances during the day, and now spent his time sitting near his sleeping quarters, ostentatiously reading medieval Chinese tomes in their original, archaic Mandarin.

'If he doesn't want to fight,' hissed Alice to her husband, 'why doesn't he at least give a hand in the hospital, or in the kitchens? Chang is pathetically anxious to attach himself to your marines – he cried when you didn't take him with you to destroy those guns.'

Fonthill nodded. 'Yes, the difference between the two is amazing. You would have thought it would be Chang, the native Chinaman, who would be pro-Boxer. But it's the other way around. Have you thought of having a word with your aunt about Gerald?'

'I have tried – very delicately – to raise the matter, because the fellow just sits around all day and this has been noticed by the other ladies. Mind you,' she sniffed, 'there are plenty of others. The Italian minister, for instance, the very noble Marchese Salvago Raggi, can't be more than thirty-six years old and looks perfectly fit. Yet he sits in a chaise longue most of the time chatting to his beautiful wife. And you know about that pathetic creature, Monsieur Pichon . . .'

Simon grinned. 'Yes, but what did your aunt say about Gerald?'

'Oh, she says that he is a very studious boy who is not cut out to be a soldier and, of course, she mothers him.' Alice sighed. 'Also, of course, she is still grieving for her husband. She is doing sterling work in the hospital, which keeps her mind off things. But I can't help thinking that she is a bit jealous of me – the fact that my husband is still alive.' She put her hand on Simon's arm. 'I feel so sorry for her, my dear, but I can't help her.

'The trouble is,' she went on, 'it has been a long time since you and I – with old 352, of course – were in danger, like this. But in those days I was serving with you, alongside you, sharing the dangers. You know: in Matabeleland, the Sudan, Afghanistan and so on.' She sighed. 'Now you go off, leading bayonet charges, putting guns out of action, and I'm stuck here, trying to wash bandages in muddy water.'

Fonthill regarded his wife with surging affection. One of the reasons he loved her so much was her intrepidity. All her life, she had remained cool under pressure, whether it was scribbling under fire to record a battle for the *Morning Post* or shooting a Boxer swordsman with a Colt revolver at forty paces.

Their life together had been marred by misunderstandings at first, but since their wedding more than fifteen years ago, they had loved each other with an intellectual and physical passion. Their son, conceived in the sands of the Sudanese desert, had died in childbirth and Alice had been unable to give birth again. Now, in their middle age, they had settled into a strange but loving trio, with Jenkins, as comrade and servant, sharing in their affection.

Simon tucked a lank strand of her hair back under her headscarf. 'I know,' he said. 'I'm too bloody old to be leading bayonet charges, anyway. And Jenkins says if I get on a horse I will fall off it.'

'He always did say that.'

'He did and it's true – well, partly, though I would never admit it to him.' He pushed her away to look steadily into her eyes. 'You don't need to be soldiering, my love, you are doing wonderful work in the sickbay. And,' he smiled, 'I've noticed that you've been scribbling again. A letter to your lover? How are you going to smuggle it out?'

For a brief moment, Alice looked embarrassed. 'Yes,' she said, 'that's going to be the problem. You know the tall doctor in the hospital, Dr Morrison?'

'Well, I've seen him but I've not actually shaken his hand. At a quick glance, though, he should make a very satisfying lover, I would think.'

She gave him a playful push. 'Don't be silly. I only found out recently that, apart from his medical practice, he is the Peking correspondent of *The Times* – although, of course, he can't get any stories out of here now.'

'Quite. So?'

'So, he has stimulated me to start writing again. I've been keeping a diary so that, as soon as this siege is ended, I can write features, as well as report the news, for the *Morning Post*. I can't let the opposition get away with one of the best stories for years. I haven't really had anything published in the *Post* for months, apart from the odd piece I cabled from America. Although we can't know it, I bet the eyes of the world are on this godforsaken place, now. There will be great demand for stories from inside.'

Her eyes in her perspiring face were bright – brighter than Simon had seen them in weeks. He kissed her. 'Good,' he said. 'You could outscoop the stuffy old *Times* any day.'

Then Alice's eyes clouded over momentarily and she frowned. 'There is something I feel I ought to mention to you,' she said. 'It's probably absolutely nothing at all to be concerned about but . . .' She tailed away. 'Back to Gerald.'

'Yes. What about him?'

'Well . . .' She hesitated again, in some embarrassment.

'Go on.'

'Well . . .' Another pause. Then the words came out in a flood. 'He has started to pay me some sort of . . . er . . . attention. I don't think I am misunderstanding it, but he is being very, well, friendly.'

'Nothing wrong in that. It's about time he was friendly to *somebody*.'

'No, I mean . . . He has bought me flowers, little bundles of almond blossom, although goodness knows where he gets it from. And he finds an excuse to touch my hand. That sort of thing.' She gave an uncertain smile. 'It's ridiculous, I know, but I think he rather . . . you know . . .'

Fonthill's mouth dropped open. Then he recovered. 'But that *is* ridiculous. Oh, I'm sorry. That's rude of me. What I mean is that you are more than twenty years older than him and, dammit, you're the man's *cousin* for goodness sake. And, anyway, you're married.'

Alice put her hand on her husband's arm. 'I know all that, my dear,' she said with a touch of asperity. 'And, more to the point, he knows it too. I have done absolutely nothing to encourage him, I assure you. In fact, on the contrary, sometimes I have been almost rude to him, what with him lolling about while others are fighting, and so on. I've shown my disgust. I just don't know what's come over him.'

Simon sighed. 'Well, at least he is showing good judgement. You *are* an attractive woman, my love, and I suppose, what with the heat and everything . . .' He shrugged.

'Well, I wish he'd turn his attention somewhere else. There are plenty of very pretty Chinese girls about the place.'

'Would you like me to have a word with him? Play the aggrieved husband and that sort of thing. Warn him off, so to speak?'

'Oh, good Lord, no. There's really nothing one can take exception to. And if he does get out of hand, I can handle him. I'm a big girl now, Simon.'

Fonthill smiled. 'Hmm. Yes, I have noticed.' He pulled her to him and kissed her again. Then he wiped the perspiration from his brow and looked up at the sky. 'I don't blame young

Gerald for getting broody. This bloody drought is enough to unbalance anybody. If only we could have a spot of rain. I can't remember when last I had a bath.'

The next day, as though on cue, the heavens opened.

Torrential rain thundered down on Peking, flooding the trenches in the compounds and beating down the precarious shelters and many parts of the barricades. The defending troops were forced to leave their posts to bail out and repair the defences, under rain that stung them like flying pebbles. If the Chinese had not been similarly hampered, they could have attacked and stormed unhindered into the legations.

Then, as suddenly as it had begun, the rain ended and the sun reappeared, not at all daunted by what had gone before. Immediately, the temperature rose to one hundred and ten degrees in the shade and a dreadful humidity descended to torture the defenders anew.

Fonthill was helping to shovel mud out of the trenches when a messenger found him and brought a request for him to report to Sir Claude's office. After a quick douche from a bucket and a rub down with a towel he complied.

His apologies for his appearance were waved aside by the minister. Some of the old imperturbability seemed to have left the tall, elegant man, although, despite the humidity, his tie was correctly knotted and his moustache still fiercely waxed. He smiled and nodded to a chair.

'Whisky?' he asked.

'No thank you, sir. Too early in the day for me and too hot.'

'Quite right. Shouldn't fall into bad habits, despite this bloody heat and the . . . er . . . conditions here.'

Simon nodded and waited. Something clearly was to be demanded of him, but better to keep quiet and wait for it. The minister looked tired and on edge. There was no doubt about it.

'Fonthill,' he began, sitting back in his chair. 'I have something to request of you.'

'Sir?'

'I would like to make clear that it is a request, not an order, you understand?'

Simon nodded again. Whatever it was, it was going to be difficult. Still he waited.

'Yes. Now.' MacDonald leant forward. 'This morning I received a message from a Chinese who managed to slip through the enemy lines. He came from Tientsin.' He gestured to a small slip of paper on his desk. 'It seems that there has been fighting there for some weeks now, with the result that the city is under some sort of siege, not quite as tightly as we are here, but surrounded nonetheless.'

Fonthill felt his jaw drop. So Gerald had been right! He waited for the minister to continue.

'There was a force sent to relieve us, of course, some time ago, but it couldn't get through via the railway and was rather badly mauled and had to fall back on Tientsin. War has broken out – although I am unsure if it has been formally declared on either side – but the Taku Forts at the entrance to the Pei Ho river have been taken by the Foreign Powers. All is by no means lost and reinforcements are expected

140

daily from other foreign stations. Another relief force will be mounted. We are urged to . . .' MacDonald allowed his long features to lapse into a smile '. . . hold on.'

The minister settled back in his chair. 'And this,' he continued with emphasis, 'is what we *shall do*, of course. But the pressure here is tightening. The position on the Tartar Wall is particularly difficult, for the Americans and the Germans are exposed on the skyline, as you know. Indeed,' he flipped another piece of paper on his desk, 'the American minister has today asked my permission to abandon the barricade there. I have refused, of course. It would expose all of the southern part of the Quarter to fire from the Wall. The minister has accepted this and promised to hold on.

'You will also know that we are under great pressure on the Fu. The Japanese there are doing a wonderful job and, unlike some of the other nationalities, I get no complaints from them. No panic-influenced requests from them for reinforcements. When *they* ask for men, I jump to it, I can tell you.'

'Nevertheless, the point is, my dear Fonthill, that we *can* hold on. But I must be realistic. Food and ammunition are low – we have only fourteen rounds left for our little Italian gun, for instance. We have just enough men to man the perimeter, we don't have the space to reduce it further and our casualties are mounting. You see . . .' He let the words hang in the air for a moment. 'We really don't have all the time in the world and our people in Tientsin must be told that we need to be relieved as a matter of urgency – of *prime* urgency, in fact. They seem unaware of this.'

'Ah.' Simon nodded his head, seeing the point of the interview at last. 'And you want someone to take this message to the relief column?'

'Indeed.'

A silence hung in the heavy air for a moment. It was broken by Fonthill. 'But why me? Wouldn't it be better – safer and more effective – to send the request via a Chinese messenger? Someone who would be better equipped to slip through the enemy lines and a hostile countryside. Surely, a European would stand out like a sore thumb?'

'Quite so. These seem the obvious points. But there are strong reasons why I do not wish to entrust this communiqué to a Chinese.'

He leant forward in his chair. 'I have sent four separate messages, containing questions, to Tientsin since we have been besieged. They have been carried by native Chinese whom I thought I could trust. It seems clear to me now that none of these messages has been delivered, for this message now received seems to be singularly relaxed about the urgency of our position here and it answers none of my questions. I am sure that if these messengers had been captured, then I would have heard. There would certainly have been some references to them in this strange dialogue I continue to hold with the Manchu court.'

'So – what happened to them, do you think?'

'I believe that the messengers just absconded with them without making any attempt to deliver them. The Chinese are like that, you know.' He gave a sad smile. 'No. This time, I want someone reliable – someone resourceful – to get

142

through to the relief column. There is an additional point in this context. I want the messenger to have a strategic appreciation of our position here. Someone with military – not diplomatic – experience, who can advise the commander of the relief column on the best way to enter the city and to attack our besiegers. I can't think of anyone who could do this better than you, my dear fellow. After all, you got through the Mahdi's hordes surrounding Khartoum to get a message through to Gordon, did you not?'

Fonthill smiled wryly. 'I was a bit younger then, sir.'

MacDonald sighed. 'My dear Fonthill, in the last few weeks you have led at least two bayonet charges against the enemy, you have climbed a forty-five-foot tower and destroyed two large guns and you have worked seemingly non-stop to keep our defences in good order. Indeed, I am told that when you received my request to come to the office, you were working with the coolies digging out a trench. I can't think of a fitter, more qualified man for this dangerous mission.'

'Well, thank you, sir. There is, however, the question of appearance. A European surely would be recognised quickly in this countryside. It would be particularly difficult to get through the besiegers here and at Tientsin.'

'I have thought of that. Both you and your man – er . . . 352, isn't it?'

'Well done, sir. Yes.'

Sir Claude gave a distant smile. 'Yes. I presume that you would wish to take him with you?'

'Yes, indeed.'

'Well, both you and he have high cheekbones and are not extraordinarily tall. That's a good start. I suggest that we disguise the pair of you as Kansu soldiers from the north. They are more Mongolian than indigenous Chinese and their facial features change considerably from man to man. We have captured several of these chaps and their uniforms are quite distinctive. They straight away proclaim that the fellows wearing them are Kansu. We can dress you up quite well.'

'What about a guide? Jenkins and I just don't know the territory.'

The minister stirred in his chair, a trifle uncomfortably. 'I can offer you your choice of a dozen or more reasonably reliable Chinese. Trouble is, I fear they are not completely to be trusted. But I agree you must have someone.'

'Ah!' Simon slapped his thigh. 'I have it! We will take Chang, the Reverend Griffith's adopted son. He is as keen as mustard, speaks the language like a native, of course, and I know has made the journey to and from Tientsin several times.'

'Good.' The faint smile returned to Sir Claude's long features. 'You will accept, then?'

'Of course. I see the importance of it, although,' he frowned, 'I know my wife won't like it.' He leant forward. 'And I have to confess that I am worried about leaving her here. Without myself and Jenkins, who would protect her if the worst comes to the worst?'

'On that point, Fonthill, you must be assured. I will personally undertake responsibility for her safety, even if the Chinese do break through. She will be as important to me as is my wife. She will be part of my family, so to speak, and, in any case, I am confident that the Empress will not wish to see any of the ministers, or their families, harmed, in the unlikely event of there being a breakthrough. It would mean the end of the Manchu court, for the revenge of the Western powers would be punitive. The Empress will know that.'

Fonthill was not convinced but he decided to say nothing. 'Very well. When do you wish us to go?'

'As soon as possible. We have garments for you. I suggest you leave the Quarter at night, perhaps tomorrow, just after sunrise? The safest way, I suggest, is through the sewer hole in the wall. Not pleasant, I fear, but, as far as we can see, it is not guarded by the Chinese. It is quite small but men singly can slip through it easily.'

'Very good, sir. Tomorrow night it shall be.' Fonthill and the minister rose and shook hands.

As he predicted, Alice was incensed at the news. She argued strongly that two Occidentals would easily be detected, from their physical appearance and their language. Capture would be inevitable and it simply would not be possible to talk their way out of it. If they insisted on undertaking the mission, then she would go with them. A woman with the party would reduce the risk of being taken for spies and, anyway, she was damned if she was going to be left behind to become another widow holed up in Peking!

It took all of Simon's persuasive powers to induce her to change her stance. It would be far more difficult to disguise her appearance, with her fair hair and grey eyes. And the worry of having her with them, he argued, would adversely affect his ability to lead the mission.

Then the problem arose of how to explain Chang's absence to his mother. The youth was anxious enough to take part but, if Gerald, for all his new seeming affection for Alice, was, in fact, relaying information to the enemy, then he must not be made aware of the mission. In the end, it was agreed that Chang would leave a message for Mrs Griffith, explaining that he had been seconded to the American Legation for special duties and that, long after their departure, Alice would find a way of explaining, as diplomatically as possible, the real reason for his absence.

The next morning, the trio assembled in the privacy of MacDonald's office to be fitted by Lady MacDonald with their disguises. The minister's wife, tall and as elegant as her husband, bestowed as much enthusiasm for getting their costumes right as she did for dressing the participants in her very popular annual pantomimes.

None of the garments, which had been stripped from prisoners and washed carefully, fitted, but they were sufficiently voluminous for this not to matter. Each wore a canvas cap reminiscent of that of a scullery maid in an upper-class British house; long, smock-type coats, emblazoned with Chinese symbols proclaiming their allegiance to their leader, Tung Fu-hsiang; baggy cotton trousers; and single-strap sandals, through the front of which their toes poked. Heavy bandoliers were carried, either crossways or around their waists, and straight, short swords were thrust through their belts.

'What about rifles?' asked Jenkins. 'I don't fancy going halfway across China without our Henry-Martinis.'

'Certainly not,' replied Fonthill. 'Carrying two British rifles would betray us straightaway. We take the two Mausers we picked up at the tower. And Chang still has one of our two Colts. I wish to leave the other with Alice.'

'What if we are stopped?' asked Chang. 'What do I say about you not speaking Chinese? And where do I say we are going? This could be frightfully difficult, don't you think?'

Sir Claude, who had been an interested observer of the dressing-up, smiled at the young man's colloquialism. 'Some of these Kansus,' he said, 'are really Tartars from over the northern frontier who don't speak any of the Chinese tongues. I suggest you explain this and say that you are anxious to take part in the fighting at Tientsin and that you are guiding them there.'

Chang nodded. 'Yes, thank you, sir. I think I could do that jolly well.'

'You look Oriental enough at a quick glance,' said Lady MacDonald, standing back to admire her handiwork. 'Just keep your hats well down over your foreheads. And if you, Mr Jenkins, could grow the ends of your moustache so that they trail down either side of your mouth, in the Chinese style, that would help.'

'Well, I'll try, milady. But this moustache has had a life of its own for nearly forty years, now, and it takes no notice of me, see.'

'Yes, well try, there's a good fellow.'

They all shook hands, wrapped up their Chinese clothes

into bundles and went to their bunks to try and gain some sleep before their departure. Then, as desultory firing marked the end of the daylight, they followed the open sewer down to where it swept through a passage in the Legation wall. Alice, who had accompanied them this far, held her nose and then kissed her husband goodbye.

'If you don't come back, I shall kill you,' she whispered into his ear.

Then to Jenkins: '352, if it looks as though he's going to try something heroic, shoot him in the leg.' She was smiling but also crying as she spoke.

CHAPTER SEVEN

The trio were able to pick their way through the tunnel on the banks on either side of the odiferous water and crawl round the low gates. There, they paused. The moon had not risen and the street was dark. To the right, in the distance, figures could be seen but there was no one to their left.

'That way,' said Fonthill. 'Stride purposefully, as though we know where we are going.'

'Mind you don't trip over my moustache,' said Jenkins. 'I'm growin' the ends, yer see,' he explained helpfully to Chang.

'No talking,' hissed Simon. 'Take the lead, Chang. Get us out of the city as quickly as you can. Will the gates be guarded?'

'I do not know, cousin. But if they are, I think they only question people coming in, not going out.'

'Good.'

Even though the hour was late, they met many people as they made their way through the narrow streets, including small groups of Boxers, distinguished by their youth and the red bands they wore round their foreheads, midriffs and ankles. They also had to thrust their way through milling crowds of garishly uniformed Imperial soldiers. But they kept their heads down and no one accosted them. In fact, they were given respectful passageway whenever there was a crowd and Simon recalled being told that the Kansu soldiery had a reputation for fierceness – to friend and foe alike.

They passed through the Tung Pien Men Gate as the moon rose, and Fonthill hardly recognised the countryside from what he remembered from their entry into the city less than a month ago. The rains, although short, had been very heavy and the fields had blossomed as a result. The road had become muddy and the ditches were now running with water.

There had been no time for a proper consultation about their route. Chang had been relied on to find the best and quickest way to Tientsin, some eighty miles away. Although making haste was imperative, it had not been possible to provide them with transport. There were now only nine ponies left within the Quarter. But there would have been no way for them to have ridden out through the defensive perimeter and, anyway, the mounts were needed for food. It was presumed that they would walk to Tientsin and somehow pick up either the relief column limping back to the town or the new one marching – for the railway link had been broken – to the north-west to relieve the legations.

Now, however, lifting one muddy foot after another, Simon had another idea.

'Where are we making for?' he asked Chang.

'We make for my home village. It is on the way to Tientsin. Perhaps we can shelter for the night in our home.'

'No. Too dangerous. You might be recognised. We march through the night and lie up somewhere during the day. It will be safer that way. But Chang, tell me: the River Pei Ho is somewhere quite near, to our left as we look now. Is that right?'

'Oh yes. Quite precisely, cousin.'

'And the river has traffic on it? Trading junks and so on?'

'Yes.'

'Where does the river come out at the coast?'

'At Taku, where ships of Great Powers lie.' Chang frowned in concentration, perspiration running down his face as they walked, for the humidity remained high. 'It is about twenty miles past Tientsin. Everyone think Tientsin is big seaport. But, in fact, it is river port, lying inland.'

Simon nodded. 'Yes, I know. Well, Chang,' he spoke deferentially, 'if you agree, I think we'll change our plans. It will take us a long time to walk to Tientsin at this rate and we are likely to be picked up and questioned at any time.'

'Quite so. Oh, I agree. But . . . er . . . what do we do?'

'We make for the river on our left. I have money. We hire a junk that is sailing south-east, towards the coast. We get off when we have news of either the old expedition retreating or of a new one advancing. With the current taking us to the

151

sea we will be much quicker and,' he frowned, 'time is of the essence.'

Jenkins looked up and beamed. 'What, sail instead of walk? What an incredibly good idea, bach sir. 'Ere, just a minute. Are there any crocodiles in this river, Changy?'

'No, Mr Jenkins. I don't think so.'

'Good. Not that I was worried, mind you. But they . . . er . . . do tend to clog the river, look you. And we want to get a move on.'

Chang smiled. 'I think it excellent idea, cousin. We are here, I think, about six, seven miles to river. Turn off at next crossing.'

It took them, however, about another three hours of trudging through the mud before they found the turning, onto a smaller track that now wound through fields of *kaoliang* that stood well over head high following the rains. At first, this gave Fonthill a feeling of security, for visibility was now considerably reduced and he did not feel as exposed as when on the open plain. This was soon replaced, however, by unease as he realised that they could stumble upon a Chinese patrol in the darkness without warning. He called a halt.

'We are all tired,' he said, 'so I think we will try and get a couple of hours' sleep before we go on. Let us try and find sufficient space among the maize to lie down. It should be safe enough on this little road to walk in daylight, so we will press on at dawn.'

They found a gap in the *kaoliang,* on slightly higher and drier ground, big enough for them to lie down, wrapped in their waterproof capes. Before trying to find sleep, Simon had second thoughts on their story, if stopped.

'We must change our explanation now if we are accosted,' he told Chang. 'Say that we are going to the river to pick up a junk to take us to Tientsin because we have a message from our general, what's his name?'

'Tung Fu-hsiang.'

'That's the fellow. Say that we are taking a message from him to the general commanding the Imperial forces at Tientsin and that we are taking a boat at the river.' He smiled at the young man. 'If we do get stopped, Chang, we must rely on you to talk us out of it.'

'Oh yes. I do that well, I think, cousin. Rely on me.'

Simon nodded and offered up a silent prayer that the missionary's son's Chinese was less stilted than his English. Their reliance on him was total.

That reliance was called into play far quicker than he would have liked after they rose, shortly after dawn, and continued their journey. Within minutes they rounded a bend in the path and came upon three horsemen, dressed in the flamboyant colours of the Imperial cavalry, topped by black turbans, walking their horses towards them.

Taking the lead, Fonthill stepped to one side deferentially, into the maize, to allow the horsemen to pass. He gave a stiff incline of the head to acknowledge the seniority of the lead horseman and kept his eyes to the ground.

The horseman, seemingly an officer, pulled to a stop and addressed a question to Simon, who gestured mutely to Chang. The two exchanged words for a moment and Fonthill clutched to himself a half-forgotten statistic that less

153

than nought point one per cent of Chinese people had ever seen, let alone talked to a European. He just hoped that this cavalry officer was part of that majority.

The conversation went on interminably, or so it seemed to Fonthill. Out of the corner of his eye he saw Jenkins, his black eyes gleaming from underneath his cap – no subservience here – slowly unsling his rifle.

Then, with a grunt, the officer kicked in his heels and the three horsemen rode away slowly, disappearing as quickly as they had appeared. Simon put his finger to his lips then gestured with his head and the three walked on.

After two minutes, Fonthill called a halt. 'What did he say?' he asked Chang.

A thin line of perspiration had appeared on the young Chinaman's upper lip. 'He don't seem to believe me,' he said, his eyes wide. 'He said that he had served in Peking and knew that Kansu soldiers were manning northern parts of the legations' defence and fighting particularly in the Fu, and that Kansu soldiers not allowed in the southern part of city. He asked me name of Chinese commander in Tientsin to whom we take the message.'

'Oh Lord. What did you say?'

'I invent a name – in Chinese like English Smith. I very afraid he would know man. But he rode away.'

Simon smiled. 'You did very well, cousin,' he said. 'But I think we should move quickly now and get to this damned river.'

'Shush.' Jenkins held up a hand. He was lying prone, with his ear to the ground. 'They're coming back – and galloping.'

'Quickly. Into the maize. If we have to fight, we use swords. No shooting. There might be other patrols about.'

Chang's face paled. 'Oh golly.' But he followed Simon into the *kaoliang*, while Jenkins ducked into the other side.

Within seconds, the three cavalrymen thundered round the bend, their heads low over the mane of their horses and their swords drawn. They swept by with scarcely a glance into the tall growth on either side and disappeared once again, in the direction of the river.

'They will be back.' Simon stood for a moment, deep in thought. Then: 'Chang, you walk back a few paces and then lie face down across the path . . .'

Chang gave an exclamation in Chinese, and was joined by Jenkins. 'Blimey, why . . . ?'

Fonthill tossed his head impatiently. 'I want to disconcert them. They will stop for a moment wondering what the hell to do. You and I, 352, will be in the maize behind them by this bend. As soon as they have passed us and their attention is drawn to Chang, we will spring out behind them and bring them down. Swords, remember. No shooting.'

'Then I get up and fight, yes?' Chang's eyes were bright.

'No, be lying on your sword but don't move until we do. If you are attacked run back into the crop. Quick now. They will be back soon. Further back into the maize this time, 352. They will be looking for us in there.'

Once more the two comrades plunged into the tall crop, but this time Fonthill's heart was in his mouth. Leaving the boy out there was taking an awful risk. Would they be able to bring down the two men in the rear before the lead rider realised what was happening? And would he ride on and attack Chang anyway? The boy would stand no chance against an experienced cavalryman. He gulped. But there was no further time for introspection. There was no sound but suddenly, peering low between the stalks, he saw the officer, walking his horse slowly and looking carefully into the *kaoliang* on either side of him. Then the other two came into view, walking their horses side by side. Simon offered up a silent prayer that Jenkins had penetrated deeply enough to be out of sight.

Then he heard a loud exclamation. Chang had been seen. Simon plunged through the tall stalks, crushing them, and emerged in time to see Chang, sword in hand, standing and defying the officer, whose horse was rearing. Damn! The stupid boy was fighting! The cavalryman on Simon's side of the path was trying to quieten his own horse and had his back to him. Fonthill paused for a split second and then he gulped, sprang forward and, reaching up, he thrust the point of his heavy blade through the man's side, feeling it scrape bone. With his other hand, he grabbed the man's belt and pulled him to the ground and delivered the *coup de grâce* to his breast. As he did so he felt a thunderous blow to his back, sending him pitching forward and his sword spinning away.

He lay for several seconds as the hooves of horses crashed to the ground all around him, one of them delivering a second blow, this time to his calf. He heard the cry of 'Roll over, bach, to yer right' and he did so, his hands to his head to protect his face. Half into the maize, he staggered to his feet and saw Jenkins, the blade of a bloodstained sword between his teeth, standing between the two rear horses in the narrow path, holding onto their reins and trying to sooth them. To his right and ahead, however, a far more fascinating battle was taking place.

The officer was trying to control his rearing horse and, at the same time, deliver slashing blows to Chang, who was ducking and weaving away from the blade. As he watched, he saw the boy slash at the soldier's thigh, causing blood to burst out from just above the boot. Then he slapped the rear of the horse with the flat of his blade, causing the beast to rear again, sending the wounded cavalryman sliding to the ground, where the young man thrust his blade through the man's throat.

"'Old on to that bloody 'orse, Changy,' roared Jenkins. 'We don't want to walk anymore. Don't let 'im charge away.'

The boy threw down his sword and grabbed the reins of the startled beast, holding on and circling with it as it continued to rear and whinny, as though in despair at the death of his master.

Fonthill stood, his breast heaving, and surveyed the scene. The three cavalrymen all lay on the pathway, in different postures but all dead from sword thrusts. The three horses were now becoming quiescent. Chang and Jenkins seemed unharmed and Simon straightened his back gingerly and lifted his leg. There were two stabs of pain but neither was severe. Probably the result of bruising; nothing broken, it seemed. He walked forward to take one of the horses from Jenkins.

'Well done, lads,' he said. 'Bit of a bloodbath, I'm afraid. Good Lord, Chang. You fought like a dervish.'

The boy, his face glistening with sweat, grinned. 'What is "dervish", cousin?'

'I hope you never have to find out, old chap. Let's say he's just a bloody good fighter. Like you. Now, Chang, take the reins of the horses, they seem all right now. 352 – are you all right?'

The great chest of the Welshman was heaving, but he nodded. 'Yes, thank you. But I'm gettin' a bit old for this sort of thing. I think all this effort has opened up this old wound in me arm, but it's not bleedin' much. Got an earwig in me ear, though.'

'All right. You take the horses, then. Chang, help me lift these bodies into the side, out of sight into the maize. I don't want to leave any evidence. That's it. Good man.'

Within ten minutes the site was cleared, only three distinct patches of blood staining the pathway to show where three men had died. Simon pushed dust over them with his sandal. Then he walked to study the saddles and accoutrements of the horses.

'If we are going to take these horses – and we definitely are – then we don't want us to appear to be riding Imperial cavalry mounts,' he explained. 'Here, lend me your knife, 352. I think I can cut this fancy stuff away. Rough old Kansu infantrymen wouldn't be riding like bloody medieval knights.'

In a moment the job was done. Fonthill delayed long enough to inspect the old wound in Jenkins's arm, which had now stopped bleeding, and the three of them mounted and resumed their trek to the river. Once on horseback, Simon realised that he was trembling. Killing a man at long range with a rifle shot was one thing. Stabbing him from the back with a sword was another and his lip curled and he shook his head. Was he becoming some sort of monster? What would Alice think of him if she had witnessed the mini battle on the pathway, not to mention the bayoneting of sleeping men at the tower? And was he training a sixteen-year-old boy to become a killer? He rode in silence for a while, his head down.

Jenkins noticed and gently urged his mount forward so that they rode side by side. 'She said you were to come back, bach sir,' he said, eventually. 'So you've got to think of yourself, like. It's the old story. It was them or us. Same as it always is. Goodness gracious me, we've done it enough times. Can't be 'elped. It's the life we lead, see.'

Fonthill slowly nodded. 'I suppose you're right. But I really felt that we'd left all that behind us.'

'So did I. But I knew somethin' was up as soon as we stepped off that ship. I sniffed the air, like, and I knew we was back in it. But we didn't look for it, now did we? So it can't be 'elped. An' those blokes was comin' back to get us right enough, weren't they? So don't think about it.' Jenkins paused for a moment, then he gave Fonthill a sly, sideways smile. 'Anyway,' he went on, 'you've got to admit that, for most of the time, it's fun, ain't it?'

Simon looked at him and returned half a smile. 'I wouldn't call it fun,' he said, 'though I grant that it's exciting.' Then the remnant of the smile slipped away. 'But sometimes it's just bloody horrific.'

They rode in silence for a while. Then Jenkins sniffed. 'As long as young Changy wasn't lyin' about them crocodiles,' he said, 'I don't mind a bit of a sail, see.' And he gave that great, moustache-bending smile of his that immediately made Simon feel better.

They came to the river without further incident: the brown, turgid, not-so-very-wide highway that, hopefully, was to lead them to Tientsin and – even more hopefully – the relief column. There was not so much traffic on it, as Simon had hoped, and Chang's questioning of a fisherman on the banks provided the reason.

'He says, cousin, that further down – about twelve miles, perhaps more – is where the great foreign army decided to turn back from the railway and go back to Tientsin by river. They take a lot of junks. That is why we see not many boats now.'

'Ah, so they have turned back, dammit.' Fonthill frowned. 'All that great expectancy and hope from the legations! Ask him if he knows if another army is coming to Peking.'

Eventually, Chang shrugged his shoulders. 'He don't know, but he think that army going back has been defeated many times. Many *yang kuei-tzu* killed. But he say we come to village soon. Can hire junk there, he thinks.'

'Good. Let's get on with it, then.'

Simon's mind turned over. How badly had the relief column been mauled? Pretty badly if they had been forced to turn back. And if Tientsin itself was besieged, what hope of another force being gathered in time to relieve Peking? The besieged in the river port would surely have enough on their plate. The prospect was depressing. He shrugged his shoulders and dug his heels into his horse's side. Their task was clear. They had to persuade somebody in command in the south that the legations' plight was desperate and that time was short.

The village was small but it was a trading point where jobbing junks called in to pick up cargoes, usually of rice or grain, to take north and south. While Fonthill and Jenkins remained watering the horses, Chang, now bearing himself with the confidence of a soldier who had killed his first man, went into the village. He came back within ten minutes, his young face carrying an earnest expression.

'There is a junk that can take us and horses downriver. He has oats for horses. It leaves soon so we must be jolly quick.'

Fonthill patted his shoulder. 'Good man. How far can he take us?'

'Ah, that is the point. He says he cannot take us to Tientsin. There is much fighting just above there. Foreign troops are there. Chinese army attack them.'

'Very well. We will go as far as we can with him. Let's go to the battle.' But Simon was not as sanguine as he sounded. Fighting! How were they going to get through the lines? If they could persuade the Chinese to let them get through to the actual combat, how to prevent the British from killing them as the enemy? He shrugged. Ah well, they would have to face those problems when they came to them.

They trotted their horses through the hamlet to a wooden loading stage that jutted out into the river, where an old junk was moored. The two-man crew was adjusting a canvas cover over the open hold and the captain, a wizened, tiny man with skullcap and pigtail, looked with trepidation at first at the three wild men of the north, with their stained clothing, rifles and bandoliers, but bowed low and smiled over the handful of coins that Simon gave him. The horses, uneasy at the swell that rocked the boat, were tethered to a rail and given a feed from a sack full of oats. The three comrades sat down gratefully at the stern of the junk and accepted bowls of rice as the square sails were raised and the boat eased out into the gently flowing current.

'Now this,' observed Jenkins quietly, 'is the way to travel.' He looked out with approval at the unbroken, brown water. 'I don't care if there are crocodiles out there, because, look you, I 'ave no intention at all of takin' a dip today. I shall just sit 'ere all day and contemplate life. I am now too old to be swimmin' about an' killin' people.'

Chang, now a fully qualified member of the trio and having, at last, begun to comprehend the Welshman's idiosyncrasies, beamed with approval. Simon scowled. 'For goodness' sake, 352, keep your voice down. We're supposed to be Kansu soldiers.'

'With great respect, bach sir, I was merely makin' an observation in a very low voice. If these Chinese blokes pullin' on the ropes 'eard me, they would just as likely think I was speakin' Kansu talk.'

'Ah, that reminds me.' Simon looked up at the blessedly weak sun. 'Which way is east? Yes, there. When we've finished the rice, it will be time for us to pray.'

Chang nodded understandingly but Jenkins's jaw dropped. 'Eh?'

'Kansus are Muslims and Muslims are supposed to pray five times a day. We must face the east, kneel, bend down with our foreheads on the deck and say something incomprehensible. It could be important later if we are stopped and the captain is questioned.'

'Ah, very good. I'll give 'em a bit of Welsh.'

They carried out their devotions, much to the consternation of the crew, and Fonthill instructed Chang to explain the reason for them. Then Simon sat in the stern, inspecting a rough, hand-drawn map of Tientsin and its environs that Sir Claude had given him.

As Chang had explained, the city itself lay some twenty-five to thirty miles inland from the Taku Forts that guarded the entrance to the river on which it lay. Tientsin itself was a native walled city but, unlike Peking, the foreign holdings or settlements were discrete and situated outside the city itself to the south. The Pei Ho and the railway wound their way in parallel north-west from Tientsin towards Peking for some twenty miles or so before parting company at Yangtsun, where the essential rail bridge had been destroyed and from which the relief column, it seemed, had turned back and taken to the river for its retreat. But it seemed that the column had not reached Tientsin. Was it being held up by the force of Chinese arms or was it simply resting and recuperating? Sir Claude's message had implied that the city was invested, but how strongly? And was it the settlements that were under siege or the city itself? Surely, it should be possible for the defenders, whatever they were defending, to link up with the retreating relief force? Depending upon how fierce the opposition was to the remnants of the British force as they trudged south, they should not be too far from the city.

Simon shook his head. Too many imponderables! It seemed to make sense for him and his comrades to try and contact the relief force, rather than try to reach Tientsin. They must surely be nearest and, depending upon how many casualties they had suffered, perhaps the commander of the column could be persuaded to turn back towards Peking, given the dire nature of the defenders there?

Right. That was decided. He folded the map. They would get through to the British force, somewhere downriver of them. But they must make haste!

All day they bowled along, swept by a following wind as well as by the river itself. Chang and Jenkins dosed intermittently, for it was soporific, lying back in the stern, their heads on their waterproofs, sleepy eyes taking in the sparse river traffic – small junks, tacking against wind and current and skiffs, flitting across the water like insects, most of them making their way upstream, away, it seemed, from the fighting. Fonthill, however, stayed awake, his hand not far from his rifle, his eyes on the banks of the river.

Soon he witnessed signs of battle. The vegetation on the banks on both sides had recently been beaten down and the soil trampled as far as he could see. Here, the river was dominated by the railway embankment which ran parallel to it and the banks on both sides were pitted by craters – shell holes, presumably, showing that the British had come under fire from guns mounted on railway carriages. Rickety buildings creeping down to the water in a succession of villages all showed bullet holes in their walls. Leaning over, Fonthill could see the bottom of the river. It was extremely shallow. Had the British junks run aground and the men been forced to land and haul them off the shoals? And it looked as though each village had had to be taken by force before the boats could continue. It must have been a hell of a journey, under fire and in the heat.

Now, traffic had ceased on the water but both banks were busy highways for Chinese troops of all descriptions, wearing various uniforms and in individual groups. Not an army, more a ragbag collection of soldiers straggling – not marching – along. They were all heading south and curious eyes were cast towards this solitary junk.

Simon felt uncomfortable, for even though he and his two companions were not easily visible, lying low beneath the deck sides of the vessel, the horses, with their military saddles, could clearly be seen. He sat up, for, faraway but clearly, he could hear the sound of shellfire. It was time to leave the river.

He roused his comrades and looked ahead. Dusk was falling but he welcomed that. It would be safer to land in the darkness, but where? He beckoned to Chang. 'Tell the captain that we must soon go ashore,' he said. 'Is there a landing place soon where it will be easy to land the horses?'

It was clear that the captain was not anxious to keep his passengers now that gunfire could be heard. 'He says, soon,' reported Chang. 'Round the bend is landing place. Road goes away from river here but about a mile to south is great arsenal of Hsiku Arsenal. He don't know what this is but he thinks British have captured it and are fighting there.'

'Splendid.' He felt in his pocket for more coins. 'Give him these with our thanks. Tell him to land us there.'

Dusk settled on them comfortingly as the junk was steered towards where another wooden landing stage leant out into the river. Simon scoured the area with his eyes but he could see no one. He turned to Chang. 'New story now, cousin,' he said with a grin. 'Now we are just three Kansu cavalrymen from the north who were sent scouting and lost their way. We are now looking for the front line to join in the fighting.'

As the sail was lowered and the boat was held to the landing stage with boathooks, the trio led their horses ashore and then mounted them. With a wave to the sailors they clattered away in the lowering darkness.

'Nice, enjoyable little sail,' observed Jenkins. 'Now what do we do?'

'We try and find where the British are fighting and then play it by ear.'

'What is this "playing by ear"?' enquired Chang. 'Is it a game?'

Fonthill grinned. 'Not exactly, old chap. We react according to the circumstances. But we must somehow get through the Chinese lines and cross the British defences without both sides killing us. Yes, well, put like that, I suppose it is a sort of game. Trouble is, I don't know the rules. Come on. Let's ride with a sense of purpose, as though we are under orders.'

They kicked their horses into a canter and rode through a shell-scarred thicket before finding the road. Most of the groups of Chinese troops had halted their journey southwards and had bivouacked for the night. Fires had been lit and bedrolls laid out. The trio rode on determinedly. Several times they were challenged – greeted? – but Fonthill gave a cheery wave and cantered by. Luckily, they met no other cavalry and saw no other Kansu soldiers.

The firing ahead seemed to have died away with the onset of darkness but, looming up ahead, on the banks of the river, they saw the blackness of a great building. Before they could get near to it they met a Chinese sentry, rifle slung across his shoulders. Chang trotted forward and engaged in conversation with the man for several minutes.

He came back grinning. 'He think I am blooming Kansu and he afraid of me, all right,' he said.

Fonthill nodded. 'Glad to hear it,' he said. 'But what is ahead?'

'Ah yes. Big building ahead is big place for Chinese weapons, ammunition et cetera. It is called Hsiku Arsenal. British have taken it and Chinese are very mad. Imperial army is now trying to take it back. So far they don't do it.'

'Good Lord! I suppose that's the remnants of the relief column. Are the Chinese attacking during the night?'

'No. Wait till morning.'

'Good, then that's what we'll do.' He turned his head. 'Let's get back into those woods and find a place to tether the horses and lie down for a few hours.'

Jenkins grinned in approval. 'Good idea, bach sir. I've 'ad

167

a busy day. But what do we do in the morning? 'Ow do we get through the lines?'

'I don't know but I'll think of something. Come on, into the woods.'

They rested through the darkest hours, although only Jenkins slept well. As dawn was lightening the sky to the east, they rose, rubbed down the horses as best they could and mounted. The firing had not yet recommenced. They sat uncertainly for a moment.

Then: 'Have you got a spare vest in your pack?' Simon asked Jenkins.

The Welshman's jaw dropped. 'A what?'

'A spare undervest. And is it white?'

'Well, sort of. I washed it before we left.'

'Good. Get it out and tie it to this rifle.'

Jenkins shook his head in disbelief. 'Blessed and wonderful are the ways of the officer class,' he muttered as he unrolled his slender pack. He had attended Sunday school chapel as a child.

One arm of the vest was tightly knotted round the muzzle of Fonthill's Mauser and the other to the breech just before the trigger guard. Simon nodded in approval but held the rifle low so that the vest hung downwards.

'Now,' he said, 'this is no longer the disgusting undergarment of a very dirty Welsh Kansu soldier—'

''Ere, steady on,' interrupted Jenkins.

'. . . but a flag of truce, although it won't be raised until we get to the front line. There, we will ride in a V formation towards the gate of the arsenal, you two behind me, sitting very upright, and me in the lead, carrying the flag, as though we are an official delegation come to parley.'

'Ah,' nodded Chang.

'Brilliant, bach,' said Jenkins.

'Until we get to the front, though,' continued Fonthill, 'we will not display the flag and, Chang, you will lead. We shall be stopped, I'm sure, and you will explain that we have come with a message to the commander from our general in Peking, General . . . what's his name again?'

'Tung Fu-hsiang.'

'That's the chap. Explain that it is urgent and we can't be delayed. Then, when we reach the line, we will raise the flag and ride straight ahead – cantering, not galloping, mind you. Straight to the main gate of the arsenal and there we will explain that we are English and ask to be admitted.'

'What?' asked Jenkins. 'Stand there an' 'ave a chat while we get shot in the back by the Chinks and in the front by the Brits?'

'Something like that.' He grinned. 'It's risky, I admit. But I think that it's a fair bet that the English will be wary, but they won't defile a flag of truce and once they hear my voice they will let us in. As for the Chinese, I am gambling that everyone but the commander will think that it's a parley that has been ordered from on high. And once *he* realises what's up we shall be inside the arsenal.'

'Then do I get me vest back?'

'Of course. But it could have bullet holes in it. Come on, gentlemen. Let's advance.'

* * *

169

Once again, Fonthill's confidence was only reflected outwards. He would have felt happier if he could have reconnoitred the ground – particularly the Chinese lines – for himself. The main danger, he felt, would be getting through those lines. Chang's story would not stand up to much interrogation. Their main hope would be that the young man would argue with, not only conviction, but also with the superiority and arrogance that stemmed from being a general's messenger. He sighed. Once again, it would be a case of dipping a toe in the water to see how hot it was.

They rode back to where they had met the sentry the previous evening. He had been replaced and the new man made no attempt to stop them as they rode by. Confidence, reflected Fonthill, was all under these circumstances.

They rode on through scattered contingents of troops and heard intermittent firing from directly ahead of them. Luckily, they met no cavalry and no other Kansu troops, for they would surely never have survived interrogation from 'one of their own'. The dead cavalryman must have been correct in saying that these Muslim soldiers were restricted to fighting on the north of the Peking legations' perimeter.

They were stopped by one sentry, however, who was beginning to engage in a conversation with Chang when Simon interrupted, curtly gesturing them forward with an air of command that only an ex-British public schoolboy could call upon. They rode on and halted at the edge of a sad little thicket.

Before them loomed the huge, high walls of the arsenal, looking impregnable in the early-morning light. Stone outbuildings skirted the foot of the walls and these were manned by the defenders, who were directing a desultory fire at a line of hastily dug trenches some thirty yards away from the thicket and which curled down to the river. Smoke and cooking smells came from the trenches, as the Chinese soldiers prepared their breakfasts. The gap between the outbuildings and the trenches was some two hundred and fifty yards. The muzzles of light artillery pieces poked out from gaps in the line of outbuildings but Fonthill could see no artillery in place behind the Chinese lines. In any case, he mused, it would have taken very heavy guns to have made any impression in the walls of the arsenal.

He drew a deep breath. 'Right,' he said, 'no point in waiting. We will ride straight ahead towards that gap where the cannon is pointing out. Rifles slung behind us so that they don't threaten. We ride at a stately canter, now, and backs very straight. We are elite Chinese cavalry.'

'Even though we are Mussulmen who 'aven't said their prayers this mornin',' muttered Jenkins through clenched teeth.

They cantered out of the thicket, Fonthill in the lead, carrying his rifle high, with Jenkins's vest fluttering at its muzzle. They took the narrow trench in a leap, startling the troops below them huddled around their braziers, and set off across no man's land, in stately fashion as though they were leading the trooping of Her Majesty's colour in Whitehall, London.

Two bullets hissed by Fonthill's head from the direction of the British lines. He immediately removed his cap, coiled the reins around the thumb of his left hand and held it palm

171

extended towards the British, in the universal sign of peace, and raised his 'flag' even higher. He heard someone bark a command from the outbuildings and the firing ceased.

They continued to ride in an eerie silence, for all firing had ceased along the lines. It was as though both sides were watching a tableau being staged for their entertainment.

When the trio had reached about sixty yards from the outbuildings, close enough to see the faces of the British soldiers, a Chinese voice rang out sharply.

'They say, come no further,' shouted Chang.

Fonthill rose in the stirrups. 'I am an English officer,' he cried. 'My name is Fonthill. I have come from Peking with a message for your commander from Sir Claude MacDonald, the British minister in the capital. We have ridden through the Chinese lines in disguise.'

Silence fell. Then a voice displaying authority came from behind the cannon: 'If you are an English officer, state your rank and regiment.'

Fonthill muttered a curse and then responded loudly: 'I was commissioned in the 24th Regiment of Foot in 1876. I fought at Rorke's Drift and Isandlwana and I am a Commander of the Bath. If we are left sitting out here much longer presenting three fine targets to the enemy I shall make bloody sure that you are cashiered. Now, let us in. Quickly.'

There was another silence and then the voice – this time carrying an edge – ordered: 'Very well. But ride in slowly and do not touch your rifles or your packs.'

Thankfully, Simon kicked his heels into his horse's flanks and the three of them walked forward to the gap in the line.

Just before they reached it, a shout rang out from the Chinese lines and a ragged volley sent bullets singing past their ears. With alacrity, they urged their steeds forward and sprang through the gaps on either side of the cannon.

Hurriedly dismounting, Simon faced a ring of rifles and a haggard-faced young subaltern, who looked at him with some unease.

'Good morning,' he said, cheerfully, extending his hand. 'Simon Fonthill. Sorry to have seemed rude but I was expecting a bullet up the arse at any minute.'

The young man shook hands, still a little warily, and then waved down the rifles. 'Good morning . . . er . . . sir. I'm afraid you took us all rather by surprise.'

'Yes. Had no time or the wherewithal to send you a letter. Ran out of stamps. Now, who is in command here?'

'Admiral Seymour.'

'*Admiral?*'

'Yes. We are the relief mission that set out to relieve Peking. The lieutenant took out a tattered handkerchief and ran it across his brow. 'I'm afraid we've had rather a rough time. We've had to fight every inch of the way back from Langfang . . .'

'*Langfang!*' Fonthill's jaw dropped. 'But that's only about thirty miles from Peking. You got so near.'

The young man smiled ruefully. 'Yes, we all know that. But I think you had better see the admiral, if you say you have a message for him.'

'Yes please, right away. Oh – I wonder if it would be possible to rustle up some breakfast for my two companions?

May I introduce 352 Jenkins and Chang Griffith. I wouldn't have been able to move an inch without them.'

The lieutenant shook their hands – just a little uncertainly in the case of Chang – and gave quick orders to a sergeant. Then he walked with Simon back through a small post door set in the giant gate in the walls of the arsenal. They climbed a stone stairway and then Fonthill was kept waiting outside a semi-open door while a conversation took place within. Then he was ushered into a grand room, which, situated at the heart of the stone fortress, was blessedly cool. At the far end stood a tall, thin, bearded man, dressed in what was once the white ducks of an admiral of the British navy. Now they were creased, dirty and still covered in dust.

Seymour advance to meet Fonthill and held out his hand. His face was drawn beneath the beard and his eyes tired. 'Fonthill?' he asked. 'Are you the Fonthill of Khartoum and Matebeleland?'

Simon nodded and then grinned. 'I suppose I am, Admiral, though for the last two days, as you see, I have been a Kansu soldier.'

The grin was returned. 'So I see. No wonder we wouldn't let you into the lines. Congratulations on your disguise. We've been fighting Kansus for days and they and their general, Tung Fu-hsiang,' he pronounced it perfectly, 'have been giving us hell.'

'Really? I thought the Kansus and their general have been restricted to the siege at Peking.'

'Certainly not. They're down here in force. Now please

174

don't tell me – *please* don't tell me – that you have come to announce that Peking has fallen?'

'No, sir. At least not when I left two days ago.'

'Thank God for that.'

'No. But I have come to urge you to make all haste to relieve the legations. They are holding out, but only just, and I don't know how much longer they can defend the Legation Quarter. Can you turn around and march on Peking? You could be there in a few days.'

'My dear fellow, do sit down.' The admiral gestured to a chair and took the one opposite. 'Fonthill,' he spoke wearily and with heavy emphasis. 'There is no question of that. We can't relieve anyone. It is *we* who need relieving. You see, we ourselves are besieged here. And, from what I can hear, so are our people in Tientsin. I fear that, at the moment, we are losing this damned war with the Dragon Lady.'

Chapter Eight

Simon Fonthill stared blankly at the admiral. 'But,' he said, 'we were told that you had set out with two thousand men.'

'So I did.' Seymour's face was expressionless but his eyes were those of a man who realised that his career had come to an end. 'Because of the need for haste, we decided that the railway was the obvious and quickest way to advance – after all, Peking was only some eighty miles away and we were being faced not by a regular army but just a bunch of peasant rebels. Well,' he smiled sadly, 'it wasn't quite like that, I'm afraid.

'Of course, we were strung out along the line in a succession of trains and we had to keep repairing the line ahead to remedy the damage done by the Chinese, so our progress was painfully slow. The Boxers first attacked us on the third day. They came on at our lead trains just a touch north of Langfang.' The admiral's voice was soft and low, as though he were telling a fairy story to a child, but Fonthill could sense the agony behind the words. 'They attacked us with supreme courage, although they were only armed with swords and spears. We brought down about sixty of them and they retreated but then they came on again, making it impossible for our chaps to get out to repair the line. In these subsequent attacks there were more of them and better armed.

'We began to run low on ammunition and water and it was damned hot. You see, as we had advanced, we had been forced to garrison every station we passed to prevent the enemy tearing up the line behind us. We were on half rations and stretched out like a thin piece of string . . .' Seymour suddenly shook his head. 'I am forgetting my manners. You would like some tea, of course?'

'That would be kind, sir. But what about your supplies?'

The admiral waved his hand. 'That is the good news. We have found that this place is stacked with weapons, ammunition, medical supplies, fifteen tons of rice and a seemingly endless supply of tea. All left by the Chinese when we shooed them off.' He shouted and a bluejacket appeared. 'A pot of tea for two, please, Jackson. Now, where was I?'

'You were stretched out like a piece of string.'

'Yes, so we were. Then the Chinese destroyed the bridge at Yangtsun and we were cut off from our supply trains, which had to retreat back to Tientsin. We thought long and hard about pushing on to Peking overland but there was no major road, we had no transport and a growing number of

177

wounded to care for. We decided to fall back on Yangtsun, commandeer junks for our wounded and supplies, and advance up the river to the capital. But there the German force we had left as a garrison was attacked by about four thousand of the enemy and their train was pursued for some miles as it retreated back to Tientsin, from which we could now hear gunfire.'

Wearily, Seymour rose and poured tea. 'The important point here, however,' he continued, 'is that the force attacking the Germans were not Boxers but well-led contingents of the Imperial army. In other words, this rebellion was now being backed by the Chinese army, presumably on the orders of the Empress. So it was no longer a rebellion, it was war.' He sighed. 'This meant that it was impossible for us to continue towards Peking, with our wounded and cut off, as we were, from our supplies. So we took four junks and turned back for Tientsin. We have had to fight every inch of the way, deploying men at every village to take them at bayonet point and often pulling the junks containing our guns and wounded off the shoals as they grounded. We were under attack all the time. Then, suddenly, looming up out of the dusk we came upon this place, of which we had no knowledge at all. We mounted a night attack and, although it was fiercely defended, we managed to break through and send the garrison packing.'

Fonthill nodded, not quite knowing what to say, for his thoughts were beginning to turn to Alice and the beleaguered defenders at Peking. But the admiral was not finished.

'Our pursuers, of course, closed in all around us, cutting

us off. Here, we are only about six miles from the foreign settlements at Tientsin and we can hear gunfire from there, so they are clearly under siege. But we have not been able to make contact with them, of course. You see, Fonthill,' Seymour leant forward, 'we are dead beat. Of what was left of my small force when we were cut off north of Yangtsun, we have lost sixty-two dead and two hundred and thirty-two wounded. We have successfully fought off a series of counter-attacks but we are simply not strong enough to break out.'

He sat back. 'There. That's our story. Every step of the way I have thought about our people in Peking and, since turning back, I have half expected to hear that they have been overwhelmed.' He smiled wanly. 'You can imagine the frustration and even the feeling of guilt. So please tell me how things were when you left and also how you were able to get through the lines.'

Simon relayed the message from Sir Claude MacDonald and then told his own story of how he and his two companions were able to reach the arsenal. At the end, both men fell silent.

It was Seymour who broke the silence. 'You've shown remarkable courage and resource, Fonthill,' he said, offering his sad smile, 'and when the people back home hear about it, you will surely get rather more plaudits than I. But that is of no account. What matters now is that we have to get out of this place.'

'Quite so.' Fonthill's mind raced. The story of the relief expedition was undoubtedly an unmitigated disaster. Surely someone – someone, that is, with some experience of land warfare, not an admiral, for God's sake! – should have realised how vulnerable to attack would be an advance through enemy territory *by train*. Cutting the advance into segments by pulling up the line and then attacking each exposed segment would be as easy as snipping a piece of string here and there. His mind flashed again to the vulnerability of Alice now and of how the defenders of the Legation Quarter had been relying on relief and expecting it daily, scanning the sky to the south-east for searchlights and listening for the distant rumbles of guns to show that a column was near. Indignation flared within him at the incompetence of it all. Then a look into the sad eyes of the man before him, a man who had tried his best and who knew that his long and distinguished career had now ended in disastrous failure, rid him of thoughts of blame. What to do now, indeed!

'You have tried to get help, presumably, from Tientsin?'

'Oh yes. Only a Chinaman, of course, could get through and all of the reliable native people with me have refused to attempt it. I have to say that I don't blame them. Reports have come in that Tung Fu-hsiang – a vicious bandit, by all accounts – is torturing and then beheading any of his countrymen found helping the enemy. We shall just have to lick our wounds here until we are strong enough to break out.'

'Hmm.' Fonthill thought hard. 'We can tell by the sound of the guns, of course, that the Tientsin settlements are still holding out. If only we could link the two forces – here and there, I mean – then we would have a much stronger unit to attack the Kansus. Is there hope of reinforcements coming to Tientsin from the sea?'

Seymour's eyes lit up. 'Yes indeed, that is my hope. Before I left, the Foreign Powers were being asked to send troops to reinforce us from their possessions in Asia. The Russians, of course, are the nearest.'

'Good.' Simon fumbled within his long jacket and produced the rough map that Sir Claude had given him. He moved the teapot and spread the paper out on the table before them. He jabbed the map with a grimy forefinger. 'You are presumably about here,' he said, 'on the riverbank, some six miles or so from the settlements?'

'Yes.'

'And the river flows from here downstream directly past the settlements?'

'Indeed.'

'Then that is the route for a messenger to follow.'

The admiral shook his head. 'But a boat would never get past the Chinese, who are watching every inch of the river. Then, of course, there is the question of getting through the ring of Tung Fu-hsiang's troops who are besieging the settlements.'

'It should be possible for someone in disguise to get through the Chinese lines around the settlements. We have done it here. And I would not use a boat to go downriver.'

'What do you mean?'

'I presume you have access to the river?'

'Yes, after dark.'

'I have seen that there is plenty of driftwood that floats down the river with the current. It should be possible to pull some such detritus to the shore, take cover under it, in or out

181

of the water, and float downstream, swimming ashore when the settlements are reached – all under cover of darkness.'

The admiral scratched at his beard. 'It's ingenious, but highly dangerous, I would have thought. But who would . . . ? You are not suggesting that *you* would go?'

'Of course.'

'But, my dear fellow. You don't know the territory, you would not be able to control your means of travel, you would not know when you had reached your destination . . . I can think of a dozen reasons why the whole thing would be ridiculously hazardous.'

Fonthill leant forward. 'I have to confess, Admiral,' he said, 'that I have a vested interest in getting you out of here. You see, I had to leave my wife behind in the Legation Quarter in Peking. I don't know how long the defenders can hold out there but their resources are running low and unless help comes soon they will be overwhelmed. If that happens, I do not wish to think of what could happen to her. If the fit remnants of your column and the defenders at Tientsin are merged – plus, of course, any reinforcements that have been able to land from the sea – then it should be possible to mount another attempt to relieve our people in the capital. But all this will take time, of course, and we have precious little of that. So I intend to leave tonight.' He paused for a moment. Then he added slowly but with emphasis, 'I need to go myself to impress the authorities of the need for haste and for care in the planning of this second relief column. It needs to go quickly – *and it must get through*.'

The two men sat gazing at each other in silence for a

moment. Then the admiral stood. 'I admire your courage and your determination, Fonthill,' he said. 'Of course, I will do all I can to help. Now come over here and I will show you a better map.'

The two walked to the admiral's desk, where he unrolled a large-scale chart. 'This arsenal is not marked but we are roughly here on the right bank of the river, as you have indicated. The river flows more or less straight for about three miles, then it gets a bit complicated. Just above the Chinese City of Tientsin here, you see that the river bends back on itself and the Lu-T'ai Canal comes in from the left. Then the river itself becomes like the head of a buffalo, facing north; you come in on the right horn, so to speak, and the left horn goes to your right and becomes the Grand Canal, flowing past the city. You must not be swept into the canal because that takes you away from the settlements, which are down here, sou'-sou'-west, about another mile away. If you can get ashore at the northern extremity of the settlements, here, with the railway station on your left, that would be best. Do you speak French?'

'Yes. Well, reasonably.'

'Good, because the French concession occupies the northern end of the settlements and I assume that French sailors will be occupying this part of the defences. Now, do you intend to go alone?'

'Yes, I cannot ask my companions to undertake such a journey.'

'Very well. I suggest that you strip down but carry your Kansu clothing tightly wrapped in a waterproof. Rub down if you can find cover on the riverbank and then dress. You can't wander naked through the lines. Ah, one more thing.' He rolled the map up again. 'Just on the edge of the arsenal here, where it comes down to the river, there is a promontory, which juts out and collects driftwood. We should be able to find material for some sort of transport there.'

Simon nodded in appreciation. 'Splendid! I am most grateful for your help and advice. Now, I would welcome the chance to have something to eat and to talk to my companions.'

'Good Lord! Of course. I have been most neglectful.'

Moments later, Fonthill joined Jenkins and Chang, who were finishing a plate of rice and meat of indeterminate origin and drinking from large tin mugs of tea. Similar fare was provided for him and, between mouthfuls, he related the story of the relief column to his companions.

'Barmy, goin' by train,' said Jenkins. 'Did they think they were goin' on 'oliday to the seaside?'

Chang nodded and concurred. 'It is jolly regretful that they should go that way.'

Jenkins mopped up the remains of the rice with a crust. 'What's the plan now, then, bach sir?' He looked around him. 'I could quite enjoy this postin', out of the sun, like, an' with a bit of decent somethin' to eat. I suppose we will stay 'ere for a bit to get our breath back, so to speak?'

'Yes, well certainly you two will.' He then explained his plan to them. Chang, as usual, was imperturbable but Jenkins listened with mounting horror.

'What!' he exclaimed, his nose wrinkling and his eyebrows

nearly meeting his moustache. 'We float down that bleedin' river on a bit o' wood, with the crocodiles nippin' at our balls and lettin' the Chinks take potshots at us? It's barmy, look you.'

Simon sighed. 'No, my dear old comrade. *We* don't go. *I* do. Two of us certainly would present a target and, anyway, you can't swim and you are afraid of crocodiles. I love them. Nice creatures.'

Chang broke his silence. 'Three too many, cousin. I quite agree. But you need interpreter. And I can swim and I love crocodiles too. So I come.' He grinned. 'Mr Jenkins stay behind because he is not family.'

Jenkins blew out his cheeks. 'If you go, I go. Or I shoot you in the leg, as instructed by Miss Alice. I think this counts under the 'eadin' of "stupid, brave thing", or whatever it was she said.'

Fonthill shook his head slowly. 'I am sorry,' he said, 'but I do this one on my own. Three of us are too big a party. And it is far too dangerous, anyway.'

Jenkins leant across and put his hand on Simon's arm. 'Now, listen, bach sir,' he said. 'This is no time to break up our partnership. You're as brave as a lion, I know that, and you're cleverer than General Roberts and General Wolseley put together. But you *need* me, you know you do. I can do the killin' while you do the thinkin'. We're a good team, but not so good, with respect, when we split up. Whatever you say, anyway, I shall come with you.' He turned to the Chinaman. 'An' you, Changy, should stay 'ere an' write to yer mother.'

Chang, his face set, shook his head. 'You need interpreter,' he said. 'You don't get through lines without talking. I go, too.'

Simon made one last effort. 'But you can't swim and you hate the water,' he said to Jenkins.

The Welshman shook his head. 'Who was it that swam . . . well, sort of . . . across that river in Matabellyland 'oldin' on to your 'orse's tail?' He turned to Chang. 'An' you said, didn't you, Changy, that there aren't any crocs in this river?'

Chang nodded affirmatively.

'There you are, then. What time do we go?'

Fonthill looked hard at his old friend. If there was one thing that Jenkins hated more than heights and crocodiles it was water. For him to volunteer to hang on to a piece of timber and float downstream in a fast-flowing river was the epitome of courage. But for all of his idiosyncrasies, Simon had never met a braver man than Jenkins. It was not like either of them, however, to be sentimental. So he merely smiled and nodded. 'Oh, very well, but I call this insubordination. We leave as soon as it is dark and when we have managed to pull some driftwood out of the river.'

He shook his head disparagingly. 'It's going to be a big load and it looks as though we shall need something like Brunel's "Great Eastern" now. We don't take rifles, just the Colt revolver, and we will need to pack our clothes tightly in our waterproofs. Try and get some rest now. It could be a long night.'

The three dozed intermittently through the day, to a background of artillery and rifle fire. Then, just before dark,

Fonthill made his way to the rear wall of the arsenal, that which faced the river. The water lapped at its high walls but, true enough, to the right where the wall turned at right angles, a thin tongue of land jutted out, containing just enough scrub of cover to anyone watching from downriver or the opposite bank. As the water swirled up to it and round, it had collected enough driftwood to found a timber yard. Prominent amongst the detritus was the trunk of a medium-sized tree, which still had branches protruding from the base, to which a few, sad traces of foliage still clung.

Simon nodded his head. That would suffice.

As dusk settled on the river, the three set out from a little post gate near the promontory. With them came Admiral Seymour and four barefooted sailors. Fonthill and his companions had stripped down to their underpants and clutched bundles of their Kansu uniforms, wrapped in their waterproof capes. The warm air engulfed them and even the water was tepid as Chang and the four sailors waded out, their backs bent low, to retrieve the tree.

Seymour clutched Fonthill's hand. 'Remember,' he said, 'that you go to the right bank when you are abreast of the railway on your left. Be careful not to be swept to your right up the canal as you meet the "buffalo head" of the river. I don't know who is in charge at Tientsin, but tell him that we can hold out here for quite some time but that, if we hear nothing for a week, we shall try and break out to reach them.

'Good luck, my dear Fonthill. May God go with you.'

'Thank you, sir.' They shook hands as the tree trunk was pushed to the bank. Simon stole a glance at Jenkins. Despite the humidity, the Welshman was shivering. He avoided Fonthill's gaze but waded out and hesitantly climbed onto the trunk, lying prone on it, his legs slightly apart to maintain balance, with one hand clutching his bag and the other holding on to a branch that rose vertically just by his head.

'That's good, 352,' whispered Fonthill. 'The river is not turbulent so you should be quite safe if you hold on tight and spread your legs apart to keep your balance. Chang, you hold onto that branch to the right and I will take the left side. Kick with your feet if this bloody thing starts to drift to either side. Right. Here we go.'

There was a distinct muttered cry of 'Oh, bloody 'ell' as the two swimmers pushed the log away from the strip of land and the current caught it, causing it to roll a little. Then it righted itself and Fonthill and Chang kicked their feet in breaststroke fashion to propel it into the centre of the river. Once there, Simon felt the full surge of the river as they were taken up by the current.

He kept his head low, so that the water lapped his chin, and stole a glance to either side. Campfires glowed on both banks, but they were, of course, more numerous on the right bank, facing the arsenal.

He could make out no figures in the darkness and they seemed to be undetected. Thank goodness the trunk was not yawing and Simon offered up a fervent prayer that Jenkins would continue to lie supine, looking from the bank like some gnarled, knotted protrusion in the middle of the tree.

After the heat of the day, it was not at all unpleasant drifting down the river in the comparative cool of the night.

They passed several junks moored for the night on the banks but nothing was moving on the river except them, as either he or Chang kicked out to maintain their position. He soon realised that the young Chinaman was like an eel in the water and, after a time, he left it to Chang to correct their position whenever the need arose.

Fonthhill became aware that their biggest danger would arise if they met shoals of shallow water, for, despite the recent rains, the long drought had severely reduced the river level. Several times he felt his feet kick the bottom as they wandered a little from the deeper channel in midstream. He took comfort, however, from the fact that Seymour had told him that there were no rapids marked on the map above Tientsin.

As they drifted, he began to address the question of when and how they would forsake their tree and gain the riverbank. He had no watch, of course, but he tried to record the position of the pale moon in the dark sky above him and also to assess the speed of the current.

Seymour had estimated that it seemed to be between one and two miles an hour, say one and a half. That meant that, given they were six miles from the foreign concessions, they should be abreast of them after about four hours. Good, that meant that they would arrive still in darkness. How he would successfully navigate the 'buffalo head' junction, he had no idea, except to keep to the left side of the river – if, that is, he knew when they had reached the junction, for little could be seen of either riverbank at the moment.

He was startled by a sudden grunt and then a low moaning sound. He let himself slip back to the rear of the trunk and raised an enquiring eyebrow to Chang, who was on his back and allowing his feet to trail behind him, fluttering in the stream, as though he always used this form of transport to travel on the Pei Ho. The Chinaman grinned and pointed forward. Jenkins, he who was terrified of water, was fast asleep and snoring!

Fonthill crept back up the log and firmly held Jenkins's ankle. He was anxious that his comrade should not suddenly wake up and upset their makeshift boat. The Welshman came to with a start and Simon hissed, 'I told you you would enjoy the trip but don't go to sleep, for God's sake.'

'Oh, sorry, bach sir.'

A light flickered from the right riverbank and then, suddenly, a rifle exploded with a crack and a dart of flame. The bullet hissed into the water behind Fonthill, who breathed, 'Nobody move. Keep perfectly still.'

Another shot was fired which splashed even further behind and then the river lapsed into silence once more. 'I think he was just amusing himself,' called Fonthill softly. 'A bit of nocturnal target practice to amuse himself on the long night-watch.'

'As long as 'e wasn't shootin' at crocodiles,' grunted Jenkins.

The water seemed to be turning cold and a shiver ran through Fonthill. He estimated that they had been in the river for about three and a half hours, although the moon had now slipped behind what seemed like a thick bank of cloud. Ah, rain would be a good thing! Under its cover they could land easily enough. But the night remained dry.

A new and hitherto hidden danger of the river, as Jenkins had discovered, however, was that their method of transport proved to be soporific and Simon felt himself drifting off to sleep, despite – or perhaps because of – the coldness now of the water. He was rudely stirred from his drowsiness when the trunk hit the bank and was immediately sent swirling around, jettisoning Jenkins in the water with a resounding splash. Fonthill immediately struck out for him and caught him by the arm, as he began to thrash the water.

'On your back and keep quiet,' he hissed into his ear. Simon slipped behind the Welshman, thrust both hands under his armpits and began kicking to take them to the riverbank. He realised that Chang was at his side, helping to hold up Jenkins, but that the tree trunk, with their bundles of clothing caught in the thrusting branches, was floating away downstream.

At the same moment, there was a babble of voices from up above them on the bank and, looking up, Simon saw half a dozen rifles thrust towards them and as many faces – Chinese faces, of course – gazing down at them in consternation.

'Chang,' called Simon. 'Tell them not to shoot.'

They scrambled ashore under the threatening rifles and Chang shouted, 'I think they shoot us now as spies.'

Fonthill's brain raced. 'Tell them that we are not spies,' he said, 'but that we are English and come from Peking with an important message for General . . . damn . . . what's his name . . . from Sir Claude MacDonald. We came by boat but it overturned in the shoals and we have been forced to swim. Make it sound good, cousin, for God's sake.'

Chang burbled away urgently while the three stood in their underpants, water dripping from them. A shamefaced Jenkins stood, clenching and unclenching his fists, his great moustache looking as though his nose had caught a water rat. 'Sorry, bach,' he murmured, 'all my fault. I'll take this lot on while you dive back into the river and get away. That's best.'

'You'll do nothing of the kind. That way we will all be shot. And, anyway, it was my fault for falling asleep. We will just have to see if we can talk our way out of this.'

It seemed that Chang was not having much success, for a rifle butt was suddenly swung into his face, knocking him to the ground.

Fonthill strode forward. 'That's enough of that,' he said, with the confident and reprimanding air of a British colonel. 'You do not hit that man again.' And he wagged his finger in the face of the antagonist. 'We are British soldiers and . . .' The muzzle of the man's rifle was suddenly thrust sharply into his stomach, winding him and causing him to bend over and drop onto one knee.

Jenkins sprang forward and delivered a perfect left hook onto the jaw of the soldier, sending him staggering, before the Welshman was felled with a rifle butt from behind.

Grimacing, Fonthill looked up at the hostile faces all around him. They were, he realised, all Kansus. Their eyes, set in Mongolian faces, regarded him quite expressionlessly. These were the toughest, most vicious soldiers in the Empress's army, little more than bandits, rapists and killers, led by the biggest brigand and foreigner-hating man in all

China. As he watched, he saw the man Jenkins had struck walk forward and aim his rifle at the dazed Welshman's head and pull back the bolt.

Then the name came to him. He stood erect. 'General Tung Fu-hsiang,' he said firmly. 'Take us to him.' Then he repeated the name. 'General Tung Fu-hsiang.' He embraced the three of them with a whirl of his arm. Then gestured from his breast and then vaguely to the south. 'General Tung Fu-hsiang.'

Chang pulled himself to his feet, his eye half closed, and began speaking in Chinese again.

Whatever he said, that and Simon's firmness had an effect, for they were pushed forward with rifle muzzles. Fonthill became aware of the sound of artillery fire, much closer now, and they were being marched towards it. After five minutes they saw campfires and all three were forced to their knees by blows from rifle butts into their backs and left under a guard of two men on the edge of the camp.

'Are you all right, the two of you?' asked Fonthill.

'Me 'ead is singin' but it's me pride that's wounded mostly,' grunted Jenkins. 'Sorry, bach sir, for sleepin' at me post and fallin' off into the water. It looks as though I've got us into a fine mess.'

'Don't talk rubbish.'

Chang squinted across at Simon with his good eye. 'I think, cousin, that they now believe you that you have message for general and they go to fetch officer. But I think they will be jolly angry when they find you have no message.'

Fonthill shrugged. 'I'll think of something. I had to stop

them shooting us out of hand. They're Kansus, aren't they?'

'Yes. Not very nice people.'

'By the sound of the guns, we are very near the settlements, if only we can get out of here.'

Jenkins looked down at his nakedness. 'If we get through the lines, we'll probably be arrested for indecency. Or catch cold and die of flu.'

Eventually, an order was barked from out of the semi-darkness and they were bundled forward, rifles at their backs, until they reached a large tent. Inside, a Kansu was seated at a trestle table. He was dressed and looked exactly the same as the soldiers but he was obviously an officer, for he was treated with great deference by the escorts. He spoke rapidly to Chang.

'He want our names and where we come from and why we go downstream on log,' he explained.

Fonthill nodded. 'Give our names and ranks – captain and sergeant. You are our interpreter. Do *not* say that you are the son of a missionary. Explain that we escaped from Peking with a personal message for the general from Sir Claude MacDonald, the senior minister in the legations. We made for the river, where we hired a small boat. Upriver it hit an obstruction during the night and overturned, throwing us into the water. We were all asleep on deck in just our undergarments because of the heat. We found this log floating and hung onto it, because we were all poor swimmers.'

'Blimey,' muttered Jenkins. 'There's ingenious for you, isn't it?'

Chang gave his translation, while Simon watched the

officer closely to gauge his reactions. The man's face was impassive. Then he spoke curtly.

'He say, give him message and he will relay it to general.'

'No. The message is confidential and is not written. I have orders to deliver it to the general personally. Ask him to take us to him immediately.'

'He say, how you know general is here and not in Peking?'

'Word came through to Sir Claude that the general had given up his command of the troops attacking the Wang Fu to direct operations against the Tientsin settlements.'

Fonthill sucked in his breath and hoped to God that Seymour's information about the whereabouts of Tung Fu-hsiang was correct. If his gamble had failed then the odds on being shot straight away were short. But the officer's face gave no indication either way.

The Kansu fixed his gaze on Fonthill, who returned it without blinking. The two stared at each other in silence for a full thirty seconds before the officer turned and barked a command.

Chang let out an audible sigh of relief. 'We are to be taken to general,' he whispered. 'He gives orders that coats are to be found for us, for it would be insult to commander for us to appear before him naked.'

'Quite right,' muttered Jenkins. 'Well, bach sir, first round to you. But you'd better think of a good message to deliver. The general wouldn't be Sir Claude's illegitimate son, by any chance, would he?'

Fonthill frowned. 'Do be quiet, 352. I'm trying to think.'

Three dun-coloured coats were thrown around their

shoulders, their hands were bound roughly behind their backs and they were pushed out of the tent. The first signs of dawn were streaking the sky to the east and they were marched away, following the officer and surrounded by a guard of Kansus. The gunfire was louder than ever and Fonthill realised that they must be near to the line surrounding the settlements, although little could be seen in the darkness.

This was confirmed as they climbed a hill and saw ahead, just out of rifle shot, a dark outline of buildings, linked by a low and indistinct line of what must be barricades. Troops were now all around them, crawling from their bedrolls and congregating around small open fires over which cooking pots were hung. To their right and behind them, cannon were firing desultorily and the sour smell of cordite hung on the air. At the top of the hill, tucked away among stunted trees, a large, low tent had been pitched, lit from within by a dim light.

'Let's 'ope that the general 'as slept well,' muttered Jenkins.

They were forced to wait for ten minutes while the officer spoke with guards outside the tent and then disappeared inside it. Then they were pushed through an opening in the canvas.

The tent seemed even larger from within and three vertical poles supported the roof. To one side, sleeping mats had been spread and three women, dressed in traditional Chinese style but looking a little dishevelled, as if they had dressed hurriedly, were folding blankets. In the centre of the room stood a table on which a large map had been spread and, at

196

the far end of the tent, a fourth woman was ladling rice into a wooden bowl set on a smaller table, behind which sat one of the largest men Fonthill had ever seen.

Although he was sitting, it was clear that he was not tall, perhaps Jenkins's height. But he was wide – wider than the Welshman by far – and immensely fat. He was half-wearing a green tunic that had been buttoned up only to the midriff, revealing rolls of flesh. The head was either completely bald or shaven, although a long moustache adorned the upper lip, the ends of which hung down on either side of his mouth like rat's tails. The man was eating rice and meat with chopsticks, displaying a delicacy of movement that denied the grossness of his appearance.

He looked up as the trio were ushered in and gestured briefly with his chopsticks. Immediately, rifles were crashed onto the shoulders of the three, forcing them to kneel before him.

Fonthill looked with interest at the general. He knew that the man enjoyed the confidence of the Empress, because of his diligence in stamping out isolated examples of insurgency in the north of China and his oft-declared hatred of the foreign barbarians whose presence in the country was humiliating its people and the Dragon Lady herself. He was a warlord in his own right in the north but he gave devoted allegiance to the Empress and had been one of the early supporters of the Boxers. His competence as a military leader had been reflected in the fact that the Peking sector that he commanded, the Wang Fu, had posed the greatest threat to the legations, causing the diligent Japanese who defended it to concede ground regularly, if stoically. Now he regarded the three prisoners with tiny eyes, set in a round, jowled face.

Fonthill decided to take the initiative.

'Are you General Tung Fu-hsiang?' he demanded, looking directly at the general, rather than Chang, who interpreted in a diffident voice.

There was an intake of breath from the dozen or so Kansus in the tent. It was, clearly, *lèse-majesté* for a prisoner to address the general without being spoken to first and a rifle butt crashed into his back, sending him sprawling.

Chang hurriedly answered, although no one had replied to the question. 'Yes, cousin,' he said, 'this is the general. Please be careful.'

'Then tell him I have a message for him from Sir Claude MacDonald.'

The general acknowledged the statement with a wave of his chopsticks. 'Tell me the message,' translated Chang.

'No,' said Fonthill. 'I speak to no man while kneeling before him.'

There was another intake of breath, not least from Chang and Jenkins, and the general looked up, a flicker of interest momentarily lighting up his face. 'Then you will be beheaded as you kneel,' he replied, indicating for one of the guards to step forward and draw his long, curved sword.

'Then you will not hear the message,' answered Simon, still fixing his gaze on that of the general.

'Bloody 'ell,' muttered Jenkins. 'Steady on, bach sir.'

A slow smile began to spread across the general's face but he lowered his head and continued eating for a moment before looking up and growling a command to the officer. Immediately, Simon was levered to his feet.

'Very well,' said Simon. 'I wish my companions to stand also.'

Another signal was given and Jenkins and Chang were brought to their feet, rifle barrels thrust under their armpits.

'Now,' said Fonthill. 'Sir Claude MacDonald is the leader of the eleven foreign ministers who, with their staffs and families, are being kept under siege in Peking.'

'He knows that,' interpreted Chang, 'and he says that the man is a fool.'

'If he is a fool, he represents the British Empire, the most powerful empire in the world, which is three times the size of the Chinese Empire. He is also the elected leader of the ten other European powers who, with the British, have navies and armies thirty times the size of the Chinese. Sir Claude is imprisoned within the Legation Quarter but, even so, he sends his greetings to the general.'

At this, the Chinaman put down his chopsticks and leant back in his chair. Encouraged, Fonthill continued.

'He respects the general, because he knows of his prowess as a fighting man and he respects his Kansu troops, who have a similar reputation. But he is afraid for the general's life.'

Tung Fu-hsiang lifted his eyebrows and gestured for Simon to continue. 'Yes,' said Simon, 'at this moment twenty thousand Russian troops are on their way to Taku from the Russian provinces in Asia and the British are also sending troops from India. The British Admiral Seymour has captured the great Chinese arsenal of Hsiku near here and has at his disposal great quantities of field guns, machine guns, rifles, and seven million rounds of small-arms ammunition.' At this point, Chang held up his hand for Simon to slow down while he translated.

The general looked unimpressed. 'You lie,' he said. 'We have both Peking and the Tientsin settlements surrounded and there are no reports of foreign reinforcements in Taku. Even if this were so, these are matters for the Empress, not me. Why should your minister fear for my life?'

There was a muted murmur of acquiescence from the soldiers in the room.

Fonthill drew in his breath. He had no knowledge of reinforcements being imminent. They would come, he had no doubt about that. But they would probably be too late. Nevertheless, he continued.

'Because, General, the Foreign Powers, when they land and have defeated your outnumbered and outgunned army, will advance on Peking and storm the Forbidden City and the Manchu Palace. The Empress, of course, will not be harmed. She will be needed to reunite the country after the dreadful revenge that the powers will take on your people. But the generals who have supported the Boxers and led the attack on the capital and on the settlements will be killed – all of them.'

A silence fell on the room as Fonthill's words were translated by Chang, who was now speaking in a loud and firm voice, as though taking heart from the words he was conveying.

A glance from Chang showed that he had finished and

Simon hurried on. 'However, because he admires your fighting spirit, Sir Claude is prepared to guarantee that you will live after punitive actions have been taken. But you must withdraw your men from the settlements immediately.'

'Good try, bach sir,' whispered Jenkins. 'Good try.'

A slow smile spread across the round face of the general. He nodded his head slowly, as if in admiration of Simon's audacity. Then he spoke slowly, giving time for Chang to translate, which he did with increasing glumness.

'He say you speak with the honesty of a snake and the wisdom of a cow,' he said. 'The whole of China is rising against the foreign pigs who have defiled our country with their religion and allowed their missionaries to murder our babies.' The general's tone rose and his words became a rant. 'None of your so-called armies will stand against the power of the Divine Empress. Just as we destroyed your pathetic attempt to relieve Peking so we will crush any further troops that land here.'

He paused. Then went on, 'As for you three, you will die the death of a thousand lashes. Tie them to the posts.'

With a yell, the Kansus ran forward and seized the trio, untying their hands and then retying the wrists of each of them behind each of the three posts. Fonthill turned his head to issue a further threat in an attempt to save them. He saw a messenger come through the opening and say something in the general's ear, then, more ominously, six long whips being produced as six of the Kansus stripped off their shirts and took post, two to each of the intruders. It was clear that the men would take it in turns to deliver each stroke, giving the flogged no respite. The coats of the three were torn from their backs in preparation for the beginning of the torture.

Jenkins groaned and, half-turning to Simon, said, 'Oh bloody 'ell. Not again.'

Fonthill, who was pinioned to the furthest of the poles on the left, turned his head. 'I am sorry, lads,' he said. 'The gamble failed. Thank you both for—'

But he was interrupted by a cry from Tung Fu-hsiang. Immediately the whips were lowered and Simon felt a finger prod the middle of his naked back. He also felt the general's breath on his cheek. It reeked of cinnamon and other spices. The Chinaman prodded his back once more and turned and shouted to Chang.

'He says, what are those marks?'

Puzzled, Simon replied, 'They are the marks of the flogging we received from the Mahdi at Khartoum, in the Sudan. My comrade next to me was also whipped. What does it matter?' The punishment had been administered more than fifteen years before but the tan which they had both received on the slow plod on the ship across the Pacific a few months ago had not concealed the scars, which now stood out like white wheals.

'He say, how many lashes you receive?'

What was this about? Fonthill sighed. Perhaps the bastard would double the dose for them – but he had already promised a thousand, which was the death penalty, so it didn't matter. 'I had fifty lashes and Jenkins twenty-five.'

'Ah!' The ejaculation came from Tung Fu-hsiang, who immediately jumped in front of Simon and Jenkins, removed his jacket and turned his back. A gasp came from the soldiers now crowded into the tent to witness the entertainment, for the general's back also bore the signature of the lash, criss-crossed and standing out whitely, like those of Fonthill and Jenkins.

'He say,' said Chang, his voice a little louder now, 'he say he got forty lashes as young man from Empress's nephew, the deposed Emperor, a cowardly man. He salutes you two as similar brave warriors. These are marks of courage. Many men die as result.'

The general, now beaming, interrupted Chang, who listened with growing disbelief and then translated with as much of a smile as his closed eye would allow. 'He say, because of this, he will release us and let us through the lines to settlements. But, he wants you to know that this is not because of minister's attempt at bribery, which he treats with scorn, but because he admires bravery. Cousin, we are not going to be whipped to death. God be praised!'

''Ere, 'ere,' muttered Jenkins. 'Tell the old bastard that I'll vote for 'im, see, when he stands for emperor, so I will.'

Fonthill maintained a straight face and nodded sagely. 'Thank the general. We admire him as a man of courage also.'

Their bonds were cut and their ill-fitting coats restored to them. Simon gave the general a half-bow, which the others emulated, and followed the officer out of the tent, amidst a hum of – what, derision, approval, disappointment? – from the assembled soldiers.

'Have you noticed something?' asked Simon. 'The firing has stopped.'

'I think I know why,' beamed Chang. 'It all bally interesting, cousin. I tell you why when we get through lines.'

They followed the officer who picked his way through the shallow trench works that constituted the Chinese forward lines. They passed hundreds of Imperial soldiers, rifles at the slope, who were marching away from the settlements. Then the officer pointed towards a low mud wall which fronted the Chinese lines some two hundred yards away. It was studded with rifles at its crest and broken occasionally by the snout of a cannon. But all firing had stopped.

'He say, there are French lines,' interpreted Chang. 'We free to go towards them.'

With a half-smile, the officer gave them a ceremonial bow and marched quickly away, to catch up with the departing infantry.

Simon turned to Chang. 'What was so bally interesting back there, cousin?'

'Ah.' The Chinaman gave a lopsided smile. 'Just as we being tied to posts a man came in and gave general a message.'

'Yes, I noticed that. Did you hear what he said?'

'Not completely. But I hear distinctly words "thousands of Russian troops" and "retreat".'

Fonthill returned the smile, slowly nodding his head. 'I thought this "comrades-in-arms and fellow sufferers" stuff was all too good to be true. The old rascal freed us because reinforcements had arrived for the settlements and he wanted to get some credit with the Allies for releasing us. The old fraud.'

'Well,' said Jenkins, 'I don't really care what 'e thought

as long as 'e let us go. Now let's get moving towards the Frenchies, shall we?' And he began to stride forward.

'No!' Fonthill held up his hand. 'If we march across this no man's land wearing these coats, we are just asking to be shot by the French. Take 'em off and we will saunter across in our underpants, waving the coats. That should amuse the French and also stop 'em shooting at us. Come on – and try and smile. We could be having French onion soup for lunch . . .'

And so, barefooted, wearing fixed grins and nothing but their filthy and still-wet and virtually transparent underpants, the three comrades strode towards the defenders of the Tientsin settlements.

CHAPTER NINE

Alice Fonthill sat down outside the hospital, wiped her brow with a less-than-clean handkerchief and cursed her husband. The words came from a fruity vocabulary, built up originally in her Swiss finishing school and then honed and extended during her years of reporting for the *Morning Post* from various boundaries of the Empire on Queen Victoria's wars and also from campaigning with Simon. Alice had never lived a sheltered life and, although being shelled through most of the day and living on quarter rations of dusty rice and horse meat did not exactly represent tranquillity, she resented being cooped up in Peking and, most of all, being without Simon.

As a soldier's daughter, a war correspondent operating in a masculine world and as the active partner of an army scout and 'irregular' agent, she was used to hardship and danger. What she resented now, however, was being forced to play the role of the woman waiting anxiously for news of her man. She had done it before, of course, but rarely since their marriage. And certainly not when he had set off on any mission that so justified the term 'hopeless cause' as this one.

She jerked the brim of her canvas hat down over her eyes in a vicious movement to avoid the glare of the sun. How could he be asked to track eighty miles through enemy territory – an obvious Occidental in Oriental country – with not a single word of the language, no transport and no real idea of where he was going? And how could he accept such a task, without taking her with him? She picked up a handful of dust and threw it away again, immediately regretting it as it blew back in her face.

Alice loved Fonthill with a passion that had grown stronger with each year they had been together. They had made a false start when, impressed by his bearing and courage, she had married Lieutenant Colonel Ralph Covington, Simon's erstwhile commanding officer. Shortly after her engagement, she had realised her mistake but, when Covington had lost an eye and a hand in action, she had honoured her pledge to him. The arid years of her marriage had ended with her husband's death at the Battle of Tel el-Kebir and she had hurried into Fonthill's arms. But she bitterly regretted those lost years and the thought now of losing Simon filled her with despair. Where was he, what was he doing and why couldn't she be by his side, instead of sweating away here, changing dressings?

In the early days of the siege, before Simon had set off,

morale within the legations had been kept alive by rumour of imminent relief: of distant bugles and bagpipes heard and of strange lights in the sky to the south-east. Now, these had receded and been replaced by a grim realisation that things would get worse within Peking before they got better. The fighting was static but it was relentless and casualties were mounting, usually among the most efficient and courageous of the defenders.

Practicality was the order of the day. Sir Claude was proving to be a surprisingly energetic leader, with a fine eye for detail. Typical of his range of concern was the notice he posted at the Bell Tower, written in his tiny, civil service hand. It ran: 'LOOPHOLES. Loopholes should never be left open except when being used for looking through or firing through. A brick placed at the narrowest part is quite sufficient to prevent the enemy from firing through and hitting people passing.' The ex-subaltern was proving his worth as a military commander.

The previous day had probably been the worst since the siege began. The Japanese had been dislodged from their only recently installed fallback position in the Fu and had to erect, once again, a new defensive barricade; the Germans, in their sector, had been reduced to a desperate bayonet charge to save their positions; and, as ever, the Americans were under fierce attack on the wall.

Then, just before dusk, Alice, working in the hospital, had been almost thrown to the ground by two explosions from the direction of the French Legation. Two mines had been detonated under what was left of the legation there and a howling mob of Chinese had poured through the ruins, jumping between the flames caused by the explosions.

Alice had seized her revolver and rushed to the scene. She found that the French were conducting a strenuous defence amidst the debris, kneeling in the smoke and repeatedly firing into the mass of attackers, who had now halted, daunted by the French shooting. She herself joined the French but was thrust aside by a member of what was left of Fonthill's mobile reserve, who rushed to the aid of the French, alternately firing and throwing up rubble to form a new barricade. Eventually, a bridgehead was created and held but two French sailors were buried in the debris and several others were wounded, including the Austrian *chargé d'affaires*.

Wearily, Alice made her way back to the hospital, where the day had been the busiest yet, five men having died there and ten others brought in for treatment.

Every day, however, the work in the little hospital was hard and becoming increasingly demanding. Set up in the chancery of the British Legation, it was small and inadequately resourced. It had only four small iron bedsteads and seven camp beds and most of the patients were forced to lie on mattresses on the floor, stuffed with straw in which wine bottles had been packed. The windows were sandbagged and the heat and the flies were intolerable for patients and staff alike. There were few anaesthetics, fewer antiseptics and only one thermometer.

The place was run by two physicians: Dr Velde, a German surgeon, and Dr Poole, the British Legation's resident doctor.

They were given support by an overworked sickbay attendant from a British warship and an amateur nursing staff, of whom Alice and Mrs Griffith were among the earliest and most dedicated members. Latterly, Lady MacDonald, the respected wife of the British minister, had organised the ladies of the Legation to provide a deeper nursing source to assist the doctors. Dr Morrison, the *Times* correspondent, was a trained backup for the doctors but he had proved to be as brave and active a member of the defenders as any of the regular sailors and soldiers and was to be seen on the line now more than in the hospital.

He, in fact, was a factor in deciding Alice that she need not be as scrupulous a helper in the hospital as in the early days of the defence. She realised that, although he could not send any despatches back to the London *Times*, Morrison was almost certainly preparing for the day when the cable services could be reached and was making extensive notes of the incidents in the siege. She must do the same and so, given the increasing numbers of ladies to strengthen the nursing roster, she had now taken to reducing her shifts in the hospital and visiting each sector of the defences in turn.

She did so, wearing her riding breeches and boots, wide-brimmed hat and with the pearl-handled Colt revolver tucked into her belt. She had become known, in fact, as 'The Lady with the Gun' and, ignoring the protests of the officers in the line, she had several times taken part in helping to fight off attacks on her sector.

Now, squatting in the sun at the door of the hospital, Alice decided that it was pointless worrying about Simon.

She rose to her feet and brushed the dust from her skirt. It was time to visit the Fu, the most hard-pressed sector of the line.

She made her way back to the tiny room – previously a store cupboard – that she shared now with Mrs Griffith, splashed a little water onto her face, changed into her breeches, thrust her revolver into her belt and picked up her pencil and notebook. As usual, she was warned not to go further as she scurried out of the Legation and across the narrow bridge spanning the central canal. And, as usual, she smiled at the sentry and continued on her way, ducking her head instinctively as the noise of the firing increased as she neared the barricade up ahead.

Alice was full of admiration for the Japanese contingent who defended the park-like space immediately to the east, across the canal from the British Legation. Of all the contingents, these little men – no more than twenty-five of them – fought the hardest and complained the least. They presented the amazing statistic of sustaining a hundred per cent casualties, in that every single man had been hit and had to leave the line at one time or another and returned, including their commander, Colonel Shiba, the Japanese military attaché. He had become a particular favourite of Alice, for he made no fuss about her helping to man the barricade.

He greeted her now with a smile and a full, ceremonial bow.

'Quieter today, Colonel?' she asked.

'Not quiet, madam. These Muslims facing us fire all the time but they usually fire too high.'

Alice knew that the defending line here had been forced to contract regularly since the Kansus had first broken through the walls of the park. Now it zigzagged across the open space, winding its way between the various small buildings and shrines, now reduced to rubble, most of them.

'Have you had to fall back today, Colonel?'

'No, Madam. And we retreat no more. If they make frontal attack, we kill them. But we stay here.'

Alice scribbled in her pad, noting that the Colonel had a bullet tear across the right shoulder of his uniform. She drew her revolver and made her way to an open loophole in the rubble that formed the barricade. She removed her hat and peered through. The Chinese barricade, similarly made of broken bricks, gravestones and the like, seemed amazingly near. They had left open a small gap, through which, presumably, they made their now increasingly rare frontal attacks, and, through it, she could see dun-coloured figures moving. They were close enough for her to make out some facial characteristics, although most of the Kansus were dressed exactly alike. She levelled the Colt. She now had no compunction at all in killing any of the Chinese troops. One less might somehow ease the danger on Simon.

She sighted down the long barrel and then froze. Into view came a white-suited figure, disconcertingly familiar, with his Occidental features, yet wearing his hair drawn back into a pigtail and affecting a long Mandarin moustache. Her jaw dropped and her finger slackened on the trigger. Then the figure had gone.

Alice pulled back away from the loophole, her eyes wide. Could it be? Could it be Gerald Griffith, mingling with the Muslim Kansus opposite this, the most tightly pressed sector of the Legation defences?

She took another look but sharply withdrew as a bullet pinged to the left of the loophole. She scurried back to find the colonel.

'Has a man – a European-looking man – in a white suit been seen on the Chinese barricades?' she asked.

The little man immediately walked along the line and barked a series of questions to his men. He came back. 'No, madam,' he said. 'All Muslims opposite us. Very sorry.'

Alice thanked him and walked away, her head down, thinking hard. The colonel had told her previously that the Kansus seemed to know which part of the defences were the most vulnerable and on which to concentrate their fire. Could it be that Gerald – *her cousin* – was relaying this kind of information to the enemy? Although he made no secret of his admiration for the Boxers and his approval of their cause, he surely would not take that attitude to the point of betraying his fellow countrymen? Or would he?

It was true that he had taken to disappearing again during the day but Alice had given up questioning him, or even of talking to the young man, for fear of encouraging his obvious admiration for her.

In fairness, this had been restricted to glances and the odd brush of the hand. No flowers now – they would be difficult to find, anyhow. Could she face him now and charge him with betrayal? It would be a heinous crime of which to accuse him. No. She would probe gently with Aunt Lizzie, although she would have to step warily there.

She found the missionary's widow sitting outside the Legation main building, sewing a piece of cotton onto an old, torn skirt.

Alice smiled at her. She had become very fond of her aunt, despite – or perhaps because of – them being thrown together in the crowded conditions of the Legation. The old lady was a strange mixture: a diffident, modest woman whose faith and love of her husband had sustained her throughout her arduous life in China; and yet also a tough, resilient pragmatist who was not above scolding a servant with the sharpest of tongues. She had taken the death of her husband with remarkable equanimity, although she visited his plot of earth in the Legation cemetery – there had been no chance of putting up a proper headstone – every evening.

'Be careful, Aunt, sitting there,' she said. 'You are not out of range of a stray bullet, you know.'

The old lady held up her handiwork in a gesture of disgust. 'If a bullet finds me,' she said, in mock resignation, 'then it will be the Lord's will. I just can't sit inside our stuffy room any longer. And, anyway, I can't see in there.'

Alice discreetly slipped her revolver along her belt to the small of her back out of sight and squatted in the dust beside her aunt. 'Here,' she offered, 'let me do that for you.'

'No, my dear, but thank you. I can see clearly out here. Where have you been?'

'Well I finished my shift at the hospital and went for a bit of a walk.' She made a show of looking around. 'Where's Gerald?'

'Oh, I don't know. I don't know where he gets off to.' She looked up quickly. 'No news of Simon and Chang, I suppose?'

'No, dear. And I don't expect to hear anything.' She paused. 'I am sorry we had to mislead you rather about their departure.'

Mrs Griffith came near to a sniff. 'Yes, well, I didn't feel that was absolutely necessary, although I would have tried to persuade Chang not to go, you know.' She looked at her niece with stern eyes. 'He is only a boy. Hardly sixteen. I worry about him all the time.'

'I am sure you do, Aunt, and I am so sorry. But he was ideal for the purpose and so anxious to take part. We had to dissemble to you about him because of the security risk. Sir Claude and Simon could not risk news of their journey leaking out . . .'

'You mean Gerald?'

Alice started. She had never thought for a moment that Mrs Griffith ever doubted her son's allegiance to the defenders of the legations and it was startling to see her refer to the possibility now so matter-of-factly.

'Well . . . er . . . yes. But not just him, you know. It is common knowledge that this place is riddled with spies and Boxer sympathisers.'

'Gerald would never do anything like that.' The words came out like bullets from a gun.

Alice's mind slipped back quickly to the attack of the

Boxers on the cart and the discharge of Gerald's fowling piece which prompted the murder of his father. 'No, Aunt,' she said. 'Of course not.' This was *not* treading warily. The subject had to be changed. 'Is Gerald still wrapped up in his medieval texts?' she asked brightly. 'I never seem to see him now.'

A smile came at last to Mrs Griffith's careworn face. 'Oh yes. He takes *such* an interest in the history of this country, you know. He was waiting to take a postgraduate degree at the university when all this trouble started. He has such an original mind.' She paused for a moment, her needle poised. 'I suppose he is what you would call a freethinker. He has always supported the cause of Chinese nationalism against foreign intervention in this country.'

Alice decided to probe. 'And yet, of course,' she said, 'the Boxers and the people in court here who support them would blame the missionaries for so much of that intervention.'

'Certainly not!' The old lady's tone expressed extreme indignation. 'It is not the men of God who have claimed large territories of China for their own commercial ends. It was not the missionaries who encouraged the growing and selling of opium here. No. It was the politicians and empire-builders back home in Europe who made money from that loathsome trade and who have been competing against each other for years to acquire large swathes of this wonderful country, taking advantage of China's weak and corrupt central government to do so.'

She leant forward to make her point. 'You know, Alice, dear Edward had a basic sympathy for the Boxers. He felt that they were – they are – just a bunch of uneducated young men, simple peasants, who felt that they had to stand up against this Western imperialism. No. It was their unthinking brutality, their primitive violence, that he abhorred, not their basic motives.'

Alice had never heard her aunt express these kinds of views before – indeed, she had never heard her discuss politics of any sort. But she was beginning to see what had influenced Gerald's thinking. Now, she must gently steer the conversation back to him.

'So Gerald was influenced by his father in adopting his views?'

Mrs Griffith frowned. 'Well, not exactly. Gerald was always much more nationalistic than Edward in his thinking. And,' the frown deepened, 'I am afraid that there was a gulf between him and his father in later years. They did not speak together very much. It was very sad.' She returned to her sewing.

'How, then, did Gerald acquire his views?'

'Oh, I don't really know. He read many books of Chinese history – in their original Mandarin, of course – and he began mixing with a rather regressive . . . I think that would be the word . . . group in the court here.' She looked up and stared into the middle distance, reflectively. 'He's quite a good talker, a debater, you know.'

'I wouldn't doubt it. But, Aunt, what will he make of his life now? The Great Powers will never let this siege go unpunished. Whatever happens to us here, there will be a terrible revenge invoked against the Manchu court and the government. Given his views and his ethnicity, would there be a place for him in the Chinese foreign service? Would the Empress – should she keep her throne after the war – want a foreigner like him to serve her and, indeed, would the ambassadors and ministers of the powers want to deal with someone like him?'

Mrs Griffith looked surprised at the question. 'Why ever not? He will have done nothing wrong at all in this business. He would be just the sort of young man to enter the service and help to build bridges between China and the great nations.'

Alice nodded. So '*he will have done nothing wrong*'! Her aunt clearly had no doubt about her son's basic loyalty to his country – his *real* country. Or was it his *real* country? Surely a man could decide to give his patriotism to the land in which he was born and in which he had grown up. After all, Gerald had never visited England. His parents were the only influences in his life to steer him towards allegiance to Britain and its empire. And they were completely dedicated to their work in China, an empire with a civilisation and history far longer than that of those small islands off the mainland of Europe. Alice gave a tiny shrug. She could go no further with Mrs Griffith. Her mind's eye once again threw up the distinctive image of the man in the white suit behind the Chinese barricade. She *must* discover his identity. If Gerald was a spy for the Chinese court then he was a source of great danger to the defenders of the legations. The only thing to do was to question the man himself. But – again – she had to tread warily. He must not be warned that he was under suspicion. She would catch him when his guard was down.

Gerald Griffith, however, never seemed to lower his guard, nor keep to a fixed schedule. All of the able-bodied men in the Quarter were expected to play their part in the defence, but there was no mobilisation, no formal allocation of responsibilities, except to the men and women of some standing who joined the various committees set up by Sir Claude to direct the logistics of the defence. Those down the line who shirked did become the subject of social approbation but, somehow, Gerald escaped all that. His profile, of course, was not high, unlike that of the cordially detested French minister, and he kept to himself, slipping beneath the gaze of authority, quietly reading his Chinese texts, coming and going at odd times. An evasive, slippery figure.

So it was not until three days later that Alice was able to accost her cousin. She had decided that, if he did find her attractive, despite their age difference, then, indeed, she would deploy that weapon to detain and even, perhaps, intrigue the young man – Alice had never been averse in her work to using her good looks to gain a professional advantage. As a result, catching a glimpse of him sitting reading that evening in the shade cast by the hospital, she rushed to her room, applied a little face powder and rouge and a touch of her precious perfume, and emerged to walk by him, so innocently.

'Ah, Gerald,' she smiled. 'I have not seen you for ages. May I sit with you for a minute? I think there is room on that log and that shade looks so cool.'

Gerald Griffith looked up and distinctly blushed. 'Of course,' he said, standing and taking the hand she offered to help her sit. 'I was . . . er . . . just reading.'

'So I see. What is the book?'

He snapped it shut and shuffled uneasily on their makeshift bench. 'Oh, just something from Father's old library. It wouldn't interest you. It's Chinese philosophy. I hardly understand it myself.' He gave a small, self-deprecating laugh.

Alice put a hand on his arm. 'You know, Gerald, I am so sorry about your dear father's death. Do you miss him dreadfully?'

He looked at her from the corner of his eye and, almost imperceptibly, edged closer to her on the log, so that their thighs touched. She did not move away. 'Oh . . . er . . . yes, of course,' he said. 'Although, I have to confess that in the last few years we were not close, you know.' He held up the book. 'I think he became annoyed that I did not follow his faith. I am studying the Shinto religion, you see.'

'Ah, how interesting.' She gave him a sidelong look. He was wearing a two-piece suit of dark-grey cotton. 'You always look so smart, Gerald. Goodness gracious, how many suits did you bring with you?'

He gave a slightly embarrassed smile. 'Oh, only two. The other one is a white flannel. But it is too hot, really, and it gets dirty so quickly here, of course.'

'Yes, of course. Tell me, my dear, what do you do with yourself all day under these difficult conditions?'

'Well I mainly study. And sometimes go for a walk.'

'Walk? But there is hardly anywhere to go. We are so restricted here.'

'Oh, I find places.'

The firing from the Fu suddenly rose in intensity and then fell away again. 'Another attack on the Fu,' observed Alice tentatively.

'Oh, I doubt it,' said Gerald airily. 'The Chinese there have dropped their direct attacks and decided that a process of attrition is the best way forward. With so few Japanese facing them they feel it is only a question of time before they wear down the defences there. It is better to snipe than to charge across in the open, you see.'

'Really. How do you know that, Gerald?'

He looked uneasy for a moment. 'Oh, I hear these things, you know. And it is just common sense, really.'

They fell silent for a moment. Then he looked directly at her. 'Have you heard from Simon?'

The question threw her for a moment. She had never discussed his absence with Gerald – nor with anyone, for that matter, except her aunt. 'No, I have not, nor did I expect to.'

He looked smug. 'No, I don't suppose you would, would you? Nothing gets through now from Tientsin.'

She whirled round on him. 'How would you know where he was going?'

A smile of self-satisfaction spread across the young man's face. 'Good gracious, cousin. Everyone knew that he, Chang and that ludicrous Welshman were trying to slip through the lines and impress the Foreign Powers at the coast of the need to send another relief force.'

Alice looked hard at her cousin. '*Everyone* knew, Gerald? I have told no one. Who do you mean by "everyone"?'

He shrugged his shoulders. 'A lot of people. Anyway, I saw them go.'

'Gerald, they left in the middle of the night. What were you doing out at that time? Were you spying on them?'

'Oh, I was just out walking. I don't *spy*.'

'How did you know where they were going?'

For the first time the young man looked uncomfortable. 'Oh, I just put two and two together. It was not difficult to presume that that was where they were going. They were dressed as Kansu soldiers. The Chinese certainly presumed that that was where they were heading.'

'The *Chinese*?'

Gerald had now regained his composure. He seemed now to be revelling in his knowledge. 'Oh yes.' The pressure on Alice's thigh had now increased. 'You would be surprised at what I know, cousin. I have very good friends in high places beyond these walls, you know.'

Alice drew in a deep breath. She was amazed at his indiscretion. He was clearly keen to impress her and she decided to play along with his arrogance. 'You amaze me, Gerald. You mean you have contact with the people who are besieging us?'

'Oh, yes. They have confidence in me and I work at their friendship because I am sure that, when this ridiculous siege is over, I can be useful to both sides in settling the peace.' He took up her hand. 'I will be able to help you and Mother by interceding with the Chinese authorities, Alice. You can trust me.'

222

She gently withdrew her hand. 'Thank you. But you said that the Chinese knew about Simon's mission. How did they know, Gerald?'

The shifty look came back into his eyes. 'Oh, everybody knew,' he said vaguely. Then he picked up her hand again and faced her directly. His face took on a serious and troubled mien, that of a much older man, concerned for her. 'You must reconcile yourself, dear Alice, to the fact that Simon will not return, you know. The Kansus sent off three cavalrymen to apprehend the three of them and, if they resisted, to kill them. This was some time ago, so I am very much afraid that that is probably what happened. I am so sorry.'

Alice felt the blood drain from her face. She drew in a deep breath. She must retain control. She gripped the hand holding hers. 'Gerald, can you really find out what has happened to Simon? I need to know.'

'Oh, I expect so. Yes, of course. I will ask my friends. They should know by now.' The old arrogance came back to his face. 'They were so stupid, you know, Simon and the Welshman, to set out like that, expecting that my so-called brother could guide them to Tientsin.'

'What do you mean, your "so-called-brother"? Surely, he *is* your brother, even though he is adopted?'

Gerald shook his head vigorously. 'No, he is not. He is just the son of some backward peasants that were killed. My parents took him in. He is *really stupid*, with his affected accent and silly British words. He tries to be what he is not. He should be proud to be Chinese. There is no need for him to ape the British. It is preposterous. And he is so young.'

223

His mouth turned down in contempt. 'He is the last person to guide anyone to Tientsin, let alone conduct them through the Chinese army. He is just a silly, young boy.'

Alice felt that she could not stand very much more of this. How sure could he be that Simon was dead? He did not sound altogether convinced. But she must not let her emotions take over. She must continue to indulge him, however odious the task. She pressed his hand and then withdrew her own.

'Well, thank you, Gerald. Yes, please do find out what you can about Simon.' She let her voice then assume a tone of admiration and wonder. 'It sounds as though you go freely into the Chinese lines. How on earth do you do that? It must be extremely difficult.'

He seized her hand again. 'Oh no. It's not all that difficult, if you know what I know. People do it all the time. There is a secret place that is used for smuggling. I will show you, if you like.'

'Oh yes. Please do.'

Gerald then had a moment of doubt. 'Well, I will, of course. But you must not tell anyone. Will you promise me that?'

'Of course.'

'Very well. We could go tonight. I could introduce you to some of my friends, if you like.'

'Yes, please do. That would be most interesting.'

He looked around him. He had suddenly become a furtive adventurer. 'We had better make it after dark. Shall we meet here an hour after nightfall?'

'Good, I shall be here.'

'So will I.' He now adopted a proprietorial air. 'You will see and hear things tonight that will interest you greatly. I promise.'

Alice freed her hand and stood. 'Thank you, Gerald. Until tonight, then.'

His eyes were glowing as he answered, 'Until tonight, then, cousin.'

Walking away, Alice thought of her husband. Was he dead? She tossed her head defiantly. Of course not! Simon Fonthill was indestructible. But she wished – oh, how she wished! – that he was here to deal with this odious young man, *her own cousin*!

CHAPTER TEN

Within fifteen minutes of crossing those two hundred or so yards of no man's land and then climbing the bales of wool, silk, cotton and peanuts that formed the main part of the French line defending the settlements, Fonthill found himself sitting facing the senior British officer at Tientsin, Brigadier General Dorward. Jenkins and Chang had been ushered away to be given soup – alas, not onion, but thin gruel – and Simon, wrapped once again in his Kansu coat, was telling his story.

'Seymour is where, did you say?' barked the brigadier.

'Only about six miles from you, upriver. He is holed up in this great Chinese arsenal. He has plenty of supplies because he has captured them, but he is completely surrounded by Tung Fu-hsiang's forces, his command is severely depleted and he can't fight his way out. Can you relieve him?'

'My dear . . . what's your name again, sir?'

'Fonthill.'

The brigadier leant forward. 'My dear Fonthill, we are not in a position to relieve anyone.'

Simon blinked. 'But the siege of the settlements has been lifted, hasn't it? I saw the Kansus retreating. Haven't thousands of Russians arrived from the coast?'

'No bloody fear. Look. We only had two thousand four hundred men to start with – to defend a five-mile perimeter against a force that we estimate to be at least twenty thousand. More came in and then we managed to get a message through to Taku, a twelve-hour ride away, through country thick with Chinese troops. Bless 'em, they responded and scraped the barrel – or rather, the ships – to produce a mixed bag of Russians, Germans, Americans and a few British. They have fought every inch of the way and managed to get through this morning.'

He wiped a hand across his chin, scraping his whiskers. 'What this means, my dear fellow, is that we have not been *relieved*. We have been merely *reinforced*. Our defenders have been supplemented, thank God, but I can't see us breaking out of here to relieve anyone. These people surrounding us are not a bunch of Boxers. They are the Kansus, fierce fighters, as we have found out, and an organised army, well equipped with artillery.'

'But I saw the Kansus retreating.'

'Not retreating. Regrouping.'

A silence descended on the room to be broken, ominously, by the boom of Chinese cannon. Weary and hungry, Fonthill felt his heart sink. He had, it seemed, escaped from the frying pan into the fire. What hope for the Peking defenders now, with the military forces of the so-called Great Powers cooped up within rings of Chinese bayonets? He sighed.

'But Brigadier,' he said, his voice low, 'I have explained that the situation in Peking is becoming desperate. I don't know how long the people there can continue to defend the legations but it can't be long. We can't sit here and wait for them to be overwhelmed.'

The brigadier had the grace to look embarrassed. 'As a matter of fact,' he said, 'reports have come out from . . . Shanghai, I think it is, that they have already . . . er . . . capitulated. Mind you,' he hurried on, 'these are unsubstantiated.'

Fonthill put his brow in his hands. 'Oh my God. My wife is still there.'

'Ah, my dear chap.' Dorward put out his hand and touched Simon's arm. 'I am so sorry. Let me repeat that these are just rumours, and you know what China is like for rumours. Such a huge country with such poor communications. Almost sure to be rubbish.'

Simon looked up. 'Who is in command here?'

'Well . . . ah . . . nobody, really. That's the trouble, y'see. We are such a mixture. The Russians have got the most troops here but, theoretically, I suppose I am the senior officer. Look here, Fonthill. All is not lost. Let me talk to the senior chap amongst these new arrivals – Russian, almost certainly – and let us see if we can get a force to break out and get to this arsenal place. You are quite right, the effort should be made.'

'Thank you, Brigadier.'

'However,' Dorward mused for a moment. 'There is no way we could strike north for Peking without taking the Chinese City of Tientsin first. It's a walled city of about a million people and it completely dominates the way north. We estimate that it is defended by about twelve thousand Imperial troops, with something like ten thousand Boxer auxiliaries. All of which doesn't mean to say we can't knock 'em over. Now, could you lead us to this arsenal place, d'yer think?'

'Yes. Shouldn't be difficult. Skirt the Chinese City but follow the river. We wouldn't need an army but Seymour has plenty of wounded to move. We would want probably about a thousand troops who could move quickly, I would think, if you can spare 'em.'

'Hmm. Probably have to. We can't leave Seymour holed up. And we had better act quickly to take advantage of the fact that the Kansus are movin' about. Now, let's get you something to eat and wear.'

'Clothes for my two companions also, please, Brigadier.'

'Of course.'

Dorward acted with commendable speed. Early the next morning, Fonthill, Jenkins and Chang – the latter pair had refused to be left behind – set off at the head of a mixed force of men, most of them Russian, who streamed out of the settlements. The column was under the command of a Russian, Colonel Shirinsky, whose mounted Cossacks ranged ahead and either side of the infantry, who themselves marched in quick time. They were immediately opposed by a force of Imperial troops, but a determined charge by the

Cossack vanguard, wielding lance and sword, scattered the enemy. The column advanced at speed and with a sense of purpose that impressed Fonthill.

The Colonel took it in a swing away from the walls of Tientsin City and then back again to the river and soon they saw the huge redoubt that was the arsenal. With a sigh of relief, Simon saw that the white ensign of the British navy still fluttered high above the walls and he joined the squadron of Cossacks who, pennants flying from their lances, cantered up to the great wooden door.

Within moments, he was introducing a weary but relieved Seymour to the red-cheeked Russian colonel.

'Thank God you got through, Fonthill,' said Seymour, pumping his hand. 'Plain sailing, was it?'

'Oh absolutely, Admiral. Pleasure cruise, really.'

While the Cossacks ranged the surrounding country, now remarkably clear of the besieging Kansus, the remnants of the original relief column were gathered, carts were loaded with supplies and ammunition from the arsenal's stores, and the wounded who could not march were led out on stretchers.

The journey back was slower, of course, but the column was remarkably unhindered, whether because of the fearsome reputation already established by the Cossacks on their advance on the settlements, or because the bulk of the Imperial troops had retreated to bolster the defence of the Chinese City, Fonthill could not decide. He was merely grateful that the first stage in the long march to relieve Peking had been successfully concluded.

As he marched at the head of the column with Jenkins

and Chang, each of them arrayed in ill-fitting blue uniforms supplied by the Tientsin Office of Customs and carrying army issue rifles, his mind concentrated on the task ahead. How could he, a comparatively unknown civilian, move the massive diplomatic bureaucracy that surrounded the Allied army in the settlements to address the question of relieving Peking? Without a central point of control and chain of command to work with, how could he instil urgency and give focus to this loose collection of fighting men? Well, he shrugged, a start had been made, anyway.

It seemed almost as though the forces besieging the settlements had deliberately parted to let the Seymour remnants back within the barricades, for, the day after their return, the Chinese closed in again and launched a series of attacks along the perimeter. For more than two weeks the defenders fought savagely, encouraged by the new reserves of ammunition provided by Seymour's men and the fact that new men had arrived to reinforce those manning the low mud walls and bales of merchandise that formed the perimeter.

It was a hugely frustrating time for Fonthill, who, with Jenkins and Chang, took his turn at the barricades.

'This is a bit of a – whatchercall it – stalepiece, ain'it?' observed Jenkins, wiping his brow with a piece of fine silk that protruded from the bale over which he was firing.

'No, I think the word is "stalemate", is it not, cousin?' asked Chang. 'They can't get in and we cannot get out. It is not exactly checkmate, you see, Mr Jenkins, because either side can actually move, so—'

'Whatever it is,' growled Fonthill, 'I've had enough. I'm going to see Dorward.'

That evening he bearded the brigadier. Simon presented once more Sir Claude's message, with its plea for urgent action. The soldier nodded.

'There has been action, of a sort,' he said. 'We have formed a sort of council here, representing all of the powers involved, and I have informed them of your message. I should add that Lieutenant General Sir Alfred Gaselee, a most distinguished British soldier, is due to land at Taku any day, I understand, to take charge of troops here. At the moment, the trouble is that we have not been able to agree on an immediate course of action, when we have been under such pressure from the Chinese besieging us. But, look here.' He leant across his desk. 'There is a meeting tonight. Please come and present Sir Claude's message yourself. That should stimulate something.'

'Very well,' said Fonthill. 'But I warn you, I shall speak candidly.'

It was, felt Simon, a strange meeting. To a background of artillery fire, like a continuous and not-so-distant drum roll, eight men filed in to sit around Dorward's large table: Dorward and Seymour, two Russians, a Frenchman, an American, a German and a tiny Japanese, each dressed in the uniform of his country. With the exception of the Japanese, every man was bearded and each face reflected the strain of battle. Fonthill had dreaded that the language used would be French, the tongue of diplomacy, but everyone agreed to speak English. He had also feared that there would be a long agenda to get through before he was allowed to speak, but he was called upon to address the meeting immediately. Most of them, he reflected with satisfaction, were men of action, after all.

Dorward introduced him and gave a brief summary of how he and his two companions had arrived at Tientsin. Then Simon began.

'Gentlemen,' he said, looking round at the heavy, jowled faces, 'you have more than ten thousand men here, with the promise of more to come from the coast. You are fighting a defensive battle to protect the settlements. You have been able to evacuate most of the women and children of the settlements to Taku. You are fighting stoutly and you have been given fresh ammunition and supplies from Admiral Seymour's column. With the exception of the quick expedition to the arsenal, however, you have not moved from behind your barricades. It is time you did so.'

There was a sharp intake of breath, but he continued.

'I left Peking just over two weeks ago, getting here, as you have heard, with some difficulty. I did so because I was asked to bear a message from Sir Claude MacDonald, the British minister there, desperately pleading for help from you.' He looked around the table at each man in turn and then went on, emphasising his words.

'There are approximately two thousand civilians, including women and children and most of them Chinese, crowded into the legations there, sheltering, as you are here, behind makeshift barricades and walls. The difference is, though, that when I left, there were only some three hundred able-bodied men defending those walls. The little hospital there is full, the defenders are running low on ammunition and are reduced to half rations. The water they drink is warm and brackish. The enemy surrounding them is well armed and equipped with modern artillery. If they wished, they could reduce the whole Quarter to rubble with their cannon, but for some reason they do not do so, probably fearing the retribution that would fall on them from the Great Powers – that means from *you*, gentlemen.

'For weeks now, the defenders there – led by the formal representatives of your countries – have looked to you for relief. Their situation is rapidly becoming desperate. Whatever the circumstances here, you must set up a second relief column without delay. If you don't and if the Chinese break through and pour into the Legations, then the watching, civilised world will condemn you accordingly.

'It will take time to advance to Peking, through hostile country and without the service of the railway. But it can be done, following the river northwards. There is no time to be lost. You must break out of here *now*.'

He finished and sat back amidst heavy silence. Then the German, a large man with kindly eyes, spoke. 'Ve cannot move vizout taking the Chinese City. To leave vizout taking it vould leave the settlements at zeir mercy.'

The Frenchman shrugged his shoulders. 'It is a 'uge fortress. Do we 'ave the men to conquer it? Those big walls . . . ?'

The question hung in the air. 'Who would command the expedition?' enquired one of the two Russians.

'There must be a unified command,' declared Dorward. 'I suggest the country which provides the most men should provide the commander. And that,' he gave a deferential half-bow to the Russian, 'would be you, Admiral.'

'Ach no,' said the Russian, with a quick glance towards the silent Seymour, 'we need a soldier this time. You are the senior army man here, Dorward. You do it. You will have the Russian support.'

There was a low murmur of agreement around the table. Fonthill felt ambivalent. At least they had agreed to do *something*, but he had seen the size of the fortress that was Tientsin City. To break through those walls would need a serious besieging force. Could the besieged suddenly become the besiegers? How would they do it? But Dorward was speaking again.

'Very well, gentlemen, I am gratified to have your confidence. I take it that we are all agreed that we must take Tientsin City before we can think of mounting an expedition for the north?'

There were nods of agreement from around the table.

'Thank you. I will begin making a plan of attack immediately. Could each of you let me have, within the hour, a note of the forces you could provide for the attack? We must not, of course, leave the settlements unprotected and I suggest that, say, five thousand good men will be all that is needed. If we are to strike, we should do so quickly. There can be no suggestion of laying siege to the city. We must make a concentrated breakout which will turn into sudden, frontal attack on the gates. Let us meet again at eight tomorrow morning, when I shall present my plan to you.'

With that, the delegates stood, nodded to each other cordially, like city councillors breaking up after a municipal meeting, and departed, as the cannon still crackled in the background.

'Thank you, Brigadier,' said Fonthill. 'I hope to God you can take the city, for failure means that the legations must surely fall. Will five thousand be enough, do you think?'

Dorward tugged at his beard and smiled. 'Oh, I believe so. I have changed my mind. With the reinforcements we have received within the last few weeks and the way we have been able to repulse the attacks on the line in the last fortnight, I am convinced now that we can break out. Like a huge sortie, in fact. The city is just a couple of miles away and we can be upon it before the Chinese have had chance to prepare themselves. We now have some excellent men here in whom I have faith. You spoke well there, Fonthill. You persuaded us all.'

'Thank you. May Jenkins and I join in the attack? We don't want to kick our heels here.'

'Of course.'

Fonthill overruled Chang's protestations at being left behind – 'You are only sixteen, dammit, and although you have behaved magnificently in helping us to get here, you are not a soldier and this will be infantry work' – and he and Jenkins fell in with the 2nd Battalion of the Royal Welch Fusiliers, both of them delighted to be reunited with a Welsh regiment after so many years.

* * *

The attack took place on the second day after the meeting of the military leaders and, initially, the breakout went impeccably according to plan. Simon and Jenkins were with the British and French, held in reserve to the Japanese and Americans who led the attack, which was launched towards the South Gate in the walls, while units of Russians and Germans harassed Chinese positions on the north bank of the river.

The Japanese broke cleanly through the Chinese lines around the settlements, scattering the Kansus in their path and making Fonthill feel that a breakout could have been achieved long before this. The little men trotted along impassively behind their long bayonets, making for the South Gate, which faced the settlements.

The city, in effect, was one large box, formed by its stout walls, and with one gate on each of its sides. Without siege artillery, there was no way that the attackers could breach the walls of the city and the attack was therefore concentrated completely on the South Gate. The fault in this tactic, however, soon presented itself. The only way to reach the gate was by advancing along a causeway that ran in a straight line for approximately a mile, spanning open country crossed with canals, patches of marshy bog, irrigation channels and lagoons. The Japanese leading the attack, therefore, presented an easy target to the defenders firing down from the top of the walls. It was even worse for the 9th United States Infantry, newly arrived from fighting the guerrillas in the Philippines, who had to wade through the marshes to the right of the causeway.

Fonthill shook his head. 'Dorward is an idiot,' he said. 'This is just offering men up for slaughter. He should have attacked at night, targeting at least two of the gates. God help those Japanese.'

'Amen,' muttered Jenkins. 'To be honest, bach sir, I've never 'ad much faith in British generals, look you. What with Ishywander and all that lot in Zululand.'

'The man must never have commanded in battle in his life – he must have been stuck out here throughout his career. He's made an elementary mistake. We could be bogged down here for weeks before we get a chance to march on Peking. Damn and blast the bloody fool!'

As they watched, the fire from the ramparts of the city walls intensified and the Japanese began dropping like flies. To compound the matter, the Americans, struggling in the marshes, began moving to their left to find firmer ground on the causeway. Orders were shouted and the British and French began moving up behind the lead troops, deploying as best they could to deliver supporting fire upon the Chinese on the walls.

Fonthill and Jenkins were among the latter, crouching in the long marsh grass, attempting to target the distant and diminutive figures behind the puffs of smoke, high on the walls. The sun beat down and the humidity, intensified by the moisture engendered by the dykes and irrigation channels surrounding them, caused the perspiration to course down their foreheads and into their eyes. Their discomfort was compounded by the flies that rose from the marsh and settled on them like black snowflakes. They spent as much time beating them off as aiming and firing their rifles.

And so the day wore on, with the Japanese and Americans retreating in the face of the strong defensive fire and then surging ahead intermittently, only to fall back again.

As dusk approached, Simon met a sweating Dorward. 'Do you have any artillery you can bring to bear, Brigadier?' he asked.

'Only a couple of eighteen-pounders that we could ill spare from the defences of the settlements. Can't get 'em near enough to make a difference.'

'May I make a suggestion, sir?'

The two men eyed each other. They were roughly the same age and they might have been from similar backgrounds, except that Fonthill had formally left the army twenty years ago and Dorward, of course, had ploughed his way upwards through the officer ranks, albeit mostly in the Far East.

'You can suggest what you like, Fonthill. But may I enquire about your experience in situations such as this?'

'Of course you may. I served with the 24th of Foot and was at Isandlwana and Rorke's Drift in the Zulu affair. I did intelligence work with Roberts in Afghanistan and was in Kabul when the Residency was attacked. I was able to help Wolseley with his attack on the bePedi at Sekukuni and then at el-Kebir in Egypt. I commanded a couple of riverboats for Gordon at Khartoum, not that that did him much—'

Dorward held up his hand. 'Good Lord! Now I know who you are, Fonthill. You're the chap who got through to Gordon at Khartoum and was with Rhodes on the invasion of Matabeleland.'

Fonthill grinned. 'Well Rhodes wasn't exactly there, you

know. He had a habit of turning up after the fighting was over.'

'Yes, well even so.' Dorward mopped his face with his handkerchief. 'I certainly accept your experience. Frankly, I am not sure what to do next. The Japs and the Yankees have taken a terrible beating. I've lost something like seven hundred men.'

'Yes. This looks a tough nut to crack. If I may say so, I think a frontal attack in daylight is ill-advised.'

'So. What do you suggest?'

'Wait until it is completely dark. Then, get the Germans and Russians to make a fuss, as though we're going to attack the North Gate. Have you got any sappers with you?'

'Yes.'

'And dynamite, too?'

'Well, I believe so.'

'Good. Make a big thing about retreating back down the causeway now, in the failing light. I think the Japanese and the Americans are probably a bit spent, by the look of it, so let them fall back. Then bring up the Welch Regiment quietly but hold them back. Give me enough dynamite to blow that bloody big South Gate open, then attack along the causeway with the Welshmen – they're damned good soldiers but they'll have to run fast – and break through what's left of the gate.'

'What? You would plant the explosives?'

'Yes. Well, I would take my man Jenkins with me to complete the job in case I get knocked over. It needs two men. Any more would probably be spotted, even in the dark. I do think it's the best plan, Brigadier.'

'Very well. Come with me and we'll talk to the sapper major.'

Simon explained the plan to the major, who listened, nodded and produced ten sticks of dynamite, wrapped innocuously in paper in two packets of five, each eight inches long and about one inch in diameter.

The major, a short, stout man with impressive moustaches, was pompously proprietorial about his explosives. 'Look here,' he said, 'this stuff is extremely dangerous.'

'Well,' muttered Jenkins, who had come along to be briefed, 'I suppose it would be, wouldn't it, if it's goin' to blow somethin' up, like.'

The sapper ignored him. 'These sticks,' he continued, 'are made of three parts nitroglycerine and one part diatomaceous earth, or fossilised microscopic algae, with a small addition of sodium carbonate. The point about the earth is that it makes the nitroglycerine less shock sensitive, but the sticks are still extremely volatile and have to be handled with great care. For God's sake don't drop 'em on the way, otherwise the sticks will be completely wasted – and they are hugely expensive, don't you know.'

Fonthill glared at Jenkins to prevent him from uttering the sarcastic put-down that was on his lips and asked instead: 'From what I can see of these gates, they are extremely thick and about twelve feet high. Will this stuff do the job?'

'Oh yes. Knock 'em down easily. Look. They should be detonated by using these two blasting caps fired by two long fuses, creating small explosions, triggering the larger ones.'

'Where exactly should we put the sticks?'

'Well, ideally, one group at the bottom and one about

halfway up. But I don't suppose you will be able to knock nails in the gate, will you?'

'Doubt it.'

'Put them at the bottom, then, where the two gates meet. Any questions?'

'How long do we have after lighting the fuses?'

'Say thirty to forty seconds. Ensure they don't fizzle out, mind.'

'Oh we will. We will. Thank you, Major.'

'Right.' The brigadier turned back to Fonthill and Jenkins. 'I reckon you've got about an hour between now and when the moon comes up. Is there anything I can do for you before you go?'

'No, thank you. Just make sure that the Welshmen come in at the run when the balloon goes up. We don't want to give the Chinese time to shore up the gate again.'

'Of course. Forgive me now if I go and arrange things. Thank you both, and good luck.'

Fonthill gingerly deposited the dynamite in a small hessian sack and they both walked to where the men of the Welch Regiment were resting.

'Now, let me get this clear,' said Jenkins. 'When it gets really dark we just saunter up this causeway thing, steppin' over the bodies that are litterin' the place, like, an' we just pop this dynamite stuff at the bottom of the gates, ring the bell an' run away. Is that it?'

'Roughly right, old chap. I realise I've rather landed you in on this one, and I shall quite understand if you feel it's rather asking too much.'

242

'No, bach sir, thank you very much. I'm supposed to be lookin' after you on this postin', 'cos I promised Miss Alice, so I'll be goin' with you. I'll come just to make sure you don't drop the stuff and make that bloody little major shit 'is breeches about the cost of it an' all.'

'Don't be disrespectful about the major. He holds the Queen's Commission. Right. We'll take our rifles because we don't want to be left unarmed when the gates go down. But we'll sling 'em over our backs. Try and find us a pair of plimsolls, if you can in the time we have left. We want to move quietly – and run fast, if we have to. Off you go.'

Simon sat down and looked ahead of him. In the gathering dusk the walls of the Chinese City loomed high and impenetrable. Would the Chinese have a searchlight? They would be in trouble if they did. On reflection – and he gave a wry grin – they would probably be in trouble even if they didn't. This was a ridiculous enterprise. Everything depended upon the defenders relaxing their vigilance, having given the Japanese and the Americans a good hiding and despatching them, or so it seemed, back to the settlements; that and their attention being diverted by the faux attack on the North Gate.

Then he and Jenkins must get enough cover in the darkness to steal up to the South Gate, literally under the noses of the guards on the walls. Ah well. It seemed the only way to persuade these stuffy old armchair generals in the settlements to stir themselves for the real battle – in Peking. He thought again of Alice. He had no illusions. If the Chinese did break

243

through to the legations, then she would stand little chance, despite the protection offered by Sir Claude. He offered up a quick prayer for her safety and then settled back to wait for Jenkins, his mouth dry, despite the heat and humidity.

The Welshman arrived, well within the hour, bringing two bayonets in scabbards, and two pairs of unlaced canvas running shoes. 'Didn't know about your size. Bigger than mine, I thought, 'cos I've got dainty little feet. 'Ere, try them on.'

'Oh, they'll do. Now. We will begin walking along the causeway at first, then, when we get nearer, I'm afraid we shall have to take to the marsh on the side of the road. The long grasses there should provide us with a bit of cover. Once we hear the sound of the diversion from the French and Russian lines, we will edge nearer and then make a run for it along the causeway. Keep the bayonets sheathed in case they flash a reflection when the moon comes up.'

'Matches?' enquired Jenkins.

Fonthill threw back his head. 'Oh, blast and damn!'

The grinning Welshman held up two boxes. 'Oh, dearie me. I 'ave to think of everythin'.'

Simon thumped him in the chest, pocketed one of the boxes, shouldered the hessian bag to hang down his back the other side to his slung rifle, then offered his hand to Jenkins. 'Good luck, old friend,' he said.

'Good luck, bach sir.'

Together, they began their walk in the darkness. The sun to the west had not long before slipped over the horizon, leaving a slight glow in the sky. But the moon had not yet risen and they made good time on the paved way, while they could. Then, to the north they heard the crackle of musketry and distant shouting.

Fonthill kept his eyes on the black walls ahead of him, dreading the sudden brilliance of a searchlight cracking open the darkness. They were now, he estimated, about a quarter of a mile from the gate.

'Time to get off the causeway,' he hissed to Jenkins. Immediately, their progress slowed as, shoulders bowed, they trudged through spongy grass and mud and then picked their way delicately through the shallow waters of the irrigation channels, stopping occasionally to freeze and listen to ensure that the Chinese had not sent out picquets to prevent just such a surprise attack. It took them more than an hour to cover most of that quarter of a mile and they were within the shadow cast by the city walls as the moon rose behind them.

The two men crouched together while Fonthill gave Jenkins his five sticks of dynamite. 'When I give the order,' he whispered, 'you run up to the right-hand side of the gate, and flatten yourself to the wall. I will do the same on the other side. When I nod, crawl up to the gate, put the dynamite as close to the door as you can, where it meets the other door. I will do the same. Trail out the fuse your way, the way you came, and I'll do the same. When I nod, light it.'

'What do we do then? Run like hell back down the road?'

'Absolutely not. It would be easy to pick us off, if they've got their wits about them. No. We flatten on the ground, as near to the wall and as far away from the bloody gates as possible. Hands over heads and just hope that the damned walls don't fall down on top of us.'

'Very good, bach sir.'

Simon took a deep breath. He could see no sign of movement on the battlements. 'Right. Off we go and good luck.'

The two men regained the causeway and, bent double, they ran towards the massive gate looming before them. Out in the open and feeling completely exposed, Fonthill realised that they were demanding a lot from Dame Fortune, if they were to reach the wall without being seen. And so it proved.

He heard a cry from up above him and then the sharp crack of a rifle. The bullet hit the paved road and pinged away, but by the time the second bullet was released, he was up against the wall, safely underneath a large stone overhang that ran all the way along, just beneath the embrasures, so preventing anyone manning the top from firing down vertically. 'Are you there, 352?' he called.

'I'm 'ere. To the gates now?'

'Fast as you can.'

The two men ran and met at the foot of the huge pair of gates. Simon placed his bundle of deadly sticks, almost touching those of Jenkins. Behind the door, the two men could hear voices shouting and the sound of running feet. Fonthill looked up and saw that there was a small post gate, set into the massive door. He unslung his rifle.

'Light your fuse and run,' he shouted.

''Ere. What are you goin' to do?'

'Never mind. Light the bloody thing.'

Throwing his rifle on the ground, Simon fumbled with a match, struck it, lit the fuse and then ran back, unwinding the fuse as it fizzed and crackled. Then he doubled back, picked up his rifle, just in time to see the post gate open. Firing from the hip, he brought down the first man to run through the gate, worked the breech bolt, fired into the open doorway, then ran back alongside the wall, hurling himself to the ground as the night exploded with a mighty boom and a thousand flashing lights that penetrated through his spread fingers. Debris, some of it blazing, rained down on him, for he had not made the comparative sanctity of the base of the wall. Then there was a great crash as the two doors forming the gate crumpled outward, shaking the ground where he lay. He became aware of a burning sensation across his leg and kicked away at a flaming ember that lay across it. His ears were singing but he could hear a faint cheer coming from far, far away, as he lapsed into unconsciousness.

He came to to find himself lying half in an irrigation channel close to the wall. Jenkins was splashing water onto his face.

'Are you all right, bach? Ah, thank God. I thought you'd gone for a minute. You were half on fire when I got to you.'

Fonthill raised his head and realised that heavy boots were pounding up along the causeway by his head as the Welch Regiment ran towards the open gateway. Cheering came from their rear but there was firing from within the city.

'Ah, thanks, 352,' he said. 'I feel a bit warm and my head's singing, but I think the fire's out. Are you all right?'

'Right as ninepence. Blimey, but you were barmy to go back to fire into that doorway. Bloody barmy, if you don't mind me sayin' so. You almost went up with the gates.'

Simon sat up and shook his head but the singing in his ears continued. 'Had to do that,' he shouted. 'Otherwise those fellers would have been through and been able to stamp out the fuses. I should have realised that there would be a post gate. Must be losing my touch. Here, help me up. I'm all right now.'

Together the two men stood, swaying slightly as the British infantrymen charged by them, their rifles and bayonets at the ready.

From within the city the firing was now muted, although screams could be heard.

Jenkins sniffed. 'I don't think there's much quarter bein' given by them Taffies,' he said, 'after bein' cooped up for so long in them settlements. An' they've 'eard what them Boxers 'ave done to the missionaries an' their families. They'll be goin' in with the bayonets, all right.'

'Let's get back,' said Fonthill. 'I don't think I'll be much good charging in there with them. My head is still singing.'

Together, the two comrades walked through the advancing troops – the French were moving in now, behind the Welch Regiment – along the causeway and back to the settlements, where Jenkins found a doctor to examine Fonthill. His face was blackened and what was left of his Customs uniform singed and burnt, but he was found to have sustained only superficial burns and was put to bed with a soothing pill.

The next morning, he was visited by Dorward, who

248

gingerly shook his bandaged hand. 'Congratulations, my dear fellow,' he said. 'You did a wonderful job. We stormed into the city and took it within the hour. Both the Chinese Imperial troops and the Boxers fled, streaming through the East and West Gates, those that weren't bayoneted. I fear that there was quite a bit of looting, but that can't always be helped in these conditions. Anyway, everyone here is very grateful to you.'

Fonthill waved his bandaged hand. 'Glad it worked, Brigadier. I thought for a terrible minute that we had blown it – no pun intended, you know.'

'No. The gates caved in beautifully and my sapper chap is going around saying it's all his work.' He grinned. 'And there's more good news.'

'What's that?'

'Lieutenant General Sir Alfred Gaselee has arrived from the coast with God knows how many troops.'

Fonthill's eyes lit up and he pushed himself into a half-sitting position. 'Ah, that's the best news I've heard. Now, when do you think we could put together a column and march to the north, eh?'

Dorward frowned. 'Oh, my dear fellow, not for some time yet. We have got to occupy the city and sort things out here first. Can't leave the settlements denuded. It may take some weeks yet, I fear.'

Fonthill groaned and sank his head back onto the pillow.

CHAPTER ELEVEN

Alice Fonthill dressed for that evening meeting with Gerald Griffith with as much care as she had displayed for that 'chance' meeting earlier in the day. No cosmetics this time, however. Despite the heat, which never slackened until long after the sun had gone down, she wore riding breeches, her long boots, a soiled cotton shirt, a bandana round her waist and her hair tied back severely with a scarf. From a box under her bed she retrieved the small French automatic pistol and six cartridges, which she inserted into the magazine. Then she tucked the gun into her bandana and sat on the bed, deep in thought.

What exactly was she hoping that this meeting with Gerald and his friends would reveal? Well, the first priority was to try and learn something about the whereabouts of Simon, Jenkins and Chang. She frowned. It was, of course, preposterous to think that the trio might be dead. Simon's whole life had consisted of getting into scrapes and getting out of them again. It was inconceivable to think that his time had come at last; he had so much . . . so much . . . *life* left in him. And there was 352 Jenkins with him, the Great Protector. She allowed herself a smile. No. Even if they told her that Simon was dead, then they would have to provide proof before she believed them.

Alice had to admit that the original, underlying reason why she had agreed to this assignation was to probe beneath that cool, self-satisfied demeanour of her cousin. She had learnt much already this afternoon, but the key question of whether he was an active spy, working within the Quarter for the Chinese, remained unanswered. And, if it proved that he was relaying vital information to the Manchu court, what would she do about it? She tossed her head. She would hand him over to Sir Claude, without compunction. Anyone who betrayed the defenders in their sad predicament deserved to be shot – or placed in prison. The punishment would be the minister's decision.

But what about her aunt? She had lost her husband, was she now about to lose her son – and possibly her adopted son also?

Alice put her head in her hand. Despite her great inner strength, that would surely be too much for the little widow to bear. And yet – she looked up and stared unseeingly at the wall of the room – what if Gerald had deliberately told the Chinese of Simon's mission and what if this had led to his death? She thought for a moment and then stood. It was now quite dark outside and time to go. She would face all of these questions later, if she had to.

Gerald was waiting for her, crouched by the side of the hospital from the interior of which came faint groans.

'You are late, cousin,' he said.

'I am sorry. I had things to do.'

He stood before her and seized both her hands. 'Now Alice, will you promise that you will tell no one of where we go tonight and of what you learn?'

She thought quickly, for she had already been forced to give one promise and she did not wish to compound the lie. 'Oh, come now, Gerald. You are making all this sound as though we are about to embark on a sequence from the *Arabian Nights*. You are fantasising. Or are you engaged in some enterprise which will make your mother and I ashamed of you?'

The ploy worked, for Gerald coloured and avoided her eye. 'Well,' he muttered, 'these are dangerous times, cousin, and the wrong word here or there could get us all into trouble.'

'Let us get on with it, then.' She disengaged her hands. 'Where are you taking me?'

'You will soon see. Follow me.'

They walked through to the entrance of the British Legation. The sentry there, who was used to her coming to and fro during the day, looked concerned. 'Don't go far, Mrs . . . er . . . The snipers still shoot at night, you know.'

'Just going for a little walk with my cousin, Corporal. We will be careful.'

They made their way down by the canal, past the Russian Legation, picked their way between the rubble in Legation Street and crossed to where the American Legation still stood, proudly forming the southernmost point of the defences, just underneath the Tartar Wall at the section of the wall still defended on the top by the Americans and Germans. Here Gerald turned left, crossing the little bridge over the canal, to a point just past the sluice gates in the wall. There, he put his finger to his lips, pulled back some large pieces of stone and beckoned her towards him.

'Climb over,' he whispered. 'Don't make a noise or we could be shot at by the Chinese on the wall above.'

On hands and knees, Alice scrambled over the stones to find a low opening in the great wall. A drainage pipe emerged from the ground under her feet and ran forwards into the darkness of the tunnel. She realised that it was what was left of some kind of service tunnel, only about four feet high, and running ahead into complete darkness. She waited nervously while Gerald replaced the stones, leaving them so that a chink of light shone through. He seized her hand.

'It's all right,' he said. 'Just keep stepping either side of the pipe. It's quite level. I'll go first. Keep holding my hand.'

She did so, until he paused and fumbled in the dark. With a creak, a small, wooden door opened and Alice realised that she was standing in the street on the other side of the Tartar Wall. She withdrew in consternation, for she was now outside the perimeter of the defences. But Gerald pulled her forward and they crossed the street to a house opposite, whose door stood slightly ajar.

Gerald knocked on it, pushed it open and called softly inside. He was answered in Chinese and a further door opened to reveal a room lit by several Oriental lamps. It was furnished severely in Chinese style, with tapestries and several vertical banners, decorated with Chinese symbols, covering the walls. At one end there was a kind of shrine, with candles burning at it, and also a highly coloured photograph of the Dowager Empress. Ceremonial Chinese swords, sheathed in ornamental scabbards, hung from the walls. A large wall map of the Chinese Empire caught her eye and, underneath it, what she immediately recognised as a map of the Legation Quarter. Everywhere, there were the red sashes and scarves of the Boxers – flung over chairs, hanging from pegs in the doors and lying loosely on the central table.

'Oh my God,' thought Alice. This must be the headquarters, the very heart of the Boxer movement.

Four men immediately rose to their feet as they entered. They were dressed seemingly identically in nondescript, loose-fitting garments – uniforms perhaps? – with black skullcaps, and all seemed middle-aged (Alice still found it difficult to tell the age of Chinamen). They bowed to her and Alice and Gerald bowed in return.

Then Gerald spoke quickly to them in Chinese and Alice sensed that she was being introduced. Was there an acerbic note in the response of the oldest man, who seemed to be the senior of the group? He wore a single gold epaulette and Alice noted that his hands were beautifully manicured. She caught a glimpse of silver hair swept back under the skullcap. Gerald bowed to him again and then turned to Alice.

'This is General Kuang Li, the chief of staff to General Jung Lu, who commands the Imperial army in Peking, and these gentlemen,' he waved his arm, 'are senior members of the army.' Gerald looked crestfallen. 'I am afraid that the General has rebuked me for bringing you here.'

Kuang Li bowed again to Alice and then addressed her in almost accentless English. 'Yes, Mrs Fonthill, I am afraid that Mr Griffith has compromised us and, indeed, you, by bringing you here. But, nevertheless, let me welcome you.'

'I am sorry, sir,' replied Alice, 'but I had no idea where my cousin was bringing me. If you wish, I will leave immediately.'

'Ah.' The smile on Kuang Li's lips did not reach his eyes. 'I am afraid that will not be possible – at least, not yet. Since you are here perhaps you can be of use to us. I should add,' he inclined his head towards her, 'that you are in no danger here. Would you care for some tea?'

Alice's brain whirled. The threat was clear. Gerald, the vain oaf, had blundered by bringing her here and they clearly had no intention of letting her go until she had helped them in some way. At least they obviously were not Boxers and their manners were those of cultivated Chinese. So what could they want of her?

She cleared her throat. 'I should make it clear to you, sir, that I cannot, under any circumstances, reveal details of the defences of the Legation Quarter.'

'No.' The little half-bow came again and Kuang Li shot a quick glance across at Gerald. 'I would not expect that of you, madam, nor do we need it. We have very good sources of that nature already, I assure you. No. But perhaps you can be of service to us – and, indeed, yourself, in other ways. But first . . . ah . . . do excuse me.'

He reached towards Alice and she took an involuntary step backwards.

He put out a placatory hand. 'No, if I may . . .' And, very slowly, he reached towards her cummerbund. He gently pulled down the top of it and inserted two long fingers inside it, pulling out her automatic pistol. Then, he expertly opened the magazine in the butt, shook out the six cartridges, snapped shut the magazine and, with a courteous bow, offered the pistol back to her.

'Forgive my . . . ah . . . clumsiness, but we have no weapons here.' He gestured to the swords on the wall. 'These are just ceremonial trappings. Better that we speak without the thought of force, in any way. To repeat, madam, you are quite safe here. Now, won't you please sit down and take tea with us.'

Alice blushed and slipped back the pistol into her cummerbund. What an astute old rascal! 'Very well,' she said. 'Thank you.'

She sat at the table, which was rapidly cleared of the Boxer sashes. Tea was brought quickly. Fine, delicately scented tea, served without milk or sugar, the like of which Alice had not tasted since first they had landed at Tientsin. She sipped it gratefully and looked across at Gerald. No place was made at the table for him and he remained standing, drinking his tea.

Alice decided to take the initiative. 'My cousin,' she explained, 'gave me to understand that you might be able to give me news of my husband and his two companions, who recently left the Quarter for Tientsin. I would be grateful to know anything you can tell me about them.'

The General turned and spoke to his colleagues. A conversation ensued and Alice waited, her heart in her mouth. What would they say – and, whatever it was, would it be the truth? She stole a quick glance at Gerald, who was following the conversation with wide eyes.

He caught her glance and had the grace to look uncomfortable.

At last Kuang Li turned back to her. 'I shall tell you what we know,' he said, and she had the sudden and firm conviction that what he would tell her would be the truth.

'We know of your husband, of course, madam. He led the attack on our cannon on the Chien Men and he is clearly a . . .' He hesitated, obviously searching in his English vocabulary for the right phrase. 'I think you would call him a "doughty" warrior.' He smiled, happy that he had found the correct expression. 'Because of information given to us – but a fraction too late – we nearly cut him off on his return, but he broke through our men and was able to make his way back to the Legation Quarter.'

Alice frowned in impatience. She did not want flowery compliments – this was so Chinese, she thought – but only the truth about Simon. For God's sake, was he still alive?

The General continued. 'We also knew about his mission to Tientsin – again a little too late. So we were unable to prevent him leaving the city but we did send three horsemen after him to apprehend him and bring him back here. But, alas,' he held out his hands, almost in supplication, 'these men seem to have disappeared.

'The next we heard of this remarkable man, Mr Fonthill, is that he and his companions were fished out of the river above the Tientsin settlements by Kansu soldiers – very much alive, I hasten to add – and they were all brought before our distinguished colleague, General Tung Fu-hsiang and interrogated.'

Alice winced at the word, but Kuang Li went on. 'Then, a most remarkable thing happened. The general, who, what shall I say, has a reputation for the most intense questioning of prisoners he takes, let them go! We do not know why – he is not the sort of man one questions about these things. But he did so and, madam, your husband and his two companions seem to have, ah, disappeared. That is all I can tell you.'

Then he bowed to her across the table.

Alice felt a flush of exhilaration flow through her and she had to look down at her teacup for a moment to hide her feelings. Then she inclined her head in return. 'Thank you, sir. I am grateful for the information and for your courtesy.'

'Now,' said Kuang Li, 'may we ask something of you in return, now that,' he paused and looked across at Gerald, 'you have strayed into our house?'

'I will help you all I can, short of betraying the defenders of the legations,' said Alice firmly.

'We will not ask that of you. Now.' He leant back and put the tips of his fingers together. 'I am told that there is some puzzlement in the Quarter about why we do not unleash on you the full force of the artillery we have at our disposal.'

He gave a wan smile. 'We were annoyed that your husband put our two Krupp guns out of commission but not seriously inconvenienced by his action. We have much more artillery, you see, and it is quite within our power to reduce all the legations to rubble if we so wish.'

Alice remembered Simon telling her that the Chinese had other large guns and plenty of ammunition that they did not bring into play.

'Why, then, do you not do so?' she asked.

'Ah yes. Why indeed? To give you the answer, I fear that I must now take you into the labyrinth that is Chinese politics.' The fingertips came together again and Alice formed the impression that the old man was rather enjoying himself. 'You see, despite what you see here,' and he gestured towards the Boxer scarves bestrewn around the room, 'we are not all supporters of these peasant militants. There are people within the Manchu court who have attempted to persuade the Dowager Empress that it was foolhardy and even dangerous to back these uprisings.'

He opened a small, lacquered box and, with the utmost delicacy, took a pinch of snuff, which he placed into each nostril before he continued.

'Unfortunately, these people at present do not have the ear of Her Divine Majesty. For instance, although my master, General Jung Lu, is formally in command of the Imperial army, General Tung Fu-hsiang, from the north, he who commands the Kansus, has great influence. And he bitterly hates all foreigners and wishes to destroy them. It is he who is commanding the troops that are fighting the Foreign Powers around Tientsin.'

Alice adopted a puzzled frown. 'If General Tung Fu-hsiang has the power, then why does he not shell the legations?'

'Because he does not have *all* the power. So far, General Jung Lu has been able to persuade the Empress that to order a comprehensive bombardment of the legations would be going too far, given that it would almost certainly kill all of the ministers, their families and their staffs. That kind of blind use of force would, it is feared, put the whole of the Western world against us and could even bring about the end of the Manchu Dynasty.'

Alice forbore to mention that things had 'gone too far' already and that, whatever happened to the defenders of the legations, revenge on the Chinese royal house would be severe and inevitable. Instead, she said, 'But it seems as though you are fighting only half a war, doesn't it?'

He gave a smile that was completely Chinese in its impassivity. 'If you were in Tientsin at the moment, I don't think you could say that. The fighting there is severe. But you must not misunderstand me. The Imperial forces in Peking – and you will perhaps have noticed that there are very few Boxers attacking your barricades at the moment—'

'Oh, are they in the country again, butchering defenceless missionaries?'

Kuang Li bowed his head at the shaft, but continued: 'Our forces here are determined to occupy the Legations Quarter. But it is all a question now of how that is done.'

'I am sorry but I don't quite understand.'

'The Empress is at this moment considering offering, once again, a ceasefire to the fighting here on condition that the ministers, their families and soldiers agree to leave the legations and proceed to the coast, under the protection of the Imperial army.'

'But you offered this before and it was rejected.'

The General shook his head. 'Not quite. The offer was allowed to lapse.'

'But we are at war now. The Chinese nation declared war on the Foreign Powers.'

'Quite so. Because you took our Taku Forts at the mouth of the river. But the amnesty would include the offer of an armistice.'

Alice frowned, these waters were becoming deep. 'You say the Empress is only considering this?'

'Yes. You see, she is torn between the conflicting advice she is receiving in the palace, from princes of the royal blood on the one hand who would give General Tung Fu-hsiang his head, and people like my master, General Jung Lu, on the other, who would wish this stupid war to end. Now – if you could take this message back from my general to your Sir Claude . . . er . . . MacDougal . . . ?'

'MacDonald.'

'Ah yes. So sorry. I always had difficulty with Scottish names.'

Alice stifled a grin. The complexity of Chinese names had always bewildered her. It was good to hear that there was a quid pro quo. 'But what precisely is that message?'

'We would wish to know if that offer would receive serious consideration and would be likely to be accepted. You see, it would be a great loss of face to our Empress if

261

her generosity was thrown back in her face, so to speak. If, however, we could have Sir Claude's assurance that the offer might well be accepted – why then our people at the palace could, we feel sure, persuade the Empress to make it and so end the fighting and the war, both here and in the south.'

He sat back and a heavy silence descended on the room. It was clear that the General's colleagues present had not followed the conversation but that everyone was now looking at Alice in considerable anticipation.

'Of course I will take what you have said to Sir Claude,' said Alice, eventually. 'Naturally, I cannot say to you what his response will be. How should he relay that, by the way?'

'Oh,' that subtle smile returned, 'through the usual channels. They have always remained open throughout this conflict. But we here tonight were meeting to think of a way of putting our message to Sir Claude informally. Your arrival has seemed to meet our purpose very well. Would you care for some more tea?'

'You are kind, but no thank you. May I ask you one more question?'

'Please do.'

'What if Sir Claude rejects your invitation?'

'Ah yes. Then that would be a great pity. It would mean, you see, that the – what shall I call it? – the pro-Legation factor amongst the Empress's advisors will have lost the day, so to speak. As a result, the people at court who wish to see this war intensified will have their way and the attacks on the Quarter will be intensified. In fact, my general may be forced to initiate the terrible cannonade of which we have spoken.'

'I see. Very well, I shall take that message. And now I feel that I should leave you, unless there is anything further you wish to say?'

He held up one long, elegant finger. 'Only this – and I do hope that you will not think this rude of me. Please do not allow Sir Claude to think that he can attack this house here. After our meeting, you see, we will not be able to use it any more and it will become deserted. So any effort towards it will not be justified. Oh, and that little passage in the wall that has proved so useful to Mr Griffith will now be holed up at this end and will be of no further use to anyone.'

With that Kuang Li bowed ceremonially, followed by his companions.

Alice inclined her head. 'Thank you. Good night, gentlemen.'

She departed without a glance towards Gerald, who scurried behind her, and she crossed the street in long strides, thinking hard. She pulled at the little door but it refused to budge, so Gerald leant over her shoulder to exert pressure and pull it open. She whirled on him. 'Gerald—'

'No,' he interrupted. 'It is dangerous here, come inside.' He pushed her gently into the little opening, closing the door behind them, so that they were in virtual darkness, only relieved by the shards of moonlight that slipped through the gaps in the stone at the far end.

Gerald seized her arms, so that she could hardly move. 'Now listen,' he hissed. 'Don't believe what you heard back there about Simon. He is almost certainly dead. They softened it for you – I understood what they said – because

263

they wanted your help. Listen, Alice.' His tone became softer. 'You must know that I love you and I have since the first moment you arrived at our house.'

She struggled to get free, but he held her tighter.

'Your life with Fonthill, from what I hear, has been one of hardship; you must have felt that you were some . . . some blasted trooper in the army, following this madman around the Empire. Even if he is still alive – and I don't think that he is for one moment – it will be easy to divorce him and marry me. Join me in a tremendous adventure in this wonderful country. You saw how highly placed my contacts are here. You would live here in Peking in great style, when I am part of the foreign office here.' He leant his head forward to kiss her.

Alice, her arms still pinioned, moved forward into his embrace and then sharply brought up her knee into his groin. Then she pulled back her head and crashed it into his nose. He howled, released her and doubled over, holding his nose.

'Now, you listen to me, *cousin*.' Alice's tone was even but bitingly cold. 'You touch me again and I will cripple you, I promise. This has happened before to other men. I know how to do it.'

She pushed him hard so that he sat down with a thud, painfully, on the pipe that ran through the tunnel.

'My husband is a *man*, not some grovelling little spy, who slithers here and there, sometimes with the enemy, sometimes with us, but always betraying those who trusted him. As for whether Simon is still alive, I would rather – much rather – take the word of that Chinaman than yours. No, don't get up. I haven't finished with you yet.

'Now, listen carefully to what I tell you because it is important. It is quite clear to me that you have betrayed the defenders here. You informed the Chinese that Simon was going to make his attempt on the guns. Thank God you were – what was the phrase? – ah yes, "a little too late". You told them also about his mission to Tientsin – a little too late again, it seems. But my dear Simon could have been taken and killed out of hand.

'You hunt with the besiegers. I know this because I saw you with the Kansus in the Wu, on the *wrong side of the barricade*, cousin. You must really get rid of that distinctive white suit, you know. I now believe that you fired off your fowling piece that day in the cart on the way here deliberately to put your father – *your own father*, cousin – in danger. In fact, my dear, you killed him.'

Suddenly, Gerald was on his feet albeit stooped over in the low tunnel. His voice was high-pitched and it echoed in the confined space, bouncing back off the low walls. 'The man was an idiot,' he shrieked. 'Always was. His religion is stupid, *stupid*, I tell you, compared to the elegance and deep truth of Shintoism. He and his kind – the *missionaries*,' he spat out the word with contempt, 'were ruining this wonderful country, with its fine past and magnificent future. The Boxers were right – right, I tell you – to rise up against them.

'Now you listen, *cousin*. The Chinese, the true Chinese, like Tung Fu-hsiang, are right to fight the Foreign Powers, who just want to partition China between them. And they will win, I promise you that. And the first card to fall in

265

the line of dominoes will be this artificial piece of foreign territory, the Legation Quarter. You will see.'

He finished, gasping for breath and holding a handkerchief to his bloodied nose.

Alice nodded. 'Now, at last, Gerald, we know where we both stand. Listen hard. I will give you half an hour – no more – to pack some belongings and to tell your mother what you intend to do. I don't care what you tell her, but don't you dare make her worry on your behalf. She will hear nothing from me about tonight. You will have just thirty minutes to do that and then scramble back down this rathole to join your Chinese friends, before they wall it up. Then I shall wake Sir Claude and tell him everything that has happened tonight. So you will leave the Legation Quarter and you will not return until this siege is ended, if you value your life.' She turned to go and then turned back. 'And if you try to stop me now, I promise I will kill you. To repeat, I know how to do it.'

She scrambled back towards the shafts of light, half-fearing a sudden attack on her. She had never killed a man with her bare hands – although she had fought a few off – and she had not the faintest idea how to do it. But no attack came and she was able to reach the stones, pull them back and climb through. Then she broke into a run towards the British Legation, startling the guard on her arrival.

CHAPTER TWELVE

If the news brought to Fonthill that it could take some weeks yet before the relief expedition could be mounted was bad, that which was brought by Jenkins shortly after Dorward's departure was even worse.

The Welshman sat on the edge of the camp stool by Simon's bed and waved the flies away. 'I don't know 'ow exactly to say this to you, bach sir,' he said.

Fonthill frowned. 'You can't find a decent pair of trousers for me?'

'No, no. It's not that. It's just, well, I can't find old Changy anywhere.'

'What do you mean, you can't find him? Where the hell did you leave him?'

'Well, we both left 'im, so to speak, when you told 'im 'e couldn't come along with our bit of gate blowin'. 'E was really fed up with that, you may remember, an' went off in a bit of a sulk. I 'aven't seen 'im since.'

Simon elbowed himself to a sitting position. 'I wondered why he hadn't been to see me. I thought he was just miserable with me for not letting him join in the attack. Have you asked around?'

'Course I 'ave. Though goin' around this place sayin' "Excuse me but 'ave you seen a Chinaman?" is a bit of a waste of time.'

'Hmm. So he's been missing since last night?'

'About that.'

'Have you made enquiries with the Royal Welch?'

'No. They're still in the Chinese City, probably enjoyin' a bit of rape an' pillagin' an' that.'

Simon thought for a moment. 'It is not like him to go off and sulk. I can only think that he would have watched us go and waited with the Royal Welch and then charged with them when we set off the fireworks. He's excitable enough to have been caught up in the glory of the charge and all that. He would have not seen us in that ditch and probably charged straight past us and gone off with the Taffies into the city.'

'Yes, but, where would 'e be now? 'E's only a lad, look you, an' wouldn't 'ave got caught up in the roisterin' stuff inside.'

'I agree. Here's what you do, 352.' Simon began scribbling a note. 'Take this to the CO of the Welch Regiment – I think he's Colonel Davies. I only met him briefly but he owes us one for opening the door for him into the city. He'll probably get a DSO for that, if he hasn't blotted his copybook by letting his lads loose on the civilian population. This explains what you're after. The NCOs might help. After all, Chang wasn't just another anonymous Chinaman – he was strangely dressed as a customs officer and there were no Chinese charging with the Welsh. Someone might have seen him. Report back to me here as soon as you can. I'm getting out of this bed.'

'No, no. You stay there. It's too early for you to get up yet. Leave this to me.'

'Very well. Off you go.'

As soon as Jenkins was out of sight, Fonthill pushed back the bed sheets and swung his legs to the floor. He had sustained burns to his right ankle and calf, as well as his hands, but he could stand and, best of all, the ringing in his ears had stopped and his head seemed clear.

A Chinese orderly bustled over. 'No go yet, sir,' he said.

'I have General Dorward's permission,' he lied. 'Now,' he fumbled in the little drawer in the bamboo table at his bedside. He produced a handful of Chinese coins. 'Can you do something for me?'

'Ah, yes, sir.'

'Good. I want some Chinese clothes. Ordinary clothes used by Chinese workmen. Something that will fit me and the man who has just left. And we shall need two coolie hats. If you can do that, I will double this. Bring them to me at my billet, at this number, as soon as possible.'

The orderly's face broke into a big grin. He bowed over Simon's hand and took the money. 'Can do that, very good, sir. Bring to you quickly.'

'Good.'

Still in his tattered underwear, Fonthill walked out of the makeshift hospital to the billet which he, Jenkins and Chang had been allocated on arrival. It was little more than a wooden shed with three bunks, but it was private and suited Simon's purpose well. There he found his and Jenkins's rifles but Chang's was missing.

Simon sat on his bunk and tried to think logically. There was no way that Chang would have run away, he would consider that to be deserting his post. He was as keen as mustard and now regarded himself as a soldier. In addition, after their capture by the Kansus and the rough treatment they had received from them, he had become their sworn enemy. Nor would he have wandered off disgruntled. One of the endearing qualities of Chang, he reflected, was his lightness of spirit and his ability to take hard knocks, both literally and metaphorically. No, it made sense that he would come after his two comrades to join in the battle in the city. And then . . . and then what? He shook his head. There was no way that he could shrug his shoulders and write off the loss of Chang as just another casualty in the Boxer uprising. He could never face Mrs Griffith – or Alice, for that matter. The boy had to be found. But where the hell to look?

Jenkins brought some news, at least. Colonel Davies had, indeed, been helpful and one of the corporals vividly remembered Chang, in his navy-blue jacket, charging by his side as the Royal Welch swept into the city. At first, they had met strong resistance from the Kansus and there had been fierce fighting, street by street, until the Muslims seemed suddenly to disappear, as they fled the city through the gates not under attack.

'Yes, but what about Chang?'

'You know, bach sir, you shouldn't be up. The surgeon major would cripple me if he felt I had encouraged you.'

'Bugger the surgeon major. What about Chang?'

'I was comin' to that, if you 'ad just a touch of patience. Now, the corporal – nice chap, from Rhyl, see, in the north of Wales, just like me—'

'For God's sake get on with it.'

'Well, 'e saw one of the bullets fired by the Chinks 'it the wall just above where old Changy was kneelin' an' firin', see. This bullet knocked a chunk off the wall and it fell an' seemed to knock poor old Changy out.'

'What do you mean, "seemed to"? Did it or didn't it?'

'Well, I wasn't there, was I, so I can't vouch for it. But the corporal said that Changy fell and lay still. 'E couldn't stay to 'elp 'im, because the Chinks counter-attacked an' they 'ad to retreat. When they fought their way back, Changy 'ad gone. That's all 'e could say.'

Fonthill pulled at a stray piece of bandage on his left hand with his teeth and then tucked it back in. 'Does he remember where it was?'

'Oh yes. 'E took me there. In a cobbled street just outside an 'ouse.'

'I don't suppose for a moment that you could find your way back there, could you?'

Jenkins looked indignant. 'Course I could. I marked it well.'

'Good. We'll go there tonight.'

271

''Ang on. You should be back in bed.'

'Balls. We'll go as soon as some clothes I've ordered arrive.'

'Brand-new suits, is it?' Jenkins grinned and looked down at his once-smart customs uniform, now burnt in patches and covered in dust.

'Not quite. I have a feeling that we are going to have to go out into the country again. And we go as Chinamen.'

'Oh bloody 'ell. Not in the river again . . .'

'We'll go where we have to. But we must find Chang.'

'Ah, amen to that, bach sir. 'E's a good lad.' But the Welshman's face darkened and he sucked in his moustache under his lower lip. 'Trouble is, as I've pointed out, this place is full of millions of Chinamen, 'cos it's their country, isn't it? It's goin' to be like lookin' for a bloody needle in an 'aystack. I mean, where do we start?'

'We start at the house where he fell, if you can find your way to it, which I truly doubt. But we are going to need an interpreter.'

The orderly arrived, the broad grin still in place, carrying two parcels. They were unwrapped and revealed two virtually identical garments: loose, pyjama-like trousers, pulled in at the ankles, high-button shirts and shapeless, cotton working overalls. Sandals and conical coolie straw hats completed the outfits, neither of which was too clean. But they fitted, more or less.

The orderly was suitably rewarded and Simon pulled him to one side. 'Are you in the British army?' he asked. 'Can you get away from the hospital for a few days? You will be well paid.'

The man's eyes lit up. 'I not a soldier,' he said. 'Work for English lady in settlements. She gone to Taku. I can leave hospital and work for you. Where we go?'

'Into the Chinese City to start with. Then we shall see. What's your name?'

'Lady calls me Sam.'

'Very good, Sam. Here, help me into these clothes.'

By the time Sam had finished with them, Jenkins and Fonthill looked exactly like a pair of Chinese coolies, quite nondescript in their earth-coloured, none-too-clean overalls. The fact that they didn't fit was of no matter. Sartorial elegance was not desired. By keeping their heads down under their cone-shaped hats, their comparatively long, Occidental faces, with their prominent noses and strong chins, could not be seen. At first glance, they looked exactly like the thousands of anonymous figures who peopled the settlements and the city.

'Do we take the rifles, bach sir?'

Fonthill sighed. 'I'd like to, but coolies don't carry British army issue rifles. Here, how well do you know the quartermaster?'

'Played cards with 'im last week. 'E won.'

'Good. Hand me that pad. Now . . .' He scribbled a note, signing it 'S. Fonthill, Major, General Gaselee's staff', and handed it to Jenkins. 'Tell him we are off upcountry on an intelligence mission. That will explain your garb. I want him to accept our rifles in temporary exchange for two Webley service revolvers, officers for the use of. It might work and we'd be better off with something we can tuck out of sight. Don't be all day.'

Simon set about unwinding his bandages and, with Sam's help, cut them down to a less unwieldy size. Jenkins returned within the hour, discreetly carrying two Mark 4 revolvers and a box of .455 cartridges. Then the three set off for Tientsin City.

A smell of cordite and smoking timber hung over the South Gate and the city itself seemed subdued, after the excesses of the night before. The streets were patrolled by a mixture of Russian, German and British soldiers but Simon and his two companions merged easily into the indigenous Chinese who walked by, going about their business, albeit with their heads down and eyes averted from those of the soldiers.

The trio halted just inside the gate, confronted by a maze of narrow cobbled streets. 'Which way?' hissed Fonthill.

'Ah. Just a minute. Bloody 'ell, these streets all look the same now.'

Simon looked up to the heavens. Jenkins, he knew, had an inbuilt inability to find his way from A to B, even if the route was marked by flaming torches. 'Concentrate, man,' he urged. 'This is important. We haven't got much time.'

'I *am* concentratin'.' Jenkins tipped back his hat and studied the streets that all opened onto the small square behind the gate. 'Ah. This one,' he said. 'I recognise that funny sign there, tho' God knows what it means. Yes, it's up this 'ill, it's an 'ouse on the left, just past an archway.'

They walked up the hill and it was clear that the street had recently been the scene of heavy fighting. Bullets had scarred the stone of the buildings and tiles were hanging over gutterings.

Dark patches of dried blood showed where men had fallen and Simon was glad he had missed this part of the battle, for there was practically no shelter to be had in the terraced street, hardly a doorway in which to escape the bullets.

Jenkins stopped with confidence outside a one-storey house, roofed with the distinctive Chinese terracotta wavy tiles. He pointed to where a sizeable piece of stone had been taken from the wall. 'Accordin' to that Taffy corporal, this is where old Changy was knocked down, obviously by this stone, 'ere.'

Simon scrutinised the cobbles underneath and, indeed, there was a distinctive bloodstain. He nodded and turned to Sam. 'Now,' he said, 'knock on the door of this house and ask them if they know anything about a young Chinaman who was knocked down just here during the fighting last night. He was wearing a blue coat and carrying a rifle. And he was fighting for the British. Tell them there is a reward for information – but only if it is correct. Do you understand, Sam?'

'Understand well, sir. I talk to them.'

The door was not opened at first and when it was, after repeated knocking, it was pushed only slightly ajar. Then, when the occupant, a very old woman with tiny, bound feet, saw that it was a Chinaman and not a soldier knocking, she opened it wide. Fonthill and Jenkins kept their heads down while a conversation ensued.

Eventually, Sam turned to them with a satisfied smile. 'Yes, she remember man falling and hitting door. They afraid to open but did so when firing stopped and Chinaman on his knees holding head . . . what you say?'

'Bleeding?' offered Simon. Sam nodded.

'Young or old man?'

'Very young. He asked to come inside and bathe head, but then Kansu soldiers come before he could go inside and take him away.'

'Damn! Did she hear them say where they were going to take him?'

Sam turned and again questioned the woman, who had been following the exchange in a foreign language with frightened eyes.

'She say she think them say take him to Peitsang, where soldiers have their . . . what you say . . . ?'

'Headquarters?'

'That the word.'

'Thank her and give her this.' He handed over several coins. 'Sam, how far is this Peitsang?'

'It about ten mile north, along railway.'

'Right. Let's go there.'

Jenkins gave a frown so face-distorting that his great eyebrows nearly met his moustache. ''Ere, you know you should be in bed, and, look you, you won't be able to walk that far with that burnt ankle, see. An' 'ow are we goin' to stroll through all these Kansu buggers? They'll see we're not Chinese and then we *will* be bloody well whipped if they get another chance.'

'Don't argue. Thank you, madam,' and he gave the startled woman a most ceremonial bow. Then to Sam: 'Which way?'

'Through city and through North Gate. I take. Follow me.'

They set off, Fonthill hobbling slightly. Jenkins hissed, 'What if we get to this Pete Sang place? What do we do there? Surround it and attack from all quarters?'

'Yes. Good idea. Save your breath for the walk. It's going to take me some time at this rate.'

Sam knew his way through the Chinese City and they soon found themselves at the North Gate, a similarly impressive entrance at the opposite end of Tientsin. There were Russian guards at the gate but they paid no attention to three coolies shuffling past them, on their way to the parched *kaoliang* fields stretching away before them. Turning to his right, Sam led them to the railway track and the wide path at its side.

'We follow track,' he said. 'Lead us to Peitsang.'

Fonthill had been concerned that, once out of the city, they would be met by dug-in entrenchments of the Imperial army, but it seemed clear that, following their defeat at Tientsin, the Chinese had decided to retreat further north. They would realise that the Foreign Powers' next move would be to launch a column in some strength – not two thousand sailors this time, with officers in their white ducks, sitting in railway carriages – to the north-west to attack Peking. But Simon had no illusions. The Chinese army would stand and fight at some place – or places – along the way. Where would that be, he wondered? More to the point, was Chang still alive and, if so, how the hell would they be able to release him? As they trudged along, heads down under the burning sun, Simon recalled a maxim from his then newly opened officers' training course at Sandhurst: 'No time spent on reconnaissance is wasted.' They would have to trust to their disguises to allow them to reconnoitre the place and then form a plan. A plan. Ah yes. *A plan*. He sighed. He would have to think calmly and rationally – and hope they had a lot of luck. But would Chang be alive? From what he had seen of the Kansu, it would be unlikely. He sighed inwardly and walked on.

It took them nearly five hours to walk the ten miles to Peitsang and it was dark by the time they saw the name, written in Chinese letters of course, so Sam had to translate, on the side of the small station platform. They had followed the railway all along and had met only three people, peasants, like themselves. To their surprise, a locomotive was standing at the station, no carriages, just the engine.

Fonthill concluded that the line was still open back to Tientsin and engineers were working on the locomotive. Steam was hissing from behind the wheels but somehow it looked as though it was going nowhere, waiting, presumably, for trucks or carriages.

The town itself was little more than the rail stop and Fonthill felt uncomfortable walking through it in the semi-darkness, particularly as they passed several groups of Kansu soldiers. There was obviously a depot there for these men and he thanked their lucky stars that they would all be Muslim, otherwise they might well have been accosted by a drunken Kansu or two. But would they have Chang and, if so, where?

On the far side of the town they came upon a large field containing tents that seemed to have been hurriedly pitched. So irregular was the grouping of the tents that Simon felt sure it could not be a military camp – although they had passed nothing else that resembled one. Then he saw the rifles stacked, pyramid-style, along the rows. Two low wooden buildings stood on the periphery of the field.

'This must be the Kansu headquarters for the region,' he said.

'Yes,' said Jenkins, looking round carefully. 'But if it is that, then the old general with the fancy initials cut into 'is back ain't 'ere. 'E 'ad a damned great marquee of a tent, if you remember. There's nothing like that 'ere.'

'True. But one of those huts on the far side has got bars to its windows. And there's a guard outside. Could be a jail.'

The field had no fence or other means of delineating the boundaries for the camp, except that there was a slightly larger tent on their edge of the field, outside of which two soldiers stood guard. The guard tent?

They walked by unhurriedly, without looking at the sentries, and went round a bend in the path. Simon beckoned to Sam.

'Sam,' he said, placing an arm on his shoulder. 'I would like you to do something a little dangerous. Can you do it, do you think?'

'If not too dangerous, sir.' The young man looked nervous. 'I not soldier, remember.'

'Of course not. All I want you to do is to walk back to one of those sentries and ask him if they have captured a young Chinaman in a blue coat. Say you think he was in Tientsin. Say you come from the same village and his mother is worried about him. Do you think you could do that?'

'Ah, that easy, sir. I don't argue with guard, eh?'

'No. Just walk up easily and ask if the man is in the camp. Just say you need to tell his mother.'

'Very good. You wait here?'

'Yes.'

The young man nodded and slowly walked away. Jenkins blew out his cheeks. 'That's takin' a bit of risk, ain't it, bach sir? What if they run in old Sam as well? Then we'll be buggered and very far from 'ome, look you.'

Simon shrugged. 'We just don't have time to walk around half of China,' he said. 'If they feel Chang was important enough to arrest in Tientsin and bring back here – or wherever, for that matter – then I'm afraid they're going to torture him to find out what he was up to. There he was, wearing a British customs office coat, fighting with the Brits, remember. So we really have no time to waste. We just must take a risk.'

Jenkins nodded. 'Poor bugger. I hope he is in there and we can snaffle 'im, then.'

Fonthill's heart lifted when Sam reappeared a few minutes later, beaming.

'Yes, sir. Chinese man in blue coat taken here from Tientsin. In wooden hut.' The smile disappeared. 'They hit him, I think.'

'Is he still alive?'

'Ah yes. Wait for big officer to come tomorrow.'

Simon nodded. 'Right. That means we get him out tonight.'

'Blimey.' Jenkins's nose wrinkled. ''E's on the edge of the bloody army. They're camped all round 'im, with a guard with a rifle standing outside the door. ''Ow are we goin' to do that, then?'

'I will create a bit of a diversion and then we nip in and take him.'

'What? Just like that?'

'Yes, Just like that. We are miles from the front and they'll all be resting from their exertions in the Chinese City and the march back. By the look of it, most of the troops here are sleeping in their tents. They will not be expecting an attack and certainly not an attempt to take their prisoner. But it is vital that what we have to do we do quietly and quickly. Now listen. This is the plan.

'We are lucky in that the hut is on the edge of the encampment and that the guard tent for the camp is virtually on the other side of the field to the hut. We are also lucky that this wood seems to go to the edge of the field for two-thirds of the way round, so giving us cover when we get out with Chang. However, we are a bit unlucky that the entrance to the hut faces inwards, into the field, and that is where the guard stands, of course.' He grinned. 'That's odds of two to one in our favour.'

'Oh, bloody marvellous,' said Jenkins. Sam was listening carefully, his mouth open in concentration.

Fonthill continued: 'When we are in place on the edge of the wood, I will walk around to the guard and engage him in conversation.'

'What,' asked Jenkins, 'in fluent Chinese?'

'Of course. Now, while I have his attention, you creep up behind him, 352, and kill the bastard. Quietly – with your

281

knife. It's important, though, that you prop him up with some kind of stick – there's plenty around in this wood – so that it appears as though he is still on guard. Got that?'

'Oh yes. Kill him and stand him up. Very easy.'

'Good. Then you, Sam . . . are you following all this?'

'Hah. Think so, sir. But not a soldier, remember.'

Fonthill sighed. 'No. We are not asking you to kill anyone. Then you, Sam, come inside with me. There will probably be a guard inside who will have the keys to where Chang is being kept. I will need you to interpret. We will threaten this man and take his keys and then . . . er . . . knock him out so that he cannot raise the alarm. Unlock Chang and escape through the woods.'

Jenkins nodded solemnly. 'An' then we all 'obble back to this Tiensingy place?'

Simon shook his head. 'No, my ankle is killing me. I can't march far. I suggest we go by train.'

A slow smile crept over Jenkins's face. 'Brilliant, bach sir. Bloody brilliant. I just 'ope we 'ave a bit of luck.'

Fonthill's face was set hard. 'So do I, old chap,' he said. 'So do I. We are going to need it. Come on. Let's go.'

They slipped off into the wood, leaving the path behind them, treading carefully in the dry timber along the edge of the field, stopping only for Jenkins to pick up a long, sturdy stick, until they came to the dark outline of the second building, nearest to the wood. Fonthill held up a hand and they stayed listening quietly. Nothing could be heard.

Simon indicated with his hand. 'I will walk around the hut this way,' he whispered. 'Give me fifteen seconds, 352, and then walk around the other side. With any luck the guard will have his back to you. I'm afraid it means stabbing him in the back, but it can't be helped. You come with me, Sam, but wait out of sight behind the hut while I approach the guard. All right?'

'Good luck, bach.' The absence of the customary 'sir' betrayed Jenkins's anxiety.

Fonthill took a deep breath and left the protection of the wood. He walked quietly round the hut and came upon the guard who was half-dozing, leaning against the door. 'Excuse me,' said Simon, his head down.

The guard immediately presented his rifle and grunted something.

'Ah, sorry to trouble you, old chap,' Simon spoke low but clearly. 'Could you tell me the Greenwich Mean Time, please?'

The question had the effect of making the soldier half-turn to face Fonthill. 'Huh?' he grunted. It was the last word he spoke. Jenkins materialised behind him, put his left hand over the guard's mouth and plunged his knife into his back, high up and slightly to the left of the vertebrae. He held it there as the man uttered a half-groan, dropped his rifle, which Fonthill caught, and began to slip to the ground as his knees buckled.

'Quick, prop him up,' hissed Simon.

Together they dragged the man to the wall. Fonthill caught a glimpse of Sam watching, his mouth open in horror, and then Jenkins had rammed the staff into the ground and put the other end under the collar of the guard, who swayed for a moment and then stayed perilously erect.

Fonthill propped the rifle against the figure and then drew his revolver. He waved it to Jenkins. 'Open the door.'

The Welshman did so and the two of them sprang inside, to be followed seconds later by the wide-eyed Sam. One man, in Kansu uniform, was sitting at a desk, his head down on his folded arms, fast asleep. Behind him were two cells, separated from the office by vertical bars. One cell was empty. In the other, lying on the earthen floor, lay the familiar figure of Chang. A familiar, but now sad figure, for he lay hunched, in the foetal position, but with blood oozing from a wound in his head and another from his upper arm. He seemed to be sleeping but his mouth was open and he was sucking in air with a rasping sound. There was nothing left of his blue jacket but a few shreds hanging from his shoulders.

'Bloody 'ell,' exclaimed Jenkins. 'I don't feel so bad about killin' that feller now. The bastards.'

'Open the outside door a fraction and keep watch, 352,' hissed Fonthill. 'Sam, when I wake this man, tell him that if he makes a sound I will shoot him.' He grabbed hold of the sleeping man's hair – cut short, so no pigtail – pulled his head back sharply and thrust the muzzle of the Webley into his nostril.

Sam spoke quickly to the man and also put his finger to his lips in the universal demand for silence. The Kansu was awake in a second and his eyes widened in terror.

'Good. Now tell him to unlock the cell door. Quickly now.'

The guard stood, wavered for a moment, and then took down a large keyring from a peg on the wall. He selected a key and unlocked the door to Chang's cell. 'Now tell him to remove his coat and his trousers.'

Before the demand could be translated, however, Jenkins called from the doorway. 'Soldier coming. From the guard tent, I think.'

'Damn! Only one?'

'Looks like it.'

Fonthill turned to Sam. 'Tell this man that I will shoot if he utters a word. Now sit him down, with his back to the door. That's it. Now, you two, either side of the door, backs to the wall. We'll grab him as soon as he enters.'

Sam was pushed behind the door, which was left slightly ajar, and Jenkins and Simon flattened themselves against the wall on the other side of the opening. There they all waited, holding their breath, until they heard a gutteral question delivered outside, followed almost immediately by an astonished 'Hah!'

Fonthill bit his lip. Would the guard immediately give the alarm or investigate inside before doing so? It was a life-or-death question.

Then, with almost agonising slowness, a rifle was pushed through the opening. Seeing the man seated at the desk must have given some assurance because the newcomer half-advanced into the room, asking a question of the seated man. Immediately, Simon grabbed the barrel of the rifle and pulled it and the soldier into the room. At almost the same moment, Jenkins sprang forward and sank his knife into the soldier's stomach, clutching the man to him as he did so. With a gasp, the guard slumped slowly downwards and Fonthill delivered the *coup de grâce* by crashing the butt of his revolver into the man's head. It was all over in seconds.

Fonthill poked his head round the door. The dead man outside was still standing, although he had lurched to one side. There was no sound from the rows of tents and, through the lines of canvas, he could see the flicker of lamps from within the guard tent. He shut the door. 'All clear, I think,' he said. 'Maybe this man was the relief. Now,' he waved his revolver at the key holder, who was visibly trembling, 'Sam, tell him he won't be harmed if he does as we ask. Tell him to remove his coat and trousers.'

With frightened eyes, the man did so.

'Now, Sam, see if you can find rope or a belt we can tie his hands and feet with. And something to stick in his mouth to gag him. I will keep him covered. 352, see if you can wake poor old Chang and bring him out here. He's got to get into these clothes, or we'll never get him out of here.'

With a heavy heart, Fonthill watched as Jenkins knelt beside the sleeping – sleeping or unconscious? – Chang and gently began to bring him to consciousness. Blessedly, he seemed only to be sleeping but it took nearly a minute to rouse him. At last he opened his eyes, immediately flinched as he saw Jenkins's face close to him, but then he smiled, as best he could. His nose had clearly been broken and his face was a mass of blood. His jaw had been injured and he found it difficult to speak.

'What's he saying?' asked Simon anxiously.

'I think 'e said that 'e's frightfully glad to see us,' grinned Jenkins.

'Get rid of those rags and see if you can help him to stand and get into the jailer's clothes.' Still covering the Kansu with his revolver, Fonthill edged towards Chang. 'We are going to get you out of here, old chap,' he called. 'But we can't have you walking naked through the streets, so we will need to have you dressed like a Kansu. Can you walk?'

His arm around Jenkins's shoulders, the boy gave half a nod and immediately almost fell over.

'Steady, lad,' said Jenkins. ''Ere, sit down at this desk a minute.'

Sam now appeared carrying what appeared to be a clothes line. 'Bind him, 352,' said Fonthill gesturing towards the jailer. 'Hands behind and feet together. Don't bother about making him comfortable. And tear his shirt up, stick part of it into his mouth and tie it in, so that he won't make a sound. We need a head start.'

Simon found a tap, returned with a cupful of water and raised it to Chang's mouth. The young man gulped it down eagerly and then spat out a little blood. Fonthill took what remained of the Kansu's shirt and, dipping it into the refilled cup, gently began wiping the injured youth's face. Chang tried to say something but was urged to be quiet. Tearing the shirt remnant into strips, Simon dipped them into the water and did his best to bind the Chinaman's wounds and staunch the bleeding, which had begun again as he stood.

Eventually, Chang was dressed and the jailer was trussed up and deposited in his own cell, with the door locked. Then, with Jenkins and Sam walking either side of the injured youth, clutching his arms, and Fonthill walking cautiously ahead, they left the jail hut and gained the shelter of the wood and, then, the path that led through the town.

'If we are challenged, Sam,' said Simon, 'say that our friend has drunk too much rice wine and we are taking him home.'

By now, however, it was approaching midnight and the streets of the little town were deserted. They were able to walk along unchallenged until eventually the hiss of steam ahead told them that they were nearing the station.

'Sounds as though the engine is still there, thank God,' muttered Jenkins. 'But will it have steam up?'

'If it hasn't, we'll get it up,' said Simon. 'The problem will be if the line down to Tientsin has been torn up. Seymour told me that they were shelled from the rail track on their way to the arsenal, so the chances are that we can get as near as dammit to the city – if, that is, we can persuade those engineers to get the thing moving.'

'Oh, I think we can manage that,' said Jenkins grimly, drawing his revolver from beneath his coat.

Chang was now staggering badly and had to be virtually carried, so Fonthill left him at the station entrance, leaning against a tree under the care of Jenkins, while he and Sam went onto the platform. Since they had first passed the station, a line of open wagons had been shunted and had been coupled to the locomotive, which was still being fussed over by two engineers, although no one else was in sight.

'Come with me,' said Simon to Sam, 'and translate for me.'

One engineer was on the footplate and the second bending down by the front bogied wheels as the pair approached. The man by the wheels stood up and truculently asked a question of them. Fonthill produced his revolver. 'Tell him to get back onto the footplate, now,' he said. 'And tell him if he makes a noise I will kill him.'

The engineer's jaw dropped and he turned and climbed up to stand beside his mate, who was now looking down in astonishment into the muzzle of Simon's Webley.

Fonthill climbed up beside them and waved Sam to come up onto the footplate too. 'Now,' he said, 'I want to know how long it will take to get steam up and if the line to Tientsin is still open. Explain that we have just killed two men and I will shoot them if they try to raise the alarm.'

Sam asked the questions and gained surly replies. 'They say they have had problem with . . . hah . . . valve but is all right now. Steam is already up. Track good to Tientsin. But they push these trucks north with soldiers at dawn.'

At this, Fonthill's interest quickened. If the track towards Peking was open again, then the destination for the soldiers could give an indication of where the Imperial army intended to make its stand against a relief column from the south.

'Ask them where they take the soldiers.'

'They say, Yangtsun. Is about ten miles to north, I think.'

'Ah, good. Now, Sam, go and fetch Jenkins and Chang. I will keep these two covered. Make haste.'

Sam nodded and scampered down the steel steps. Fonthill realised that his burnt ankle was now causing him pain and he looked around on the footplate for somewhere to sit. As he did so, he caught from the corner of his eye a quick movement. Instinctively, he turned and fired in one movement, shattering the chest of the nearest engineer, who had seized a shovel and was about to bring it down on his head. Immediately, Simon swung the revolver round to cover the other man, who fell onto his knees and raised his hands high above his head.

'Shit!' The noise of the heavy revolver had shattered the stillness of the night. How near were the nearest soldiers? He hung his head over the side of the locomotive in the general direction of Sam and Jenkins and shouted, 'Come on, quickly. We've got to get out of here.'

He turned and motioned to the engineer to get to his feet. He gestured to the controls, made a 'shushing' sound and then pointed behind him to the south. The man looked blankly at him. 'You stupid bastard,' shouted Fonthill. 'Get steam up.' He made a shushing sound again and then made a circular motion with both hands.

'Hah!' The engineer nodded and immediately turned, picked up the shovel – an action which made Simon start backwards – and then began shovelling coal into the open furnace. He turned back and adjusted a lever, which made more steam escape. Then he was back shovelling coal.

Keeping a wary eye on the man, Fonthill leant out of the cab once again and saw Jenkins and Sam, with Chang in between them, his limp arms around each of their shoulders. They were making slow progress and Simon fingered his revolver nervously. Had the shot raised the alarm? He moved to the other side of the footplate and looked along the line of trucks, stretching ahead of him. There, in the distance, he saw Kansu soldiers, rifles in hand, running towards the train. Oh hell! The two bodies and the bound jailer must have been found and the revolver shot would have given away the direction taken by the fugitives. He rushed to the other side of the footplate.

His three comrades were now some twenty yards from the steps up into the cab but, as he watched, three soldiers materialised onto the platform behind them. The nearest knelt and raised his rifle to his shoulder. Disregarding the engineer, who was now stoking furiously, Fonthill steadied his revolver with two hands and took careful aim. The shot ricocheted from the stone of the platform immediately in front of the Kansu and took him in the stomach. He clutched his midriff and fell, causing his two companions to dive into the station waiting room.

'For God's sake, hurry!' shouted Simon.

'Nearly there,' cried Jenkins. At the foot of the steps, he lifted Chang like a baby, so that Fonthill was able to reach down, clutch the young man round the waist and drag him onto the footplate, where he lay, breathing heavily.

Simon let him lie and rushed to the other side of the cab and leant out. A bullet immediately clipped off the side of the locomotive and winged its way past his head. Sighted awkwardly with his left hand, he released two shots at the advancing soldiers, causing them to duck and take cover under the trucks.

Sam at last followed Jenkins onto the footplate. 'Tell him to start the engine and reverse out of here, that way,' Fonthill shrieked at him. 'Revolver, quickly, 352. Take the other side and keep the Kansus at bay. I'll take this side.'

Their revolvers were operating at too long a range but they had the effect of keeping the Chinese from advancing along the line of trucks until, suddenly, with a lurch and a hissing of steam, the locomotive began slowly to reverse out of the station.

'Hey,' shouted Jenkins. 'We're pullin' a whole line of trucks, look you.'

'It doesn't matter. It'll slow us down a bit but it will also stop the Chinese from loading them with their troops to take up north. Keep a sharp eye, though, in case any of those Kansus have climbed onto the wagons.' Simon looked down at Chang, who was looking about him with a bewildered air. 'Chang, my dear cousin-in-law,' he shouted above the roar of the engine, 'we're taking you to the seaside – well, not far off it, anyway.'

The young man tried to force a smile. The locomotive gathered steam and soon they were rushing through the night air, with the click-clack of the rails imposing a reassuring rhythm to match the hiss from the open furnace. Sparks from the locomotive's funnel flew over them, dancing like glow-worms against the dark sky.

Suddenly, a strange 'woo, woo' made Fonthill whirl round. Sam was hanging out of the side of the cab, shouting, grinning and waving his free arm at the hidden countryside hurrying past.

Jenkins exchanged smiles with Simon. 'Enjoy yourself, son,' he shouted at the Chinaman. 'You're a soldier now.'

CHAPTER THIRTEEN

The train sped unhampered through the night, with Sam, Jenkins and Simon relieving the engineer in stoking the boiler. Their free passage convinced Fonthill that the Imperial army had, indeed, retreated en masse to the north and was about to regroup. Nevertheless, it was a great relief when the locomotive and its line of wagons steamed into an empty and echoing Tientsin station and hissed to a stop.

The engineer was given money – which further bewildered him – but was warned that his locomotive and the wagons were now the property of the Great Powers and that, under pain of death, he should not attempt to steam north again. Chang was gently eased down onto the platform and, after some discussion with passing coolies, a stretcher was produced and he was carried to the hospital and delivered into the care of the surgeon major, who demanded to know where the hell Fonthill had been. As soon as Simon was able to find his store of Chinese currency, hidden in his billet, Sam was further rewarded and returned – not without protestations – to his duties at the hospital.

The next morning, Fonthill and Jenkins sat at Chang's bedside and were relieved to be told that, although his nose had been broken, his chin was bruised and not fractured and that he had only lost two teeth. He was able to speak much more clearly now and they heard his story.

He had, indeed, charged with the Royal Welch, anxious to join in the action. Dazed by the piece of masonry that had fallen on his head, he was recognised in the street by one of the Kansu soldiers who had pulled them out of the river above the settlements.

'Damned bad luck, that,' said Simon. 'A chance in a million.'

'Your trouble,' added Jenkins helpfully, 'is that you look too Chinese. 'Ave you ever thought about growin' a moustache, a big black one? You might just pass for a Welshman then, see.'

Chang tried to laugh but it hurt him, so he was encouraged to continue to mumble his story. Convinced that he was a spy, the Kansus had marched him back with them in their retreat – 'very fast,' he said – and he had then been interrogated about why he was wearing a British Revenue coat and carrying a British rifle. This had involved having a rifle butt crashed into his face and bayonet points thrust into his ribs and upper arm. But he had stuck to his story that he had escaped from Peking and that, as a half-brother of an

Englishman, he was fighting on the side of the Great Powers. His inquisitors had promised that he would be beheaded the next morning.

He gave a weak smile. 'I was so glad to see you, even Mr Jenkins.'

'Well, that's an admission,' agreed Simon. 'Stay resting, dear old Chang, and then you can join us in the relief column that leaves for the legations – if one is ever mounted, that is.'

This remained Fonthill's greatest worry. The sense of urgency that possessed him seemed to have no echo in the comings and goings that now surrounded the military leaders in the settlements. There was no doubt that the fate of Seymour's original expedition was casting dark shadows across the preparations for the relief. Seymour himself, having failed with his enterprise, had a vested interest in portraying the strength of the Chinese forces and spoke of forty thousand troops being required. The need for even greater numbers was bandied about.

But nothing like these numbers could be found in Taku or Tientsin. Then the question of the leadership of the relief column arose. Far away, in Berlin, the Kaiser entered the fray. He claimed that, because of von Ketteler's murder, Germany must have priority in this matter and, after he had lobbied the governments of Japan and Russia, it was agreed that a commander-in-chief should be appointed in the form of the German Field Marshal Count von Waldersee. But the field marshal was six weeks' voyage away, in landlocked Berlin.

When Simon heard rumours of this, he was plunged into greater despair. Taking advantage of the fame he had gathered in the attack on the Chinese City he demanded to see the newly arrived commander of the British forces, General Gaselee. This was granted with promising alacrity and Fonthill, still wearing his Chinese coolie garments, found himself facing the general shortly after he had left Chang's bedside.

Gaselee was white-haired, wore a huge, equally white walrus moustache and had twinkling eyes set in a face that seemed always to wear a kindly, rather puzzled expression. He advanced across the room to meet Simon with outstretched hand.

'My dear Fonthill,' he said. 'Congratulations on your magnificent effort with those damned gates to the city. And I hear that you've just returned after plucking one of your chaps from the very midst of the enemy.'

'Thank you, Sir Alfred. You are very kind.' Fonthill took a deep breath. To hell with the compliments, he wanted action. 'When can you set off for Peking? We can't wait for some blasted Prussian field marshal to get here, can we? The legations can't hold out for another six weeks, that's for certain.'

Gaselee chuckled. 'Ah, I'd heard that you were a touch impatient. Now take a seat and we can talk this through.'

'Seriously, sir. We just can't afford much more talking. Lives are being lost up there.'

'I quite agree. As you know, I have only just arrived, but I have been arguing for immediate action with my international colleagues since I set foot here. And I promise you, Fonthill, that we won't wait for this Prussian to arrive. Nevertheless, there are problems.'

He held up his hand as Fonthill made to interrupt. 'Now, hear me out. My own personal problem is that the British army is not well represented here. As you know, we are still fighting a war with the Boers in South Africa – a war that we thought was over weeks ago – and that continues to make demands on our manpower. In addition, I have been ordered to put a brigade into Shanghai to defend our considerable interests there. The result is that we can muster only about three thousand troops for the relief expedition, which doesn't give me much of a voice in our councils here.

'Mind you, my colleagues have difficulties, too. The Americans, who don't have much of a standing army anyway, have got their hands full in the Philippines; in Manchuria the Russians are fighting Boxer-inspired uprisings; and the French have got internal problems in Indo-China. Only the Germans and the Japs are not involved in any overseas fighting.

'Nevertheless, I believe we can muster about twenty thousand men between us and I think that that is enough. Now, we know we can't use the railway past Yangtsun – although,' he smiled, 'it's most kind of you to present us with a locomotive and wagons. So what's your advice on the best way to get to Peking, eh?'

Fonthill smiled, half in apology for his brusqueness and half in relief at finding a senior army officer with a refreshing sense of urgency and one who was *prepared to listen*! 'There's only one way to go, General,' he said. 'Put heavy stuff on the river – you may have to pull the junks from the banks over shoals, or even to pole them – and march by its side. It goes virtually to Peking. There's no major road but in view of this drought you can cover the ground pretty well. It looks to me as though the Kansu troops have retreated or are retreating at least to Peitsang, so you should have a head start. And they were the main and by far the best of the enemy facing us.'

'Good. And I trust you will come with us and guide us when it comes to getting into the legations?'

'Of course, sir. My wife is there and I am anxious for all sorts of reasons to get back there.'

'I can well understand that. Now, are you happy to stay in native dress or shall we rustle up some kind of uniform for you?'

'I will stay "blacked up", so to speak, sir. It's been a long time since I was in uniform, anyway, and I don't think it will quite suit me to get back into it now. But thank you for the offer.'

'Good. Now, if you'll excuse me, I have much to do. I have a feeling, Fonthill, that we can get those twenty thousand men marching within the next few days, whoever the hell is in command.' His eyes twinkled. 'Perhaps it ought to be you, eh?'

'Thanks for the compliment, but I would have more faith in you, sir.'

Fonthill left with a heart far lighter than when he had arrived. At last, a general who wanted to move! Again, his thoughts turned to Alice. He knew just how self-sufficient she was, so well able to take care of herself. Yet, if those fragile defences broke, he had no confidence in Sir Claude's assurances that she would be protected. Gaselee certainly seemed to understand the need for speed, but it was clear that establishing a unified command was rather like getting an elephant to perform in *Swan Lake*. As he walked back to his billet, Simon decided that, if no real progress had been made within three days, then he and Jenkins would attempt the perilous journey back to Peking on their own. Alice could be left alone no longer.

The good news produced within those anxious few days came from the hospital. Chang had made excellent progress and was discharged after two days with light dressings on his wounds and following a successful operation on his nose that did little for his appearance but helped his breathing considerably. That same evening, Fonthill received an invitation to revisit General Gaselee.

'I know you are anxious,' said the old man, 'and you have certainly done enough down here to receive a progress report. I think I am getting agreement at last.'

'Thank God for that.'

'Quite. The Russians have a new leader here – a general named Lineivitch – and he is all for waiting, and the Yankee chap, General Chaffee, is worried that he hasn't got any artillery. But I have talked the Japanese into starting virtually straight away and as they have about ten thousand troops here, which is by far the largest national contingent, we are beginning to sway the doubters, because I have let it be known that the British and Japanese will go it alone, if necessary.' The general's eyes twinkled under his grey brows. 'This has frightened the life out of 'em because the Russians, the French and the Germans, in particular, would lose so much face in the international community back home if they didn't help to relieve Peking that I am sure they will join the party. It's blackmail, my dear Fonthill, but it's working.'

'Well done, General. So when do you think we can set out?'

'If we can't get moving within three days, that's by the fifth of August, I will eat my hat.'

'Who will be in command?'

'Can't say. We can't agree. So we will lead our own contingents and probably have a sort of council of commanders to tackle problems as they arise.'

'Isn't this a recipe for disaster?'

The general shrugged his shoulder. 'Quite probably.' Then he shot a shrewd glance at Fonthill. 'What would you rather we did, Fonthill, hang about here and sort out these xenophobic haggles or press on and get to bloody Peking as fast as we can?'

'I think you know my answer, sir.'

'Quite so.'

'So, may I enquire the size of the relief force and its breakdown?'

'Here, look at this.' Gaselee threw a sheet of paper across his desk. 'This is my estimate, but we will probably set off with less than this.'

Simon read:

Japanese	10,000
Russians	4,000
British	3,000
Americans	2,000
French	800
Germans	100
Austrians and Italians	100
Total	20,000

Fonthill looked up: 'Artillery, cavalry?' he asked.

'Should have adequate guns,' grunted Gaselee, 'but I must confess that we are light on cavalry, so we shall be hampered when it comes to reconnaissance and pursuit. The Japs have one cavalry regiment but their horses are too light and probably useless. We have some Yankee cowboys landed at Taku but their mounts will probably not have recovered in time from the sea voyage. So we shall be left, I think, with a few Cossacks and, thank God, the Bengal Lancers.'

'And your plan, sir?'

'We shall follow the course of the Pei Ho, as you recommended, taking a train of junks and sampans for our supplies. We are desperately short of road transport, although the Americans have some good mules and wagons. Most of the way there will be only one road, I understand, and God help us if it rains, because we shall be bogged down. Our strategy, my dear Fonthill, will be to launch a frontal attack on the Chinese whenever and wherever we are opposed. And our aim will be to move bloody fast, like some battering ram, until we see the walls of Peking before us.'

Simon grinned. 'At least, General,' he said, 'your plan has the advantage of simplicity.'

Gaselee gave a sad smile. 'There is no choice, Fonthill. You see, this force will be unique. Never before – except probably in the case of the Crusades, centuries ago – has there been such a polyglot, cobbled-together army. Given these circumstances, we cannot afford sophistication. We must advance as quickly as we can and go straight at 'em. I am gambling that the Chinese will not be well led and that . . .' he paused for a moment and the smile widened '. . . as always, God will be on our side.'

'Good luck, sir.'

'Be ready to march with us in three days' time.'

'We shall be ready.'

In fact, the energy of the old general proved so effective that the 'army of the nations' was brought together a day earlier and the relief column set out from Tientsin at dawn on the morning of 4th August, forty days after the siege of Peking began. Fonthill, Jenkins and Chang marched in the van. Ahead of them it was estimated that fifty thousand Chinese troops were assembled to deny them passage.

CHAPTER FOURTEEN

So it was that the three comrades found themselves retracing their steps to Peitsang – this time, though, in daylight under a scorching sun. Simon had been introduced to the council of war as someone who could guide the relief column but, in fact, his services were not needed, since it was a simple enough matter to follow the river, and he, Jenkins and Chang therefore allowed themselves to drop back through the marching men to allow Chang to walk at a less punishing pace and to join the British at the rear.

This, in fact, proved to be a mixed blessing, for the rearguard marched, not only in appalling heat, but in the dust cloud caused by the long column stretching ahead. Whenever the column halted, the weary, parched British found that all the shade had been taken and many of the wells drunk dry. It was whispered among the ranks that the amenable Lieutenant General Gaselee had volunteered to take this unenviable place on the first day as a gesture to his international colleagues.

It was the Japanese, in fact, who led throughout the day, in recognition of their numerical superiority, and it was they, therefore, who encountered the enemy first. On the basis of what he had learnt concerning the rail trucks at Peitsang, Fonthill had advised Gaselee that it was unlikely that the column would meet any serious opposition at that first small town, but the Japanese met the Chinese dug in at its front.

The engagement that followed was brief but conclusive. The Japanese advanced remorselessly in close formation, supported by artillery fire, and the Chinese, after first firing a couple of volleys, turned and fled, taking their guns with them.

At the rear, Fonthill and his companions knew little of the encounter, for the guns up ahead seemed to cease firing almost as soon as they had begun. Gaselee, riding by, paused to explain to Simon what had happened. 'They've got away, dammit,' he said. 'I knew we would have to pay for not having enough cavalry.'

The advance continued at a fast pace and by the early afternoon of the next day the column had reached Yangtsun, some twenty miles from Tientsin, where, as Fonthill had warned, a more formidable Chinese force was waiting for them, firmly entrenched in several defensive lines, supported by artillery. This time it was the British and Americans who were in the van and who consequently led the attack.

Simon, whose burns now appeared to be on the mend,

had requested permission for himself and Jenkins to join the ranks for the attack, although Chang had been firmly posted to the rear. To avoid being mistaken for the enemy, they had been issued with Royal Welch jackets, although for comfort's sake they would have wished to retain their cool cotton overalls. Now, as the Allied artillery played along the Chinese positions, they waited, rifles and bayonets at the ready, for the order to advance. Perspiration trickled down their faces as they stood in the smoke and heat.

'I can't see a bloody thing,' said Jenkins, licking his lips. 'I'm just as likely to stick this lunger into a friend as into a foe. What's the plan, bach sir? Do we just march up to them trenches?'

Simon nodded. 'Looks like it.' He thought back to his conversation with Gaselee about strategy. 'I don't think there's much scope for flanking movements in this war. For one reason there's not much room, with the river on our right. And for another, we haven't the faintest idea where our support might be – or, for that matter, who they are. This campaign is going to be chaotic, mark my words.'

They exchanged weary grins and then a bugle sounded and they were off, heads down, marching through the cannon smoke, half-blinded by perspiration. It seemed almost at the last minute that the smoke cleared and they saw the first line of the Chinese trenches immediately before them. A ragged cheer broke out from the British – led, once again, by the Royal Welch Fusiliers – and Fonthill and Jenkins, with the rest of the line, broke into a shambling trot.

Simon was dimly aware of flashes of rifle fire very close

up ahead and of the hiss of bullets. Then he was jumping into the enemy trench and firing at one green-clad Chinamen who rose before him, and then wheeling to engage his bayonet with that of another to his right. A shot rang out and the man slumped to the ground. Fonthill was dimly aware of Jenkins, at his side, sliding the breech bolt of his rifle to insert another round, when a sergeant's voice rang out in the mellifluous tones of the Welsh valleys. 'Don't hang about, lads. Onto the next trench. We've got'em on the run!'

Using his rifle butt as a crutch – his ankle was beginning to burn again – Fonthill levered himself up the side of the trench and lumbered ahead over uneven ground to where he could see the Fusiliers jumping down into the next line of entrenchments, stabbing and firing. He was conscious, among the chaos, of glimpsing Chinese banners in the distance and then he too was down in the trench, pausing amongst the bodies that lined its floor and realising that he was completely out of breath.

'I'm too bloody old for this now,' he gasped to Jenkins. 'Not to mention a wonky leg. Let me get my breath back.'

'Ah, bach sir. Now you know what it's like being a poor bloody infantryman.' He, too, however, was gasping for breath.

They stayed, perhaps for three minutes, at the bottom of the trench before crawling up the far side and advancing once more towards where rifle flashes through the smoke showed where the Chinese, at their third line of entrenchments, were putting up a stronger resistance. Now they were among a platoon of gaitered Americans, wearing their wide-brimmed hats, whose advance had been halted by sweeping fire from a machine gun embedded immediately ahead of them. The men were lying spreadeagled, hugging the soil, attempting to take advantage of the undulating nature of the ground but not moving forward.

Fonthill crawled alongside a corporal. 'Why don't you try and outflank the gun?' he asked.

The young man turned a startled face towards Simon. He looked him up and down, taking in the Royal Welch jacket, with no chevrons or other badges of rank and the coolie trousers and sandals. 'Who might you be, then, buster?' he demanded.

Simon sighed. 'Captain Simon Fonthill, British Army. Intelligence. Where's your officer?'

'Haven't got the faintest idea, bud.'

'Say "sir" when you speak to me. Now, take three men and follow me and Sergeant Major Jenkins here. Crawl and keep your heads down. Come on. Now!'

For a moment, the corporal considered refusing. Then the tone of command in Fonthill's voice and his air of authority prevailed. He turned to the men on either side of him. 'Foster and Schumann follah me and this . . . er . . . Limey officer. Come ahn and keep yoh heads down.'

The five of them crawled to the right, slithering on their bellies and sometimes across the front of other American soldiers, similarly taking cover. Then, when they were outside the arc of the machine gun, Fonthill led them at a tangent towards the Chinese line, again taking advantage of each patch of cover he could find: a stunted clump of millet, cut down by rifle fire; a rare rocky outcrop; or a dried-up irrigation ditch. Fonthill used every bit of knowledge he could dredge up from his days as a platoon commander, leading ground craft exercises on the Welsh Beacons.

Somehow, they managed to get within about fifty yards of a section of a Chinese trench from which only desultory rifle fire was showing. Still on his stomach, Fonthill turned to the three Americans.

'Which part of the States are you from?' he asked.

'We're all from the South . . . suh. From Virginee.'

'So you can do a rebel yell – a real yell, from Virginia?' (Simon had studied the American Civil War during his time at Sandhurst.)

A puzzled smile crossed the corporal's face. 'Sure can.'

'Right. All five of us will discharge a volley and then we'll up and attack that trench with the bayonet. But give a bloody great yell. Pretend, if you like, that you're going at a bunch of Yankees. Right?'

All three grinned and nodded.

'Right. Five rounds rapid fire and then up and at 'em.'

The resultant volley was not the most impressive that emerged from either side on that day at Yangtsun, but it caused fragments to fly from the soil bags lining the top of the Chinese trench and sent one of its defenders falling back with a bullet hole in his forehead. Then the five rose to their feet – Simon with the aid of a push from Jenkins – and charged across the intervening ground, their bayonets glinting, as the three Americans and one Welshman let out piercing screams.

It was enough to send the already demoralised Chinese – for they had seen the occupants of the first two lines of their trenches leap over them in wide-eyed retreat – drop their weapons and run to the rear.

'Where to now, bud?' cried the corporal, turning to Simon as they grouped together in the trench.

'Don't call me— Oh, never mind. To the left. Clear the trench till we come to the machine-gunner. Run on now. I have a problem with my foot but we'll be right behind. Oh, and keep up the yell. Shout for Dixie.'

Hobbling behind with the help of Jenkins, Fonthill found the trench cleared most ably by the three Americans, whose rebel yell preceded them and seemed to strike terror in the Chinese manning the line. Then he found the three Southerners crouched behind a traverse in the trench, on the other side of which they could hear the machine gun still chattering.

'Thought we'd wait for yoh heah, suh,' the corporal explained, a trifle diffidently. 'Don't know what's on the other side, yah know?'

Simon nodded. 'Dammit,' he frowned. 'Wish we had grenades. Nothing for it but just to charge round. At least the Maxim will be in a fixed position and firing forward. I'll lead. You four follow.'

'No, bach sir.' Jenkins thrust him aside. 'This is a job for a Welshman. Our yell is much better than any Yanks.'

'Hey, man.' The corporal was indignant. 'We ain't Yanks.'

But with a scream completely Celtic in its origin Jenkins charged around the traverse, closely followed by Fonthill and the three Americans. Three Chinese were manning the heavy machine gun in a specially built mini salient jutting out from the line. They stood no chance as five rifles fired as one.

'Stand guard at this other traverse,' shouted Simon to Jenkins. Then to the corporal, 'Lend me your hat.' Fonthill seized it, then stood up on the embrasure protecting the gun and waved it towards the American line. 'Come on, boys,' he shouted. 'We've put the gun out.'

Immediately, there was a cheer from the line and scores of figures rose from the ground and, bayonets fixed, ran towards the Chinese trench. Fonthill waved them on and then, exhausted, slumped onto the line of sandbags. The Americans ran by him down into the trench and then up and over, continuing their attack.

Jenkins squatted next to Simon and shouted to their three companions, 'Go with 'em, boys, we're a bit knackered, see.'

The corporal seized Simon's hand and shook it. 'Keep the hat, bud,' he grinned. 'Consider yourself an honorary Dixie Boy.' Then the three of them ran after their comrades, now all disappearing into the dust and gun smoke ahead of them.

'Well done, bach sir,' said Jenkins. 'We could 'ave been there all day in front of this bloody gun.' He turned to inspect it. 'Looks brand new,' he muttered. Then, 'Ah bloody 'ell. It says 'ere, "Made in Birmingham".'

Fonthill had no time to reply before the ground seemed to erupt all around them and they were in the middle of an artillery barrage. The two dropped to the salient floor and covered the back of their heads with their hands as earth, rocks and things indefinable rained down on them. The noise was deafening and Fonthill flinched as a piece of rock hit his injured ankle. He tried vainly to press himself further into the ground that seemed to shake beneath him.

Eventually, the barrage lifted and Simon lifted his head and reached out a hand towards Jenkins. The Welshman raised a face covered in soil and debris.

'Are you hurt, 352?'

'No. You all right?'

'Yes. Where the bloody hell did all that come from suddenly?'

Jenkins wiped soil from his moustache. 'It was a bit late, look you. We'd already captured all the bloody trenches. Do you want to carry on?'

'No. This leg is giving me trouble. I shan't be able to march if I don't rest it. Let's stay here for a minute.' Fonthill gave a wan smile.

'It looks as though the Taffies and the Yanks can manage very well without us.'

The two were clambering out of the trench when the thud of hooves announced the arrival of General Gaselee and his ADC. The general looked down on them in disapproval.

'What in God's name are you two doing here?'

'Sorry, sir,' gasped Fonthill. 'I'm afraid I couldn't quite keep up with the charge. Gammy leg and all that. Jenkins stayed behind to give me a hand.'

'Good Lord, man. I wasn't rebuking you. Well, I was. You have no right to be charging with the infantry. I am going to need you when we come to Peking and try to get through those bloody walls into the legations. You mustn't risk your life at this stage. We've got plenty of damned good infantry who can do that. Now, get back out of it as soon as you can.'

'Will do, General. Where the hell did the Chinese suddenly produce that artillery barrage from? It was a bit too far in the rear to catch our chaps but it certainly caught us two.'

General Gaselee brought the head of his horse around as it tried to prance away. 'Bloody mess, Fonthill, I'm afraid. Those weren't Chinese shells. They were ours. It was the Americans in the second wave who mainly caught it. I've just come back from investigating it – the Chinese, by the way, have retreated once again. But we lost four men of the Yankees and another fourteen wounded, most of them fatally.'

'Good Lord! How did that happen?'

Gaselee pulled at his moustache. 'Two batteries involved. Ours and the Russians'. Nobody's exactly sure what happened but it seems that the Russians were unlimbering next to our battery and asked us for the range. We gave it to them in yards and it's my belief that they thought it was metres, so they dropped short before we could stop 'em. Anyway, the Yanks caught it.' He shook his head. 'This is what happens when you get a polyglot collection of units fighting alongside each other in complete bloody ignorance, without any overall coordination. Can't be helped. Probably won't be the last time it happens. Now get back and rest that leg.'

With a forefinger touch to his cap brim, he turned and galloped away. Fonthill and Jenkins exchanged glances.

'Well, there you are,' sniffed the Welshman. 'Nearly drowned in that blasted river, narrowly avoiding gettin' whipped to death by the Chinese, nearly blowin' ourselves up with dynamite and now just escapin' by our teeth from a shellin' by the Russkies. This is a bloody dangerous war, I'm thinkin', bach sir. Too dangerous for me.'

'Rubbish. We've been through worse. Now give me a hand to get up. I wonder if the cooks are brewing any tea back there.'

The relief column spent that evening and the next day resting at Yangtsun, waiting for the supply junks to catch up and, in the words of one senior officer, 'sorting itself out'. Having been present at the council of war held at Tientsin on the eve of departure, Fonthill knew that the original plan had been to advance no further than Yangtsun until reinforcements had arrived. Some fourteen thousand troops had reached that town, a number originally felt to be insufficient to push on to Peking. But the comparatively easy victories in the two battles experienced so far had firmly put the bit between the teeth of the Allied generals involved. The old competitiveness had also reared its head.

'I fear that this is no longer going to be an advance, more a damned race,' observed Fonthill, when orders were given to break camp and resume the march on the morning of the eighth, just four days after leaving Tientsin. The field had now thinned out and of the eight starters, only the Japanese, British, Americans and Russians were sufficiently well organised in terms of transport and commissariat logistics to be able to continue. The much smaller German, Italian, Austrian and French contingents were forced to return to Tientsin and reorganise, without having fired a shot in anger.

Nevertheless, the four nations that now comprised the column were determined and quite undaunted by being outnumbered – at least in practice – by the enemy. It was, however, a gruelling march. Much of the plain now was covered in the tall *kaoliang* which provided ideal conditions for ambushes. None came, however, and it was the sun and the lack of drinking water that were the worst enemy for the column.

The British were once again forming the rearguard, with Fonthill, Chang and Jenkins marching with them. Despite the harsh conditions, both Simon and Chang had recovered from their injuries well enough to be among the 7th Rajputs of the Indian contingent when the latter marched through an American detachment.

'Blimey,' whispered Jenkins, 'look at 'em. 'Alf 'ave got their eyes closed and it looks as though they're goin' to fall over at any minute.'

'Yes, Mr Jenkins,' said Chang. 'But they're plodding along, you see. They're not giving up. They're making a splendid effort.'

The Welshman grinned. 'Yes, Changy, but you can see 'ow them Injuns beat old General Custard. Take away their 'orses and make 'em march an' the Yanks are buggered.'

Fonthill shook his head. 'Well, they fought well in that trench and on the wall at Peking. And I hope to God they're still doing that last bit.'

More and more his thoughts were turning to Alice and the Legation defenders. He was relieved and delighted when the commanders of the column decided to push on from Yangtsun without waiting for reinforcements. He kept telling himself that they would have heard if the Legation compound had fallen. But the fear grew that, as the news of the advance neared the capital, so, too, would the efforts of the attackers there. If, in breaking through, the Chinese took prisoners, then the better they would be able to bargain with the relief column outside the walls. So, despite his aching body, Simon put down his head and trudged on amongst the dust at the rear.

One night, around their campfire, Fonthill took advantage of their close proximity to question the Chinaman about his half-brother, Gerald. How well, he asked, did he know him?

These days, Chang took time to consider his answer to questions, as though in the light of the new understanding of the ways of the world that his experiences of the last few weeks had given him. His recent injuries – particularly his broken nose – had also changed his countenance, making him appear older. So, his head on one side, he pondered the question for a moment before answering.

'Well, cousin,' he said, 'he was, I think, about seven or eight when I was introduced, so to speak, into the family. As a result, there has always been a gap between us. Mainly because of age, of course, but also perhaps because of our ethnic backgrounds.'

'Yes, Chang, I understand that. Yet it seemed to me that Gerald appeared to be more Chinese than you in many ways.'

Again Chang considered the question. 'Yes, I can understand that. Perhaps it was because we were both of us, for different reasons, trying to change our . . . what is the word? . . . ah yes, our *ethnicity* to match the surroundings into which we had been placed. Me, you see, to be more English, to match my mother and father, and Gerald to be more Chinese to match his surroundings and the many Chinese friends he had made.'

'But did you notice that Gerald, perhaps, took this rather further than you? You have never, as far as I can see, become anti-Chinese – although, I hasten to add that I know you do not like the Boxers, and with good reason. But you have never expressed your dislike of the Chinese people in general. Gerald, on the other hand, seems to have become almost virulently anti-British.'

Another pause. Then: 'Yes, I think that is probably so. He has studied history, you see, and he has become very annoyed at the way the Foreign Powers have, in one way or another, colonised parts of China. And I think he has never forgiven the British in the way that they created the Opium Wars so that they could take their own share of our country and also continue to benefit by the trade in opium.'

'But you know these things too, Chang, and you seem to have less antagonism towards us than your brother.'

The old smile came back to Chang, lighting up his battered face. 'Ah, that is because I like you more, you see. And I think your culture is as great as ours – Shakespeare, Milton, Pope and so on. If you can't beat the jolly old British, I say, then you should jolly well join them.'

At this, everyone grinned. 'Blimey, Changy,' said Jenkins, 'you'll be playing cricket soon.'

Chang's face lightened again. 'Oh, but I do already, Mr Jenkins. I can bowl this new googly that everyone is talking about. Look, I can show you how you do it—'

Fonthill held up a hand. 'Not just now, cousin,' he said. 'Perhaps some other time.'

The advance continued, as did the hardship, particularly the heat and the lack of water. The Russians and the Japanese seemed to stand it best, despite the fact that the Japanese remained in the lead now and bore the brunt of what fighting was left. On 12th August, they blew up the South Gate of the City of Tungchow and the Chinese garrison streamed away without a fight. The Allies made camp, resting there and replenishing their supplies. The city was the site of a large American mission that had been brutally sacked by the Boxers with much loss of life in the early days of the uprising. One officer suggested that what was left of the mission should be burnt as an example to the local populace. Fonthill was with General Gaselee when the suggestion was made. But the old general demurred.

'My dear fellow,' he said, putting a paternal hand on the officer's shoulder, 'I do not agree. I intend, in fact, to establish a market here, right away, so that it is operating before we leave. A place where the local populace can come in and trade with us. Now don't you think that would be better than setting these ruins on fire again? After all, we do not wish to antagonise the three hundred and fifty million people of China, now, do we?'

He turned to Fonthill. 'Would you be so kind as to ask your Chinese chap – Chang, isn't it? – to write a suitable notice in the local dialect, asking the people to come in and bring their local produce to sell to us. We will put it up here. So much better, I think, than more burning. Don't you agree?'

'Oh, very much so, sir. I will ask him right away.' He turned away and smiled to himself. How refreshing to meet a military commander who considered the feelings of the civilian population!

Very tentatively, the Chinese who had fled their city began to drift back, bringing rice and other vegetables to trade with the column. Rumours also began to flood into the camped army as it rested at Tungchow. It was said that the general commanding the retreating Chinese forces, the xenophobic Li Ping-heng, had poisoned himself and that Yu Lu, the viceroy of the Chihli province, had blown out his brains – stories that later were found to be true. More concerning for Fonthill, however, was the rumour that the legations had fallen and that all of the foreigners within had been murdered. This was quickly quashed, however, when a cavalry patrol sent out from Tungchow to probe the state of the country between the city and the capital was able to ride virtually to the walls of Peking without meeting any organised resistance. The patrol reported, however, that it could hear heavy gunfire coming from within the city. So the siege continued!

Simon, of course, was vastly relieved but was also full of frustration once again at the seeming sanguineness of the Allied leaders who were resting their troops almost within sound of the Chinese cannon at Peking.

He expressed his concern to General Gaselee, whose own patience was beginning to show signs of fraying at the repeated demands of his fellow countryman.

'You know, my dear fellow,' he said, fixing Fonthill with his kindly eyes, 'we cannot trot up to Peking non-stop. This relief force has done remarkably well to get this far so quickly, with such success and sustaining so few casualties – particularly considering that we are more a not-so-mobile Tower of Babel than a military force. We have marched for some seventy miles in this burning heat and with very poor water supplies and we have defeated the Chinese whenever we have met them. To charge on to Peking without pause for breath or consideration of how we are going to get through those great walls would be the very negation of well-established, military, strategic thinking. And you, as a former soldier and a distinguished servant of the Empire over many campaigns, ought to know that.'

The general's tone softened and he leant over and put a hand on Fonthill's knee. 'I well understand your concern about your wife,' he went on, 'but we now know that the defenders are still holding out. In addition to the report of our own cavalry, one or two messages have filtered through from Chinese sources to say that the legations are still manning their barricades, although we understand that they are hard-pressed now.' He sighed. 'But the attack on Peking will be by far the most difficult thing we have undertaken. It is vital it succeeds.

'Now, the council is meeting tomorrow and – I may say to my great relief – we will then formulate a plan in detail to allocate roles and to decide on our tactics for the final attack. We have already decided to press on immediately afterwards and to regroup within three miles of Peking from where we shall spring forward to the attack. I promise that I will report back to you and inform you on those plans, because, as I have already said, I would wish to use your local knowledge. You have already explained that the only way to penetrate the outer walls, given that we have no siege artillery – nor time, for that matter – is to attack the great gates. We shall need you, once we are inside the Chinese City, to show the best way through to the legations. So, my dear Fonthill,' the eyes under the great bushy brows were twinkling again now, 'do rest content for the moment, I implore you.'

Simon responded with a slow smile. 'I accept all that you say, of course, General, and I really am most grateful to you for taking me into your confidence in this way. It goes without saying, of course, that my companions and I will do all that we can to assist in the attack. I look forward to hearing from you tomorrow.'

That night, Fonthill did not sleep well. He had to confess to himself that he had no real confidence in the ability of the generals leading the relief force to prepare an attack based on military principles rather than national considerations. Each would want to report back to their anxious governments and peoples back home that they and their own troops had performed gloriously in the relief of Peking. There would be honour and medals to be won. And, he reflected sadly, lives to be lost. He just hoped feverishly that one of them would not be Alice's.

The council took place the next day and lasted for some time. True to his word, Gaselee, whom Simon suspected was beginning to grow in stature among his international colleagues, not only for his seniority in rank but because of his sagacity and experience, summoned Simon to his tent.

He explained that the Russian commander, General Lineivitch – a soldier of similar seniority to Gaselee – had reported that his men were too exhausted to carry out an assault immediately on completing the approach march and he had persuaded the generals that the attack should be carried out in two phases. The column would bivouac three miles from the walls and the army would put in a coordinated attack on the morning of 14th August.

'Coordinated?' enquired Fonthill with a lifted eyebrow.

'Oh yes. For once, we have agreed on the details. Each of the five nations will attack one of the four gates in the walls on the eastern side of the city, swinging round in a synchronised attack—'

Simon interrupted him. '*Five* nations, sir?'

Gaselee smiled. 'Yes, the tiny French contingent, which, you will remember, had to retreat to Tientsin, have burst their buttons to catch us up and are at this moment very, very proud of themselves.' His smile broadened. 'You know what the French are like. So . . . the plan is as follows: the Russians will attack the Tung Chih Men Gate in the north, on our right flank; and the Japanese will go for the Chi Hua Men, the next one down in the wall, so to speak. They will both attack on the north side of the Imperial Canal. We and the Americans will be on the south side of the canal. The

Americans, with the . . . um . . . no doubt gallant assistance of the French, will attack the Tung Pien Men and we will go for the Hsia Kuo Men, the southernmost gate in the eastern wall, leading directly into the Chinese City.'

The general's virtually permanent half-smile lapsed now into a broad grin. 'You will be glad to hear, Fonthill, that our target is quite near to the Legation Quarter, which, my dear fellow, you will take us to with the utmost alacrity. So, with any luck, we just might be the first nation to free the defenders of the Legation. Not, of course, that being the first in is of any concern to any of us.'

Fonthill did not return the grin. 'I just hope that we shall be in time, General,' he said. 'Those poor folk in the Quarter must be down to eating tree bark and hurling bricks at the Chinese by now.'

Gaselee gave a sympathetic frown. 'Quite so. Quite so. But I have every confidence, Fonthill, that we shall break through and get there in time. Now, as usual, you will march with us.' He stood. 'Good luck, my dear fellow.'

They shook hands. 'And good luck to you, sir.'

That evening, Gaselee's ADC, a young man of boundless good humour and, even in China, elegant trousers, approached Fonthill. 'I say, sir,' he said. 'Have you seen this?' He held out a piece of paper covered in writing in a rough and ready hand.

'What is it?'

'Well, as you may have heard, the jolly old French have just marched in – all hundred and fifty or so of 'em. They're in pretty parlous condition, don't you know, but their commanding officer – he's a general, no less, called Frey; he's the chap who's marched the poor buggers up and down from Tientsin . . . but anyway,' he paused for breath, 'one of our chaps has caught sight of his orders to his men for the final attack on Peking, although the place is still bloody miles away and we ain't ready to attack yet anyway.'

'Yes?' enquired Fonthill coldly.

'Yes, well sir, our chap has translated it from the French and this is what it says. I think the little chap thinks he's Napoleon. Do have a read, sir.'

Simon did so and read:

'This evening the German, Austrian and Italian columns will lie alongside the French troops. Tomorrow, under the walls of Peking, when the foreign national anthems are played, a complete silence will be maintained; each anthem will be heard with respect. When the French national anthem is played, it will be sung as loudly as possible, in tune, by the whole of the French Expeditionary Corps. Our compatriots and the occupants of the foreign legations beleaguered on the other side of the walls of the Chinese capital will know, when they hear our noble war chant, that deliverance is at hand.'

The ADC regained his paper and chortled again. 'You see, sir, the French haven't fired a shot yet and the German, Austrians and Italians are miles away down the road to Tientsin and will never arrive in time. All a bit vainglorious, don't you think? Eh? What?'

Fonthill recalled the far-from-gallant part played in the

defence of the Legation by the French minister, Monsieur Pichon, and couldn't stifle a smile. 'Well,' he said, 'at least the Frogs have arrived. Let's hope that their national anthem frightens the hell out of the Chinese. Eh? What?'

His smile had disappeared as soon as he turned away, however. The attack on Peking was not some point-scoring contest between the Great Powers, for God's sake! Lives were at stake here, not national glory. He just hoped that the various contingents would work together when it came to attacking the great walled city. The eyes of the world would be upon them.

CHAPTER FIFTEEN

Alice did not go to her bed on reaching the British Legation after leaving Gerald, for she realised that the man must have time to see his mother, with whom she shared a room, and explain to her why he would be leaving the Legation. Nor did she wake Sir Claude MacDonald, of course, for Gerald must be given his half an hour to pack his belongings and get out. Tomorrow would be time enough to see the minister.

In the end, she crept into the hospital and explained to the duty nurse that she was having trouble in sleeping in the same room as Mrs Griffith (she felt guilty at complaining about her snoring, for her aunt was a deep and silent sleeper) and begged permission to doze on a makeshift stretcher for the night. Comfortable it was not, but better than having to face Aunt Lizzie in these early hours.

She was forced to dissemble again when she met her aunt

the next morning. The old lady looked withdrawn and grey and Alice wondered what excuse Gerald had given her. It did not matter, as long as it did not involve *her*. The young man, of course, was a skilled and compulsive liar.

In fact, Mrs Griffith seemed more concerned about the fact that her niece had not slept in her bed that night. 'Wherever have you been, my dear?' she asked.

'Oh, Aunt, I am sorry. I should have sent a message to you. I altered my shift at the hospital and did night nurse duty, together with Mrs de Courcy. I am sorry if you were worried.'

'Well, I was. The next time, do tell me, please?'

'Yes, it was remiss of me.' She had no intention of telling her aunt about her son's treachery. Mrs Griffith would have to learn some other way, but what had he told her about his intentions? She tried to be nonchalant. 'Have you seen Gerald?' she asked. 'He . . . er . . . wanted to borrow a book of mine.'

For the first time, the old lady looked uncomfortable. 'Oh, he has gone to stay with a friend in the American Legation, I think,' she said. 'He may stay some while, I understand . . . er . . . something to do with working together on a project.' She put up a stick-like hand to her head and pushed away a wispy, grey lock.

Alice felt a sudden surge of affection for her aunt. She was obviously worried about her son and Alice yearned to comfort her. But it was impossible. Better to stick to the lies and brazen it out.

Shortly after breakfast, however – an unappetising

bowl of millet porridge – she made her way to Sir Claude's quarters and requested an interview. He saw her immediately and listened quietly and with surprisingly little emotion to her story.

At the end, he nodded. 'Thank you, Mrs Fonthill. I am grateful to you for telling me all of this. We have always known, of course, that information was somehow getting to the Chinese about our fortifications and so on.' He gave a sad smile. 'This place is rather like a colander, you know, in terms of leaking things. With so many Chinese within the legations it was impossible to keep everything tight, so to speak. But I have to say that I have long suspected that young man of being up to something. Lolling about all day and declining to take his part in the defence – it was all rather suspicious, you know. But I couldn't bring myself to consider him to be an out-and-out traitor. Does his mother know?'

'No – at least I am fairly certain he has made up some excuse to leave the British Legation.'

'Very well. I will, of course, keep this matter confidential, but if the young fellow turns up again in the Legation I will have no hesitation in putting him behind bars.'

'Thank you. But will you respond to the Chinese invitation?'

'Certainly not.' His winged, tightly waxed moustache twitched as he allowed himself a dismissive smile. 'I am quite aware that there are certain elements at the Chinese court – and particularly in the foreign service there – that have always quite genuinely disliked the Boxer Uprising and deprecate the attack on the Quarter, but I could not possibly advise the ministers to trust them to the point that we lay down our arms. Chinese politics are far too volatile and I sense that the hatred of Her Royal Highness the Dragon Lady,' his smile widened at his daring in using the colloquialism, 'for we foreigners is far too deep-seated for us to put ourselves completely at her mercy. No, Mrs Fonthill, we hang on here and continue to fight.'

Alice nodded. 'I am sure you are right. But I sense that conditions here are becoming much worse. Am I right?'

His face returned to its customary solemn mien. 'I am afraid so. We killed our last pony last night and therefore I am afraid that meat will shortly drop off our menu. I am concerned about the number of casualties that we continue to sustain, our ammunition is running low and I live in constant fear that the Chinese will, as you have mentioned, subject us to a sustained artillery bombardment. Nevertheless,' and his eyes brightened, 'our morale is high as is our spirit. For all their shouting and blaring of trumpets, the Chinese are clearly frightened of our firepower and no longer seem to threaten any direct attacks on the perimeter. I could not wish to have better people to man our barricades. No, Mrs Fonthill, we will endure and we will prevail. Yes, we will prevail, I am certain of that.'

Alice bowed her head for the moment, so that Sir Claude could not see the moisture in her eyes. Then she looked up. 'Of course, you would have told me if you had heard any news of my husband?'

'Indeed. But it has been my experience so far in this highly unusual situation that bad news will almost always find its way to me quickly. I would expect to have heard if he had been intercepted. I have heard nothing. But I do know that there has been heavy fighting in Tientsin. I remain confident that we will be relieved.'

'How long can we hold out, then?'

He rose to his feet. 'The answer to that question, my dear lady, depends upon too many imponderables, so forgive me if I do not attempt to answer it. And also forgive me if I ask you to excuse me now. There is much to do, I am afraid.'

'Oh, of course, Sir Claude. It is good of you to give me so much of your time.'

They shook hands. Then the minister held her hand for a moment or two longer. 'I would like you to know, madam,' he said in a low voice – one that seemed to contain a hint of embarrassment – 'that I admire your courage in following that young scoundrel out of the Quarter and appreciate all that you do in the defence: your hospital work and the other, more . . . ah . . . active roles you play. You set a splendid example, madam.'

Alice felt the colour rise to her cheeks. It was so unlike this withdrawn Scotsman to distribute compliments. She felt unable to speak, so she bowed, smiled and left him.

She was relieved and glad, however, that the minister had rejected out of hand the proposal that the defenders should lay down their arms and allow themselves to be escorted to the coast by the Imperial army. She recalled similar instances – in Afghanistan and India not so many years ago – when such trust had been broken and massacres had resulted. She shuddered.

Nevertheless, Alice did not need MacDonald to tell her that conditions were worsening within the Quarter. A rare batch of newly hatched eggs was offered for sale in the market on the lawn before the British Legation for five cents each. They were all snapped up within minutes. Dog meat, which had been the staple diet of the Chinese within the Quarter since the siege began, was now on offer to everyone. It was the many children, white, brown and yellow, within the compounds who were suffering the most and Alice became more and more depressed as she noticed how malnourished they were becoming. The Chinese converts, who crowded within the legations, were particularly hard hit. The men who worked on the barricades or who did other labouring work were granted extra rations but those who could not work were nearing a state of near-starvation. The trees in their corner of the Fu were stripped of leaves and bark to eke out their food. Marksmen contravened the order to conserve ammunition by firing at crows to help them.

Small incidents played their part in lifting spirits. The British contingent heard with glee that the fiercely unpopular Monsieur Pichon, the French minister, had protested to Sir Claude that the Union Jack, which had always flown proudly from the Legation lawn, was attracting Chinese fire and was therefore a danger. He demanded that it should be removed. The demand was rejected curtly and the dapper little Frenchman was sent on his way, to the rejoicing of the British.

Alice had struck up a friendship with Dr Morrison, the correspondent for *The Times,* and a faux rivalry had ensued between them, for both knew that the other was now keeping extensive notes of the siege, for publication at its end. Pichon, with his histrionic pessimism and complete inactivity, was a welcome source of amusement for them both, particularly when it was learnt that the Frenchman and his brave counterpart in the Russian Legation had both been seen burning their records.

'Huh,' said Morrison. 'I'd give fifty thousand dollars for a sight of the Russian papers.'

'How much for Pichon's?' asked Alice.

Morrison grinned. 'Possibly . . . maybe . . . perhaps, on a bad news day, I would run to five thousand.'

Alice was not at all sure, however, that Sir Claude's practice of publishing the list of killed and wounded was conducive to maintaining morale. The latest list showed that in the four weeks since the siege had begun, fifty-seven of the defenders had been killed and eighty-seven wounded. It was disconcerting to find that the British, with three killed and seventeen wounded, were among the highest casualties. The Japanese, who, as always, bore the brunt of the fighting at the Fu, the most vulnerable part of the defences, had suffered almost equally, with eight killed and thirteen wounded.

She tried to comfort herself with the thought that, if Simon and Jenkins had stayed within the Quarter, they might well have been included in the casualty figures, given their energy and bravery. But it was of little solace. Where, oh where were they?

Then, at last, a strange quiet fell over the Quarter once more. The defenders had been conserving their ammunition for some time now, only returning fire when it was absolutely necessary.

But gradually the Chinese fire fell away, too, although there was no formal restoration of a truce. The Dowager Empress compounded the surrealism of the moment by sending Sir Claude a personal gift of melons and other fruits.

Alice met the British minister when he was distributing the fruit to Chinese children. 'What's it all about, Sir Claude?' she asked.

The tall man shrugged his shoulders. 'The unpredictability of the Chinese never fails to astound me,' he said. 'They must know that we are in a weakened state and yet they relax their attacks. My own feeling is that this must reflect the fact that our people in Tientsin have won some sort of victory. The old lady may have heard that a relief column is on its way and the pro-foreigners at the court have won a hearing at last. I don't think it's likely to last, but let's enjoy it while we can.'

And so they did. Spirits were sent soaring when it became known that a message had got through to Sir Claude to say that, in fact, the foreign settlements had been relieved, Tientsin had been taken by the Allied powers and that a relief column at last was on its way to Peking. So many false alarms had been sounded from various quarters but it was clear that this news was real. Alice clutched her hands together. Was Simon on his way, too?

To the besieged within the defensive ring, the decline in the intensity of gunfire was somehow intrusive, as though a vital element in daily life had been withdrawn. Once again birds could be heard singing in the Quarter and, almost inevitably, the British began playing cricket on what was left of their Legation lawn. Even more surreal were the reports of fraternal exchanges now taking place between the Chinese and the defenders across the barricades.

Alice had made friends with one of the student-interpreters in the consular service, Lance Giles, whom she met on his return from one such exchange.

'Strange business, Mrs Fonthill,' he said. 'I went to the German Legation, which is very much of a wreck in parts, you know?'

Alice nodded.

'Well, the German and the Chinese positions there are separated only by a wall, seven or eight feet high and about two feet wide. It is loopholed and so can be a bit of a death trap. It's probably the thinnest and most fragile of the interfaces between us and them in the whole of the perimeter. I took my camera to take advantage of the truce and climbed up the wall to take a picture.'

'Bit of a risk, Lance.'

The young man looked a little sheepish. 'I suppose so, but it all seemed so peaceful. Anyway, at the top I looked down on some Chinese soldiers on the other side. They shouted, in Chinese of course, "What do you want?" I replied, "*Yao chao hsiang*" – I want to photograph you. They shouted back, "*Yao k'ai ch'iang ma*" – Do you want to shoot us? I told 'em I didn't, of course, and showed them my camera, so the chaps stood there a bit sheepishly, posing for me. I would have had a good picture of them but suddenly one of their officers came out and shooed them away.' He grinned. 'It's all a bit mad, this war, isn't it?'

* * *

The madness took another strange turn when the guns crashed out again with a noise that seemed all the more frightening because of the greater intensity of the firing. It was as though the Chinese had suddenly become ashamed of their strange lethargy.

Alice had half hoped, half feared that Gerald would show up during the comparative quiet with some cock-and-bull story about the reason for his absence and hope that his cousin's affection for his mother might have prevented her from revealing his treachery. But there were no sightings of him, either in the legations or beyond the barriers. It was, then, partly with expectations of catching a glimpse of him, but also to see how Colonel Shiba and his gallant Japanese were resisting the renewed aggression, that Alice retrieved her Colt from under her bed and scrambled to the Fu hotspot. It was, of course, from there that she had caught sight of Gerald fighting with, or at least present among, the Chinese.

She found that Shiba was, as ever, glad to see her, welcoming her with a full ceremonial bow. Resourceful as ever, she also found that the little colonel had commandeered the old muzzle-loaded gun to repel an attack by loading it with scrap iron. He reported that many, if not all, of Tung Fu-hsiang's Kansu soldiers had left the Fu – presumably, he said, to take part in the fighting at Tientsin or even to oppose the relief force. It seemed another confirmation that help was on its way – as was, surely, the intensity of the new firings. But if Tung Fu-hsiang had left for the south, who was now influencing the Dragon Lady?

While she was musing this, there was a cry of warning and Shibo rushed to the wall. The Japanese all began firing rapidly and it was clear that the Chinese had launched an attack. The wall of rubble was loosely loopholed and Alice suddenly realised that, in a far corner where the wall angled away, a rifle was being poked through from the Chinese side. She ducked away and ran towards it as fast as she could, drawing her revolver as she did. She arrived just as it fired and, from the corner of her eye, she saw one of the defenders twist around and fall.

Alice seized the muzzle of the rifle and, in the same movement, presented her Colt through the loophole. She fired as she felt the Chinese gun being pulled away from her and then the rifle went limp in her hands and she pulled it through, throwing it to the ground. Without exposing herself, she fired twice more through the aperture then jammed a brick into the hole.

She sat for a moment against the rubble, the perspiration running down her face, and realised that she was shaking. Ah, this would never do! She shook her head dismissively. She was in the middle of a war and this was not the first time she had killed a man, for goodness' sake! Why else did she carry a heavy .45 calibre Navy Colt? Certainly not as a fashion accessory. She looked up into the smiling face of Colonel Shiba, who held out a hand to help her to her feet.

'Very good, madam,' he said. 'Very quick. You have gained us a rifle and removed one of the enemy. I could not ask more. Now, please come away or they shoot you. That must not happen.'

'Thank you, Colonel. I am quite all right, thank you. Just the heat, you know. Made me want to sit for a moment. Now please get back to the wall.'

'Attack over, madam. But we must watch.'

'Indeed. Do go back to your post.'

Alice retreated to one of the many ruined buildings in the Fu and cautiously climbed up the shifting rubble until she could see over the top of the barricade towards the Chinese line. Shielding her eyes against the glare, she looked to where, out of rifle range, the enemy soldiers were moving. She was searching for a white-coloured suit, but nothing stood out amongst the dun-coloured uniforms and occasional green jackets that moved there. But then she frowned. Was that . . . ? Was it a man in a white – but now severely discoloured – jacket and trousers? She couldn't be sure. She scrambled down the half-destroyed wall, disregarding a cut to her ankle, and ran to Colonel Shiba.

'Colonel,' she panted, 'may I borrow your field glasses for a moment?'

'Of course, lady.'

Grabbing them less than courteously, Alice ran back to the ruin and clambered back up to the top of the wall. This time she rejected thoughts of safety and exposed herself, the better to get a view. She levelled the glasses and attempted to focus them. Yes, there he was. A man in a white suit! She adjusted the focus more delicately and Gerald's face came into view, partially concealed by— Hell! He was looking at her through a pair of binoculars. They were undoubtedly studying each other. She resisted the ridiculous instinct to wave. Was he armed? She moved the glasses just a touch downwards and there, leaning against his leg, was a rifle. She put away the glasses for a moment and wiped her eyes. She must be

336

sure. Then she focused the glasses again and held them steady. Gerald – it was undoubtedly him – had put down the glasses and was looking directly at her before turning to move away. There was no doubt about it, it was her cousin: tall and thin, the rather sallow face, and the mandarin moustache.

And he had a rifle.

That settled it. Whatever doubts Alice had about her cousin's treachery – and very few remained – they were dispelled now by that fact. Carrying a rifle meant that he was actively taking part in the attacks on the Legation Quarter. He had now completely thrown in his lot with that of the Boxers and the Manchu court. The final count in his indictment had been proven.

Alice climbed down the rubble with care this time but deep in thought. She must inform Sir Claude, of course, for there could now be no chance of allowing Gerald back into the Quarter. The question was, should she now tell Aunt Lizzie about her son's treachery? She would have to know sooner or later. Better now than later? No. Alice shook her head. Leave it for the moment. Who knew what the future held? There might be some twist of fate in store that could affect the decision. She would let it lie – and she immediately felt better for having made the decision. But oh, Simon . . . !

The enemy now seemed to have new energy. From all around the perimeter the Chinese trumpets blared and the old cries of 'Sha! Sha!' were heard from the other sides of the barricades. All day the fire poured down onto the defenders and, as dusk neared, a new sound was heard. It came from a two-inch, quick-firing Krupp, brought to an emplacement high up in the wall of the Imperial City – a site not used before. Immediately Sir Claude – the former subaltern now proving himself to be a skilled defensive soldier – ordered up his two machine guns, the American Colt and the Austrian Maxim, and had them trained on the gun. It was ten minutes before they could be set up to open fire and, in that time, the cannon had begun causing heavy damage – the worst of the siege. Once *in situ*, however, the two machine guns began firing over fixed lines, despite the fall of darkness, and, within minutes, the Krupp was silenced.

The other firing, however, continued. Alice joined her aunt and the rest of the ladies in doing double duties at the hospital as the casualties mounted. Rumours reached the hospital that the defenders were running out of ammunition and Alice retrieved her Colt and tucked it into her waistband as a precaution. Would the relief, now said to be so near, come too late, right at the end? Alice and her hard-working companions in the sweltering heat of the hospital carefully avoided eye contact and got on with their jobs. So, too, did the defenders on the walls and barricades and, although those at the flimsiest defences who were linguists could hear the Chinese officers urging their troops forward, no breaks were made at any point in the perimeter.

The fury continued for two days and, on the evening of the second, Alice was sitting on the ground taking a break outside the hospital, drinking a cup of brackish, lukewarm water, when a Chinese coolie approached her, bowed low and asked: 'Mrs Fonthill?' She nodded and he pressed an envelope into her hand, bowed and walked away quickly before she could question him.

She opened it and read:

Dear Alice,

I must speak to you. The so-called relief column is still far away and is meeting strong opposition. It will not get through. My mentor, General Jung Lu, has lost influence and, as you have seen, the decision has been taken now to overwhelm the defences. Once the breakthrough has been made the Boxers will be given their head and I fear for your safety and that of my mother. There will be wide-scale slaughter. But I can save you. I also have news of your husband. Meet me tonight at midnight (safest time) at the same tunnel as last time. It has been reopened. Come alone.

Gerald.

Alice put her hand to her head and sighed. Then she read it again. It was all almost certainly rubbish. And yet . . . Jung Lu, who seemed to have been a moderating influence, had obviously lost the ear of the Empress, if this new, fierce attack was any indication. And did Gerald really have news of Simon? She drew in her breath. She must know. So she would have to go. Tell Sir Claude? No. He would almost certainly try to stop her going or even try to arrest or perhaps even kill Gerald. And that would be disastrous for Aunt Lizzie. She would meet Gerald, for she had nothing to lose. He would not dare to try and restrain her.

She got up, tossed her head and returned to the hospital. Luckily, she was not on the night shift and so, at ten-thirty she returned to the room she shared with her aunt, who was now fast asleep after a hard day at the hospital. Alice lay sleeplessly on her bed for just over an hour and then rose, pulled on her long riding boots, pushed the Colt into her midriff sash and set off. After ten paces, she returned, retrieved the little French automatic pistol and slipped it into the top and at the back of a riding boot and continued on her way.

Gerald was waiting for her, peering from the low entrance to the tunnel. She paused by the pile of debris. 'I am not coming in there,' she hissed.

'You must. We can easily be overheard outside by the guards on the walls. Come on.'

He held out a hand to her from the blackness and, reluctantly, she climbed the pile of stone and bricks and, ignoring his hand, bent her head and stepped into the tunnel. Immediately, strong hands grabbed her, pulled her far inside and then pinned her arms to her side. She was aware of two men on either side, holding her firmly, and realised that Gerald was pulling bricks back into the entrance, leaving only a shaft of light to penetrate at the top.

'You little swine,' she said. 'So it was all a trick.'

'Not at all.' His voice was bland in her ear. 'Seeing how badly you behaved the last time we met, I felt I needed a little help. These two men are good friends and will do anything I ask, so please do not try and struggle. Now,' he reached down and withdrew the Colt from her cummerbund and threw it to the ground, 'you won't need that.'

'What do you want? Tell me about Simon.'

'What do I want? I want you, my sweet, and, one way or another, I will have you.' His face was close to hers and she could see, now that her eyes were accustomed to the dim light, that he was perspiring. She could smell tobacco and traces of something sweet – opium? – on his breath. The two men holding her were Chinese. Their faces were quite expressionless.

'As for Simon, I was telling the truth when I said that he is dead. If he was not, surely you would have heard from him by now, eh?'

'I don't believe you. Give me proof.'

'Alas, dear cousin, I can't do that. But I have it on good authority that he was blown up, together with that Welsh brute of his, at the gates of Tientsin as he tried to plant dynamite there. Proof will undoubtedly emerge when you come with me.'

Alice felt herself trembling. Was he lying? He was a born liar. Simon Fonthill, her brave, bold, fearless husband could not be dead, particularly not with Jenkins at his side. And yet something about the picture that Gerald had painted so briefly had the ring of truth to it. Planting dynamite at a fortress's door – that is exactly the sort of thing the two would attempt to do. They had undertaken such daring, hare-brained schemes so often in the past that eventually their luck was bound to run out. Had it happened now? She refused to believe it. She felt her eyes brim with tears. That would never do. She must never give this brute the satisfaction of seeing her crying.

But Gerald was continuing, now with a softened voice. 'I ask you again to come with me, Alice, to a new life. Here, in

China. After this mess, the court and the Foreign Office will be reconstituted and I have been promised a most senior post here. You will be a widow – you *are* a widow – and will need support. With my mother we can live together well in one of the most cultivated countries in the East.'

'What? In a land where brutal young peasants butcher missionaries and their wives and children? No thank you.'

'Look, I am trying to be reasonable. The alternative is horrible to contemplate. These flimsy defences in the Quarter will be torn down, if not tomorrow, then the next day, and you, my dear, will be raped and then subjected to a terrible death. The executioners these days take a hell of a long time to behead someone. I know. I have seen it. I could not prevent that but I can if you come with me now to a safe house. Fetch my mother and we can all leave this horrible place.'

He paused and put his face close to hers. Once again she felt his breath on her cheek. With hardly a thought, Alice gathered a mouthful of saliva and spat in his face.

Her two guards hissed and Gerald staggered back, drew a handkerchief and wiped his face.

'You bitch,' he swore. 'You spoilt, Christian bitch. Very well, you can go back but not before I have finished with you.' He gave a command to the two men and Alice felt her feet forced apart so that she was spreadeagled against the curved wall. She heard the Chinamen laugh and realised with horror that Gerald was unbuttoning his trousers.

'I love older women,' he said, 'even as old as you.'

She felt a rough hand undo her cummerbund and then the belt beneath it. Then her riding breeches were forced down and fingers inserted between her legs. He pushed his cheek against hers and then inserted his tongue into her ear.

With sudden inspiration, Alice slumped completely, letting her head fall forwards, her legs bend and her forearms and hands flop, so that she suddenly became a rag doll and a weight upon the two Chinese and upon Gerald himself. It was as though she had fainted. The guard to her right, anxious to assist in the rape, relaxed his grip on her arm to hold her upright around her waist and she reached forward, grasped his testicles through the loose cotton pantaloons and squeezed hard. With a cry, he pushed her away and Alice slumped down, lifted her right leg, grabbed the little automatic from the back of her boot and shot blindly downwards, to her left.

The shot boomed and echoed in the tunnel and it took the man on her left in his foot, so that, cursing, he staggered backwards and then fell over, clutching his foot. Alice stuck the muzzle of her revolver into Gerald's stomach.

'Get away from me, or I will blow a hole in you.'

He jumped away, bumping into the Chinaman who was bent over, both hands holding the ache in his loins. 'Don't shoot,' Gerald cried, holding up his hands. 'Don't shoot. It was a joke. Don't kill me.'

'Why not? No one would ever find you in here.' Alice put her left hand onto that which held the gun to stop it shaking and backed away slowly, breathing heavily, but covering both men. A dozen thoughts ran through her head, then she spoke in a low but steady voice. 'Tell your two partners in rape to get out of this tunnel, otherwise I will kill them and you. But you stay. I want to talk to you.'

Falteringly, Gerald spoke to the two men and jerked his head, his anxious eyes all the time on his cousin. The Chinamen hobbled away, one bent double, the other leaning on him, hopping on one foot and leaving a trail of blood behind him. They let in a shaft of light as they opened the door to the tunnel.

Alice watched them exit to ensure that no one entered and then she turned back to Gerald. 'Now listen to me. You are a coward and a traitor, cousin,' she said, her voice now trembling with emotion. 'You undoubtedly caused the death of your father and you were going to rape me. So you deserve to die. But as you are the son of my father's brother, I will give you a chance. Now,' she held up the pistol. 'I have five more cartridges left. I will let you turn and run towards the opening at that end, the one that leads into *your* world. I will count to six and then I will start shooting. That's the only chance I will give you. Go. Go on. Go. Now! One . . . Two . . .'

He turned and half-fell over the pipe that ran along the length of the tunnel, scrambled on his hands and knees for a moment and then continued slipping and sliding towards the far end of the tunnel. Alice let off one parting shot, aimed directly at the ground well behind him to hasten him on his way. Then, as she saw him disappear, she adjusted her breeches, picked up her Colt from the ground and trod carefully back the way she had come, scrambled through the hole and then replaced the bricks to cover the entrance.

Anxious not to draw the attention of the guards on the wall high above her, she walked quietly away, begging the god that she had followed trustingly all her life not to make her a widow.

CHAPTER SIXTEEN

Their plans laid for the attack on Peking, the troops of the strange, multinational army of the Foreign Powers marched on from the city of Tungchow, turned to the west and left the river behind them. They reached their agreed bivouac site, some three miles to the east of the capital and well within sound of the gunfire that sounded from within the walled city. The march had been difficult, although no attack had been launched on them. The humidity and heat had remained high and the Bengal Lancers in the British contingent looked bizarre as they rode with long maize fronds tucked under their helmets and hanging down their backs to avoid sunstroke. Then heavy rain fell, turning the main path and numerous rutted tracks that the troops followed into slippery channels.

On the eve of the planned attack, therefore, it was with relief that the men erected their tents under the heavy downpour and tried to snatch some sleep before the final approach to the city.

Fonthill, trudging along with his two companions, had considered leaving the column and walking across the fields of *kaoliang,* the sunken paths and the irrigation ditches and finding some way through the black walls of the city to satisfy himself that Alice was still alive. But then he realised that he must keep his promise to Gaselee to take the British troops into the Legation Quarter once they had fought their way through the outside walls.

And, as Jenkins had pointed out, ''Ow the 'ell would we get through them bloody great gates? We can't blow 'em down on our own.' So now Jenkins, Chang and Simon were huddled together in their small bivouac tent, surrounded by the Sikhs, Rajputs and Welshmen of the British contingent, listening to the rain and trying to sleep.

Fonthill's thoughts, as ever, concentrated on Alice. He knew her temperament and he was convinced that she would not be content to stay with the other women, tending to the sick in the hospital. She would want to be on the walls and the barricades, fighting with the defenders and consequently putting her life at risk. These thoughts did nothing to help him find sleep and his mind wandered to the events of the last few weeks and of how his life, perforce, had been plunged back into violence.

He speculated with a sinking heart that he had probably been involved with the killing of more men personally since his arrival in China than in all of his previous career as an infantry officer, member of the Corps of Guides in India and army scout in two continents and only God knew how many countries. Simon stirred under his blanket. This had to stop. He was becoming a butcher.

He must have dozed off because he was suddenly woken by a hand on his shoulder. He sat upright. 'Listen,' said Jenkins in his ear. 'Gunfire. Much nearer. Either we're bein' attacked or somebody's launched our attack too soon.'

Fonthill put his head outside the tent. The rain had slackened somewhat but it was still bouncing off the canvas. He saw bright flashes to the left, due east, at the base of the great black mass that was the walled city of Peking. 'That's just about where the Tung Pien Men Gate should be,' he mused. 'That's the Americans' objective. They must have jumped the gun.'

'No, cousin.' Chang materialised from out of the blackness. 'I couldn't sleep so I went to look. All the Americans' tents are still standing and their guards are posted.' He frowned. 'It is all frightfully strange, is it not?'

'Frightfully,' echoed Simon. 'Well, if anybody has stolen a march to be first into the legations, I want to be among them.' He ducked back into the tent and began pulling on his boots. 'You two needn't come with me. I will rejoin the British contingent as soon as I can.'

'You're not going without me,' grunted Jenkins, throwing aside his blankets.

'Nor me,' said Chang, ducking back into the tent and grabbing the tattered cloak that he used as a mackintosh.

'Very well. Keep the breech blocks and magazines of your rifles dry under your jackets. Come on.'

The three set off in the rain across the muddy fields, guided by the flashes of the cannon fire that stood out from the blackness of the city walls. They had not gone far when they met Gaselee's young ADC riding back towards the camp, his smart, upwards-brushed moustache now looking decidedly bedraggled.

He recognised Fonthill. 'It's the bloody Russians, old boy – oh, sorry, I mean sir,' he said reining in. 'What a capital mess! They're the very people who wanted us to rest here before attacking because their general said they were tired. Now they're going at that gate hammer and tongs. What's more, the bloody fools are attacking the wrong gate. They're supposed to go in the morning for the Tung Chih Men in the north, but they're attacking the Tung Pien Men in the south.'

'What, the whole Russian contingent?'

'In fairness, sir, no.' Steam rose from his horse's flanks as he curbed the bridle. 'It looks as though what happened is that their general sent a fairly strong force – a battalion and half an artillery battery – to reconnoitre the approach to their objective ready for the attack in the morning. But their leader – they've even got a bloody general in charge of that, a whole general, mind you – saw that the outer guardhouse was lightly defended and couldn't resist attacking. But the fool's got the wrong gate, don't y'know.'

'Has he broken through?'

'His artillery is pounding the gate now. Now you must excuse me, sir. I must report to General Gaselee. He'll be furious when he knows what's happened. Mind what you're doing . . . er, with respect, sir. The Chinks seem to be fighting back hard.'

'Thank you. We will.'

'I don't like the sound of all that, bach sir.' Jenkins's face looked lugubrious in the rain, with his black hair plastered over his forehead and his moustache – he had long ago given up trying to grow it Chinese fashion – looking like some feral excrescence under his nose. 'We know 'ow difficult them gates are to knock down an' these Russkies sound barmy to me. Shouldn't we wait until our lot comes up in the mornin', look you?'

Fonthill shook his head. 'No. If they break through I want to be among them. I've got to see if Alice is all right. You two go back if you want to.'

'No. We'll stay.'

The three pressed on, sometimes wading thigh-deep through the irrigation channels which, bone dry for the previous four months, were now running high in rainwater. As they neared the gate, they could see that the walls above the gate and on either side were manned by Chinese riflemen, who were pouring a steady stream of fire down onto the Russian infantry, who were desperately trying to find cover in the featureless landscape. Two Russian pieces of field artillery, their crews protected by their gun shields, were punching holes into the iron-clad gates and, as they watched, the doors were breached. With a cheer, the leading company of the infantry battalion ran towards the opening, pushed aside the wreckage and rushed through.

'Hell!' cried Fonthill. 'They should have tried to clear the walls first.'

Jenkins frowned. 'Why is that, then?'

'Because Chang tells me that there are always two gates in these big Peking walls. So they will rush into a courtyard only to find another door. And they will be fired down upon and caught like fish in a barrel. It's all very medieval-castle stuff, really.'

Simon had retained the wide-brimmed slouch hat given to him by the American in the attack on Yungtsun and, wearing it now in the rain and half-light, he looked at first sight as though he were a Yankee soldier. He caught the sleeve of a Russian officer. 'Do you speak English?'

'A leettle.'

'Why are you attacking this gate?' Fonthill demanded. 'This is the American target. Our objective.'

The Russian shrugged. 'Same city,' he grunted. And moved away.

From beyond the broken gate a fusillade of musketry could be heard, mingled with cries as the bullets found their targets. 'They'll be ages trying to get through there,' muttered Simon. He turned to Chang. 'Is there any other way we can get through these outer walls?'

The young man shrugged his shoulders. 'Afraid no, Simon. These are big walls and meant to be defended. Gates only way in.' He paused and then frowned thoughtfully. 'Except perhaps . . .'

'Yes, yes. What?'

'Well, when I was a boy, with other boys, we sometimes climbed the walls, you know?'

Jenkins scowled and ran his eye along the sheer, forty-foot-high brick face. 'You must 'ave been like monkeys then, Changy, that's all I can say.'

The Chinaman's face brightened. 'No. Not so very difficult. Because, you see, these walls are very old and are cracked in many places. Cracked vertically, you know. Gives spaces to put toes in. Almost like ladder.'

Fonthill looked dubious. 'Impossible to climb when riflemen are firing down on you, of course. Can you remember where these cracks are, Chang?'

'Ah yes. Think so. Let us go along here.'

'Wait a moment. You might be able to get up but neither Jenkins nor I could, with or without bullets coming down on our heads. We need a rope. We passed a couple of hauliers' carts back there, 352, behind the guns. See if you can filch something.'

Jenkins sniffed. 'I'll find a rope but you know what I'm like with heights, bach sir. You'll never get me climbin' up that bloody wall.'

'Just find a rope. That's all. If the top of the wall is manned, then there's no way any of us can get up. But it's worth investigating. Get us a blasted rope, there's a good chap. We'll walk on this way, right close to the wall, so, hopefully, we won't be seen.'

Mumbling to himself Jenkins departed and Simon and Chang walked away from the gate to the right, away from the shooting, until Fonthill could see no sign of life on top of the castellated wall. Then the two scrambled quickly to the base and huddled there for a moment.

Fonthill looked up, his rifle at the ready. There seemed

to be no one on the top. 'It looks as though the Chinese have gathered their defenders around the gates,' he said. 'If there's one of your cracks along here, we might be able to get up. Though God knows how we're going to get old 352 up there. Best not be underneath him when he tries because he's bound to soil his breeches.'

Chang grinned. 'I think there is big crack along here, if I can remember right. I think by this old, stunted tree.'

Sure enough, the wall bulged outwards at this point and had cracked visibly where water had cascaded down, revealing a zigzag of broken bricks leading to the top. It glistened now in the rain. *Not an easy climb*, thought Simon. And what if troops appeared?

'Let us wait to see if the top is patrolled,' he whispered. 'If it isn't, do you think you could get up?'

'Oh yes, cousin. I think so, if no men on top with guns.'

They waited, scanning the battlements above them, for about five minutes before Jenkins materialised out of the gloom, predictably carrying a rope, coiled round his shoulder. 'Got it from a Russky,' he said, gloomily. ''Ad to tap 'im on the 'ead to get it, mind you. But it would never take my weight now, would it?'

Simon tested it. 'Of course it would,' he said. 'Strong as steel.' He turned to his cousin. 'Now, Chang. It looks as though this part of the wall is not even patrolled, thank goodness. We will watch down here, rifles at the ready, while you climb. Coil this rope around your head and shoulder. Yes, that's it. When you reach the top take a good look before you climb onto the walkway. Be very careful. If the coast is clear, climb over, tie the rope firmly around one of the battlements and throw the end down. Jenkins will come up—'

'Oh bloody 'ell.'

'. . . And then I will follow.'

'What do we do then, Simon?'

'We will make towards the gate and attack from the rear the riflemen firing down. We should be able to take them completely by surprise, coming from out of the darkness behind them.'

'If we can get up 'ere, that is,' added Jenkins.

Thankfully, the rain had now stopped but, looking up, the climb still looked daunting, with the bricks glisteningly wet. Even Chang, slim, young and fit, now looked a touch disconcerted. 'I think I take off my shoes,' he said. 'Easier to climb.'

'Don't worry about anybody appearing up above,' assured Simon. 'We will pick them off with our rifles.' But his fingers were crossed.

His shoes tied around his neck, the youth took a deep breath, hung his rifle by its sling over his back, reached up with his hands and began the climb. It soon became apparent why he needed to go barefooted. Some of the crevices between the broken bricks were too narrow to take a shod foot and he needed to insert his toes to gain a foothold. Slowly, however, he began to scale the wall, reaching high up with his fingers, pulling himself upwards and then finding, somehow, a precarious foothold with his toes.

'Oh bloody 'ell,' exclaimed Jenkins, 'I can't look at 'im.'

'Then don't,' said Fonthill testily. 'Keep your rifle trained on the top of the wall. If you see a face, make sure you put a bullet through it. With all the firing at the gate, no one will hear. But we mustn't let anyone get away to raise the alarm.'

It seemed an eternity to the two men standing below, their rifles at their shoulders and sighted on the embrasures above. But, eventually, Chang reached the top. Holding on to the stone battlement, he poked his head through the opening, looked to left and right and then hauled himself through. Within seconds, the rope was firmly fastened and its end thrown down.

'Right,' said Simon. 'Hold the rope tightly, put your feet on the wall, lean back and just walk up. It's easy.'

'Look, bach sir. You go first and sort out old Changy up there and I'll follow you up. That would be better.'

'No it wouldn't. You would just walk away and get yourself killed at the gate. We will need you up there on the walkway when we take on those riflemen. Now, don't be such a bloody coward. Go on. Up you go.'

His face pouring with sweat, the Welshman seized the rope, leant back and put his foot against the wall. Immediately, it slipped off and he fell backwards. 'There you are,' he said. 'I told you, see. It's just not possible, look you. I'm too bloody 'eavy, isn't it.'

At the back of his mind, Fonthill noted once again how Jenkins's Welshness increased exponentially to the danger of the situation. 'Nonsense, you're just not trying. Go on. We can't leave Chang on his own up there. He will be shot if we hang about much longer. Look, this is how to do it.'

Simon demonstrated and took about five steps up the wall, gritting his teeth at the pain shooting up his leg from the burnt ankle. 'There.' He slid down. 'If I can do it with a buggered-up leg, you can do it easily. Get up that bloody wall. Now!'

Jenkins closed his eyes, seized the rope and tried again. In fact, the strength in his arms and shoulders were such that he could have hauled himself easily up the rope without using his feet but, as it was, he made remarkably good progress – with his eyes firmly shut all the way. At the top, Chang seized his jacket and pulled the Welshman through the embrasure head first, where he lay on the walkway, panting. Then Chang waved for Simon to make the ascent, which he did but not without considerable difficulty, to Jenkins's evident joy.

'No trouble, then, bach sir, was it, eh?'

'Oh, do be quiet. Pull the rope up, Chang, we might need it again. That's it. Good. Right, now, a bullet up the spout in each rifle and off we go. We'd better fix bayonets but don't fire until I give the order. We are going to be severely outnumbered, so surprise is the thing. Stay quiet.'

Simon checked himself and looked at Chang. The youth was now so self-confident and competent in most things that it was easy to forget that he was only sixteen. Slim and fit, certainly, but not as strong nor as skilled in battle as a professional soldier. They could certainly do with his rifle in clearing the battlements above the gate, but it would be thoughtless and heartless to pitch him into a confrontation that would demand all the experience and guts of a seasoned warrior.

'I think, Chang,' he said, 'that it would be better perhaps if you stayed here, fixed the rope again and defended it in case we have to double back and make a quick exit.'

The young man stared at his cousin in consternation and tears came into his eyes. 'Oh no, Simon,' he cried. 'You do not leave me behind. I can fight. There will be plenty of enemy. You will need me. I don't stay here.'

Jenkins interrupted softly. 'He's right, bach sir,' he said. 'We're goin' to need 'im and I couldn't think of a better bloke to 'ave up there, look you.'

Chang shot him a glance of gratitude and Fonthill sighed. 'Very well,' he said, 'but stay close. If you get killed your mother will never forgive me.' He grinned. 'Good. Let's go.'

Rifles at the trail, the three set off trotting along the wide walkway that formed the parapet. Fonthill was surprised that they met no one and then he heard, from the north, firing and shouting. He realised that the Russians' *coup de main* had forced the rest of the column to bring forward their attacks and that the other gates were now under fire. The Chinese had obviously concentrated their forces at these entrances to the city, the most vulnerable points in the defences. To their eyes, the walls were unclimbable and the city's long perimeter therefore needed no defenders all the way round.

The tall tower above the gate loomed up out of the darkness and the steady rattle of rifle fire showed that the Russians were still pinned down in the courtyard in front of the second gate. A row of Chinamen were lined up, leaning over the parapet as it turned to overlook the courtyard, and were firing down upon the Russians.

Simon held up his hand and whispered: 'I've just about had enough of killing and I'll be damned if I'll shoot men in the back. There's not many and, given their record on the way here, I reckon we can frighten 'em off. Shoot to kill only if we have to. There's no cover up here, so line up across the walkway and kneel to present the smallest target. Then fire rapidly, *over their heads*, when I give the order.' Then to Chang, 'That means work the bolt in the breech as quickly as possible, reload and keep firing. Right?'

The boy nodded, wide-eyed.

'Good. Now kneel, just over their heads, aim, fire!'

Despite the noise from below, the resultant volley sounded startlingly loud on the narrow walkway and the Chinese riflemen turned, as one man, their eyes wide in fear. One brought his rifle to his shoulder to fire but Jenkins's second shot caught him in the chest and he fell. Simon and Chang worked their breech bolts and sent two further shots close over the heads of the remainder and they, seeing rifles flashing in the darkness from so close behind them, turned and fled through the open door of the tower – all except one.

Made of sterner stuff, this man jettisoned his rifle, drew a sword and hurled himself at Chang, the nearest of the three, who was reloading, as was Fonthill, and in no position to defend himself. It was now that Jenkins, a terrified coward on the wall face, revealed his colours as a warrior.

The Welshman caught the descending blade with the tip of his bayonet, which shattered. His assailant gave a jubilant yell and brought the sword around in a great sweep, catching Jenkins's rifle and sending it spinning away. Chang fired but missed. Fonthill worked the bolt of his rifle and found that the round had jammed within the breech. Cursing, he reversed his grip on the gun to attack with the bayonet but he was not needed. Jenkins, as light as a cat, had dodged the next sweep of the sword, bent low and hooked his leg around that of the Chinaman, pushed hard with his elbow and upended him. Chang quickly swept the sword away with his own bayonet and then, Jenkins, in a quick, seemingly effortless movement, picked up the man by the front of his tunic, swept away his legs, hoisted him on his shoulders, whirled around to gain momentum and tossed him over the edge of the parapet.

The Welshman regained his rifle, wiped the perspiration from his bow and nodded to Chang in appreciation. Then he grinned to Simon. 'They don't fight as well as the Zulus, now, do they?'

'Bloody well done, 352. Here, lend me your knife to get this damned cartridge out.' Fonthill took Jenkins's blade, inserted it into the breech and flicked out the offending round. The parapet before them was now unmanned, so he ran to the door in the tower. 'It looks as though this leads down to behind the inner gate,' he shouted. 'We'll go down, fire a volley at whoever is down below and then you, Chang, will open the gate while we keep off the Chinese to give you time. Get behind the bloody thing when it's open, otherwise those mad Russians will kill us all. Ready? Go.'

They thundered down the stone, circular steps and came out behind the great doors, which were now being assaulted by some sort of battering ram, fashioned by the Russians. Iron-bound, however, they were showing no signs of breaking. A handful of Chinese away to the right were hastily assembling a machine gun mounted on a tripod, preparing to mow down the attackers if they broke through. Others were trying to erect a barricade.

'Bring down the gunners,' ordered Fonthill. The resultant volley killed the men at the gun and, as one man, the others at the half-assembled barricade turned and fled, no doubt thinking that the attacking army had somehow scaled the walls. Simon and his comrades were now sole custodians of the gates, which were held in place by two sturdy pieces of timber slotted horizontally into brackets and a great, iron lock in which the gatekeeper had conveniently left the huge key. Two large iron bolts completed the security.

'Wait,' shouted Fonthill. He was conscious that, on the other side of the gates, the battlements were still manned by armed Chinese. He ran to the door leading to the top of that wall and the tower and found that it, too, had a key in its lock on the inside. He heard someone running down the steps, so he withdrew the key, slammed the door shut and turned the key in the lock.

'Now,' he called, '352, see if you can turn that damned great key. Then we'll lift off these cross-beams and pull back these gates. Stand well behind them as they open or we'll get shot.'

With great effort, the key was turned, the bolts pulled back, the beams lifted off and the three struggled to pull back the doors. There was no immediate result. It was as though the Russians were too dumfounded, after all their aggression, to find the gates suddenly opened for them – or perhaps they suspected a trap. Then, after some thirty seconds, there was a great roar and the troops rushed through, immediately spreading out to make their way up the network of streets that opened up before them and from which came the sound of gunfire, showing that the Chinese had by no means given up.

Fonthill and his comrades were still wearing their Welch Regiment khaki jackets and these, together with Simon's angry gesticulations, certainly saved them from being shot by the Russians, who had been denied entry for so long and who had lost so many men in the courtyard. The three made their way through the throng of attackers out beyond the walls, to find that the rain had stopped completely and that the dawn was now well established, colouring the sky to the east in shafts of orange and red.

'I thought you wanted to go straight to the British barracks, or whatever they're called,' said Jenkins.

Fonthill shook his head. 'I reckon that the Russians will have a bit of a fight on their hands to get through the streets of the Chinese City till they get to the Legation. I promised I would lead General Gaselee through the inner walls to the British Legation. Our men are supposed to be attacking the Hsia Kuo Men Gate further down the wall and I want to get there as quickly as I can. It's this way. We just follow the wall down. Come on.'

Fonthill seemed to be possessed by a surge of almost demonic energy and his two comrades now followed him doggedly, as the sound of rifle fire intensified from within the city as the Russians began their struggle to penetrate the narrow streets. Then, as they moved southwards the sound died away, making Simon wonder why it was not replaced by that of the British attacking further along.

The tower above the Hsia Kuo Men soon came into sight and, milling before it, Simon could see the troops of the British contingent in their recognisable khaki, the turbans of the Sikhs standing out in particular. Behind them, a battery of the 12th Regiment, Royal Field Artilley, were unlimbering.

'Good Lord,' cried Fonthill. 'There seems to be no firing.' They pushed their way through the troops to where they could see a knot of officers on horseback, prominent among them the portly figure of Lieutenant General Sir Alfred Gaselee.

'Where the hell have you been, Fonthill?' demanded the general. 'I thought you were anxious to get in. We're just about to attack and get these damned gates down.'

As briefly as he could, Simon explained what had happened and that the Russians had now broken through. He looked up at the seemingly undefended line of battlements before them.

'I think it's quite possible,' he said, 'that the Chinese are not defending these gates, suspecting that our attacks will be launched on the gates in the eastern walls, the direction from which we have approached the city.' He cast a glance at the light cannon now unlimbering. 'And, with respect, sir, it is going to take you some time to bring those gates down – they're iron-clad, you see – with those guns.'

'Well, is there any other way in?'

Fonthill looked at Chang. 'I think so.' He explained how

they had climbed the walls on the eastern face. 'Let Chang here find a way up, while we make sure he's not fired on from up top, then he can let that line down and I suggest that your Sikhs could be up that wall in a flash – as long as they took their boots off.'

The general's white eyebrows descended in a frown and he turned to his staff. 'What d'yer think, eh?'

There was a general chorus of approval and Chang once again was despatched to find a convenient crack in the wall. No Chinese appeared on the ramparts, although rifle fire could now be heard more clearly from within the city. Within minutes, Chang was lowering his rope down and a whole group of bootless Sikhs, their dark faces split by great watermelon grins at the unusual nature of the task given them, were forming a line to climb up the wall. Some shots were exchanged as they disappeared from sight but it was not long before the great gates of the Hsia Kuo Men were being grindingly pulled back. The British contingent of the relief force had gained admission to the outer Chinese City of Peking with the exchange of only five shots and without sustaining a single casualty.

The strange tranquillity was broken, however, as soon as they began forming up, inside the gates.

'Which way, Fonthill?' cried Gaselee, astride his horse.

'To the right, sir. But I suggest that you and your staff dismount because you will present too obvious a target if we meet trouble within these narrow streets.'

Trouble, in fact, was not late in arriving. Uniformed troops of the Imperial army were to be seen running towards them down several streets and an irregular firing began. The alarm had obviously been given and soldiers from the Imperial City, only a few kilometres away, had been summoned.

The British contingent consisted of the Royal Welch Fusiliers, the Bengal Lancers, 1st Sikhs, 7th Rajputs and 24th Punjab Infantry, the Chinese-based Weihaiwei Regiment, the 12th Regiment Royal Field Artillery, the Hong Kong Artillery and a small detachment of Royal Engineers. But it was the Indian infantry now who led the way through the winding streets, firing from doorways, occasionally charging with the bayonets to clear specific knots of dedicated resistance, but all the time moving forward, towards the inner wall which marked the southern boundary of the British Legation.

Fonthill, Jenkins and Chang were with them, Chang pointing the way whenever there was doubt. This was urban fighting, street warfare, and among the most dangerous form of conflict in the world, for the range was short, the options for cover limited and the terrain narrow and constricted. But the Rajputs and the Sikhs, accustomed to putting down rebellious conflagrations in the towns of the British Raj, were good at it: light on their feet, flitting from doorway to doorway like cat burglars and as brave as lions.

Nevertheless, the Chinese gave ground reluctantly, firing steadily as they retreated and making Fonthill wonder why this kind of sturdy resistance had not been met on the march to Peking, where the countryside offered so many more opportunities for ambush and counter-attack.

The danger from Chinese rifle fire in the narrow streets was compounded by fragments of masonry and brickwork that flew from dwellings on both sides as bullets went astray. Fonthill was cut in the cheek by one such as a man in a white suit shot at him from an upper storey. He responded quickly with his own rifle but the man ducked away. Across Simon's brain flashed the thought that it was strange to see a Chinaman dressed in European clothing fighting with the Imperial troops, and then it disappeared as he strained to see ahead to catch a precious glimpse of a legation flag. In fact, this street alley fighting was so perilous that his mind had had little time to dwell on the agonising questions: were the legations holding out and, most of all, was Alice still alive?

The first question was answered when, at last, they broke out of the Chinese City to emerge facing the Tartar Wall, beyond which lay the Legation Quarter. And there, to everyone's blessed relief, the American Stars and Stripes was flying proudly from the top of the wall to show that the Foreign Powers at least still held this most southerly of the Quarter's defences. 'Thank God for that,' murmured Fonthill, as he looked up.

To their left stood the stunted tower of Chien Men, from which Fonthill had toppled the Chinese cannon, and beneath it the firmly bolted gate leading to the inner city. 'Do we attack that gate?' demanded the perspiring captain commanding the leading company of Rajputs.

'No,' said Simon. 'There's an easier way through. Here to the right. Come on, but we must watch our backs, for we could be fired on from these houses.'

He ran across the road to the foot of the wall, moving to the right until he found the sluice gates through which he had led the sortie to attack the guns. They were closed, of course, but, as before, there remained enough space for men singly to slip through the space between the grill and curved wall of the opening, avoiding most, at least, of the putrid effluent underfoot by hugging the wall on either side.

Fonthill rolled up his cotton pantaloons and led the way, followed by Jenkins and Chang and then the first of the Rajputs, their boots slipping and sliding in the mud that banked the noxious stream. Above them, as they emerged from the archway, they heard cheering as the Americans on their sector of the wall welcomed their liberators now pouring into the streets below them.

For the Rajputs, it was a momentous victory to have beaten their great rivals the Sikhs to the sluice gates and therefore the Legation Quarter by a few yards. This would be recorded in their histories.

Once clear of the archway, Jenkins seized Simon's hand and shook it. 'My God, we've made it,' he gasped. 'Well done, bach sir.'

Chang joined in the celebrations. 'Splendid effort, my dear cousin,' he said, characteristically. 'Very fine indeed.'

But Fonthill showed no sign of elation. 'But are we in time?' he asked. 'Are we in time? Come on. Come on.'

CHAPTER SEVENTEEN

Alice had decided that she would not tell Sir Claude about seeing Gerald with the rifle, fighting for the Chinese at the Fu, nor about the attempted rape. Time enough to face up to that problem when the relief column arrived and she could confide in Simon. He would be with them. Of course he would.

Nevertheless, she could not but be depressed by the increase in the rifle fire that now rained down on the Quarter, not merely that which crashed along the wall and the barricades but also in the activities of the snipers, whose firing from the high points of buildings outside the perimeter made walking within the grounds of even the British Legation dangerous.

To this was added the fact that she knew that she had made a mortal enemy of Gerald Griffith. She had no doubt that her humiliation of him in the tunnel meant that he would have no hesitation in killing her, should he have the opportunity. And if the Chinese broke through . . . ! She took to wearing the long-barrelled Colt revolver everywhere, except when working in the hospital.

The Quarter had always been a hotbed of rumour but now the place seethed with story and counter-story. The relief force had been defeated right under the walls of the Chinese City and then, no, it had been forced to turn back again deep in the countryside. The distant rattle of machine gun fire that could be heard, it was stated authoritatively by *someone who knew*, undoubtedly came from the Chinese, who had recently bought fifty British Maxims. The rumours, it seemed, were always pessimistic.

Part of the problem for the civilians crowded in the British Legation was that, after nearly two months of the siege, everyone within its confines was now suffering from some form or another of claustrophobia. Unlike for the defenders of, say, Lucknow, during the Indian Mutiny, there were no high battlements from which to scan the surrounding countryside for a glimpse of the banners of the relieving force, no positions of advantage from which to listen for the sound of distant trumpets or bagpipes. Even from the part of the Tartar Wall held by the Americans and Germans, the view was only of hostile dwellings, almost, it seemed, only an arm's length away. And for everyone else, it was of ruined buildings and barricades of rubble and furniture, pressing in, always pressing in.

Those who suffered the most within the Quarter were the Chinese converts to Christianity, who far outnumbered the foreigners and who now lived in appalling poverty. At the bottom of the pecking order, they lacked decent food and, often, a roof over their heads. They suffered from the sudden downpours that were a feature of recent weeks and also from the appalling heat and humidity that were even worse than the rain. Pitiful Chinese mothers crouched against piles of masonry desperately seeking shade and shelter and constantly flicking the flies away from their babies.

The number of casualties recorded by Sir Claude had now risen to sixty-eight of the besieged foreigners killed and more than one hundred and fifty wounded. His figures, however, made no mention of Chinese deaths or casualties from within the Quarter. Alice had taken to gathering whatever scraps of food she could beg from the white families and doling them out to the Chinese Christians. She lost count of the number of pathetic little forms she saw, wrapped in fragments of cloth and lying near to their sobbing mothers, awaiting burial.

When she was not working in the hospital Alice took to spending much of her time with Colonel Shiba, still manning his barricades in the Fu. Her admiration for the Japanese soldiers had grown the more she saw of them. As far as she could see, they always remained cheerful, they never complained and they were completely resolute in their defence of this most attacked and vulnerable section of the Quarter's perimeter. She reflected this in the diary she kept every day and in the series of features that she was writing for eventual publication – she hoped and expected – in the *Morning Post*. In his spare moments, the colonel spoke to her of his home and of his yearning to return there and this had turned Alice to thinking of the future.

She had married Simon Fonthill in 1885 and their only child had died at birth. Her time with Fonthill and their beloved servant and comrade, Jenkins, had been a strange mixture of tranquillity in Norfolk and the excitement of travelling and campaigning abroad. She had followed Simon and Jenkins in their many adventures, not only from love and faithful duty, but also because of the access it provided her in reporting on these wars for the *Morning Post*. She knew that the attention of the great capitals of the world would be on the siege of Peking and she was determined to be the first to report on it and on its relief as soon as cabling facilities became available again. And this work had to be done despite the fact that at the back of her mind increasingly now was the cry 'Has Simon survived?'

Alice prayed night and morning that her husband would be spared and she resolved, as do all lovers in such circumstances, that, if he was, then she would be a better, more supportive, less harping wife, worthy of such a hero. If only . . . if only . . . ! Then she sharpened her pencil and returned to her despatch for the *Morning Post*.

So it was that, a little after midday, on 14th August, on the fifty-fifth day of the siege, Alice was scribbling away. Mrs Griffith had been on night duty at the hospital and was fast asleep, so, to avoid disturbing her, Alice had taken her writing pad and found a corner in a vastly overcrowded office of the British Legation. Although deep in concentration, she suddenly became aware of a deal of hustle and bustle around her. Sir Claude strode through, cutting a gangling, elegant figure in his cream-coloured cotton suit and wearing a startlingly white shirt topped by a polished, starched collar under his best wide-brimmed Manila hat. Outside, she glimpsed women she had hardly noticed before now wearing the most tightly waisted of dresses and smart garden-party hats. What was happening?

'They're coming, they're coming!' shouted a young clerk. 'Some have got through the sluice gate already.'

There was no need to ask who 'they' were. Alice felt the colour drain from her face. What if he . . . what if he was not among them? She banished the thought and looked down at herself. She was wearing patched jodhpurs without the riding boots, broken sandals and an unwashed cotton shirt. This would never do. No way to welcome back . . . Putting away her notepad, she hurried to the room she shared with her aunt, who was still sleeping peacefully. Quickly but quietly, Alice shook out the creases from her best dress and slipped smart and high-heeled sandals on her feet. She brushed her hair feverishly, applied a little rouge to lips and cheeks and stole a look at herself in the one mirror the two women shared. Ah, how she had lost weight! The dress positively drooped around her midriff. She found her red bandana and tied it round her waist as a cummerbund. A hat. She must wear a hat! She found her old straw boater and looped a scarf of matching colour to the bandana over its top and under her chin and then ran outside.

The lawn and tennis courts in front of the Residency were thronged with men wearing unfamiliar best suits and women dressed as though for Ascot. But no soldiers were to be seen. Alice saw Dr Morrison and seized his elbow. 'Is it true?' she cried.

'Absolutely, my dear Alice. They're on the way up now. Don't know who they are, though.'

Suddenly a shot rang out and a Belgian woman of Alice's acquaintance screamed and fell to the ground, blood streaming from her blouse.

'Take cover.' Sir Claude was waving his arms unhurriedly, as though quelling excited schoolchildren. 'Snipers are still active. You all know the lines of fire. Stay away from them, but there is no need to panic.'

Indeed, there *was* no panic. After weeks of being under fire, most of the occupants knew exactly where the danger points of the Legation were and no one was going to miss seeing the relieving troops arrive. The wounded lady was helped inside and given treatment. Alice, however, frowned, thought for a moment, and then retreated to her room, where Aunt Lizzie was still sleeping, and retrieved the Colt from the box under her bed and slipped it into her cummerbund behind her back. Then, biting her lip with anxiety, she rushed out again onto the crowded lawn.

At last they came. Not the tanned British, or American or German soldiers they all expected – not even the little nut-brown men of Japan – but bashful Indian troops, wearing exotic turbans and with their boots and calves covered in black, foul-smelling mud. Someone had broken open several cases of champagne and these grinning men of the subcontinent were being offered and sheepishly declining the sparkling wine served from long-stemmed glasses. Thirsty as they were, alcohol was not for them.

In growing agony, Alice scanned the crowd. *He was not there.* And then she heard a shout. 'Alice!'

At first she did not recognise any of them: three men – a broken-nosed young Chinaman, a squat, broad man with an unkempt moustache and a slim, taller man. All wore strange cotton trousers, splashed with mud, and filthy khaki jackets. The slim man was beaming at her from underneath a peculiar hat at the base of which three acorns rested on its broad brim and his arms were spread wide.

'Oh, thank you, God!' she shouted and ran into her husband's arms, knocking his hat off and kissing him desperately. They stayed locked in each other's arms until Alice broke free and caused extreme embarrassment to Jenkins by kissing him on the lips and then embracing Chang.

'I have been *so* worried,' she said, tears coursing down her cheeks. Then she kissed Simon again. 'My God,' she exclaimed, trying to grin through the tears, 'you smell foul.'

'Ah well,' said Jenkins, 'that's because the captain would insist on comin' in 'ere up the back passage.' He then realised that he had delivered a scatological double entendre and added lamely, 'so to speak, that is.'

Everybody laughed. 'May I enquire how my mother is?' asked Chang with his customary gravity.

'Oh, she is well, Chang.' Alice smiled at him. 'I hope she approves of your new nose. I think it rather becomes you. Look, she is asleep but I will run and warn her. She will want to look her best when she sees you. So excuse me just for a moment.' She looked at them all in turn. 'Don't you dare run away again, any of you.'

She ran to the Residency and gently woke Mrs Griffith who smiled with relief and immediately knelt in prayer. 'I will be out in a moment,' she said. 'I must say thanks.'

Alice ran out into the heat and sunshine again and then her eye caught a movement to her right, a flash of white, where the rubble wall of the Legation met the old battlefield of the Mongol Market. She stopped, frozen. Along the top of the wall a man in a white suit was lying and about to level a rifle at the crowd on the lawn. She turned her head. Nearest to him on the edge of the crowd, and offering a perfect target, was the broad back of Simon, who was talking to Sir Claude. Away from them, Jenkins had found a lady with a silver tray of glasses filled with champagne and was offering one to Chang.

Focusing on the figure on the wall, Alice immediately recognised her cousin Gerald. She stood transfixed as she saw him slowly draw back the bolt on his rifle and aim at Simon.

'No, no!' Alice screamed. But there was still desultory rifle fire from outside the Legation and people were still cheering somewhere. Her voice was lost. Reflexively, she whipped out the Colt revolver from the cummerbund, held it with both hands in front of her, held her breath, took careful aim and then squeezed the trigger.

The sound of the shot, away from the crowd, was lost in the background noise but Simon and Sir Claude heard it and whirled round. They saw Gerald start, turn his head towards

Alice, drop his jaw in surprise and then slump over his rifle, a red stain growing under his left armpit before he fell away, out of sight behind the wall.

Fonthill ran towards Alice, who was staring white-faced at him.

'Alice,' he shouted as he ran, 'what have you done?'

She could not answer for a moment, then she dropped the Colt onto the grass, stared at her husband and said, 'I think I've killed Gerald.'

'For God's sake, why?'

'Because he was trying to shoot you. I knew he would try to kill either you or me. But it was you he was aiming at.'

MacDonald had now joined them. 'Your wife is right, Fonthill,' he said. 'I suddenly became aware that I was staring right at his rifle when the bullet hit him. He could only have been aiming at either you or me.' He turned to Alice. 'Damn fine shooting, madam. Now, go inside and sit down. You are understandably shaken. I will get a couple of chaps and go and see if the man has been finished or merely wounded. Frankly, I hope it is the former, from what you have told me. Excuse me.'

Alice had now begun to shake. 'What can I tell Aunt Lizzie?' she asked, white-faced.

Simon put his arm around her and walked her away to a bench under the wrought iron balcony. 'Here. Sit down, darling. I think you had better tell me what has been going on.'

Slowly, and then with increasing urgency, Alice relayed the story of Gerald's treachery, his twice-repeated proposal and his attempted rape. Then, at the end, she put her hand to her mouth and asked, once again, 'What am I going to tell his mother? How am I going to explain that I've killed her son. She's lost her husband and now her son. Oh, Simon.' She buried her face in his tunic.

He patted her head. 'Look, we don't know yet that he is dead, my love. But if he is, I know exactly what we are going to say to her. Gerald died a hero's death, right at the moment of relief. He saw a sniper aiming into the crowd from a house beyond the Austrian ruins over there. There are still plenty of them about. He rushed to get his rifle but before he could fire, he was hit. He died well. That is what she must remember. Now, Sir Claude is coming back. If the man is dead, let me see if he will concur. I'm sure he will. It's a harmless subterfuge and solves all the problems. Just stay here a moment.'

He was back within minutes. Alice had dried her tears and was staring sightlessly at the ground. Simon took her hand. 'I'm afraid Gerald is dead, my dear. Shot through the heart. Sir Claude knew of the little swine's treachery and it was confirmed when he saw him aim at me. He agrees completely with the subterfuge. By far the best way out. It seems no one noticed the incident in all the excitement.' He released her hand. 'Now wipe your face, my love. Here comes Jenkins with a glass of champagne for you.' He grinned. 'Rescuing us all, once again.'

Jenkins handed her the glass. 'Cheer up, Miss Alice. I know we all smell a bit, but you shouldn't turn your nose up at us, you know. We're all you've got, see.'

Alice accepted the glass and a sad smile crept across her face. 'Oh yes, my dear 352,' she said. 'And I couldn't wish for better. I am very, very lucky.'

EPILOGUE

Mrs Griffith accepted the death of her son with the typical stoicism and faith of a missionary's wife. She always knew, she said, that he was engaged in dangerous work somewhere – 'intelligence work for Sir Claude, you know.' Too secret to be admitted even now, but it did explain his absences. She was sure that her husband would have been proud of him and so it was fitting that he should be buried next to him in the Legation's little cemetery.

Even so, Alice realised that she could not face her aunt on an everyday basis for long and she urged Simon to make haste to get them away. First, however, she had to complete her despatches and send them off as soon as cable facilities were re-established in the Quarter. This was done and accepted with enthusiastic alacrity by the *Morning Post* in London's Fleet Street. She had filed a separate story on

Simon's adventures in getting to Tientsin and on his part in the attack on the city there, as well as the relief of Peking. This was, of course, her scoop on Dr Morrison's despatch for *The Times* and it made Fonthill a celebrity in the war-torn capital, much to his embarrassment.

The siege of Peking and its relief had made front-page news in all the great capitals of the world. Yet the atmosphere in the Legation Quarter, particularly in the impossibly troop-crowded British Legation, was now one of anticlimax. Free from the danger, the noise and the rumour-fed tension of the last fifty-five days, the inhabitants of the Legation were at a loss. The civilians wandered around, rather dreamily, inspecting the barricades and complaining now of the crowded living conditions. Monsieur Pichon, the despised French minister, made it known that he was already halfway through his account of the siege and that he had secured a publisher for it in Paris. The hard-pressed medical staff in the hospital were relieved of their duties by the army doctors and orderlies and, with more sophisticated care and supplies now available, the wounded began to make much quicker progress.

To Alice's relief, her aunt announced on the day of Gerald's burial that she intended to return immediately to her home and recommence her work in the mission there. Somewhat to everyone's surprise, however, Chang decided that he wished to take holy orders and help his mother in her work in the village.

'I think I am not really a soldier,' he confided to Simon and Jenkins. 'I find I get afraid too much, you know.'

'Blimey, Changy,' said Jenkins, 'don't we all?'

Chang gave a smile that wrinkled his battered nose. 'Oh no, Mr Jenkins,' he said. 'Not you two. No, not you two.'

So the five of them sadly retraced their steps to the house in the little village that they had left in such a hurry two months before. They found it still locked and untouched. The Fonthills and Jenkins stayed just long enough to ensure that Mrs Griffith and Chang were safely reinstalled before returning to Peking. There, Simon began to make arrangements for their passage home to Norfolk, England.

These were not completed when a cable arrived addressed to him. This was unusual because, although Alice was now in frequent touch with her editor in Fleet Street, Fonthill rarely received urgent mail.

'It's a knighthood, darling,' said Alice. 'No more than you deserve.'

'Don't be ridiculous. It's probably a bill.'

He tore it open, read the message, reread it and then silently handed it to his wife. She read:

WE NEVER MET IN SUDAN BUT WARMEST CONGRATS ON YOUR WORK CHINA STOP WAR WITH BOERS HERE FAR FROM OVER STOP DESPERATELY NEED YOU HERE FOR URGENT TASK STOP CAN YOU SHIP CAPE TOWN SOONEST STOP LETTER FOLLOWS STOP KITCHENER

Alice looked up, frowning. 'Kitchener. He was an intelligence major when we were in the Sudan, wasn't he?'

'Yes. Never met him. Of course, he became a general and beat the Sudanese finally at Omdurman two years ago and I understand that he has taken over from Roberts in command of the British army in South Africa. So the war there continues.'

'Seems like it.' Alice looked hard at him. 'You are getting famous, my love.'

'Umph. Don't know about that. I'm also getting old. I wonder what "urgent task" means?'

'Don't you think we ought to go home via the Cape and find out?'

'What? Do you mean it? Honestly?'

'Of course. I think Jenkins would get awfully bored in Norfolk again, don't you?'

He grinned and kissed her. 'You're marvellous,' he said. Then he called through the open door, '352, can you spare a minute?'

AUTHOR'S NOTE

The War of the Dragon Lady is a novel, of course, but I have tried to relate the main events of the Boxer Rebellion and the Siege of Peking as accurately as a study of respected accounts of the conflict allows. It is important, however, to distinguish between fact and fiction. Fonthill, Jenkins, Alice, Chang and the Griffiths sprang from my imagination, as did Gerald's mentor, Kuang Li. However, Sir Claude MacDonald very much existed, as did the Generals Jung Lu, Tung Fu-hsiang, Lineivitch, Frey and Gaselee, Admiral Seymour, Brigadier Dorward, Colonel Shiba, Dr Morrison, Monsieur Pichon – who published a best-selling memoir of the siege, portraying himself as a hero – and the Dragon Lady herself, of course, the Dowager Empress.

A way into the Chinese City of Peking *was* found by barefooted Sikhs, who climbed up cracks in the great outer wall; the Rajputs *did* enter the Legation Quarter via the sluice gate and were the first into the Quarter; the Russians *did* attack the wrong gate; and a Belgian lady *was* shot by a sniper as she stood on the Legation lawn to welcome the relieving troops. Other individual incidents I relate as occurring during the siege – such as the destroying of the Chinese guns on the Chien Men tower, the counter-attack at the destroyed Austrian Legation, and the 'friendly fire' falling on the Americans at Yangtsun – did take place. It is also true that spies frequently found easy methods of entry and exit into the Quarter throughout the siege.

I must confess, however, to diverting from the truth a touch here and there in recounting the detail of the siege. For instance, the gallant and popular Captain Strouts was not killed on the attack on the Krupps guns but during a defence of the French Legation. By the same token, I have taken liberties occasionally in the timing of the events of the Uprising, mainly so that I could involve Simon, Jenkins and Chang in them without stretching chronology and geography too far. I believe, however, that these indulgencies have not altered the overall veracity of my story of the rise of the Boxers and the Siege of Peking. This is a novel, after all. Nevertheless, I extend my apologies to scholars of the period who may be offended by these minor departures from fact.

The Boxer Rebellion shocked the world by the ferocity with which the Boxers attacked foreign missionaries throughout northern China in 1900. Stories emerged of elderly Europeans and their families being brought into village squares and beheaded, one by one. Wives of missionaries were forced to watch their husbands decapitated, as, holding the hands of their children, they waited their turn. On one such occasion, more than three hundred men, women and children were killed.

The Foreign Powers, of course, took their revenge after the relief of Peking. Punitive columns were sent out into the provinces to find the perpetrators and shoot or hang them. Some of the Chinese military leaders were executed and others, as related, committed suicide. Financial and other reparations were levied on the Chinese Government that ended the long reign of the Manchu dynasty, held back the growth of that country for generations and led to the eventual coming to power of the Communist Party.

And the Dragon Lady herself? With the relief column at the eastern wall, she hurriedly packed and escaped to the north before setting off on a seven-hundred-mile 'tour of inspection' to the south and west. She was not pursued and eventually returned to the capital two months later. As she stepped down from her ceremonial chair at the entrance to the city, the wall was lined by survivors of the siege. She looked up at them, gave a distant smile, clasped her hands together and bowed. Immediately, the survivors applauded her. It was a strange ending to an even stranger conflict.